London Calling

Also by James Craig

London Calling

An Inspector Carlyle Mystery

JAMES CRAIG

WITNESS
IMPULSE
An Imprint of HarperCollinsPublishers

This book was previously published by Constable & Robinson in 2011.

EPub Edition SEPTEMBER 2014 ISBN: 9780062365262

Print Edition ISBN: 9780062365255

10 9 8 7 6 5 4 3 2 1

Acknowledgements

I started writing about John Carlyle not least because I thought I could do it on my own. Of course, that was never going to be the case. There are many people to thank for their help, so, in no particular order, I doff my cap to Polly James, Paul Ridley, Michael Doggart and Peter Lavery, as well as to Krystyna Green, Rob Nichols, Martin Palmer and all of the team at Constable & Robinson.

Above all, I have to thank Catherine and Cate, who have put up with all of this when I should have been doing other things. This book, as with all the others, is for them.

'Where there is no publicity there is no justice.'

JEREMY BENTHAM

Chapter One

SHUFFLING INTO THE tiny kitchen of his one-bedroom flat in Tufnell Park, north London, George opened a cupboard above his head and pulled out an economy tin of baked beans. After opening it, he poured about half of the contents into a small pan resting on the stove. What was left in the tin went into a small fridge that was otherwise almost empty, containing only a pint of milk and a couple of bottles of Red Stripe beer that had been on special offer in the local minimart.

Taking a box of matches from the worktop, George lit the gas and began stirring. When he estimated that the beans were on their way to being hot, he fished his last two slices of white bread out of their wrapper, and carefully dropped them into an ancient toaster. Switching it on gingerly, he stepped back quickly, fully expecting the machine to blow up at any moment. Returning his attention to the stove, he also kept half an eye on the bread. George knew that multi-tasking had never been his strong point, and more often than not something got burnt. It was quite stressful, really. Giving the beans another stir, he had a quick taste.

Though bubbling away nicely, they were still quite cold. He then decided to pop the toast; the bread was barely coloured, but that was, he always thought, better than waiting too long and incinerating it. *Err on the side of caution* was his motto. Or, at least, it had been for a long time now.

Happier that he could now focus exclusively on the pan, George relaxed. As he stirred the beans, he listened to the background hum of city life. George liked to listen.

Tonight, he could hear the television in the flat downstairs over the ever-present rumble of traffic from the road outside. After a few moments, his ears picked out the sound of footsteps coming up the stairs. He heard them stop outside his front door. After a couple more seconds, the buzzer sounded, harsh, flat and insistent.

At first, George didn't react. He couldn't imagine why anyone would want to ring his bell. When was the last time he'd received a caller? With no intention of answering the door, he carefully speared a bean and dropped it on to his tongue – still not quite hot enough.

The buzzer sounded again: another short, authoritative burst. George hesitated. Maybe he should see who it was. But would he have time to answer the door without the beans getting burnt? He remonstrated with himself for even debating about it. Why should he bother? It would only be some door-to-door salesman, a cold caller, wanting him to change his electricity supplier or something similar.

Dropping the toast on a nearly clean plate, he wondered if he should have any butter. The buzzer sounded again, longer this time, as if the person outside knew for sure that he was there.

'Go away!' George hissed, under his breath, as he gave the beans one last stir. Turning off the gas, he decided against the butter and poured the beans directly over the toast. Sticking the pan under the tap, he half filled it with water and dropped it in the sink.

He was hunting for a knife and fork when the buzzer went again, a series of short staccato bursts that said: *Come on, answer the bloody door. I'm not taking no for an answer.*

'All right, all right, I'm coming.' George turned away from his dinner and shuffled into the tiny hallway. As a matter of routine, he put his eye to the spyhole. There was no one there. *Typical*, he thought, *bloody kids. They'll be hiding up on the next floor, thinking this is hilarious.* With a sigh, he turned back to his plate. Before he'd even taken a step, the doorbell went again, much louder this time, the buzzer right above the door drilling harshly into his skull.

'You little sods.' Turning on his heel, he swung the door open and stepped on to the landing, his chin making perfect contact with the fist that had been waiting for it all this time.

WAKING UP, GEORGE had a nasty taste in his mouth and a throbbing headache that made him want to cry. He was sitting in the living room, his hands and legs tied to the only upright chair. His upper chest had also been taped to the back of the chair, to ensure that he was totally immobile. There was another strip taped across his mouth. Realising that even utility companies would probably not go this far in order to convince customers to switch their accounts, he started to panic, gnawing at the tape with his teeth, and trying desperately to push himself out of the chair.

'Relax, relax.' The voice was quiet, soothing. 'Just try to keep breathing.' But the hand on his shoulder did nothing to help calm him down. It was wearing a rubber glove like the kind doctors wear, or those you see killers snapping on in movies, just before they butcher their victims.

Forcing himself to draw in a few deep breaths, George noticed the plate on the coffee table in front of him was empty now, save for a few breadcrumbs and a couple of stray beans. His stomach rumbled in protest, even though dinner was the least of his worries right now. Next to the plate was a large kitchen knife with an evil-looking serrated edge. George knew that the knife had not come from his kitchen. In a moment of bowel-freezing clarity, he realised that you wouldn't bring along a knife like that if you weren't intending to use it.

Shaking his head, George started to sob. Big, fat tears rolled down his cheeks, and over the tape covering his mouth. Surely this couldn't be the end? His time had gone so quickly. He had squandered it so badly. There hadn't even been enough that had happened in his life for anything exciting to flash in front of his eyes. What he saw was more of a short loop that kept repeating, like the trailer for a film that you know is going to be really quite disappointing.

'Compose yourself,' said the voice.

George sniffed. He could hear the banging of pans in next-door's kitchen. A young Asian couple. There were voices, laughter. He didn't know their names, but he had nodded to them on the stairs once or twice. A couple of times, he'd overheard them having sex through the paper-thin walls. Once he'd even jerked himself off to the rhythm of the woman's cautious groans. That was the best sex he'd had in a long time. The memory of it caused a twinge of arousal in his groin, sparking a flicker of fight in his belly. Rocking backwards and forwards on his chair, he started screaming through the tape. All that came out, however, was a cautious moan, not unlike that of the careful lovemaking next-door, which he'd liked to listen to whenever he had the chance.

'Enough.' Again, there was the hand on his shoulder. 'Don't wear yourself out.'

Head bowed, George nodded.

For a moment, there was silence. Then the voice continued. 'You have a very modest abode here, don't you, George? All that education. All that money. All those opportunities. All that ... privilege. How did you end up like this?'

George shrugged. He badly wanted to blow his nose. It was a question he himself had pondered many times.

The hand reached over and picked up the knife. George felt himself gag. The tip of the blade tickled the back of his neck. 'You know why I'm here?'

George nodded.

'You know what I'm going to do?'

Again, George tried to scream.

The blade appeared at his left cheek, reflecting the light from the sixty-watt light bulb overhead. 'It can happen either when you're dead, or while you're still alive, but I would suggest the former.' His guest finally stepped in front of him and brought the point of the blade to the tip of George's nose. George felt himself go cross eyed as he tried to keep it in focus. The blade was moved a few inches back as if to give him a better look. 'You have a choice. I'm not a sadist. Not like you.'

George vigorously shook his head, eyes wide. Along with the rubber gloves, the visitor was wearing a thin, clear, plastic raincoat, the kind that tourists bought when caught out by the weather. It hung all the way down to the floor and looked ridiculous.

'Oh, you'd say that now. But then ... when you had the chance.'

George felt something press into his flesh, then a burning sensation, then the agony of the knife chiselling into one of his ribs. He reached deep into his lungs and bellowed. The sound that emerged was like a constipated man trying to pass a cricket ball.

'The harder you make it for me, the worse it will be for you. I'm no expert in this kind of thing, but I should be able to make a decent effort at cutting your throat. Sit still now ...'

George was trying for one last deep breath as he watched the knife disappear under his chin. Looking down, he was distracted by the sound of something splattering off his killer's raincoat. The knife flashed in front of him for a second time but by now his head was slumped on his chest, as if he was mesmerised by the blood that had filled his dinner plate to overflowing.

Chapter Two

INSPECTOR JOHN CARLYLE of the Metropolitan Police dropped the copy of *Vogue* back on to the coffee table in front of him and yawned. In the corner, his sergeant, Joe Szyszkowski, was snoring away quietly. Above Joe's head, on a large television screen, a news reporter was standing outside Buckingham Palace speculating that the prime minister was finally going to call the long-awaited General Election. All manner of important things were going on in the outside word and here he was, sitting in a private health clinic on Harley Street, waiting for some Italian crook to finish having a tummy tuck.

'How long is this going to take?' he asked no one in particular.

The sour-faced receptionist looked up from her computer and gave him an exasperated look. Having a bunch of policemen camping in the clinic's reception did nothing for the atmosphere of the place. Not to mention her ability to spend the morning talking to her mates on the phone while updating her Facebook page. 'The doctor said Mr Boninsegna should be coming round in the next few minutes,' she said slowly, as if talking to a particularly dim child who needed everything repeated several times. 'He will let you know as soon as his patient begins to regain consciousness.'

'You are very kind. Thank you.' Commissario Edmondo Valcareggi, of the Italian State Police, smiled at the girl like a wolf contemplating the lamb that was about to be lunch.

You dirty old bugger, Carlyle thought sourly, *you've got to be even older than I am.* Having to babysit this old lech from Rome was a major pain in the arse. With his shock of white hair and sharp features, Valcareggi looked like something out of a Ralph Lauren advert. The expensively casual clothes he was wearing looked as if they must have cost many months of Carlyle's salary. How much did Italian police get paid, anyway? 'You're sure that the man in there is actually Ferruccio Pozzo?' he asked for the umpteeth time. The man recovering from his operation down the corridor was registered in the name of Furio Boninsegna.

Valcareggi smiled indulgently. 'There is no question of it. We are absolutely sure. He's had plastic surgery before, and is travelling on a fake passport of course ...'

'Of course,' interjected Joe, who had woken up and was helping himself to a fresh cup of coffee from the pot by the reception desk. Taking a sip, he smiled at the receptionist, who made a show of blanking him. Shrugging, he sat back down next to Carlyle.

'... but we have a DNA match,' Valcareggi continued. 'It is definitely the right man, and he is very worth catching. Pozzo has links to the various crime clans in the 'Ndrangheta syndicate. He has been a fugitive for almost two years now, and this is his second round of liposuction. We almost caught up with him the first time, at a clinic in Nice, but he left it about an hour before we arrived.'

'It happens,' said Joe sympathetically.

'This time,' Valcareggi beamed, 'we've got him. No problem.'

'Anaesthetic always slows them down,' Carlyle quipped. 'I don't know why we don't use it more often.' Reaching down, he picked up another magazine and quickly flicked through the pages until he came to a large picture of two well-dressed men hovering on the cusp of middle age. The pair beamed at him as if they had just won an Olympic gold, taken the casino at Monte Carlo for ten million dollars *and* fucked Scarlett Johansson all ends up, all on the same day.

The strapline read: *Better than you, and they know it.*

Tossers, Carlyle thought. But he started reading anyway.

THE GOLDEN TWINS TAKE CENTRE STAGE

The Carlton brothers will be running the country soon;
Eamonn Foinhaven profiles a new political
aristocracy in the land.

One is known as 'the Sun King', the other 'the dark prince', nicknames they picked up on their fabled journey from the playing fields of Eton, the forge of leaders down the centuries, through Cambridge University to the House of Commons, and now on to the very gates of power, in front of No 10 Downing Street itself.

If the perception in Westminster is that Edgar Carlton is the prime minister in waiting – the odds on him taking the top job shortening every day, after every new fumble and misjudgement by the current incumbent – his younger sibling (by two minutes), Xavier, is hardly living in his shadow.

The political classes are now agreed that Edgar Carlton has all the necessary skills for great office: the charm, the drive, the appetite to lead from the front. Xavier, on the other hand, who is as likely to be found in the gossip pages as in parliamentary reports, has more doubters. Already handed the post of Shadow Foreign Secretary by his brother, it seems increasingly certain that he will get the chance to prove these doubters wrong. It is even whispered that the twins have agreed a secret pact, with Edgar promising to stand down as PM in favour of Xavier once a second term is secured.

The Carltons fit perfectly with the mood of the moment, the country's new taste for austere glamour. Their story is now well known: the sons of the celebrated union between Hamisi Michuki, the Kenyan model who stormed London society in the 1960s, and Sir Sidney Carlton, a rakish tycoon who rose to the heights of Paymaster General in successive governments in the early 1960s, before his political ambitions were derailed by an unfortunate incident with a pair of strippers from the Cowshed Club, a notorious haunt of gangsters and other pre-Swinging Sixties lowlifes.

Happily for the boys, the best genes of both parents have been passed on; they acquired their mother's stunning looks and their father's political nous. Now, they are poised to sweep away both the gloom of the 'new austerity' and also the soul-destroying cult of the working-class rapscallion, or 'cheeky chav', both of which have plagued the country in recent years. In the class-ridden twenty-first century, the Carltons are the ultimate 'anti-chavs', standing against everything that is common, vulgar and ugly. Surfing a popular wave of optimism and glamour, they have, quite simply, left routine politics behind. 'They are so in touch with the zeitgeist, it's frightening,' declares Chelsea-based style guru Sally Plank. 'Their peers are footballers, pop stars and royalty, rather than other politicians. They realise that becoming a credible celebrity is ninety per cent of the job done; because if you're a celebrity, the public will forgive you for being a politician.'

Potentially the first brothers to hold senior government office together since just before the outbreak of the Second World War, they are fiercely loyal to each other. 'It's almost like a gay political marriage,' remarked one colleague who declined to be named. "They have an almost telepathic understanding and are constantly watching each other's backs.'

Not that they have much to worry about in that regard at the moment, for whatever reservations ordinary members may have about the brothers' grip on the party is more than offset by the current opinion polls. After many years in the wilderness, power once again beckons. Lucky or not, Edgar and Xavier Carlton are in the right place at the right time. They look young, modern and in touch with the public.

'They will win, that much is certain,' says pollster Martin Max of pressyourbutton.co.uk, the UK's leading 360-degree sentiment-sampling service, 'the only question is by how much. The Carltons could end up with the biggest majority in modern history, eclipsing the 232-seat majority of the Spencer government in the early nineteenth century.'

Joe Szyszkowski tapped him on the arm. 'Look ...'

Carlyle looked up at the television screen just in time to see a sleek Jaguar carrying the current prime minister sweep through the gates of Buckingham Palace.

'Here we go,' Joe said. 'Election time.'

'Big surprise,' Carlyle grumbled. 'The silly old sod left it as late as possible. Not that it's going to do him any good.'

'Who will you vote for?' Valcareggi asked bluntly.

'That's between me and the ballot box, Edmondo,' Carlyle said stiffly. He held up the magazine so that the *commissario* could see the article that he had been reading. 'But you can safely assume that I won't be supporting this bunch of over-privileged chancers.'

'The inspector is a real inverted snob,' Joe laughed, whereupon Valcareggi gave him a look that indicated he didn't understand the phrase. Before the sergeant could explain, a nervous-looking man in a white coat appeared. Reflexively, Joe reached for his handcuffs.

'Gentlemen,' the doctor said quietly, 'Mr ... er, the patient is just waking up.'

'Excellent!' Carlyle pushed himself to his feet. 'Let's go and arrest the now not-so-fat fuck.'

Chapter Three

KITTY PAKENHAM, A.K.A. Catherine Sarah Dorothea Wellesley, Duchess of Wellington (1773–1831), wife of Field Marshal
Arthur Wellesley, first Duke of Wellington, KG, KP, GCB, GCH,
PC, FRS, looked down benevolently from above the library fireplace, her gentle, amused smile no doubt reflecting the fact that
the St James's gentlemen's club that bore her name had never –
and would never – permit women to become members. Beneath
Kitty's gaze, Edgar Carlton, MP, leader of Her Majesty's opposition, sipped gently on his Cognac de Grande Champagne Extra
Old and watched a series of familiar images that flickered on the
television screen in front of him. The sound was muted – club
members didn't like noise, particularly when it was the news – but
that didn't matter, for Edgar knew it all off by heart. After grimly
clinging on to power for as long as possible, the prime minister –
the man Edgar would be replacing at No 10 Downing Street in
a month's time – had finally announced that a general election
would be held on 5 May. The Queen had agreed that Parliament be
dissolved next week. The election campaign had begun.

Edgar took a large mouthful of his cognac and let it linger on his tongue. A wave of ennui passed over him, since the prospect of spending the next three weeks scrambling across the country, meeting 'ordinary people' and begging for votes in marginal constituencies, was singularly unappealing. It was such a damn bloody chore. He knew, however, that there was no way round it. At least he didn't have to worry about losing at the end of it all.

Finally letting the brandy trickle down his throat, he gazed at the television screen and scrutinised his opponent. Looking back at him was a tired, beaten, middle-aged man who had achieved nothing other than to feed his ego for a few squalid years. Even with the sound turned down, Edgar could interpret the man's soundbite: *'This election is a big choice. The British people are the boss, and they are the ones that will make that choice.'*

'I think that they already have, my friend.' Edgar smiled. As if on cue, a graphic appeared on screen, displaying four opinion polls that had been published earlier in the day. They confirmed that Edgar's lead had strengthened to between ten and sixteen points. *Short of being caught* in flagrante *with a couple of altar boys, there is no way I can lose,* he thought. *Simply no way.*

Raising his glass to Kitty, he turned his back on the television and savoured the peace of the empty room. With a shiver, he realised that he wouldn't be seeing much of this club from now on. Pakenham's was almost two hundred years old, and for a while it had been the headquarters of the political party that he now led. Previous club members had included various princes of Wales, the writer Evelyn Waugh, and Joseph White the media magnate who rose to number 238 on the *Sunday Times Rich List*, before fraud and obstruction-of-justice convictions landed him in a Florida prison. If it was good enough for people like that, Edgar thought, it was good enough for him. Pakenham's was one of the few things in life that gave him any sense of identity. Certainly, it was one of the few places where he could get any peace.

Catching sight of himself in a nearby mirror, Edgar smiled. *Black don't crack*, as the saying went, and so it was with him. He had his Kenyan model-turned-mother to thank for that. The Audrey Hepburn of Africa, they'd called her, and she'd given him the good genes, the good looks and the non-receding hairline. He had his father, Sir Sidney Carton, to thank for everything else. Truly he deserved his 'Sun God' moniker. He let his gaze linger on the image in the mirror, and gave a small nod of approval. The flowing locks had gone, replaced by a number-one crop on back and sides and a number four on top, inspired by the new American President. On the edge of extreme, it was just on the right side of suggesting a football hooligan or a squaddie: utilitarian, athletic, a no-nonsense haircut that talked about control and focus. It worked well, too, with today's ensemble: sober two-button grey suit, white shirt and gentle pink tie, rounded off by a pair of sharp, well-polished Chelsea boots. Suited and booted indeed! Not for nothing had he been placed in the top five in *Modern Men's Monthly* magazine's list of the world's best-dressed men for the last two years, beating the likes of David Beckham, Daniel Day-Lewis, James McAvoy, Jude Law – and, best of all, his twin brother, political colleague and sometime rival, Xavier.

A polite cough drew Edgar from his reverie. He half turned to find William Murray standing behind him. One of the more important minions, Murray was one of twelve 'Special Advisers' in Edgar Carlton's team. Now that he was on the brink of power, it was a team that had swelled to more than fifty people, and seemed to be getting bigger by the day. Murray was in his mid-to-late twenties, only four or five years out of Cambridge, and appeared charming, cynical and energetic. With an indeterminate brief, he was a general fixer who could turn his hand to PR, lobbying, and one or two other things that Edgar didn't need to know about. Of somewhat brittle temperament, the young man had no pedigree to speak of, and was a 'bit of rough' who could take the fight to the other side whenever the going got heavy.

Of course, Murray was not a club member, but sometimes you had to let the hired help into the inner sanctum, in the course of performing their jobs. The young aide crossed the room, nodded a greeting to his boss and stood to attention by the far end of the fireplace. Pulling a sheaf of papers out of an expensive-looking briefcase, he waited expectantly.

It suddenly struck Edgar that the face looking back at him could be his clone from twenty or so years ago: when younger, fresher, smarter. Before he had time to get too annoyed by this thought, he felt his mobile vibrating inside his jacket pocket. Pulling it out, he quickly read the text that had just arrived. Smiling, he flashed the screen at his aide, not giving the boy time to read it. 'It's a good-luck message from my old headmaster. That's very nice of him.'

'Yes,' Murray agreed, a little bemused. His own headmaster – at the Terence Venables Comprehensive in Hammersmith – had been sacked for getting one of the sixth-formers pregnant. Why anyone would want to keep in touch with their old schoolteachers was beyond him.

'I will be the nineteenth boy from my school to become prime minister,' Edgar explained. '*If* I am elected, of course. It's quite a list: Walpole, Eden, Gladstone, Macmillan ...'

'Indeed,' Murray nodded.

'Assuming I do win,' Edgar continued, 'all the boys then get a day off in celebration. So there's a lot riding on this.' He smiled his most patronising smile. 'So ... no pressure.'

'Did you see the latest polls?' Murray asked, trying to move the conversation along. 'Spectacular.'

'Another month and we'll be there, Mr Murray,' Edgar beamed. 'I'm heading for Downing Street, and I'm taking you with me.'

'Absolutely!' The young man bowed his head slightly, as if in prayer. When he looked up again, it almost seemed as if he might start crying out of gratitude.

'So,' Carlton lowered his voice even though there was no one else in the room, 'let's just make sure that there are no mistakes during the next few weeks, shall we?'

Murray lent forward to whisper back, 'Yes.'

'Now is the time for the utmost focus and complete profession-alism,' Edgar added. 'We most definitely do not need any slip-ups at this stage.'

'No.' Murray smiled. 'I fully understand.'

'I know you do, William.' Carlton stood up and gently grasped the young man's shoulder. 'You are a very smart young man. Your parents must be very proud.'

Once again, the boy bowed his head slightly and, for a second, Edgar thought that he could indeed see tears welling in his eyes.

'Yes, sir,' he whispered, 'they are.'

'Good,' Edgar murmured. 'That's very good.' Unsettled by such emotion, he took a step backwards. 'Make sure you tell them just what an important job you are doing here. I know that I can rely on you.'

XAVIER CARLTON SAT listlessly at his kitchen table, watching the second hand tick round on the wall clock. He was resplendent in his cycling outfit, an eye-wateringly tight pair of black and grey Lycra shorts, and a lime-green and pink cycling jersey bearing the logo of an Eastern European biscuit manufacturer. His advisers had been on at him to stop wearing the jersey ever since the cycling team in question had been thrown off the Tour of Italy for a spectacular range of alleged doping offences. But it had been the only clean jersey he could find in the house that morning. And, anyway, he quite liked it. It was just so vulgar ...

PR-wise, Xavier couldn't see how the jersey was much of a problem. The great British voting public knew nothing about bike racing and cared less. As Eddie Paris, his portly communications guru who actually cycled for fun, liked to say, the plebs wouldn't know the difference between Lance Armstrong and Louis Armstrong. Or Neil Armstrong. Or ... well, any other famous Armstrong you could mention.

Xavier was no expert on cycling, but he had worn one of Lance's yellow 'Live Strong' bracelets a while back, when they were briefly fashionable. Signifying that he was cool, compassionate, committed, it was a handy prop for his image at the time.

The jersey was just another prop. In fact, Xavier's whole life was littered with them. Next to his crash helmet, at the centre of the table, was a pile of thirty-three hardback books. Xaxier knew that there were thirty-three because he had counted them. Twice.

This was Edgar's summer reading list, which had recently been handed out to all of his MPs in an attempt to raise their standing with the voters, make them seem better read and altogether more ... well, *thoughtful*. Xavier sighed. This morning, one of the books had to go into his right-hand cycle pannier. This would demonstrate willing to Edgar who, Xavier felt, was beginning to question his commitment to their great project. It would also provide a picture for the *Mail* photographer who would be waiting to snap him on his bike this morning, as he cycled to the House of Commons. The plan, agreed with the paper's political editor the night before over a couple of mojitos at the Pearl Bar in the Chancery Court Hotel, was to have something suitably erudite peeking out of his bag as he swept into Parliament Square. This nice image, athletic and cerebral at the same time, would be garnished with a headline like '*Who's a clever boy, then?*' The media beast would be fed for another few hours, and another microscopic gain in the final push for power would be duly recorded.

So which book to choose? For the umpteenth time, he scanned slowly down the heap, searching for one that vaguely attracted his interest:

Terror and Consent: The War for the Twenty-First Century,
    Philip Bobbitt
Influence: The Psychology of Persuasion, Robert Cialdini
Muqtada al-Sadr and the Fall of Iraq, Patrick Cockburn
*Empires of the Sea: The Final Battle for the Mediterranean
    1521–1580*, Roger Crowley
How Christian Holyrod Won London, Edward Giles and
    Isabelle Joiner-Jones
*Rivals: How the Power Struggle Between China, India and
    Japan Will Shape Our Next Decade*, Bill Emmott

Xavier's eyes glazed over. His mind evaporated. God, it was impossible! If it had been his own list, it would have been much more user-friendly. With a lot more pictures. He thought of *The Big Penis Book*, a recent (joke) present from his wife. Now if *that* had made the list, it would have got people's attention! Some of their colleagues might even have already read it.

> *Munich: The 1938 Appeasement Crisis,* David Faber
> *A Million Bullets: The Real Diary of the British Army in*
>   *Afghanistan,* James Fergusson
> *A Choice of Enemies: America Confronts the Middle East,*
>   Laurence Freedman
> *Fixing Failed States: A Framework for Rebuilding a Fractured*
>   *World,* Ashraf Ghani and Clare Lockhart
> *The Rise of Christian Holyrod,* Graham Quentin
> *The Pain and the Privilege: The Women in Lloyd George's Life,*
>   Ffion Hague
> *Inside the Private Office: Memoirs of the Secretary to British*
>   *Foreign Ministers,* Nicholas Henderson
> *Good Business: Your World Needs You,* Steve Hilton and Giles
>   Gibbons
> *Dinner with Mugabe: The Untold Story,* Heidi Holland
> *Politicians and Public Services: Implementing Change in a*
>   *Clash of Cultures,* Kate Jenkins
> *Carlton on Carlton,* Joan Dillinger

The BPB aside, Xaxier couldn't remember the last time he'd read a book of any description. He seriously doubted whether he'd read thirty-three books in total during his whole bloody life. His advisers had provided two-page summaries for him (two lines on each book), so that he had something to say on each, just in case he got quizzed by a journalist, but he couldn't even rouse himself to look at that briefing.

Vote for Caesar: How the Ancient Greeks and Romans Solved the Problems of Today, Peter Jones
The Return of History and the End of Dreams, Robert Kagan
Five Days in London, John Lukas
Hitler's Empire: Nazi Life in Occupied Europe, Mark Mazower
Paradise Lost: Smyrna 1922: The Destruction of Islam's City of Tolerance, Giles Milton
1948: The First Arab Israeli War, Benny Morris
Thinking in Time: The Uses of History for Decision Makers, E Neudstadt and Ernest R May
Britain in Africa, Tom Porteous
A Problem from Hell: America and the Age of Genocide, Samantha Power
Descent into Chaos: How the War against Islamic Extremism Is Being Lost in Pakistan, Afghanistan and Central Asia, Ahmed Rashid

None of this stuff mattered a jot, Xavier thought. No one actually expected the books to actually be read. Putting together the list, the thought that went into it, was the thing. It had taken a panel of three of Edgar's most senior advisers – i.e. the ones aged over twenty-five – three months to trawl the book-review pages of *The Times* and come up with a satisfactory selection. It was just more quality Carlton content, another small PR morsel, like the list of Edgar's favourite music downloads or his favourite Premiership footballers; a way to appear in touch without ever listening to an iPod or watching a football match, even on TV. Or, for that matter, reading a book.

> *Political Hypocrisy: The Mask of Power from Hobbes to Orwell and Beyond*, David Runciman
> *Good Manners and Bad Behaviour: The Unofficial Rules of Diplomacy*, Candida Slater
> *Nudge: Improving Decisions about Health, Wealth and Happiness*, Richard H Thaler and Cass R Sunstein
> *Decline to Fall: The Making of British Macro-Economic Policy and the 1976 IMF Crisis*, Douglas Wass
> *Mr Lincoln's T-Mails: The Untold Story of How Abraham Lincoln Used the Telegraph to Win the Civil War*, Tom Wheeler
> *The Post-American World*, Fareed Zakaria

Xavier reached over and picked the book from the very top of the pile. He would ask his wife to drop the rest of them off at the local Oxfam shop. Lilli wouldn't be too happy about it, having to mix with the hoi polloi, but they had more than enough clutter here in the house already and it was better than just dumping them in the rubbish bin. Safer too. Their rubbish was regularly sifted by journalists and other cranks, looking for things to embarrass them with. The binning of Edgar's selected books would be a serious gaffe.

The book he'd picked up was substantial, about half the size of a shoebox. It felt surprisingly good in his hand. He felt more thoughtful already, if not more energetic. Still lacking the energy to rouse himself from the table, he sat back and closed his eyes. The house was empty and the peace was luxurious.

Lilli had left for 'work' about an hour ago. For several years now, his wife had enjoyed a sinecure as 'senior creative director' for a luxury goods retailer, the kind of place that charged £200 for a cufflink box, £250 for an iPod case, and £1,000 for a handbag. Xavier had no idea what a 'creative director', senior or otherwise, actually did. The job had been secured for her by her father in Milan, in return for various, unspecified, favours done for the retailer's chief executive. Privately, after a few drinks late one night, Walter Sarfatti had told his son-in-law that these 'favours' had helped keep the CEO out of prison. Xavier didn't really believe that, though. As far as he could see, no one went to jail in Italy for white-collar crime. And if the slammer had beckoned, Walter would surely have got much more for his services than just a job for his daughter.

Whatever the 'job', however she got it, Xavier didn't see the point of his wife going out to work. They certainly didn't need the money. The net gain to the family finances, once you factored in the childcare costs and the amount Lilli spent on clothes and networking and so forth, was negligible. For all Xavier knew, it could easily be *costing* him money to send her out to work. He personally would rather let the kids have their mother around more often. But the job kept Lilli happy and that was the most important thing. An unhappy Lilli was not good. Not good indeed.

One problem created by their domestic arrangements was the constant turnover in the hired help. Full of enthusiasm and brio, they came from around the world, from China, from Turkey, from South Africa, from various places that Xavier had never even heard of, only to slink off months if not weeks later, crushed by the reality of trying to deal with the Sarfatti-Carlton brood. If anything, the rate of churn was accelerating. They had gone through three au pairs in the last nine months alone.

The current nanny was from Venezuela. She was called Yulexis, so Xavier had nicknamed her 'Christmas'. She was almost two months into her stint and he hoped that she would last longer than the others, not least because she was only twenty-two, *extremely* hot (she had been a semi-finalist in the Miss Venezuela pageant, the year before coming to London) and took a very broad view of her job description. This meant that he was fucking her at every opportunity. Banging the nanny was, he knew, embarrassing, a total cliché, but he wasn't about to give up his droit de seigneur just because of that consideration. If 'Christmas' lasted for six months to a year, that would be perfect. Any less than that and he would feel terribly frustrated (in various ways). Any longer, and she would go from being a bonus to becoming a liability.

He finally worked up the energy to rise from the table and head towards the front door. Standing in the hall was his Cannondale Super 6 Dura Ace Compact Road Bike. Costing more than four grand, it depressed the hell out of Xavier. His brother had talked him into cycling to the Commons as another grand statement, demonstrating the party's vitality, as well as its 'green' credentials. When had everyone gone green? The whole eco-thing was so ubiquitous now that you forgot that only a very few years ago, no one had mentioned it at all, or had cared in the slightest about the melting ice caps or the fate of bloody polar bears. It was such a bore, and such a fraud. Xavier was sure that it was only a fad that couldn't last. He certainly hoped so.

Whatever he hoped, he knew that all this green business wouldn't fade this side of the election. So, in the meantime, he was stuck with the harsh reality that they had set the bar too high for him, bike-wise. Now every time he stepped into a car, even his much trumpeted hybrid, he faced cries of '*hypocrite!*'. The bike thing had become a complete liability, but Edgar insisted that he couldn't give it up. Even though he was followed every morning by a chauffeur-driven limo containing his suits and papers, he still had to get on the bike. It was ridiculous that he couldn't just jump in the back of the car and have a well-earned snooze or read the *Sun*. It wasn't like the cycling image-wise was risk-free; there were several videos of him on YouTube breaking basic traffic laws and almost mowing down pedestrians. He had been dubbed '*The most dangerous thing on two wheels*' and some joker had started an online petition to get him back in his car. Xavier had signed it himself, using twenty-five fake names, in a failed attempt to get Edgar to relent.

At one stage, almost inevitably, the bike had been stolen. Xavier had been ecstatic but to his horror, in defiance of statistical possibility, it had been found again. He couldn't believe it; he owned the only bloody stolen bike in the whole of London ever to be safely returned to its rightful owner. It was just his rotten luck. Xavier dropped the book in his pannier, sticking a bulky fleece underneath, so that enough of the title was visible for the photo op. With gritted teeth, he grabbed the machine and pushed it towards the front door. It was light as a feather and an object of genuine beauty and craftsmanship, but the first thing he was going to do, after their election victory, was to throw the sodding thing under a bus and jump back into his official Jag.

Chapter Four

IAN COULDN'T BELIEVE his luck. Naked and sated, he stretched out on the bed and savoured the cool white crispness of the hotel sheets beneath him. Hooking up with people in chatrooms was, he knew from bitter experience, hit and miss at best. But tonight had been an epiphany. Closing his eyes, and grinning like an idiot, he recalled the gentle but insistent pressure of cool, unyielding enamel on tender flesh and the demented explosion that followed. His heart rate was only now beginning to return to something like normal. Looking down, he ran his left foot over the nine-inch 'Heart of Glass' ribbed dildo lying on the bed and felt a shiver of anticipation. But even here, even now, he was a pragmatist. He didn't want to push his luck. There would be other times. For now, he told himself that he should be happy to let the mixture of endorphins and champagne bliss him out as he waited for sleep.

'Turn over.' He felt playful fingers on his warm, damp balls, and the cool, wet probing of a tongue on his penis.

'I'm done,' he croaked.

'Turn over!' The voice was half laughing, half ordering. 'I haven't finished with you yet.'

Ian opened his eyes and smiled. 'Oh, well,' he sighed, 'if you insist.' Rolling on to his stomach, he buried his head into a plump pillow, groaning slightly in anticipation of the pleasure to come. Immediately, he felt his legs being moved gently apart. He let his mind drift off, thinking about nothing in particular. A few moments later, he was brought back to the present as a pair of fingers slipped between his buttocks and began gently probing his arsehole. He grunted in anticipation.

'Be my guest,' he mumbled into the pillow. 'It's clean.'

Under the slow, steady caresses that rippled up his spine, he finally dozed off. After what could have been a few minutes, could have been half an hour, he woke with a start as cold oil was poured over his shoulders and trickled down his back.

'Ahh!'

'Sorry. It's just geranium and orange oil. I should have warmed it first.' The voice was solicitous, calm, mature, compelling. 'Go back to sleep.'

'OK.' He relaxed back into the pillow and felt the oil turn warm as it was rubbed into his shoulders. Once again, his eyes closed and sleep came quickly.

'Ian?'

He was woken for a second time, with a whisper in his ear. At the same time, a pair of hands gently lifted his hips off the bed, pulling his buttocks apart. Smiling, he automatically tensed his cheeks. *Buns of steel*, he thought. *Not bad for a man my age.* Sleep fell away as a hand grabbed his cock and the 'Heart of Glass' was pushed firmly up his backside. Cool and insistent, he felt the skin stretch and threaten to tear. He gasped, unable to distinguish the pleasure from the pain. Pushing the hand away, he grabbed his now firm member and began pumping furiously.

For ten, fifteen, twenty seconds, they established a rhythm. Rapidly reaching the point of no return, he dismissed the idea of holding back and gave one final stroke, before coming for the second time. There was less semen this time, but still a respectable amount. With a grunt of satisfaction, he collapsed back on the bed, taking care to avoid his own mess.

Still well embedded up his arse, the dildo came to a stop. 'Ian? I'm not finished yet.'

'Do what you will,' he said yawning, as he stuck the pillow over his head. 'I am spent. Take me as you please.'

With more than a hint of petulance, the dildo was thrust roughly further inside him.

'Gently!'

'I'm not hurting you, am I?' A hand gently stroked the back of his neck.

'No … Well, maybe just a little. Be careful. Don't damage the nerve ends.'

The dildo probed a little deeper and resumed its steady movement. The hand began rubbing his neck more firmly, as if to provide a distraction from the increasing pain. Ian's eyes darted from side to side but, so close to the pillow, could see nothing. He could feel his heartbeat thumping against the mattress and a sudden spurt of adrenaline reignited his earlier feelings of pleasure. He tried to push himself up, but the hand on his neck forced him down, kept his face firmly into the sheets. Just as the sense of panic threatened to overwhelm him, the dildo slid out of him. The trapped wind made a farting noise, and they both laughed. The pressure on his neck was also released, and he felt a gentle kiss descend behind his left ear. Relaxing back into the sheets, he closed his eyes and waited for his heart rate to slow.

'Don't worry.' Another kiss. 'If that dildo is too much for you, I have something else.'

'Just be gentle,' he murmured. From deep in the pillow, he could see that the bedside clock read 1.05 a.m. He had to be at work in just over four hours so this time he really did have to get some sleep. 'It's late, and maybe we've had enough for tonight,' he said, sounding as casual as possible. 'We can do this again some other time. I need to get some rest now, but you can stay if you want to.'

'That's OK.' He felt the mattress shift and heard the sound of bare feet padding across the thin carpet. 'I will have to get going, but, first, I've got something to round the night off nicely.'

Whatever. Having called time, Ian had already moved on in his mind, and was thinking about the people that he had to meet in the morning. They were Chileans, dealers in 'specialist' technology, and very nice clients. Happily, they were also undemanding types, which would be just as well on this particular occasion.

He was just dreaming about demolishing a full English breakfast when he felt a sharp, burning pain explode through his abdomen. 'What?' he cried, his eyes welling up before he could even open them. This time, the flesh was definitely tearing. There was another blow before he could throw off the pillow and flip over on to his back. The sheets beneath him were turning red. Then he saw the blade, dripping with blood, his blood, being waved in front of his face. *I should scream*, he thought as he watched the knife scything through his cheek, extending his mouth all the way to his left ear. *Help!* his brain screamed, but all that came out was a gurgle.

A series of blows rained down on his face, neck and torso. Even as he was bringing his arms up to his head in a futile attempt to defend himself, he was mesmerised by the weapon. It was almost as if it was working on its own. Once, twice, three times, he tried to grab it, simply attracting gashes to his hands and arms. Grabbing a pillow, he tried to hide from the attack, but a swift knee to the balls sent him sprawling. As he fell off the bed, his head bounced off a side table and he landed on the floor.

Dazed, he tried to curl up into a ball but found himself being dragged back on to the bed. Maybe he cried for his mother; or maybe he just imagined that he did. For what seemed like an eternity, the blows kept descending. Even the repeated moaning, as metal penetrated flesh, and the occasional grunt of his assailant could not drown out the whirr of the air-conditioning.

As he drifted out of consciousness for the last time, Ian could not believe his bad luck.

Chapter Five

Yorkshire, June 1984

'SIT STILL, SUNSHINE. This is going to hurt.' The voice was tired, bored, provincial. Not friendly, not interested.

Fresh out of Hendon training college, Constable John Carlyle felt a long way from home.

'You'll feel just a little sting. Move around and it will get worse.'

'Shit!' Carlyle screwed up his face and closed his eyes tightly. The sweat trickled down his forehead from beneath his recently refreshed number-one buzz cut, mingling with the TCP liquid antiseptic that had just been rubbed into the gash above his right eye. Although barely two inches long, it felt massive and deep, and Carlyle could feel it opening and closing as he wiggled his eyebrows. He was sure that his skull was now exposed to the elements. *Maybe my brain will slip out*, he thought. Assuming that he still had one.

'Sit still! Surely you London boys can take a bit of rough-and-tumble, can't you?' The pasty paramedic, dressed in a green jumpsuit, his gargoyle face looking washed out in the glare of the intense sunlight, stood back to admire his work. He pronounced himself satisfied, then quickly slapped a plaster the size of a cigarette packet on Carlyle's forehead.

'You're done,' he said.

Carlyle opened one eye. 'It hurts.'

'I told you it would.' The gargoyle took a quick swig from the TCP bottle, swilled it around his mouth and spat it on the ground. He offered to share a taste. Carlyle shook his head and looked away. Wiping more sweat from his forehead, he felt the heat rising from his face and felt the snot desiccating and solidifying in his nose. This was not where he wanted to be, stuck in the middle of a row of terraced houses in the middle of some hapless, downtrodden, down-at-heel village in the middle of the north of England.

Even the weather was wrong. In the middle of his dark mood, summer had finally arrived, exploding on the scene in all its glory. What little breeze there had been earlier had vanished. The sky was a deep blue of infinite promise, suggesting long summer holidays, vanilla ice cream with strawberry sauce on top, and deckchairs on Brighton beach. Across the street, a radio began blasting out 'Electric Avenue' by Eddy Grant. Think long enough and hard enough, Carlyle told himself, and maybe you could think yourself somewhere else. Maybe ... but not for very long.

According to the weather forecast, it was supposed to reach thirty-one degrees this afternoon. Sitting here in the sun, it felt a whole lot hotter. Inside the various layers of his riot gear, it was probably well above 40 degrees, possibly even 45. Up since 4 a.m., he had spent four hours sitting on a bus, and then more than six hours standing around in the sun, with the PSU (the Police Support Unit, the riot squad) ranged in front of him, and the mounted officers lined up behind. Their horses were ready to go into action at the sound of the Commander's whistle, bolting towards the strikers whether Carlyle and his colleagues got out of their way in time or not.

Waiting.

Waiting.

Fucking waiting.

Nothing to do but stand around, with only the occasional hurled insult and the promise of a ruck offering some diversion.

This was nothing new. More than three hundred police officers bussed in from around the country had been living in a hangar on the airbase at RAF Syerston for almost a week now. Syerston was an hour down the road, in Nottinghamshire, where only twenty per cent of mineworkers were on strike. Here in Yorkshire, where Carlyle was currently pressed into service, the figure was more than ninety-seven per cent. That meant dozens of pitched battles up and down the county; and thousands of arrests. The working day consisted of fourteen-hour shifts, with the rest of the time divided into six hours' sleep and four hours of wishing you were either working or sleeping.

APART FROM THE minor head injury, today was a fairly standard day. Peeling his tongue off the floor of his mouth, Carlyle tried to swallow. His head throbbed viciously, nastier than any bastard hangover he had yet managed to inflict on himself during his first two decades on the planet. Behind the pain, 'I Fought the Law' by The Clash was playing on a continuous loop deep within the mush of his brain. Under different circumstances, the irony would have made him smile. Now he just wished that Joe Strummer, Mick Jones et al. would kindly shut the fuck up and get out of his head.

Carlyle looked up at the gargoyle. 'Got any aspirin?'

The paramedic grunted and tossed him a small foil-covered tray of pills pulled from his pocket. Carlyle popped two, and then another two, shoving the remainder into the inside pocket of his overalls. He grabbed a bottle of water from the low wall on which he was sitting, and took a cautious sip. His throat felt raw and it didn't feel as if the pills would stay down. He felt the aspirin fighting their way back up, and swallowed hard.

'Will I need stitches?' Carlyle asked hopefully. Naturally squeamish at the best of times, he wasn't a big fan of hospitals, but a couple of hours spent in one this afternoon would do nicely. He was in the market for some sympathy, and some hands-on care from a nubile nurse would go down a treat.

'You'll be fine,' the gargoyle said, as he stripped off his rubber gloves and groped for the packet of cigarettes in the breast pocket of his uniform. 'The brick, or whatever it was, basically bounced off your helmet. You should have a nice scar though. I'm sure it will look good for the girls.'

'Thanks a lot,' Carlyle grimaced, filing the comment away for future reference, all the same. Anything that helped with girls would be more than welcome. He wondered if he would have to pay for a new helmet. The old one had gone flying when he went down, and was now probably destined to become a trophy in someone's living room.

'Leave the plaster on for a couple of days,' advised the gargoyle in a detached tone, sounding as if he was reading from a book of instructions. 'If the cut opens up again after you take it off, go to the hospital.' He glanced back down the road, whence the noise of the crowd ebbed and flowed. It was like listening to the spectators at a football match when you were standing two streets away from the ground itself. 'I wouldn't visit one round here, though, if I were you,' he added, grinning.

'No,' Carlyle nodded. Round here, the police weren't exactly popular.

'You wouldn't want another crack on the head,' the medic added.

'No.'

'And you wouldn't want to get yourself lynched.'

'No.'

The gargoyle pulled an unfiltered cigarette out of his packet of Capstan. Carlyle smiled as he recognised the sailor logo. Capstan Full Strength (*For men who feel strongly about cigarette taste!*) had been his grandfather's chosen brand. Ever since Carlyle could remember, his granddad's fingers had been stained yellow from the nicotine and his cardigan pocket marked with cigarette burns. He'd always have a cigarette in one hand, often with a glass of Johnnie Walker Red Label in the other. Carlyle was no expert, but reckoned that the cigs and the booze didn't do much for the old fella's health. He had died two years previously, having barely made sixty but looking as if he was twenty years older.

Lighting up, the gargoyle ran a hand over his shaven head to wipe away a sheen of sweat that reappeared almost immediately. After a deep drag, he took the cigarette from his mouth, lent over and coughed up a large lump of brown phlegm which he deposited into the gutter, before plonking himself down on the back step of the ambulance. In the front cab, a radio chattered away, but he paid it no heed.

Along the road Carlyle counted another three ambulances where various policemen and strikers – coal miners who had been engaged in an increasingly messy and bitter industrial dispute for several months now – were being attended to for their minor injuries. One of the policemen was busy arguing with a photographer who had just taken his picture. Rather than wait to get thumped or, worse still, have his camera smashed into the tarmac, the snapper turned on his heels and marched off as quickly as he could manage, without quite breaking into a trot. The copper obviously thought about going after him before deciding that it just wasn't worth the effort.

Further in the background, the hum of the afternoon's struggle continued: five thousand police versus five thousand strikers. The scuffles that had been raging all across a worthless couple of acres of scrubland – outside the coking plant in an exhausted village called Orgreave, about five miles south of Sheffield, in the self-proclaimed Socialist Republic of South Yorkshire – showed no sign of abating.

Smoke rose lazily into the sky from a car that had been cremated, by accident or design, on the edge of the skirmishes. The gargoyle took a final monster drag on his cigarette and tossed it next to a discarded yellow *Coal Not Dole* sticker lying on the pavement. Stubbing it out with the toe of his liver-coloured Doc Martens boot, he wandered into a front garden a couple of doors down, to take a piss behind a bush.

Carlyle looked around, wondering what to do next. This wasn't what he had signed up for. Pouring most of the last of the water from the bottle over his head, he promised himself that, once this nonsense was finally all over, he would scuttle back to London and bloody well stay there.

CONSTABLE JOHN CARLYLE's badge number was V253. Like all of the police officers, however, today he was not wearing any number. The normal identification worn on their shoulder straps had been taken off before the start of the day's proceedings, to help avoid any trouble involving legal action and civil-liberties claims later. This divestment had become part of the daily pre-ruck ritual on the coach, as the officers were delivered to whichever picket line they were policing that morning.

'Right, lads,' barked their Scottish sergeant, Charlie Ross, 'numbers off. Stick 'em in your pockets. We are not going to have any problems today.'

'No, Sergeant.'

'Rest assured, gentlemen, that no one will be pissing all over your fine work accomplished here at a later date.' A general murmur of agreement rose from the seats closest to him. 'And, remember, what happens on the picket line, stays on the picket line. We watch each other's backs.'

'Yes, Sergeant,' came back the weary reply.

The smell on board was foul. The air was thick with stale sweat, body odour and nervous excitement. Carlyle stared out of the window and tried to breathe through his mouth. Sitting next to him was Dominic Silver, another recent recruit from Hendon. Dom was a genuine, one hundred per cent cockney, an east London lad, complete with regulation cheery-chappy grin plastered across his face. He was considered a 'mate', the kind of bloke who you should never confuse with a friend. Still, under the circumstances, Carlyle was more than happy to have someone he knew on the bus with him that morning.

Dom rocked back and forth, playing an imaginary set of drums on the back of the seat in front of him. He was speeding his tits off, but so was Carlyle. Dom knew where to get his hands on the best amphetamine sulphate, and half a teaspoon in a mug of black coffee set the day up nicely. Tired and wired was a million times better than just tired.

Dom broke off from his drum solo, nudged Carlyle in the ribs and stuck his hand up. 'Sergeant?' he gestured, like a hyper five year old. 'Sergeant?'

Carlyle rolled his eyes to the heavens, knowing what was coming.

'Yes, son?' Charlie Ross grinned, enjoying such banter. In his fifties, he was at least twenty-five years older than anyone else on the bus. Carlyle couldn't decide whether that made him super-hard or merely super-sad. On the brink of retirement, Charlie was small and gaunt, with sunken cheeks and a biker moustache straight out of Village People. When he rolled up his sleeves, you could see a Japanese dragon tattoo on his right forearm. There was an evil twinkle in his eye at all times, except when the booze took hold and he was about to keel over.

Despite the crushing schedule, all of this rushing around York-shire and Nottinghamshire had given Charlie a new lease of life. He looked twenty years younger than he had done when Carlyle had first seen him three months earlier, outside Cortonwood col-liery, just down the road from where they were today, frogmarch-ing a striker towards a Black Maria.

Dom put his question slowly and thoughtfully: 'Didn't I read in the paper that the new Home Secretary has promised that *all* transgressions on the picket line, committed by *either* side, will be dealt with properly, without fear or favour?'

The sarky little bugger had been reading the *Daily Telegraph* again. Not for the first time, Carlyle wondered why Dom hadn't gone for some career that would have been better suited to his restless spirit and sharp brain. Surely, it would have been easy for him to get into the City and make shitloads of money as some kind of trader. He was just too sharp to be a plod.

Laughter trickled round the bus. The small minority aware that the relatively exotic Leon Brittan had become Home Secretary only a week before did not have much time for *his* views on their current battle. A CV that included Haberdashers' Aske's Boys' School, Trinity College Cambridge, President of the Cambridge Union Society and a career as a lawyer certainly did not impress these young police officers. They knew that such a background didn't give him the right to pass comment on those obliged to do the dirty work.

Charlie stuck his thumbs into the breast pockets of his tunic and thrust out his chest. 'Well' – he had been given his cue and was preparing for the big build-up – 'I can tell you this ...' he then glanced up and down the bus to make sure his audience was paying attention, '... there are three things in life that are of absolutely no use to man or beast ...'

Carlyle grinned. He had heard it all before, several times, but he knew that Charlie's monologue would still make him laugh.

Charlie ploughed on: 'These are the Pope's testicles ...' pause, smiles all round, 'tits on a man ...' another pause to acknowledge the cheers, 'and ...' extra pause, 'a politician's promise.' A fierce round of applause ran through the bus, accompanied by cheers, whistles and truncheons being beaten against windows. Charlie made a small bow and, having milked it enough, let the smile fall from his lips. He began prowling the aisle, eyeing up his charges, looking for any signs of doubt or apprehension. 'These fuckers aren't going to give us any trouble today. Am I right?'

Nervous laughter filled the coach. A couple of cheery voices responded to Charlie's rallying cry: 'Yes, Sergeant!'

'So don't be shy.' Ross chuckled as he watched a group of mounted police gathering fifty yards down the road. 'Show 'em who's boss.'

A few more joined in this time: 'Yes, Sergeant!'

'Don't be a bunch of fucking poofs. Show those fucking communists who's fucking boss.'

'YES, SERGEANT!'

As the din died down, a voice came from the back of the bus: 'Where are we, Sergeant?'

Charlie Ross gazed dreamily out of the window. 'Dunno, son. Some DNS or other.'

'DNS?' someone asked.

'Dirty Northern Shithole.'

More laughter.

Another voice piped up: 'And what are we doing here, Sergeant?'

'Precisely?' asked another.

'Exactly?' Carlyle laughed.

'Specifically?' queried another wag.

'What is this?' Charlie snarled in mock fury, though loving every minute of it. 'Twenty fucking questions?' He smacked his truncheon against the side of a nearby seat and fixed his stare on one of the questioners. 'We are here, lads, as you very well know, to maintain law and fucking order; to allow the ordinary working man do his job without interference; to protect the innocent; and,' he paused again, to unveil his final and most winning smile of the morning, 'most importantly of all, to break some fucking heads.'

CARLYLE'S HEADACHE WAS getting worse. He swallowed another aspirin and pocketed the foil wrapper. Sitting motionless on the wall, he shut his eyes in an attempt to try to keep out the light, which seemed to be bouncing off every available surface in order to assault his brain with the maximum violence possible. He took a couple of slow, deep breaths. Finally, his heart slowed to a more recognisable beat. Now he could at least count the various different components of his all-round discomfort. Under the uniform, his T-shirt had melted into his chest. Sweat trickled down his spine and between the cheeks of his bum. Right on cue, his piles started playing up and he felt as if he had a knife stuck up his arse. He could feel his stomach churning and felt a chill wrap itself around his shoulders. Being so dehydrated, at least Carlyle didn't also have to worry about needing a piss. With all the gear on, it would have taken him the best part of an hour to expose his dick.

Somewhere along the road, he could hear the hooves of a pair of police horses clattering over tarmac. Beyond them, a roar went up on the field of combat, as one side charged the other. Carlyle closed his eyes tighter and refocused on his breathing.

After a few minutes, he tried to stand and felt his legs buckle. His mouth was still dry and sticky and his stomach heaved. He leant over the nearest wall and vomited into the garden. That brought some temporary relief, and he tried to puke again but nothing more would come out. Carlyle pushed his fingers down his throat. No joy. Spent, he just sat there, feeling useless.

After a few moments, the dizziness eased. Sticking another couple of aspirin in his mouth, he took a final swig of water and swallowed quickly. Standing up, he began moving slowly up the street, away from the din of conflict. A police Alsatian had become separated from his handler, and was casually walking along the road too, heading away from all the noise and confusion. Like Carlyle, the dog looked as if he'd had more than enough for the day.

Carlyle kept his eyes on the ground, quickly jumping backwards as a piece of brick exploded near his feet.

'Fuck off, pig!'

Carlyle looked up. Almost twenty feet away, he saw a kid of maybe ten or eleven flipping him the finger. Laughing at the disorientated policeman, the kid turned on his heels and started sprinting off down the road. Almost immediately, he tripped over his feet and crashed on to the tarmac, skidding along the street in a ball of blood, snot and tears. *Serves the little shit right,* Carlyle thought. Resisting the temptation to go over and give him a kick, he kept on walking.

What he wanted was some shade, but there was none to be found. He was in a regular terraced street of straightforward two-up, two-down red-brick houses, each with a cobbled yard at the back and a small garden at the front. It was a typical Northern working-class neighbourhood, the kind of road where trees were in short supply.

In the end, he settled for the shade provided by an overgrown hedge, about five feet tall and seven feet wide, bordering a garden maybe eight doors along from the ambulance. He slipped through the open gate and slumped down on the threadbare grass, before crawling under the bush in search of a little respite from the relentless sun and the blinding light.

CARLYLE WAS WOKEN by a man's scream, followed by the sounds of a struggle nearby.

'Get off me you, bastard ...'

'Bite me, would you?' the male voice growled.

'Stop it.'

'C'mon ...'

'Fuck ... right ... OFF!'

'Bitch!'

He slowly realised that they were somewhere behind him, in another garden, three doors further along. Getting to his feet, he squinted through the intervening hedge. Unable to see anything, he stepped back into the street and moved towards the arguing voices.

He saw the woman first. She was wearing worn blue jeans and a grubby white V-neck T-shirt. Behind her stood a policeman, sweating profusely in the same protective gear as Carlyle. His helmet had been knocked to the ground, and he had one arm wrapped around her neck. His other hand was firmly clamped on her left breast, which he was pawing slowly in a clockwise direction.

As he stepped closer, Carlyle could see that the woman was not wearing a bra. Her nipples were erect, clearly visible through her T-shirt. He had not had sex – of any description – for more than a fortnight, and now felt a sharp twinge in his groin. The stirring of it brought him a welcome distraction from the headache, but he was embarrassed all the same and felt his cheeks flush.

Looking up, both of them eyed Carlyle warily.

She was about 5'4", with short blond hair. This was clearly one of the enemy within, one of the women that supported the strikers on the picket line; probably someone's wife or girlfriend. Her grey eyes were hard and blazed with hatred. Aged anything from twenty-five to fifty-plus, she looked pinched, tired and thin, with the same washed-out, grubby, bleached complexion they all had.

The absence of any badge numbers didn't stop Carlyle from recognising Trevor Miller. They had come up from London together at the beginning of the tour and, although the two of them didn't always end up working on the same picket line, Carlyle had noticed him on each of the last three days. Maybe five years older than Carlyle, Miller was far too full of himself, a mouthy so-and-so only too eager to hold forth on what he was going to do to these 'stupid Northern wankers'. Carlyle had last seen him earlier the same day, chasing some bloke over a patch of waste ground in the no man's land intervening between the police and the pickets. The striker had been wearing a toy police hat covered in union stickers, as he flipped Miller the finger and headed off like a scalded cat. Trevor, truncheon at the ready, struggled to catch up with him through a barrage of catcalls and the occasional missile hurled by other strikers.

That had been several hours ago. So what was Miller doing here, now?

Recognising Carlyle, he sized up the situation for a second or two, preparing an explanation. 'It's OK,' he said, his expression blank, 'I've got this sorted.' He glanced down at his hand, which remained clamped on the woman's breast, rising and falling with her breathing.

'What's going on, Trevor?'

The woman belatedly piped up: 'He's touching me up, the dirty bastard.'

Carlyle took a step closer. Miller automatically took a step back, half dragging the woman with him. 'Just fuck off out of it, Carlyle,' he snarled. He was six foot plus, which Carlyle knew gave him about four inches in height and probably about forty pounds in weight. Miller could beat him to a pulp with one hand tied behind his back, but Carlyle knew that he was all front. He could face him down.

The woman started squirming again. 'Get him off me!'

Carlyle stepped through the gate and into the garden. 'What did she do?'

'She assaulted me.'

'Fuck off,' the woman spat in fury. 'You assaulted me, put me in a headlock, grabbed my tits and started squeezing them. Fucking pervert.'

Unbelievably, Trevor started grinning.

'Trevor,' Carlyle sighed, 'she's half your size.'

'So?' He seemed genuinely surprised by the idea that there might be a problem with what he was doing.

'So,' Carlyle shouted, 'the only way she could have assaulted you is with a loaded AK47. Let her fucking go!'

Miller looked at him blankly, a bead of sweat hanging from the tip of his nose.

'Now!'

Stepping sideways, Miller tramped some flower or other into the dirt. Maybe it was even a weed. Staring off into the middle distance, he gave Carlyle's request several seconds' thought. 'Mind your own business, you wanker,' was his considered reply.

It was time for a change of tack. Carlyle spread his arms wide and adopted what he hoped was his most philosophical tone: 'Mate, think about it. You don't want a complaint. It could seriously hurt your career.'

Trevor grunted. 'I'm making an arrest.'

'This is the kind of thing that could cost you your job.' Carlyle was about five feet away from them now, edging closer.

'I've done nothing wrong here, Carlyle.' Trevor looked and sounded like a little boy. A *monster* of a little boy.

'Let her go ... c'mon we have to get back.'

'No!' Trevor shook his head.

Carlyle took another step towards him, trying not to stare at the woman's nipples which seemed to be getting even bigger. *Maybe I'm becoming delusional*, he thought. 'You have to.'

At last, Trevor recognised that Carlyle wasn't going to just walk away. Finally, he let go of the woman's breast and loosened the neck hold slightly. The woman immediately sank her teeth into his arm and bit him as hard as she could.

'Fuck!' Trevor grunted.

With all the gear he was wearing, Carlyle doubted if she even broke the skin, but Miller instinctively recoiled and pushed her away. The woman took this as her cue to make a dash for freedom. She bolted past Carlyle, a bottle-blonde blur that was out of the garden and down the road before he could react. Showing a nice turn of speed, and, Carlyle noticed, a very shapely arse, she was round a corner and out of sight in a matter of seconds.

Trevor struggled with his options as he tried to decide whether or not to give chase. In the end, the final decision was no decision. He shrugged, and the spell was broken.

Carlyle stood there, wondering what to do next. His headache was returning with a vengeance, and he needed again to find some shade.

Eventually, Trevor picked up his helmet and slowly trudged out of the garden. 'You stupid bastard,' he hissed, pushing past Carlyle. 'You stupid bloody bastard, next time try to remember which fucking side you're on.'

Chapter Six

NOT WISHING TO dwell on his rampant stupidity any longer than was absolutely necessary, Inspector Carlyle headed back in the direction he'd come from only ten minutes earlier. The fact that it was such a short walk did nothing to improve his mood. Grinding his teeth in frustration, he lengthened his stride and tried not to think about the bed he could already be lying in. There was no one about to catch a middle-aged policeman talking to himself like a demented dosser, and so he took the opportunity to curse himself loudly. Tonight wasn't the first time this year that he'd arrived outside his flat, stuck his hand in his jacket pocket and realised that he had left his house keys at the station and, therefore, couldn't get in. There was no way he would dare wake his wife at this time of night, so he turned round and headed back to Charing Cross Police Station.

Keeping up a brisk pace, Carlyle cut across the north side of Covent Garden piazza, whose cobbles felt hard and unyielding under the soles of his shoes. This was his home territory, just three blocks north of the biologically dead waters of the River Thames at Waterloo Bridge.

Carlyle passed an imposing mansion standing at number 43 King Street, in the north-west corner of the piazza, which was now home to a flagship shoe store. Back in the nineteenth century it has been one of London's first boxing venues. Then, as now, the prizefight game was so bent that many of the bouts descended into farce. One of the most famous King Street matches ended in chaos after *both* fighters took a dive even before a single punch had been thrown. Not surprisingly, the disgruntled punters sought to take out their frustrations on the two boxers, one of whom found the presence of mind to feign blindness in order to escape a beating from the mob. Legend had it that this 'blind' boxer was declared the winner, and awarded the purse as well.

Glancing up at a poster advertising a new computer game, Carlyle stumbled on a loose cobblestone. He steadied himself in front of the life-size image of a cartoon commando letting fly with a machine-gun in each hand. The game's strapline promised 'a new kind of war'. That's just what the world needs, Carlyle thought sourly, as he resumed walking. Almost immediately, he was passing in front of St Paul's Church. Known as the actor's church, it was currently flanked on one side by an Oakley sunglasses store, and on the other by a Nat West bank. Inigo Jones, the architect, would doubtless be proud, Carlyle thought, to see his celebrated creation now keeping such august company. God would probably be quite chuffed, too.

In front of the church's outsized portico, an acne-scarred youth wearing last season's Arsenal away shirt sat on the kerb, with his head buried in his hands. Oblivious to his suffering, a couple of insomniac pigeons pecked at the large pool of golden vomit shimmering under the orange street lights nearby. Behind him, a very young-looking girl in an insubstantial silver dress stood motionless, expressionless, apparently disinclined to comfort him or to leave him, as their night on the town struggled to die.

The pair paid Carlyle no heed as he walked on. For his part, Carlyle gave the girl a hard stare, saying a silent prayer that his own daughter wouldn't be found in a similar situation in seven or eight years' time.

Reaching the corner of Agar Street, Carlyle looked up and took in the hulking mass of Europe's largest police station. Covering a whole block of some of the most expensive real estate in the world, it stood a couple of blocks north of the eponymous train station. It was a squat, featureless building, rising to six economical storeys, bristling with CCTV cameras on every corner, peppered with windows too small for its bulk; windows for seeing out of rather than for looking in through. The half a dozen old-fashioned blue police lamps placed in random locations around the building looked just as fake as they actually were. The same blue lamp used to be found outside every police station, reminding the public that the police were always ready to serve. Now they were just design accessories.

The station building was painted in an off-white colour that always looked grubby. The finishing touch was a small portico, as if copied from the nearby church in the piazza, framing the front entrance and making it look more like a provincial town hall than a major cop shop.

Charing Cross was one of a hundred and forty Metropolitan Police stations located across London, and Carlyle had been stationed at this one for almost ten years now, making it his longest posting by a considerable margin. In the previous decade and a half, he had made various random stop-offs around the capital in the fairly random circuit of stations that had constituted his 'career' – including Shepherds Bush, Southwark, Brixton, Paddington Green and Bethnal Green. He had moved slowly through the ranks, from constable to sergeant to inspector, having a go at most things: vice, drugs, fraud, homicide and even a short and inglorious spell at Buckingham Palace in the Royal Protection Unit.

Despite picking up more than his fair share of commendations, Carlyle knew that he had never really been considered as part of the team. He was not 'one of us', nor was he a 'safe pair of hands'. Somehow, he had survived, though, without ever becoming part of the family. How had that happened? The powers that be were doubtless as surprised as Carlyle himself that he was still around. Over the years, he had evolved into a jack of all trades and master of none. He had put down roots of a sort, like a tree stuck in the pavement: stable but not necessarily happy.

Climbing the steps, he glanced at the rather modest Charing Cross Police Station sign, which sat below a small and very grubby royal crest. Above the crest, a chaotic rainbow-coloured flag hung limply from its pole, the usual Union Jack having been replaced in recognition of Lesbian Gay Bisexual Transgender Month, whatever that was. Inside, the place was unusually empty, save for a lone figure slumped comatose in the corner.

Walter Poonoosamy, commonly known as 'Dog', was a drunk, a regular nuisance or a local mini-celebrity, depending on your point of view. Dog's moniker came from his habit of approaching tourists who were aimlessly wandering about the piazza and asking for their help in finding his pet Labrador, called Lucky. Lucky, he explained, was his one companion in life, and as luck would have it he had gone missing that very day. As far as anyone knew, there never had been any such animal, but he fitted the stereotype of a down-and-out's faithful friend, which, combined with Dog's not inconsiderable acting ability and persistence in the face of a raging thirst, was usually sufficient to tug at the heartstrings of the gormless enough to easily cover the cost of a couple of 1.5 litre bottles of Diamond White cider, which was his preferred tipple. It was urban legend that one tear-stained performance had prompted a middle-aged American lady from Wyoming to hand over a fifty-pound note and tell the bemused tramp to 'Go get yourself a new dog'.

Tonight, Carlyle could smell evidence of the comprehensive but unscheduled toilet stop which explained why no one had yet tried to move Dog on from his bench. Carlyle observed a sensible exclusion zone around the wino, as he stepped towards the desk where the duty sergeant – an amiable, middle-aged guy called Dave Prentice – was tossing a pair of latex gloves to a disgruntled, sleepy-looking PCSO whom Carlyle didn't recognise. There was a large bottle of disinfectant on the desk, alongside a mop and a bucket of recently boiled water mixed with some industrial-strength disinfectant. The cleaners wouldn't arrive until at least six-thirty, which meant a PCSO had to be press-ganged into action meanwhile. Police Community Support Officers were volunteers who signed on to help the regular police in their spare time, though, with no power to arrest suspected criminals, they were widely derided as 'plastic policemen'. Bored and unmotivated, they were responsible for most cases of gross misconduct among Metropolitan Police staff, usually involving drinking offences and motoring crimes. Twenty or so got sacked each year and, in general, Carlyle tried to have as little to do with them as possible.

'Hurry up and get him out of here,' Prentice grumbled to the PCSO, knowing that there was no question of Dog going into a cell tonight. Ever since a report from the Metropolitan Police's Custody Directorate had calculated that a night spent in the slammer cost a whopping £667, considerably more than the likes of the Dorchester Hotel (£395) and the Ritz (£390), the pressure was on to keep as many of them empty as possible. The hospitality at Charing Cross was therefore reserved for celebrities (C-list and above) and serious criminals only. Definitely no drunks, therefore. Equally, no local hospital would admit Dog, so it was a matter of finding somewhere else to sleep off his stupor.

'Just get him round the corner and stick him in a doorway,' Prentice suggested. 'He'll find his way home soon enough.'

The PCSO grunted and pulled on the latex gloves. He didn't even acknowledge Carlyle as he moved gingerly towards the snoring wino. Carlyle mentally wished him luck and headed in the opposite direction.

Prentice eyed him quizzically as he approached the front desk. 'Back already, John?'

Carlyle made a face. 'Forgot my bloody keys.'

For a man who could really not care less, Prentice did a good job of managing a small grimace of sympathy. 'Unlucky.'

'Yeah, I know. I got almost all the way home before I realised,' Carlyle replied, sounding suitably sorry for himself. 'If I buzzed the front door, Helen would go bananas,' he added, 'even if I didn't wake Alice up, too, what with her having school in the morning.'

Prentice nodded sympathetically. He had three kids himself, two girls and a boy, and knew all about the ups and downs of family life. At the same time, he lived near Theydon Bois, a village on the north-east periphery of London, near Epping Forest, which was famous for not possessing any street lights. Fifteen miles from Charing Cross, it took the best part of an hour on the Central Line for Dave to get home, so he would have had no qualms about waking the kids and getting his missus out of bed if he found himself stuck on the doorstep in deepest, darkest Essex.

Conscious of someone behind him, Carlyle turned to see a skinny, blond-haired, twenty-something man approaching the desk. He wore a pained expression – all cheekbones and attitude – and was fashionably dressed in an expensive-looking, two-button, single-breasted black suit and a crisp white shirt. As he reached the desk, Carlyle could read the legend *The Garden* in tiny grey script on his breast pocket. The Garden was an upmarket 'boutique' hotel only two minutes' walk away, on St Martin's Lane, just up the road from Trafalgar Square. It was a haunt of minor celebrities and gossip columnists, always full of self-important people doing self-important things.

The young man ignored Carlyle. Without saying a word, he handed Prentice a white envelope and turned to leave.

'Hold on, there.' Carlyle placed a gentle hand on the visitor's shoulder. 'What is this?'

The man stopped, turned and gave him a neutral look. 'I guess it's a letter.'

'I can see that, *sir*,' Carlyle said, with considerable effort, not least because 'sir' was not a word he felt comfortable in using. He took the envelope from Prentice and looked at the address in black capitals on the front: BY HAND – FAO THE DUTY OFFICER, CHARING CROSS POLICE STATION. He glanced back at the young man. 'Who gave you this?'

'The chief concierge at the hotel.' The man shrugged, like that should be obvious.

Carlyle felt his mood harden. He could be obtuse himself often enough, when he felt like it, but he didn't like it in others. Not when he was on the receiving end. He glared at the man, who took a step backwards till he was leaning against the desk.

'What's your name?' Carlyle growled.

'Anders.'

'Second name?'

'Brolin. Anders Brolin. I am from Sweden.'

'No shit,' Carlyle looked at Prentice and grunted, 'straight out of central casting.' Prentice raised his eyebrows but said nothing.

'Excuse me?'

'Nothing.' Carlyle looked the young man up and down. 'Where in Sweden are you from?'

'Skåne.'

That didn't mean anything to Carlyle. 'Where?'

'It's in the south of the country,' the man said slowly, clearly, to accommodate both the geographical ignorance of the English and the fact that he was talking to a couple of policemen. 'I am from a town called Ystad.'

'Never heard of it.'

Brolin seemed to perk up a little at the thought of home. 'It's nice but very quiet. Nothing ever happens there.' He almost smiled, then thought better of it. 'It's a good place to be a policeman.'

'Not like London.'

'Not like London, no. Here there are too many ...' Brolin paused.

Carlyle stepped in: 'Too many wankers?'

'Yes,' Brolin gave a tired smile, 'far too many.'

'So,' Carlyle waved the envelope gently in the air, 'what about this?'

'This is nothing to do with me,' Brolin said, making an involuntary jerk of the head in the direction of the front door. 'I just do what I am told.'

'Don't we all.' Prentice chuckled.

'Anyway, my shift is finishing soon,' Brolin added. 'Why don't you just see what it says?'

'OK.' Carlyle sighed, recalling that his own shift had finished over an hour ago. *This is what happens when you dick around,* he told himself. He'd forgotten his keys two or three times recently. Maybe his mind was going: short-term memory loss. Maybe he should start carrying a spare set at all times. That was a good idea. He'd just have to try to remember it.

Into his head popped a mental image of his wife snoring happily under the duvet in his beautiful warm bed. Then it slowly, cruelly, receded into the distance until it faded to black. With a sigh, he tore open the envelope and pulled out a single sheet of paper. 'Let's see what this says and then we can both go home,' he murmured. Dropping the empty envelope on the desk, he unfolded the sheet of paper and scanned the contents.

It was a standard piece of hotel stationery, but good quality, heavy grey paper with the hotel name and email address embossed at the top. The same writing as on the envelope simply stated: *BODY IN 329. NOT THE FIRST & NOT THE LAST.* Beneath the text there was a couple of dark splashes that looked like blood. They had soaked into the paper but hadn't yet dried.

Carlyle waved the handwritten note first at Prentice, then at Brolin. 'Know anything about this?'

'No,' said Brolin sulkily, 'I told you I didn't.'

This note was, Carlyle already knew, 99.9 per cent certain to be time-wasting bollocks. A body in a hotel room, if there even was one, would be suspicious, but not necessarily criminal. Charing Cross Police Station had registered seven 'suspicious' deaths last year, five of which were subsequently deemed murder or manslaughter. All of those cases had been duly solved, and none of them had involved tourists or hotels. Halfway through the current year and they had already had six suspicious deaths, five of which were criminal, with the other one still a matter of some debate. The law of averages told Carlyle that this note was someone's idea of a joke. People, as he knew only too well, did some incredibly stupid things. And, as he knew even better, they usually got away with it, leaving other people chasing their tails or cleaning up the mess.

Of course, bollocks or not, he now would have to go and look for himself, just in case. Carlyle saw several hours of time wasting ahead of him and felt his body sag. He gritted his teeth to help keep hold of his anger.

'This,' he said, pointing a finger at Brolin, 'had better not be one of your fucked-up guests pissing about.' Aching with tiredness, Carlyle could feel himself starting to go off on one, but he was saved by Prentice putting a hand on his arm, gently telling him to give it a rest. It was a timely intervention, and Carlyle acknowledged it with a nod. He understood the sergeant's point: don't shoot the messenger – even if he does appear to be a moron.

Brolin held up his hands in supplication. 'All I did was bring you the letter.'

Carlyle scratched his head. 'OK, fair enough.' He took a deep breath and tossed the sheet of paper next to the envelope lying on the desk. 'Better bag those up, Dave, just in case this is for real. Get one of the constables down here now, and then we'll go and take a look.' He turned to Brolin: 'You wait here. I'll be back in a second, once I've collected my keys.'

Chapter Seven

THE GARDEN HOTEL on St Martin's Lane, just north of Trafalgar Square, was a 1960s office block which had been bought by in the early 1990s by Mexican billionaire Jeronimo Borgetti. Borgetti had then hired an über-cool American designer called Alan Wall to turn it into a luxury boutique hotel. For the billionaire, it was a nice addition to his global property portfolio, as well as somewhere to stay whenever he too was in town. It was one of those places that always made Carlyle uncomfortable, however. The place tried *soooo* hard to be *soooo* stylish that mere mortals like him could never hope to keep up. He always had to first ask the price, and so could never afford the product.

Waiting for the chief concierge to arrive, Carlyle stood in the pale yellow and green light of the lobby, thinking again how he really should be in bed. Even at this hour, a regular stream of people moved in and out of the place. To Carlyle, they all looked too confident, too complacent. The sound of laughter drifted over from the Light Bar at the rear of the building, where there was still half an hour to go until closing time. What kind of people go out drinking at two-thirty on a Monday morning, Carlyle wondered sourly. Young and rich, he supposed, the kind of people who didn't have to worry about going off to work in an hour or two.

Tapping a shoe on the immaculate Portuguese Moleanos honed beige limestone, Carlyle picked up a copy of the hotel brochure and instinctively sniffed it. It smelled expensive and felt heavy in his hand. Flipping through the pages, he smiled at the marketing copy which spoke of 'an utterly original urban resort', 'a new paradigm', and 'a manifestation of the cultural *Zeitgeist*'. The expensively printed booklet just confirmed that The Garden was not his kind of place, not that its owners would be losing any sleep over that. A rather shabby, middle-aged policemen was definitely not the kind of target customer for a high-end establishment aimed at an 'itinerant "tribe" of world travellers who routinely stop off between the twenty-four-hour international gateway cities of London, Paris, Milan, New York, Los Angeles, Miami and the like ...'

Actually, off duty, Carlyle had been here more than a few times with Helen before they were married. Back in the 1980s and early nineties, they had regularly come to visit the old Lumiere Cinema which had then resided in the basement of the hotel building. They had visited the hotel bar once, but the damage done to Carlyle's wallet was so severe that he was never short of a credible alternative nearby thereafter. The thought of that one bill still made him shiver, more than twenty years after the event.

The Lumiere was another matter, however. He recalled it with affection, if not outright nostalgia. His now-wife would take him to see French movies like *Betty Blue* and *Les Amants du Pont-Neuf*. Waiting for the concierge, Carlyle thought about those days for the first time in ages. Early-afternoon matinees in an empty cinema. *Perfect*. Perfect and long gone, for now the Lumiere had been turned into a gym.

Patience was not Carlyle's strong point. He quickly found himself tapping the ridiculously expensive floor with increasing fury, as the concierge still failed to appear. It had been more than five minutes now and he was getting ready to shout at someone, when Alex Miles finally appeared from behind one of the lobby's pillars, offering a cautious hand and a pro-forma smile.

'Inspector ...' the smile had drained from Miles' face before the whole word was out. Dressed in a pair of polished brown brogues, freshly pressed blue jeans, a crisp white shirt and a Prince of Wales jacket (grey with tan and green in the check), Miles was thus signalling that he was off duty and therefore being even more gracious with his time than usual.

'Alex ...' Carlyle eyed him blankly, signalling – as if it needed signalling at this time of night – that this was strictly business. More than that, it indicated that the very least he would be leaving with later this morning would be another debit written against Miles' name in the Carlyle favour bank, the ongoing details of which were held in the policeman's brain at all times.

'Sorry to keep you waiting.' Alex Miles bowed his head in supplication. 'It's all kicking off tonight. We had some problems with Carlton Jackson's people ...'

'The boxer?' Carlyle asked. Jackson was an American heavyweight recently arrived in London for a fight. Before the bout could take place, he had been arrested for being drunk and disorderly, and assaulting a police officer. 'I thought he'd been deported.'

'Not yet,' Miles smiled. 'Anyway, it's sorted.'

'Good,' said Carlyle, impatiently. 'Now, about the matter in hand ...'

'Yes.' Miles bowed again. Carlyle wondered if he might have some Japanese blood in him somehow. More likely he was just taking the piss. Miles straightened up and started playing with a button on his jacket. 'How can I help?'

As chief concierge at The Garden, Miles had acted as the hotel's senior fixer for their more important and demanding guests for more than five years now. The Garden popped up on Carlyle's radar once or twice a year and, consequently, their paths had crossed maybe three or four times. Miles was what Carlyle would describe as a low-level acquaintance. He operated in that grey area between upstanding citizen, usually of no use to Carlyle, and actual convicted criminal, the kind of person who kept the inspector in his job but was a pain in the arse at the same time.

Doubtless, Miles broke various laws of one sort or another, mostly relating to drugs and prostitution, on a daily basis. But he did so in a way, and in an environment, that meant his misdemeanours were of little or no concern to Carlyle. Both men understood that socially acceptable levels of behaviour were in a constant state of flux, and invariably strayed beyond the letter of the law.

Like Miles, Carlyle believed in self-interest, enlightened self-interest. This was as good a basis for their relationship as any, requiring no real thought and the minimum of action.

Like any good policeman, Carlyle very rarely concerned himself with the self-obsession and self-indulgences of the rich. He knew that, when it came to money, the law was only partially blind. Most of the time, the best way to deal with the well-off, with their acute sense of entitlement, was merely to ignore them. He always thought that he inherited such pragmatism from his father, who had never tired of advising his son: 'Don't get into pissing contests you can't win.' For Carlyle, after more than forty years on the planet and more than twenty years on the job, this rule only broke down with the extreme cases ... like murder, for instance.

Like any good fixer, Miles knew where to get anything and everything. That was a basic requirement of the job, since the hotel's 'itinerant tribe' could be very demanding. It was his ability to acquire specific, reliable, up-to-date information for his clients that became of occasional interest to Carlyle. Once Miles realised that the inspector was a pragmatist, and otherwise not in the least bothered about the needs of his 'tribe', he felt comfortable in doing business with him. As a result, the two men had casually established a modest relationship, just one of the hundreds that populated each man's professional life.

There were now four of them standing around the concierge's table. It was a mahogany Regency writing desk, largely hidden behind an oversized sofa in the left-hand corner of the lobby, and which did not fit in with the rest of the décor in any way, shape or form. Carlyle and Miles had now been joined by the obtuse porter, Brolin, and by PC Tim Burgess, a rather pretty but callow-looking youth who was currently half hiding behind a pillar.

Burgess had arrived with Carlyle from the station, but rather stood out here in his uniform, and also seemed rather overawed by his surroundings. Within two minutes of arriving in the lobby, the young constable had received an interested, wolfish glance from a clearly inebriated middle-aged woman wandering across the foyer from the bar towards the lifts. Carlyle was amused to see Burgess blush dramatically and he half expected the woman to come over, throw PC Burgess over one shoulder and carry him upstairs. Without a doubt, frozen with fright, Burgess would have been powerless to resist. *Thank God I've got the help,* Carlyle thought. *Let's hope the killer, if there is a killer, has already left the building.* He tossed the brochure back on the desk and turned to focus on Miles.

'Has Brolin told you about the note?' he asked.

'Yes,' Miles nodded. 'How bizarre. Do you think it's a joke?'

'Probably,' Carlyle smiled slightly, 'knowing your clientele.'

Miles frowned. 'That's a bit harsh, Inspector. I've never experienced anything like this before.'

'I suppose it makes a change from them trashing hotel rooms, shitting out of windows and beating up hookers,' Carlyle mused, referring back to a previous incident, where one member of the entourage of a visiting American actor had ended up making the short trip from the care of Mr Miles into the care of Mr Carlyle, and back again ... before either the judiciary or, more importantly the media, had become involved.

'There's not a lot of that kind of stuff either, these days.' Miles sounded almost disappointed. 'It's one of the consequences of the credit crunch.'

'I've read about that.' Carlyle smiled the sickly smile of a public servant who knew that the shortcomings of the international credit markets remained someone else's problem. At least until some bastard politician started hacking away at his pension. If this crash took some rich tossers down with it, that had to be a good thing. But the sense of *schadenfreude* was fleeting, knowing that people like that always seemed to get by. 'It must be tough for your customers ...'

Miles raised his eyes to the heavens. 'It's squeezing us quite hard.'

'Anyway,' Carlyle continued, 'let's keep it to ourselves 'til I've had a proper look. Who gave you the note?'

Miles jerked one shoulder in the direction of the desk. 'It was left on the blotter. Twenty quid on top of it. I was in the bar at the time, so I didn't see who put it there.'

'Cameras?' Carlyle asked. He couldn't immediately see any, but there had to be some. 'Will they have recorded anything?'

'Maybe.'

Carlyle told Burgess to make a note about checking the closed-circuit television later, if it became necessary, and turned back to the concierge. 'How long ago was this?'

Miles made a face. 'Maybe a couple of hours.'

'And you didn't bother to read it.'

'Never thought about it.'

'No?'

'No.'

'A surprising lack of curiosity,' Carlyle mused.

'You get something like that,' Miles reasoned, 'how likely is it to be something that I am really going to want to know about?'

Carlyle acknowledged his point and changed tack. 'So it took you an hour to get it round to us?'

'We were busy. A party of Chinese tourists arrived late, after their plane was delayed six hours. Their luggage was sent to Reykjavik, and the Heathrow Express was up the spout. You know the sort of thing.'

'I suppose so,' said Carlyle, who cared not a jot about the totally shit nature of Britain's transport infrastructure. Rising from the recesses of his memory, Gang of Four's 'At Home He's A Tourist' started playing in his head. Leave home to see the sights and you're asking for trouble. The sensible thing was just to stay at home, surely there was more than enough for them to see in the People's Republic – was it still a People's Republic? – anyway. He looked expectantly at Miles. 'Have you still got the twenty?'

Miles shook his head. 'I nipped up the road to Epoca for a quick macchiato and bought a packet of Marlboro at the same time.'

Par for the course, thought Carlyle. It would have been far too straightforward for him to have just kept the bloody thing. At least it should still be in the café's cash register, as no one would be asking for a twenty in change at this time of night. He quickly despatched Burgess to try to recover the note from Epoca. It was only twenty yards down the road, so hopefully the young PC would not get lost, mugged, raped, or otherwise distracted on the way.

Carlyle watched Burgess leave the premises and then looked around the lobby one more time. It was fairly quiet now. The noise from the Light Bar had subsided to a gentle murmur, and even the party animals seemed to have called it a day. 'OK,' he said, 'let's go see the manager.'

Miles danced around from behind the desk and led Carlyle past the sofa and the pillar, and various other eclectic furnishings, as he headed further into the lobby. 'The night manager is Anna Shue,' he said, nodding in the direction of a tired-looking brunette in the hotel's uniform, who was just coming out of the lifts. She had her hair pulled back in a ponytail, making her look quite austere, and her lack of make-up – a big plus in Carlyle's book – added to this overall effect.

Carlyle stepped forward. 'Fine. Stay down here. Make sure that Brolin stays, too … and keeps his mouth shut.' He put on a frown. 'If this *is* a load of bollocks, we'll forget all about it and you'll just owe me another favour.'

Miles took a theatrical step backwards and put on his best bemused expression. '*Another* favour?'

'Yes, indeed,' Carlyle nodded.

'And if it's not bollocks?' Miles asked.

'It'll be a lot more than *one* favour.'

Miles sighed. 'Understood.'

'Good man! That's the spirit.' Carlyle gently punched him on the shoulder. 'Go and have a cigarette. If I'm not back in five minutes, it means we'll have to start conducting some formal interviews.'

LOOKING TIRED AND hassled, Anna Shue did not seem surprised by Carlyle's sudden appearance in front of her. Doubtless, Alex Miles had already tipped her off about what was going on. Not that it mattered anyway, but it annoyed him. Why did people find it so hard to keep their mouths shut? This was just another way in which Alex Miles' unreliability shone through.

After the introductions, Carlyle followed Shue back over to the reception desk, which was now manned by a younger, prettier blond girl. Shue spoke brusquely to the girl in something that wasn't English, but instead might have been Russian or Polish, or maybe even Finnish. The girl promptly disappeared, leaving the night manager to tap a few keys on the computer. After staring at the screen for a few seconds, she picked up a telephone receiver and hit 329. After letting it ring for a good fifteen seconds, she put the phone down again and looked up at Carlyle.

'No reply?' he asked.

She nodded. 'Probably asleep.'

Carlyle frowned. He didn't like bullshit. 'Surely the call would wake him up?'

Shue thought about that for a second. 'Not if he's taken something. Or he could be … busy.'

'But he checked in alone?'

Shue glanced at the screen again. 'Yes.'

Carlyle waited for Shue to say more, but she just stood there silently. 'And?'

Shue snapped to attention. 'Number 329 is registered to a Mr Ian Blake. He booked in for just the one night. He checked in at seven twenty-five last night, had some food and champagne delivered just after nine, which he signed for. He has an alarm call booked for seven-thirty tomorrow or, rather, this morning.'

Carlyle thought about that. The information was useless: it told him nothing. They were just putting off the inevitable visit upstairs. He took a deep breath: 'OK, let's go and pay Mr …'

'Blake.'

'Mr Blake … let's go and pay him a visit. I need to take a look inside room 329.'

Shue frowned. 'Are you sure, Inspector?'

This was a necessary part of the job, trampling over people's reluctance to get involved, dragging them unhappily into a little bit of the mess that comprised his regular working life. Sometimes he did it with relish, but not tonight. Tonight he was painting by numbers.

She pulled a key card out of a drawer behind the desk and held it up for him to inspect. 'Well …'

Are you sure? Carlyle looked down at his shoes, trying not to smile. He'd been asked that question a million times before. He was a policeman, for fuck's sake. Of course, he was sure.

'… we could end up getting a guest out of bed by mistake.'

'Yes,' he nodded, 'we could.'

Her face brightened slightly, as she mistakenly assumed that he was considering her point of view.

'Or,' Carlyle met her gaze with a grin, 'we could be ignoring something serious – maybe a murder.'

'Um.' She took a step backwards, with a look of annoyance as if he'd just tried to grab her arse.

Carlyle ignored her irritation. 'So,' he said firmly, 'do you see where the balance of risk lies here?'

THEY RODE THE elevator to the third floor in silence. Stepping out, Shue led him along a silent corridor that was lit by low-wattage lighting at floor level, like the emergency lights on a plane. Their footsteps were hushed by a deep blue carpet and, with even the normal background hum of the city for once blocked out, the silence had a strange completeness to it. The scene, Carlyle reckoned, had that 'middle of the night in the big city' feel to it, although, with no windows to look out of, it could just as easily have been the middle of the day.

At the end of the corridor, Shue turned right into a shorter corridor, which led to a dead end. She came to a stop outside door 329 in the middle of a cluster of six rooms, three ranged on either side, towards the back of the hotel building. Outside the door, the remains of the room-service order were stacked neatly on a tray, beside an empty champagne bottle.

Shue nodded at the label. 'Krug. From the 1995 vintage; the good stuff. It costs five hundred pounds a bottle.'

Carlyle shrugged.

For a moment, she just stood there, pass key in hand. 'God,' she whispered, turning to Carlyle, 'I hope you're right about this.'

'What?' Carlyle asked, with gentle amusement. 'You mean that you're hoping that he's really dead?'

'No.' Shue smiled weakly. 'You know what I mean. If he's asleep ... or shagging or something ...' Her unease seemed genuine.

Despite his aching tiredness, and against his natural instinct, Carlyle took a deep breath and summoned up the energy to try some empathy: 'You must have seen all sorts in your time?'

'No.' She took a step away from him, looking strangely put out. 'No, not really. I've only been doing this for six months.'

Giving up on the small talk, Carlyle pulled his shoulders back and assumed his most official tone, the one that didn't normally sound like him. 'Don't worry. This is formal police business and I will take full responsibility for upsetting your guests.' He rapped gently on the door and counted to ten. There was no response from inside. He knocked on the door, harder this time, before again counting to ten. Still nothing. He gave Shue a knowing smile. 'Please, unlock the door and then stand back.'

The night manager did as requested. Carlyle opened the door firmly but slowly. Without saying anything, he stepped inside the tiny vestibule. To his left was an empty wardrobe; on the right was an equally empty bathroom. Ahead of him extended the room proper. It was illuminated only by the light from a floor lamp in the far corner, and Carlyle could see one foot dangling off the end of the bed. There was no snoring to be heard, and there were no noises suggesting than any sexual activity was in progress either.

Closing the door behind him, he took two steps into the room proper, in order to confirm what he already knew.

The note had not been a joke.

Chapter Eight

Cambridge University, June 1984

LIFE IS SHORT, but the day is long.

There were signs. Signs everywhere. It was the hundred and sixty-ninth day of the year. It was one hundred and sixty-nine years to the day since the English had triumphed at Waterloo. It was a time for history. A time for destiny. And, above all, a time for pain.

In the here and now, it was the end of the summer term, the end of the academic year and the end of life at university. The big, wide world was out there waiting for them, ready to shower them with money, status and power. Of course, they would make it wait until they were damn well ready. That was their right. They had been taught from birth that the world waits for gentlemen, not the other way round.

Liberty was being traded for power. All of this would be missed.

The celebrations had lasted for more than thirty hours now, an endless tour of bars and parties, running into the same people again and again. Now, drawing deep on their second wind, they had returned to his rooms for the unspoken, much anticipated finale.

The club was in session.

It had started to rain. A heavy summer downpour at the end of a baking day was accompanied by the rumble of distant thunder. The weather only added to the *fin de siècle* feel of it all. They were washing away the past, preparing the ground for the future. Sad, weary, but expectant.

The sight laid out before him was like a porno version of *Tom Brown's Schooldays* directed by Tinto Brass – less Flashman, more Fleshman. The Italian smut king's *Caligula* had pride of place in his porn collection in one corner of the room: a stack of quality VHS tapes almost five feet high that had been accumulated over the years. On the television screen next to them, *Salon Kitty* played silently to the sound of 'She Works Hard For The Money' by Donna Summer coming out of his fantastically expensive Bang & Olufsen Beocenter stereo system.

All eyes were fixed on a space of about eight feet by four that had been cleared in the centre of the room and on the body that lay there, face down. The atmosphere was thick with the clashing scents of body odour, excrement, semen and cannabis. Despite opening all the windows, the blue smoke that had settled around head height was still thick enough to effectively obscure the print of Hockney's *Mulholland Drive* on the far wall. Someone had crashed through a glass coffee table, the remains of which had been pushed into a corner. Empty champagne and Absolut vodka bottles littered the floor. A half-eaten pizza was left peeking out from under the sofa.

Their quarry was three years in the grooming. The networking, the lobbying, the oiling, it had all led up to this night. Now, he would be three hours, three minutes, in the destroying. Their pretty boy Icarus, flying too close to the sun. Now he had to fall to earth, to reclaim his place among the peasants. To realise that he had been flying too high.

The day is short, but life is long.

A mini-roar went up as he stepped forward, feeling like a gladiator entering the arena, confident of victory, assured of respect. Preliminaries over, he pushed the prostrate Icarus' legs apart, lent forward and eased his way inside. Gently at first, a little tentatively, and then with more confidence and some swagger, he began thrusting. His breathing soon synchronised with that of the other man as he found his rhythm. Feeling a response beneath him, he let his speed increase. This was going to be good. Better than good. This was going to be … perfection.

Sine metu. Without fear.

Reaching down for Icarus' penis, which was warm, velvety and pleasingly firm, he made a half-hearted attempt to bring him to climax, which did not survive the first jeers of the audience. Ignoring the catcalls, he tossed back his majestic black mane and felt the sweat beading on his forehead. His mouth was dry. His heart felt as if it could jump out of his chest. He sensed every beat of it as if it could be his last. He had to remember to breathe in and breathe out. The combination of Krug, Lebanese Gold and amyl nitrite coursing through his system helped relax him and further heightened the sense of satisfaction. He knew he was grinning madly, and he couldn't stop. This was what he had always wanted. This was where he was supposed to be. At the centre of things. In charge. On top. Going deeper, where he no longer had to contemplate his actions.

This was *being*, not doing.

Now it was just about the two of them. Everything else had dissolved into nothingness. Duran Duran, blaring out 'The Reflex' from the tape machine on the stereo, sounded as if they had retreated far into the upper atmosphere, along with the laughter and cheers of the others watching. The shining semi-darkness of the room was left far behind as he floated out of his body and looked down on the indistinguishable mass he had become.

A pained whimper from below brought him back to something approaching consciousness. Trapped wind escaped from the boy's anus like a spectacular fart, prompting more laughter from the surrounding gloom. The smell of shit rising from his conquest disgusted and excited him. It smelt of fear. Of corruption. Of defeat. He lent forward and breathed in deeply.

He tickled the boy's balls, pushing down on the back of his neck with his forearm at the same time. He had never felt this hard, or this strong, or this much in control. This was *it*, his John Travolta moment.

He *was* Tony Manero.

He had read somewhere that filming *Saturday Night Fever* had been such a buzz for Travolta that when he finished he wanted to head right out and fuck Jane Fonda, at that time the biggest sex symbol in the world. He knew the feeling. But she was getting on a bit now, so bring on Helen Mirren. For that matter, bring on Kathleen Turner. Bring them both on. And all the rest. Bring them all on. Line them up into the night and lay them down in front of him. At that moment, there was not a single person in the world that he did not want to fuck; to fuck them right apart.

He could go on forever. He wanted to go on for ever.

'Get on with it!' shouted a drunken voice.

Someone else giggled. 'Others are waiting, you know!'

'Hurry up!'

Something bounced off his back. A bottle of beer was poured over his head.

'He's fucking for England!'

'It's the rape of Lucretia ... part two.'

'I think he's enjoying it too much.'

'Fucking pervert.'

'Come on you ... you poofter!'

More giggles. 'Use it or lose it!'

It was time to concentrate. To cross the finish line, get it done. Holding on for dear life, he had to force himself still further inside his new-found soul mate, in search of that twitch in the groin that told you there was no way back. The moment when you were ready to shoot your load, and would have happily fucked a rabid pit bull to make it happen. A few more thrusts and he found it. He grunted and let go. Stars exploded before his eyes and behind his brain. The cheering reached a crescendo. He collapsed into one final caress, before various hands dragged him away.

Crawling on to a couch in a corner of the room, he closed his eyes and listened to the sounds of the next man taking his turn. His dick, smeared with shit, was still throbbing. He lovingly squeezed it with his right hand and felt the blood pumping through it. Gently caressing it, he felt it begin to harden again before letting it go. Reaching down to the floor, he picked up a crumpled tailcoat, pulling it over his nakedness.

He lay there feeling at one with the universe. The signals going to his pituitary gland prompted the release of a flood of endorphins, the body's own form of morphine, into his bloodstream, sending a flood of exhilaration and well-being through his body. This truly was bliss. Even if he lived for another sixty ...

or seventy ... or eighty years, he knew that this could never be bettered. However, wherever, whenever he lay on his deathbed, he would remember this moment with a smile on his face, while his wife – some pretty young thing, wife number two, or maybe number three – and his gaggle of children and grandchildren looked on, distraught as their world crumbled around them.

A cheer went up as the next man dismounted, still in a state of considerable excitement, his right arm pumping furiously. He looked up and saw an arc of semen heading towards the door. 'The cleaner's not going to like that!' someone squeaked, as it splashed across the wooden floor.

Out of the corner of his eye, he caught the amused expression on his brother's face. The place was wrecked. Food, booze, glass and god knows what else everywhere. It looked like a bunch of coked-up, incontinent chimpanzees had run amok with Uzis. Not that it mattered. Like it or not, his cleaning lady could sort it out tomorrow. That's what he paid her a more than generous £1.50 an hour to do. Tonight he cared not a jot. Oblivious to tomorrow, he lay there, panting like a dog, basking in the glow of the best sex that he had ever had. The best sex that he would ever have.

The day had gone; life is short.

Chapter Nine

WITH MONEY TO burn, the average world traveller of The Garden Hotel's itinerant tribe of global travellers would probably not expect to swing even a small cat for somewhere north of three hundred pounds a night, and in room 329 they would not have been disappointed. The room was small, but perfectly formed. 'Simple, serene, practical and pure – but full of wit, style and surprise', had been the description of the décor, in the hotel's brochure. Someone had certainly got a surprise here, thought Carlyle, as he pulled out his mobile phone and called for reinforcements.

Ending the call, Carlyle shivered. The air-conditioning had been left fully on, so the room temperature was now easily below sixty degrees. The man in front of him was naked, lying face down on a queen-sized bed that was almost too big for the room. It was hard to tell, but the victim looked about Carlyle's age, maybe just shy of six feet tall and in reasonable shape. Apart from the fact that he was dead, of course. He had a bit of a mullet, Carlyle noted, and was thinning on top. His clothes had been draped over the back of the chair (an 'École Nissim de Camondo designed Lucite chair' no less) in one corner. A pair of expensive-looking loafers, Charles Church or a similar brand, had been placed neatly beside the chair, in front of drawn curtains which were now splattered with blood.

Scanning the room, Carlyle decided that he had seen much worse. The most arresting touch was the knife gleaming, as if self-satisfied, in the room's twilight. It looked like a standard kitchen item. It was, however, sticking out of the victim's backside, in a way that set a new benchmark for London knife crime. Unable to resist, Carlyle mumbled to himself: 'That must be a real pain in the arse.' With his nose hovering about three inches away, he squinted to read the writing on the handle. It contained an image of two matchstick men, side by side, with just two arms and three legs between them. The man on the right had his arm in the air in a *walk-like-an-Egyptian* type of pose. Bloody strange logo, thought Carlyle. Next to it was the brand name Zwilling and J.A.Henckels. Otherwise, it looked like a normal knife, one you could probably buy anywhere. Nevertheless, its provenance was something to have checked later.

At a gentle knock at the door, Carlyle stepped back past the foot of the bed and into the vestibule. He pulled open the door to find a friendly blond woman called Susan Phillips smiling at him. Phillips was based at the Holborn police station, which was barely five minutes away by car at this time of night. She had been a staff pathologist with the Met for more than fifteen years now, and they had worked together several times before. 'Good morning, Inspector,' she said with an annoying cheerfulness. 'I hear you have something for me.'

'Thanks for coming,' Carlyle said, holding the door wider. He thought she was looking tired and quite a bit older than her thirty-seven years, but sensibly he kept such thoughts to himself. After all, it was the middle of the night, and Carlyle knew that he was no oil painting himself, whatever the hour.

'No problem,' Phillips nodded. 'Shall I come in?'

'Let me move out first,' said Carlyle, 'then you can get at him more easily. I won't spoil your fun, but it looks fairly straightforward.'

He stepped out into the corridor and nodded a greeting at a pair of forensic technicians he didn't recognise. A couple of yards along, Anna Shue had also returned, with PC Burgess in tow. Burgess was looking quite pleased with himself, having successfully fully tracked down the twenty-pound note tendered by Alex Miles in the Epoca cafe.

Stepping forward, Carlyle had a quiet word with both, and watched them set off to deal with their allotted tasks. Phillips and the technicians had already taken over the room and there would be little for Carlyle to do for the next couple of hours.

HE COULD HAVE been dozing, or he could have been thinking. Either way, Carlyle's reverie was ended by a knock at the door. Without waiting to be invited in, room service appeared with a breakfast trolley bearing scrambled eggs, coffee, toast, a generous selection of Danish pastries and some fruit. The waiter pushed the trolley as far into the room as possible, then turned on his heel to leave. Almost before Carlyle had the chance to mumble 'Thank you', the man was gone, seeming careful, for whatever reason, to avoid eye contact – or any other kind of contact – with the forces of law and order.

Realising that he hadn't eaten for more than twelve hours, Carlyle salivated as he eyed the spread provided. He was extremely grateful indeed to Anna Shue for opening up the empty room right next to 329, where he could park himself and organise the start of an investigation, but he was even more grateful for the breakfast. Pouring himself a cup of steaming coffee, he sucked it down in one go, letting it scald the back of his throat. Hot was how he liked it, hot and strong, and he felt the caffeine spread through his system as he poured himself a second cup, and contemplated a sugar rush to go with it. Carlyle had a sweet tooth – he could easily name ten favourite patisseries within a one-mile radius of the piazza – so he passed on the eggs and went straight to the pastries. Sitting on the rather lumpy bed, he took another slurp of coffee and took a large bite out of a cherry Danish before enjoying a contemplative chew. Not up there with the best of them but not at all bad, Carlyle decided happily, while polishing it off and reaching for a second.

While forensics commandeered the victim's room, Burgess had taken formal statements from Alex Miles and the rest of the hotel staff. For the record, they had reiterated what was previously said, i.e. not very much. The guests in the rooms immediately surrounding number 329 were also roused, to general dismay and annoyance, in order to confirm that they had seen and heard nothing too. To the night manager's obvious relief, Carlyle agreed that they wouldn't knock on any further doors on the third floor before seven-thirty. He knew that such activity wasn't likely to yield anything, so he was happy to make her that concession. Anyway, it was just a matter of ticking a particular box for the record.

There had since been few other developments. The twenty quid rescued by PC Burgess from the Epoca café had been given a quick once-over by the technicians on site. With no signs of blood, it hadn't yielded anything of immediate interest, so had been sent to Scotland Yard's Forensic Science Laboratory, at Hendon in north

London, for further tests. Finally, Alex Miles had taken Burgess and Carlyle through the hotel's CCTV footage to see what they could glean from that.

At one point, it struck Carlyle that Miles seemed to be very much leading the hotel's response to the incident. For such a high-profile hotel, in-house security was conspicuous by its absence. After some probing, Shue admitted that the chief security officer was off site, 'auditioning' a pair of Costa Rican hookers who wanted permission to work the premises.

The body itself had left for the morgue about half an hour ago. Having done her thing, the pathologist, Susan Phillips, had returned to Holborn police station to consider her findings and come up with a preliminary report. Meanwhile, the forensics guys had taken turns in going through the room with their own particular fine toothcombs. The remains of the victim's room-service meal had been bagged up and sent to Hendon, too, along with the murder knife, clothing and a few other bits and pieces found inside the room. Details of anything of interest would arrive on Carlyle's desk at Charing Cross later in the day, probably sometime in the middle of the afternoon. Business cards found in the victim's jacket pocket, as well as a driving licence in his wallet, had confirmed the man's name as Ian Blake.

It appeared that Blake had been managing director of a company called Alethia Consulting, whatever that was. Alethia herself, Carlyle vaguely remembered from various conversations with his daughter Alice, had been some kind of Greek goddess. What the company actually consulted on wasn't clear, and it was unlikely that it mattered that much right now. Blake's colleagues, or rather his ex-colleagues, would be receiving a visit within a couple of hours. Doubtless they would express their shock and dismay, portray the deceased as a latter-day saint, and reveal nothing useful whatsoever.

Carlyle drained his coffee cup and finished off the second pastry. He eyed a third but, after a few elongated seconds of emotional struggle and internal debate, he thought the better of it. Putting the empty cup back on the trolley, he sat back on the bed and let out a small burp.

The caffeine left him recharged, if not refreshed. It also inspired a thought. Sitting on the bed, he rifled through his pockets, looking for his new toy, a BlackBerry 8820. The handheld computer, only slightly larger than a cigarette packet, was one of the first two hundred to be assigned to Metropolitan Police officers – at inspector level and above – on a trial basis. Carlyle wasn't what you would call an early adopter of new technology, but then neither was the Met. It had taken him the best part of nine months to successfully apply for the thing, get his hands on the thing, and then cajole the IT guys to persuade it to talk to his desktop computer and the network at large. Even now, the little machine seemed to work only erratically, but he could see its possibilities, not least in terms of spending more time out of the office, and so had vowed to stick with it.

After typing in his password, he went to the browser and Googled 'Alethia'. Finding the company's website, he then went to the homepage, which told him that it provided 'strategic consulting services' and had offices in New York and Dubai as well as London. Struggling with the small-size script, he brought up a list of directors and clicked on Blake's biography.

Ian Blake, 47, revolutionised the consulting paradigm when he founded Alethia Consulting in 1993. His experience (over twenty years in the industry) has been focused within reputation management and evolving business strategies specifically for dynamic companies and individuals. This experience includes a wide variety of capital markets and transaction-based activities including leading multiple corporate financings, M&A transactions, personnel management and global-issues management activities. Ian works extensively with the most senior executive management – from small to large corporations, as well as not-for-profit organisations – across all sectors and markets, focusing on integrated strategic communications. He holds an MBA in international business from London Business School and a Master of Entrepreneurial Leadership degree from INSEAD in Paris.

Very informative, Carlyle thought. Maybe that's why he was killed – someone took extreme offence at his ability to mangle the English language. After another few seconds of staring myopically at the screen, he hit the 'clients' link and watched as a list of names came up which included a football club, two universities, two banks and a handful of large retailers. There were also various names that Carlyle didn't recognise, but all of these were quickly forgotten as he reached the three names listed at the very bottom: the Office of the Mayor of London, the Metropolitan Police, and the Police Federation. *Fuck!* Carlyle thought. *That's just what I need, a corpse with connections.*

The tiny screen – or maybe it was the caffeine – was now giving him a headache. He hit the 'close' button and dropped the Black-Berry back in his pocket. Resisting the temptation to take his shoes off again, which would almost certainly have proved fatal to his attempts to stay awake, Carlyle lay back on the bed and shut his eyes. Almost immediately, he felt a buzzing by his chest. He sat up and pulled his mobile out of the breast pocket of his jacket. The screen revealed 'Helen', which meant that it was his wife. Which meant that it would have to be answered.

Carlyle pressed the green 'receive' button and tried to sound awake. 'Hi.'

'You didn't come home last night?' His wife sounded just as tired as he felt, perhaps even more so. Somehow, this energised him a little.

'I know,' he sighed. 'I got waylaid.'

'Anything interesting? Or just the usual?' After all this time, Helen was used to the random nature of his working life, and the fact that it resulted in him going AWOL on a regular basis, so there was no edge to this conversation.

'A dead man in a hotel room.'

A yawn. 'Suspicious?'

'Oh, yes,' Carlyle deadpanned. 'Lots of blood and a murder weapon.'

He could feel her waking up, and seriously wished he was lying there in the bed beside her. 'Seriously?'

'Of course.' He frowned. 'Why else would I be here?'

'Poor sod,' said Helen, now totally alert. 'Well, I suppose it'll be an engaging case.'

'Maybe.' Carlyle smiled. 'Engaging' was not police language. He already knew where this conversation would be leading. His brain began to contract, and he felt the need to get off the phone.

'At least it's got to be better than the crap you've been dealing with lately.'

'I'm sure that will make Mr Blake feel better.'

'Who?'

'The victim.'

For some reason, the word 'victim' made her stiffen. 'It's not your fault he's dead.'

'No, I know that,' Carlyle said softly. He wanted to avoid irritating his wife. There would be plenty of time for that later and, for now, he didn't want to have to deal with domestic tetchiness on top of everything else. 'It's just that my heightened job satisfaction is not going to provide much of a silver lining for him, is it?'

She thought about that for a second, letting the tension ebb from her voice. 'He's not likely to care much, one way or the other, but at least it should be interesting for you. Something a bit more high-profile?'

'We'll see.' The conversation was a familiar one. It irritated him that she invariably demanded more from his job than he did.

'You know what I mean,' she said, with just a hint of crossness reappearing.

'I do,' he agreed quickly, 'of course.' And he did. A job is always just a job, whether you were a drug dealer or a postman, a fluffer or a priest. Being a policeman, the worse it got, the better it got.

Helen's voice softened again. 'Are you OK?'

He accepted the olive branch. 'Sure, I'm fine.'

That was clearly as much time as Helen was prepared to spend in getting Carlyle into the right mood. 'Anyway,' she said, moving the conversation along, 'what about this morning?'

This morning? Carlyle felt a slight wave of concern wash over him. What had he forgotten now? He tried to remain calm. 'What about it?'

Helen paused. 'Will you still be able to take Alice to the Barbican? You know I've got an important meeting at work this morning.'

Carlyle groaned, slumping back on to the bed as domestic life caught up with him. Today was supposed to be a day off. This morning he was supposed to be doing the school run. He had signed up to it several weeks ago. All the usual caveats had applied, but Helen always chose to ignore them. His Parent of the Week Award was in the post.

Helen herself normally took Alice to school before turning round and heading back across town to Paddington and the international medical charity, called Avalon, where she worked as a senior administrative manager. Carlyle knew that she spent between two and three hours a day shuffling backwards and forwards across town. It was a bugger, but that was the deal. He therefore had to do his bit.

This morning, Carlyle vaguely remembered, Helen had a very unpleasant disciplinary hearing to deal with: something involving a male doctor who, allegedly, had sexually abused a colleague. This type of problem was common in organisations like this. Apparently they attracted more than their fair share of people who hid under the cloak of liberal empathy to abuse either their co-workers or the locals, the very people they were supposed to be there to help. It had shocked Carlyle when his wife had first told him about it. On reflection, however, it made a lot of sense. Where else would you find a better balance of opportunity and risk?

How on earth you could hope to shed any light on what had or had not happened between two people halfway up a mountain in Afghanistan, much less do anything about it, was beyond him. It was hard enough trying to deal with such cases in London: the complaint rate was pitiful and the actual conviction rate was much, much worse. It was impossible, therefore, to see how his wife could ever hope to get to the bottom of this particular mini-drama. The whole thing seemed like an exercise in liberal masochism, but he knew well enough to keep thoughts like that to himself.

He didn't envy Helen the job of trying to sort it all out, but where did that now leave him? Carlyle always looked forward to his thirty minutes with Alice as they meandered towards the Barbican arts complex, home to the City School for Girls, that celebrated private school that soaked up a distressing proportion of their household income. On an intellectual level, Carlyle wasn't in favour of private education, but the idea of an all-girls school quite appealed, since anything that helped keep the boys at bay for as long as possible had to be a good thing.

Not that the decision had been much to do with him. It was too important for that. Even before Alice was born, Helen had insisted that they would go private if they (i.e. she) decided that it was the best thing to do. As they (she) had. So Carlyle waved goodbye to around fifteen thousand pounds a year (after sodding bloody tax) that they didn't really have, and Alice attended City.

At least she loved it, and for that Carlyle would have happily paid much more than fifteen thousand pounds. His principles, after all, had to coexist with the realities of being a parent. All he could do now was to hope and pray that she would be able to apply for – and win – the biggest possible scholarship when the opportunity arose. At City you had to reach the age of eleven before you could apply, and so he was counting down the days till then, much to Helen's scorn.

On the way to school, they would pick up breakfast, then he would listen to Alice's musings on a random selection of topics, ranging from pets (and why she wasn't allowed any) to the Second World War (why did Japan support the Germans?) to vampires (why don't they die?) to mouthwash (Alice had informed him one day that she liked to try the different colours because she was an 'adventurous girl'). Carlyle could not think of anything in the entire world he would rather do than walk through the streets while listening to the random thoughts of his daughter. He lived in dread of the inevitable day – at most, he guessed, three or four years hence – when she would refuse to let either of her parents take her to school, and demand to be allowed to go on her own or with her friends. God only knew what her sense of adventure might involve her in then.

So, meanwhile, his family duties were clear. On the other hand, his brain was struggling to process the current situation and come up with an answer. Preferably the right answer.

Helen knew what this pause meant. 'John?'

The threat of retaliation hung in the air, so he took a deep breath. 'Sure. Give me half an hour or so. I'll be there in plenty of time. I'll even bring you a coffee.'

'Good. Thanks.' His wife sounded wary rather than grateful. 'A latte would be great ... and a pain au chocolat.'

'No problem. See you soon.' Carlyle switched the phone off and tossed it on the bed. With monumental force of will, he pushed himself off it and headed into the bathroom. Could he maybe take a shower? He hated the feeling of intense grubbiness that he was left with after a night spent on the job. In the end, he decided that would be taking a bit of a liberty. And also it would involve too much time. Instead, he made do with a long and satisfying piss. Afterwards, he looked in the bowl. *Too dark*, he thought. *I need to drink more water.* Zipping himself up, he took a half-step to the sink and splashed some tap water on his face. After drying himself, he took a look in the mirror, where the usual quizzical, plebeian features stared back at him. He pushed his shoulders back and made an effort to stand up straighter. Stroking the stubble on his jaw, he noticed that it was flecked with an increasing amount of grey. *I won't bother shaving today,* he decided. *It'll do my skin good.* Carlyle looked himself in the eye, holding his own gaze for several seconds. He was well aware that he was a man who often felt quite uncomfortable in his own skin, but not this morning. Now was not the time for any of that introspective bollocks. Despite the tiredness, he felt good. Not bad for someone who's been up all night, he reckoned, lingering in front of the mirror. At any rate, not bad for someone of my age who's been up all night.

Having made a half-hearted attempt to tidy up the remnants of his breakfast, Carlyle wheeled the trolley into the corridor and let the door close behind him. The door to 329 was also closed, with white-and-blue *Police – Do Not Cross* tape stuck across the surrounding frame. The police would keep the room for at least another few days, while the investigation progressed. It might even be a week or more before the hotel staff would be allowed to clean it up but, the economy and current occupancy rates being what they were, that was not really much of a problem. Carlyle glanced around the corridor one last time, before leaving. Silent and dark, it looked exactly the same as five hours ago, when he had first entered it.

Heading towards the lifts, Carlyle brought up a new number on his phone and hit 'call'. There was a click and he waited for the inevitable voicemail. After the beep, he left a message: 'Joe, it's almost half-eight. *Wstawaj ty leniwy draniu!* Get up, you fat, lazy bastard. We have a new case. When you finally get out of bed, they'll fill you in at the station. After that, can you give me a call? Things are under control, so I'm now leaving the scene, and will be back at Charing Cross in a few hours. Let's catch up then. Otherwise, we could grab some lunch in Il Buffone. In the meantime, see if you can start chasing the obvious, and in particular any outstanding cases where the victim had a knife gratuitously stuck up his arse. That would be great. Say "Hi" to Anita and the kids for me. See you later.'

Chapter Ten

Shepherds Bush, London W12, March 1985

SLUMPED ON THE sofa, Carlyle tried to ignore Barbara Edwards, 1984's Playmate of the Year, winking at him from the well-thumbed copy of *Playboy* resting next to his feet on the glass coffee table. With a heavy heart, he turned his gaze from Barbara's incredibly perky breasts to a poster of the West Ham footballer Clyde Best on the wall behind the television, and then to the screen which was showing the BBC lunchtime news. The glum faces revealed that the miners' strike was finally, officially, mercifully over. It had been a long slow death and the men trudging back to work could only muster the feeblest shouts of defiance. Having lost the war, they knew that they faced a slow, relentless defeat during the ensuing peace as well.

Not that the police were celebrating victory, for many officers had enjoyed the escape from home life, the camaraderie of the picket line and the excitement of the rucks. Even more of them had become nicely accustomed to the overtime pay. Now it was back to the basics of normal life.

At least, Carlyle thought dolefully, they had lives to go back to. Not all coppers could say that. A couple of days earlier, the Irish Republican Army had mortared a police station in Newry. Nine fellow officers from the Royal Ulster Constabulary had been killed. Northern Ireland was a long way off, but the IRA also regularly attacked London. There had been a steady stream of bombings in the city over the last few years, and the most recent, a car bomb at the Harrods department store in December 1983, had killed six innocent people. Being a policeman seemed more dangerous than ever.

The terrorists might not be beaten, but at least the miners were. Carlyle himself had not been on a picket line since before Christmas, so already, the strike felt like a distant memory. After several months pounding the streets around Shepherds Bush and Hammersmith, he was finally beginning to feel like a normal copper. And now he was on the cusp of being transferred south of the river, to Southwark. That suited him fine, as a new beat would offer a welcome change.

Between his postings, Carlyle had a week's leave to use up. Two days in, though, and he was bored and restless. So when he got a message from Dominic Silver, saying that he wanted 'a chat', Carlyle was perfectly happy to oblige. He hadn't seen Dom for about six months.

The last time they had been together was outside Maltby Colliery, east of Rotherham. After a long, exhausting shift, they had played marbles on the pavement, like two kids just out of school. The recently acquired marbles already had a certain sentimental value, since they had been catapulted towards police lines by the strikers during one of the more vicious scuffles of their conflict.

'This is great,' Dom had laughed, as he won another game, taking a couple of quid off Carlyle in the process. 'If marbles are all they can fight with, we've got absolutely nothing to worry about. They are really, truly fucked.'

SITTING IN SILVER'S new bachelor pad, enviously eyeing his stroke mags and watching his new twenty-inch Philips television, Carlyle wondered where the money to pay for all this luxury had come from. It certainly wasn't from playing marbles, or even from police overtime payments. Carlyle himself was still living with his parents in Fulham, and couldn't afford to buy as much as an outside toilet anywhere within two hundred miles of London. Renting wasn't much easier. Dom's place seemed way, way out of his league. Covering the top floor of a Victorian house, Carlyle reckoned that the flat must have cost him twenty grand, maybe more. That was a hell of a lot of money for a twenty-something kid. For sure, no one would give you a mortgage for that amount on a constable's salary.

'Stupid buggers. They should have seen the writing on the wall long ago.' Dom stood in the doorway, wearing a Van Morrison Wavelength tour T-shirt, as he waved a large spliff in the direction of the television. It struck Carlyle that Dom was turning into a right old hippy bastard. What ever happened to punk? It was almost as if The Clash, still struggling along in name only, had never happened,

The smell was good, but Carlyle declined Dom's offer of a toke. Dope wasn't really his thing; invariably it would give him a splitting headache and make him puke. He liked his drugs to get him going, rather than slow him down.

Carlyle watched the embers glow as Dom took another greedy drag. Back in television land, one of the union leaders appeared on the screen and started talking about 'dignity', 'solidarity' and 'the need to keep fighting'. The man looked haggard, and so haunted that you almost expected him to burst into tears at any minute.

'Idiots!' Dominic snarled. 'Donkeys leading lions.'

'If the lions really were lions,' Carlyle asked, 'would they really allow themselves to be led by donkeys?'

'Smart-arse.' Dom took another puff.

Carlyle shrugged.

Dom failed to blow a smoke ring and coughed. 'Seriously though,' he said through the haze, 'that's a bloody good question, Johnny boy … now shift up.'

Carlyle moved to one end of the sofa and Dom flopped down beside him. For the next few minutes, Dom stared at the television screen intently, without saying a word. Eventually the news bulletin moved on to other stories. Apparently, Nelson Mandela had refused a deal from the South African government which would see him released from jail in return for renouncing armed struggle.

'Bad move, Nelson, old son,' Dom remarked airily.

'If he does a deal with them, it will damage his credibilty,' Carlyle said earnestly.

'Credibility's overrated,' said Dom sharply. 'He's been in jail for what … twenty years? He's old … what, in his sixties?'

'Something like that.'

Dom pointed the spliff at the screen. 'Now he should get out while he's got the chance. Once he's out, Botha and his boys are finished. Even that bitch Thatcher won't be able to stop him.' He clenched his fist: 'Nelson! You're a lion! It's time to roar!'

Dominic's political stance was at least as surprising as his property ownership, since Carlyle had never previously heard him speak of anything other than football and girls. Even if it was the dope talking, which Carlyle was sure it was, he sounded nothing like the Dom he thought that he knew. He certainly sounded nothing like a copper. Carlyle wondered for a minute if he might suddenly whip a pile of newspapers from behind the sofa and try to sell him a copy of *Socialist Worker*.

The smoke was making Carlyle feel giddy. Getting slowly up from the sofa, he went to the window. Opening it, he felt the cold air sneak into the room and inhaled it deeply.

Dominic looked him up and down. 'I'm leaving the Force,' he announced though the haze.

Carlyle almost banged his head against the window frame. 'You're doing what?'

'I've had enough of all this bollocks,' Dom replied, looking round for an ashtray. 'It's not for me. I'm packing it in.'

'Your family won't like that,' Carlyle said, knowing that Dom's dad was a policeman. So, too, was his uncle. Blokes couldn't do anything else in the Silver household.

'It's my decision,' Dom said firmly, stubbing out the remainder of his joint on a saucer that he had finally discovered under the sofa.

'What are you going to do?'

'I'm going into business,' he said. 'Or, rather, I am going to focus on my existing business interests full time.'

'And what might those "business interests" be?' Carlyle asked warily, not really wanting to know the answer.

'I'm looking for some help.'

Trying not to feel flattered, Carlyle asked a question that he did now quite want an answer to, even if he might not like it. 'Why me?'

'Why not?' Dom stared into space, and then wound up his short sales pitch. 'I know you. I know you're straight. I know you're dependable. I know that you're not cut out to be a copper.' That he had clearly anticipated the question wasn't as surprising as his ability to push the right buttons.

'What do you mean, cut out to be a copper'?'

Dom grinned slyly. 'Come on, John. Coming from me that's hardly a criticism, is it? Neither of us fits in. We can both see past the bullshit. I can't play the game, and neither can you. If you stay, they'll piss all over you – even more than they've done already.'

Carlyle leant against the windowsill. 'I *am* a copper,' he said, more for his own benefit than for Dom's.

'Yeah … right.'

'It was my decision,' Carlyle said, trying to sound convincing, 'and I have no regrets.' He already had his doubts – plenty of them – but he wasn't going to share them with anyone. 'Now all this coal bollocks is over, I'm enjoying it a lot more. It's fine.'

Dom swung his legs on to the sofa and stretched them out like a cat. 'Don't you realise, though? This is what it's always going to be like. There will always be something else. Last time it was the miners, next time it'll be the steel workers, or the dockers, or the anti-apartheid mob or students or … whatever. There will always be an "enemy within". We – *they* – can't do without them. There always has to be someone to fight.'

'Maybe,' Carlyle said doubtfully, 'but nothing as big as what we've had to deal with during this last year. Not like Orgreave.' Without thinking, he raised a hand to his forehead and touched the small scar that remained from the flying brick that had caught him on the picket line.

'Face it, you'll be doing someone else's dirty work forever.' Dom picked the roach out of the saucer and rolled it between his fingers. He glanced over at Barbara and smiled a proprietorial smile. 'How's the Miller thing going?'

His question surprised Carlyle. He hadn't thought about Trevor Miller for months. And he wasn't aware that Dom had heard about their little run-in the previous summer, or its unresolved aftermath.

To Carlyle's dismay, the woman in the garden that day at Orgreave, called Jill Shoesmith, had launched civil action and was claiming damages for the assault. She had tracked Miller down through Carlyle (unluckily, she had remembered his surname). Being the only witness, Carlyle's statement was crucial. The obvious thing – the expected thing – was to clear Trevor from the off, but he was reluctant to do that, basically because Trevor was such a total cunt. Letting him get off would have meant some careful 'interpretation' of what had happened that day, and for a more sympathetic colleague, he could easily have managed it. Even for Miller, he could have been persuaded – not by the useless great lump himself, of course, but by others on The Job.

The Job, however, didn't want to know. When Carlyle sought out his commanding officer at Shepherds Bush for some advice, the man was evasive and non-committal. The longer the conversation went on, the more the look on his superior's face was that of a man who had just seen a stinking pile of dog shit dragged into his office. After a couple of minutes, however, he managed a lame smile, said that he knew that Carlyle would make 'the right decision' about what to say, and unceremoniously ushered him out the door, shutting it quickly behind him. This was Carlyle's introduction to (non) man management, Metropolitan Police style.

In the end, Carlyle fell back on his father's advice – don't tell a lie but don't tell the whole truth either – and provided the investigation with a statement that was as short and factual as possible. His angst was tempered by the belief that the Met would just bung the Shoe-smith woman a few quid and get the matter over with as quickly and quietly as possible. He was surprised and horrified, a few weeks later, when his Federation rep told him that was not going to happen, and that the action would be allowed to run its course. Jill Shoesmith would have her day in court and Trevor would have to face a formal disciplinary hearing. The whole thing could take months, or even years. Worse, Miller could lose his job. If Carlyle wasn't worried about that outcome for Trevor's sake, he was cer-tainly worried about it for his own. Getting another policemen sacked would destroy any nascent reputation that he might hope to cultivate within the Force. Never mind Trevor bloody Miller, it could easily kill Carlyle's own career before it had even started.

Whatever was happening, however, Carlyle wasn't now about to give Dom a blow-by-blow account of how he was managing to fuck his own career in slow motion. 'I gave them a statement, and that's it, I think,' he said non-committally.

A drug-induced grin spread across Dom's face. 'And what did you say in your statement?'

'I simply told them what I saw: Trevor pawing the woman's chest and the woman running away.'

'Crap answer!' Dom shook his head. 'You should have let it go, John.'

Carlyle shrugged, knowing Dom was right and – not for the first time – cursing himself for being so stupid. 'It's what I saw,' he said lamely.

'He could have been arresting her.'

'He could have been, but he wasn't. He was trying to pull her tits off. You normally have to go to Amsterdam to see that sort of thing!' Like he would know.

Dom pushed himself up on his elbows. 'So you're the white knight for this slag?' he shook his head. 'How fucking noble of you.'

Carlyle had now had enough of being patronised. 'You don't know she's a slag,' he protested, 'and even if she was, so what? I just said what I saw. I didn't make any speculation or add anything that would cause the dickhead any more trouble than he'd already brought upon himself.'

Dom jumped off the sofa and started waving his arms about. 'You didn't watch his back, you idiot.'

'No one else has mentioned it,' Carlyle said sulkily, still knowing that he was right.

'Word gets around. Your card will be well and truly marked, my son.'

'Miller is an arsehole. He went too far.'

'It doesn't matter,' Dom said. 'If you don't get that, you shouldn't be on The Job. It's their game, their rules. Anyway, I hear he's up for a promotion.'

'What?' Carlyle gasped. 'You've got to be fucking kidding.'

Dom gave him a bemused 'stoner' look. 'Why would I joke about something as serious as this? Trevor Miller, useless shithead that he is, came out of the strike with two commendations. He has friends.'

'Friends?'

'Yes, friends. Friends that will make sure this whole little mess gets quietly forgotten, whether your slag gets bought off or not. Trevor will come out of this smelling of roses. Unlike you.'

'Fucking hell!'

'You can fuck in hell or you can fuck in heaven,' Dom continued. 'Either way, the only person you're fucking is yourself. Face it, Johnny, you're not a team player.' He smiled. 'At least, not when it comes to the Police. So it's just as well that I can offer you alternative employment.'

'Doing what?' Carlyle asked again. Again, he didn't really want to know.

'Just some organising, a bit of man management.' Dom grinned. 'This and that.'

Carlyle knew exactly what he was talking about.

'It's a chance for you to get in at the beginning of something big. Something lucrative.' Dom raised his eyebrows. 'What do you say?'

Carlyle looked at Dom, at his cheeky smile and dilated pupils. He needed a haircut and a shave. The man was right about Trevor Miller, but Carlyle knew that he would have to sort out his own mess. Going into business with a drug dealer was not the way to deal with that situation.

'I've got to go,' he said, smiling as best he could. 'I'll think about it.'

Dom shrugged. 'Fair enough. Let me know before you go back to work.'

Carlyle headed for the door. 'Sure.'

'OK … great.' Smiling, Dom saw him off with a friendly wave, both of them knowing that Carlyle wouldn't meet Dom's deadline.

WALKING DOWN PERCY Road, Carlyle quickly realised that he had developed a splitting headache. The world was spinning gently. He stopped and tried to breathe in deeply though his mouth, but all he got for his trouble was the taste of car fumes.

Chapter Eleven

BACK IN THE Middle Ages, a barbican was a fortified gateway, the outer defence to a castle. They fell out of use in the fifteenth century, as military technology improved with the emergence of the mobile cannon. It made no particular sense therefore that the Barbican arts centre and housing estate was located in the middle of London, in an area bombed out during the Second World War. The City of London Corporation, the guys who ran the capital's financial district, built the arts centre – opened by the Queen in 1982 – as the City's gift to the nation. However, the 1980s was not a great decade for architecture and what they came up with was a concrete ziggurat, a terraced pyramid with a multi-level layout so complex that it required different coloured lines painted on the ground to help theatre goers and tourists from getting lost on its walkways. If ever a building had a personality bypass, this was it. To no one's surprise, it was later voted London's ugliest building.

None of this was of much interest to young Alice Carlyle, who knew exactly where she was going and didn't need a yellow line to show her the way. Alice sucked greedily from a small carton of apple juice as she stood next to her father on a walkway thirty feet above the ground. Handing Carlyle the carton, she started happily munching on the last of the hoso-maki rolls from her tray of salmon nigiri that they had picked up from a sandwich shop. This was part of the usual breakfast-on-the-run routine, executed by either parent to Alice's precise specifications for that particular day. The kindergarchy was alive and well in the Carlyle household, with Alice centre stage and Mum and Dad both fretting about being reduced to the role of indentured servants. As many parents knew, it was hard to break free from the dictatorship of the child, but at least they knew that it would pass soon enough.

Carlyle finished his skinny latte, which was, annoyingly, barely lukewarm despite him asking, as always, for it to be extra hot. Irritated by the failings of Bulgarian baristas in particular and the service economy in general, he leant over the balcony and looked down at the City of London School for Girls below. It was about two hundred and fifty yards away, on the far side of an ornamental pond half the size of a football pitch. 'City' as it was known, resembled a rather small 1970s comprehensive not unlike the one he had gone to himself, six miles, thirty years and several generations away. Why it had been plonked down in the middle of this rather drab piece of urban planning, Carlyle had no idea. But, watching the other kids make their way happily in, he was glad that it was.

Work-shift patterns and criminals willing, Carlyle managed to take his daughter to school maybe three or four times a month. He knew he should make the most of it. It was 'free' time, when they could just be together, and he enjoyed the school run more than just about anything else he could think of. As far as he could see, Alice didn't think about it at all, but that was more than good enough for him. For kids there was only time; you either gave it to them or you didn't. You had a short window of opportunity, and then they were off and you were back on your own. You couldn't fake it by trying to split your life into quality and non-quality time. That was just middle-class bollocks. You either did it or you didn't.

The fact that he had spent the previous night with a corpse made the morning – Alice munching, the sun shining and the city bustling – even more enjoyable than usual. He turned away from the balcony and ran an eye over a poster announcing the imminent arrival of an exhibition of work by Lithuania's leading avant-garde fashion designers. Carlyle had never heard of Helmut & Karl. To him, they looked like a slightly hipper version of Gilbert & George, the aged English artists famous for a laugh-a-minute oeuvre with titles like Shit Faith, In the Shit, and Bloody Life. Letting his eyes slide down the poster copy, Carlyle saw that Helmut & Karl looked like a somewhat fluffier proposition:

Helmut & Karl are widely acknowledged to be the leading geniuses of the post-modern fashion industry. 'The House of Helmut & Karl' will show a selection of the designers' leading signature pieces from 1984 to the present, reborn in a newly commissioned installation that dominates the entire Esterhaus gallery on the fourth floor of the Centre. Among the highlights will be the pair's world-famous 1992 'Chinese Doll' collection. For this exhibition, emerging supermodel Madison Smith will be dressed in a series of twelve jewel-encrusted dresses until she is wearing 250 pounds of haute couture worth more than $60 million. 'What we are bringing to London is an ode to individuality and exclusivity,' say the designers. 'Unavailability is what gives fashion its aura. If it is too easy, too accessible, where is the art? We will show you the art.'

'Exclusive' and 'unavailable' took him back to the Garden hotel and the rather over-the-top claims in its brochure. *There are, what, more than six billion people on the planet*, Carlyle thought. *So why do we all struggle so hard to be unique?* One of his wife's favourite phrases, taken from Freud, was 'the narcissism of small differences'. She usually employed it when she was baiting him about the tribalism and stupidity of football fans like himself. Was narcissism the reason behind Ian Blake's death? Some drive for an exclusive experience? Carlyle filed these thoughts away at the back of his mind and cast a final glance at Helmut & Karl. Not one for his own 'must see' list, he decided.

Next to the exhibition poster was an advert for Blossombomb, the first perfume created by the same dynamic duo. That was much more straightforward, featuring an almost naked woman waving a bottle of their product in a fairly unimaginative manner. *After the bullshit*, thought Carlyle, *comes the hard sell. Is there anyone on the planet who doesn't now have their own fragrance?*

He looked over at Alice, still munching her sushi. Already, she had probably been exposed to more advertising than he had seen by the time he was thirty years old. It was relentless, indiscriminate, everywhere. What did she make of it all? Carlyle and Helen warned her that advertising was basically there to sell her crap she didn't need. Sometimes that message seemed to get through, sometimes not. Blossombomb wasn't yet the problem, but it – or something very much like it – would become one soon.

His watch said 8.52 a.m.. They had entered that ten-minute open zone before nine, when the girls could be dropped off in the school playground. Carlyle knew that they wouldn't be late, but they wouldn't be early either.

'Come on,' he said gently. 'We'd better get down there.'

'Yes, Dad,' Alice nodded, handing him the now-empty plastic tray and taking her apple juice from his hand. Draining the last of the juice, she handed the carton back to her father, the walking dustbin. Picking up her backpack, she headed in the direction of the stairs.

Carlyle followed behind, hands full, no waste bin in sight – just in case some terrorist decided to hide a bomb in it, the better to take out the Helmut & Karl collection? 'Careful on the stairs,' he called automatically.

'Yes, Dad!' replied an exasperated little voice, as its owner disappeared from view.

Back on ground level, they stood in front of the extremely over-monikered St Giles-without-Cripplegate church. Named after the patron saint of beggars and cripples, it was one of the few medieval churches left in the City of London, having survived both the Great Fire of 1666 and the Blitz. Under the benign gaze of the saint himself, out of sight of the school gate, Carlyle gave his daughter kiss. This was the agreed spot for final shows of parental affection, being deemed far enough away from the entrance so that Alice wouldn't be embarrassed in front of her friends.

'Have a good time.'

'Will you pick me up this afternoon?' Alice asked, as she finished wiping the spot on her cheek where he had just kissed her.

'No, I have to go back to work. I would love to be here, but things are a bit busy at work. It will have to be Mum.'

'Good. I like it when Mum picks me up,' said Alice happily, to Carlyle's considerable disappointment. She skipped away, moving five yards towards the school before turning back to face him. 'Was he dead?'

'Who?'

'The man last night. Mum says that's why you didn't come home.'

'Yes.' As usual in these situations, Carlyle kept it short, but he didn't try to ignore her question or change the subject. Alice, like her mother, had little time for bullshit. She was a no-nonsense girl who, aged four, had informed her parents and, rather undiplomatically, her school chums that Santa was a 'creature of myth and legend'. In terms of maturity and development, she was probably already three or four or five years ahead of where he'd been at a similar age. That was a hell of a big gap, and Carlyle knew that it would only get bigger.

'Was he murdered?' Her tone was matter-of-fact. Her look said: *You can tell me the truth, it's no big deal.*

'That's TBC,' Carlyle lied. 'We don't know yet.'

Alice looked at him more closely. 'But you'll find out?'

'Yes.'

'And then they'll go to jail?'

'The person who did it? Yes, that's the idea.'

'So that they can't do it again?'

'Yes,' Carlyle nodded. 'The idea is that they go to jail to protect the rest of us.' He thought about it for a minute. 'Maybe, when they are in jail, they learn that they did something wrong. That's their best chance of making sure that they don't do it again when they come out.'

Alice made a face. 'But that doesn't happen very often, does it?'

Carlyle laughed. 'Hard to say, sweetheart. Hard to say.'

She thought about it some more. 'It's good that you'll catch him. You can tell me about it tonight.' She started moving away from him. 'See ya!'

'See ya!'

Alice skipped inside the school, waving at her teacher, Mrs Matterface, on duty at the front gate, while scanning the playground for any of her young friends. Carlyle stood there and watched his daughter go in, safe and sound. Sending Helen a text to say that he had successfully completed his mission, he loitered for a minute longer. A lone straggler managed to just sneak in before the front doors were ceremonially closed and the school day officially began. Feeling satisfied with a job well done, Carlyle turned away and headed off in the direction of the tube.

AFTER DROPPING ALICE off at school, Carlyle returned home in search of a couple of hours' sleep. Home was a two-bedroom apartment, measuring eight hundred and ninety square feet, on the thirteenth floor of Winter Garden House, facing south towards the river, with decent views of the South Bank arts complex, the London Eye and Big Ben. WGH was a fifteen-storey, 1960s block housing thirty apartments, which sat on Macklin Street at the north end of Drury Lane. Their apartment had been bought by Carlyle's father-in-law from Camden Council for sixteen thousand pounds in 1984. With an excellent sense of timing, he had keeled over with a massive heart attack just five months before Alice was born. Helen's mother had been happy to give them the place, as she herself had moved out years earlier, about a week after her daughter had left school, dumping her husband and decamping to Brighton, the lively seaside town an hour out of London. If it hadn't been for this happy set of circumstances, the family would have found itself living far from Covent Garden, and Carlyle would have been condemned to a lifetime of commuting on London's chronically underfunded and unreliable public-transport system.

Waking just before one o'clock, he lingered in bed for a while, thinking about nothing in particular. Eventually he got up, had a shower, got dressed and headed outside. Crossing the one-lane, one-way thoroughfare, he stepped into Il Buffone, a tiny 1950s-style Italian café on the other side of Macklin Street. Inside, there was just enough room for the counter and three shabby booths, each of which could sit four people – or six at a squeeze. It was then a case of risking a random dining companion inside or taking one of the small tables outside on the street, where the exhaust fumes came for free.

Carlyle always preferred to stay inside, where he could sit under a crumbling poster of the Juventus *Scudetto* winning squad of 1984. That was the team of Trapattoni and Platini, higher beings from a different era. Even on the busiest of days, a few moments spent contemplating their achievements were, to Carlyle's way of thinking, always time well spent.

It was now after two o'clock and the lunchtime rush was coming to a close, so Il Buffone was largely empty. A couple of businessmen lingered over their lattes, discussing the chances of some big order materialising. Each was puffing on a cigarette, in casual contravention of the smoking ban. Carlyle looked questioningly at Marcello, the owner, who just shrugged and turned to the Gaggia coffee machine.

'*Ciao. Buon giorno. Come stai?*'

'I'm good, Marcello,' Carlyle replied to the back of the man's head. 'You?'

'Fine,' Marcello shouted back to him, over the hissing of the machine. 'Cathy's visiting her mother today, so I'm on my own, but it's OK. What you havin' now? Lunch or breakfast?'

It was a difficult decision to make, for Carlyle was normally a morning visitor to the café, and choosing lunch would require some extra thought. He couldn't be bothered with that, so he plumped for breakfast.

'The usual?' Marcello asked.

'*Si, grazie.*' Having now exhausted the complete range of his Italian vocabulary, built up painstakingly over the years, Carlyle nodded respectfully to Trapattoni and Platini and slid into the rear booth to wait for his regular daily rations comprising of a double macchiato with a chunky raisin Danish.

Marcello Aversa had come to London more than thirty years earlier, for a week's holiday. In that short time he'd managed to fall in love with an English girl, get engaged and find himself a job. Carlyle never ceased to feel impressed every time Marcello told the story. It must have been quite a trip. Thirty years on, still married to Cathy, he was coming to the end of a career that had seen him running various clubs, restaurants and bars in north London and the West End.

Four years ago they had taken on a lease for the café, the idea being to give their youngest daughter a start in the business. However, the reality of five-thirty starts, five mornings a week, plus dealing with customers, the council and the health-and-safety people, had proved too much for the girl. She had chucked it in after less than a month and was last heard of backpacking around Chile. Marcello and Cathy were left trying to cover the final years of the lease, while hoping to get someone to take it off their hands.

Carlyle's wife and daughter were regulars here. Marcello and Cathy doted on Alice, which meant, inevitably, that Helen loved them. That meant, in turn, that Carlyle felt obliged to go in there at least once a day. His job was never mentioned but, over time, he was drawn into the role of problem solver in chief whenever the couple ran up against various bureaucratic problems, which they did with dispiriting regularity. The only bad thing about this situation was Marcello's constant refusal of any payment. After eating, Carlyle regularly had to force him to take his money. It was embarrassing, but not as embarrassing as taking advantage of their kindness.

Marcello dropped the coffee in front of him, along with a monster pastry, and then tactfully opened the windows at the front of the café in order to let the illegal smoke out. On his way back behind the counter, he swept up the almost empty cups sitting in front of the two businessmen, in a way that suggested it was time for them to leave, giving Carlyle a wink before he ducked into the microscopic kitchen at the rear.

Carlyle took a sip of his macchiato and contemplated the pastry. It was a thing of beauty, almost the size of an old seven-inch vinyl single, but half an inch deep and covered in icing. Marcello ordered half a dozen each day from the north London kosher bakers Grodzinski, primarily for the benefit of Carlyle, who had been known to nip in and have a second one, if the opportunity presented itself.

This was a ritual definitely not to be rushed. As was his habit, Carlyle carefully cut the pastry into quarters, and took a further second to decide the order in which he was going to eat them. This was definitely going to require another coffee, so he emptied his demitasse and called to Marcello for another double macchiato.

Once that had arrived, Carlyle reached for the first quarter of his pastry. It was already in his mouth when the door opened.

'How's the gay slaying coming along?'

Carlyle chewed, swallowed and smiled. 'Afternoon, Joe.' He looked up to watch Sergeant Joseph Szyszkowski flopping into the booth, opposite him. Joe had an early edition of the evening paper wedged under his arm, and an excited look in his eye. Exercising more than a little self-control, the inspector resisted the urge to demand where the hell he'd been for the last fourteen hours or so. 'Want something to drink?'

'What can I get you?' Marcello piped up from behind the counter.

'I've had lunch, thanks, Marcello,' said Joe, 'but a latte would be nice.'

'Coming right up.'

'Oh, before I forget,' Joe said to his colleague, 'I got a call from Valcareggi.'

'And what did Edmondo have to say for himself?' Carlyle asked, hoping that he wasn't now going to have to chase down any more Italian mobsters.

'Apparently the guy we arrested later got knifed in some prison outside Rome.' Joe paused for dramatic effect. 'They killed him.'

'Pozzo?' Carlyle sniffed. 'At least he won't have to worry about his weight any more, will he?'

'I suppose not,' Joe agreed. Picking up a copy of Marcello's menu, he studied it carefully.

Carlyle gave his sergeant the once-over as he listened to the coffee machine burst into action. Joe was five foot ten, about a stone overweight, with long dark hair and a perpetually amused expression like a slightly bigger version of the actor Jack Black. They had been working together for more than four years now. Carlyle was notoriously uninterested in the backgrounds of any of his colleagues, but he had nevertheless gleaned quite a bit about Joe in their time working together. Joseph Leon Gorka Szyszkowski was second-generation Polish, born and brought up in Portsmouth before coming to London to study geophysics at Imperial College. For reasons Carlyle didn't understand, he decided to join the Met after graduating with a good 2.1 degree.

In the wider world of London, Poles were now well established. Many were heading home, as the recession began to bite, but they were still considered the benchmark of quality, reliability and value for money in the plumbing, building and other sectors of the economy. They also provided the odd footballer and many, many Catholic priests. For any ethnic minority, however, it was harder to break into the relatively closed, conservative world of the police than to gain acceptance in civilian jobs. Carlyle had so far only ever come across one 'Polish' policeman in the Met, and that was Joe. To be fair, if it wasn't for the name you would never guess his ethnic background. Joe was thoroughly assimilated, even if he would never be invited to join the Masons, that rather comical secret society (or 'society with secrets' as they preferred to be known) and home of the 'all-seeing eye' and the motto *Ordo ab Chao*, 'Order out of Chaos', which for some reason attracted policemen by the bus load.

There were about 21,700 sergeants employed in the UK police, and Carlyle knew the only one of them that could sing the English national anthem in both Polish and Hindi. Joe had an Indian wife, Anita, and together they had given their kids, William and Sarah, the most thoroughly English names that they could think of. Despite all this, there remained a strand of Joe's DNA that was deeply and irredeemably Polish, i.e. dark, pessimistic and Catholic. This background contributed to a sense of detachment, irony and – perhaps just as important – fatalism, which Carlyle could relate to. The two got on well and trusted each other. Carlyle was happy about that.

'What have they got?' he asked, as he watched Joe theatrically unfold the newspaper and lay it out on the table in front of him.

'What do you think they've got?' Joe tossed his copy of the *Evening Standard* on to the surface.

'Everything?'

Joe nodded. 'Everything.'

He waited while Carlyle contemplated the 72-point headline on the front page which read: TOP HOTEL KNIFE HORROR.

'They've got the knife, the time of death, the note,' Joe continued, 'and they're also speculating about the sexual nature of the crime.' He picked the newspaper off the table and turned it around to scan the article. 'And I quote: "Sources suggest that the frenzied attack bears the hallmarks of drug-fuelled sexual experimentation gone badly wrong."' He rolled the paper up and waved it at Carlyle. 'Drug-fuelled sexual experimentation?' He sighed theatrically. 'Those were the days ...'

'Speak for yourself,' Carlyle grinned.

'This is top-notch journalism,' Joe laughed. 'You know, I reckon that this paper has got a lot better since that ex-KGB guy bought it.'

'Better a propaganda vehicle for the Kremlin than one for our idiot mayor,' Carlyle said sourly. 'Who wrote that piece?'

Joe unrolled the paper and squinted at the byline. 'Someone called Fiona Singer-Cavendish.'

'Never heard of her.'

'Me neither,' Joe shrugged, 'but she's certainly on top of this one. I'm surprised that they don't have a picture of you exploring the dead man's orifice.'

'Wait for the final edition,' Carlyle joked. Bloody Alex Miles, he thought. The little bastard will have sold the lot just for a few hundred quid. He reflected a bit further. 'Do they know about the note?'

'They certainly know that there was a note,' replied Joe. 'They don't seem to know that it was delivered to Charing Cross, thank God! They also don't know – or aren't disclosing – what it said.'

'Do you really think there's a gay angle to all this?' Carlyle asked.

'Maybe.' Joe raised his eyes to the ceiling. 'Why stick a kitchen knife up some poor bugger's ... no pun intended ... behind if not to make a point of some crude sexual nature?'

Carlyle raised his eyebrows. 'It could mean anything. Or nothing.'

'Yeah, right,' Joe scoffed. 'Surely it's saying: *"I want to fuck you right up the arse"* ...'

'Possibly.' Carlyle went with the flow. With Joe in this kind of mood, that was always the best option. It was normally the only option.

'... *after you're dead.*'

'It could make sense,' Carlyle agreed, for want of anything else to say.

'This,' Joe smiled, 'has gay hate crime written all over it.'

Marcello placed Joe's latte on the table and retreated to a respectful distance. Carlyle thought about the story in the paper and suddenly felt his enthusiasm for the case desert him faster than an Old Compton Street hooker who's been paid in advance.

All he could see was the slog ahead of them. 'Do we care, one way or another?' he wondered out loud. 'Gay or not, does it make much of a difference?' The gay crimes taskforce had been disbanded three years earlier. Cases like this all went in the same pot now, in this case *his* pot.

Joe lent back in his chair and let out a deep breath. 'Not really.'

'What about the SCD? Could this be one for them?'

Of the Metropolitan Police's eleven Specialist Crime Directorates, the Homicide and Serious Crime Command was SCD1. It usually dispatched a major investigation team or a homicide task force to sweep up all the interesting murder cases. By definition that meant virtually all those that were not solved within a matter of hours.

'I wouldn't bet on them bailing us out,' Joe replied. 'Homicide is seriously stretched at the moment. Half of them have been sent to Belgravia to deal with the Arab billionaire who took a dive off the balcony of his Mayfair penthouse, back in March.'

Carlyle nodded. He was aware of the case.

'Lots of foreign travel involved with that one,' Joe continued, 'so everyone wants a piece of it. No one's in a hurry to call it a day, either.'

'I can imagine,' said Carlyle. Lots of foreign travel meant time away from the family *and* lots of well-paid overtime. Even better, there was no real pressure to get a result. The established consensus was that it had been a professional hit, with the killer lurking somewhere back in the Middle East, untraceable and untouchable. All in all, it was a great case to be working on. Those involved would be fighting off volunteers with a stick.

'Face it,' said Joe, 'it looks like we're stuck with this one.'

'We?'

'Yes, well, you obviously, O great one,' Joe's grin got wider, 'but, as usual, I will probably have to help out … at least a little bit.'

Carlyle nodded formally in the sergeant's direction. 'You are too kind.'

'No gratitude necessary,' said Joe, bowing slightly in return. 'We might as well try and get it sorted out as quickly as possible.'

'Quite.' Carlyle stroked his stubble and shot his sergeant a look of mock seriousness. 'No one's turned up to confess this morning?'

Joe Szyszkowski pretended to think about this for a minute, before delivering the inevitable reply, 'No.'

'Is there no hot lead that presented itself while I was in bed?'

Again, Joe pretended to think about it for a second, before shaking his head. 'No.'

'OK, OK, let's get serious.' With a tremendous effort of will, Carlyle summoned some enthusiasm for the matter in hand. 'What about the knife, then?'

'It's a nice bit of kit. No prints. Could have been bought in several hundred locations across central London, assuming it was purchased recently, that is.'

'Do we want to spend time checking on that?' Carlyle asked.

'It's already in hand.'

Carlyle moved on down his mental checklist. 'Did you see the note?'

'Yes.'

'What do you make of it?'

'There's a story here, obviously,' said Joe. 'The killer wants us to know *why* he did this.'

'OK,' said Carlyle, suddenly all business. 'So have we come up with anything else involving a similar MO?'

Joe adopted a philosophical tone. 'The modus operandi in this case appears to be fairly unique. There have been twenty-eight knife killings in London so far this year. There were eighty-six last year. Most are either domestics or kids stabbing each other on sink estates.'

Carlyle grunted. Crimes of passion or crimes of stupidity, both categories bored him silly.

'We are checking out all of the rest,' Joe continued, 'but there appears to have been nothing similar so far ... arse-wise.'

'Have you viewed the CCTV pictures from the hotel?' Carlyle asked.

'Yeah.' Joe took another slurp of his coffee. 'Useless result, though some American boxer and his groupies got into a fight with the management, just before you turned up.' He grinned. 'One of the women had her top ripped off. Wearing no bra.'

Carlyle gave him a look that said: *Let's focus on the matter in hand, shall we?*

'That was quite entertaining but caused chaos. I've got one of the lads back at the station having another look through, but I don't bet on them finding anything useful.'

'OK,' Carlyle sounded disappointed. 'Just make sure that they don't stick the groupie's tits on YouTube. In the meantime, what about the victim himself?'

Joe raised his eyes to the ceiling and began reciting from memory, rather like a third-former standing up in front of the whole class. 'His name is Ian Blake, as you know. Forty-seven years old. Owns a flat in Chelsea – there's a team investigating there now. He works in that most noble of professions, public relations, at a firm called Al ... something.' Joe paused the recitation and pulled a torn piece of paper out of his pocket to scan the notes scribbled on it. 'Alethia. They have an office near Park Lane.'

'Alethia was the goddess of truth,' Carlyle explained. 'Daughter of Zeus.'

Joe raised an eyebrow. 'And we know that because?'

'We know that because Alice explained it to me on our school run this morning.'

'Top girl!'

'Yeah,' agreed Carlyle happily, 'she certainly is. She's into all that Greek mythology stuff, big time at the moment.'

'It's good to know that at least one member of the Carlyle family is showing an interest in culture,' Joe smirked.

Carlyle feigned indignation. 'I'm not taking any crap from someone whose kids spend all their time playing with their Nintendo DS,' he grinned, 'and who wouldn't know a book if they were smacked in the face with one.'

'They are just at one with the *Zeitgeist*, chief,' Joe quipped serenely. 'We don't want them to get bullied in the playground, now, do we?'

'I suppose not. Anyway, what about this Alethia?'

'PRs,' grunted Joe. 'What a name, then! They really understand irony, don't they?'

'Yeah,' Carlyle agreed. 'Apate would have been a better choice.'

'Because he is?' Joe asked, happy to play along.

'*She* was,' said Carlyle pointedly, 'the goddess of deceit.'

'Ho-ho, very good. Anyway, as well as being incapable of irony, PRs also don't know how to hide their light under a bushel. In present circumstances, this is a very good thing. It means we are making good progress in building up a picture of the victim.'

'We are?'

Joe laughed. 'Oh, yes. Blake's picture and a short bio were prominent on his company's website.'

'I saw that.'

'And he's also on Facebook.'

'Why am I not surprised?' Carlyle grunted. 'And what does that peerless source of information tell us?'

'In a nutshell?' Joe grinned.

'Yes, please, Sergeant,' Carlyle nodded, hoping for something good. 'In a fucking nutshell.'

'Well, he's a "spurmo". Or, at least, he wants us to think he's a spurmo.'

'A what?'

'Spurmos,' Joe intoned, 'are straight, proud, unmarried men over thirty.'

Carlyle yawned as he was introduced to yet another tedious media fabrication. 'So that's like a metrosexual?'

'Maybe. Kind of. Perhaps. I have no idea.'

'As opposed to a retrosexual,' Carlyle smirked, 'who hasn't had any in years.'

'Yes, well … we'll leave your domestic problems out of this, shall we?' Joe laughed. 'It's not always *all* about you, you know. If you were a bit more culturally literate, you would know that the spurmo god is George Clooney.'

'OK,' Carlyle reluctantly tried to get a bit more serious, 'so straight and proud doesn't seem to suggest a gay angle to this killing.'

Joe made a face. 'He could have been in denial. Reluctant to come out of the closet? Maybe the whole spurmo thing was a front.'

'Come on, no one is in the closet these days. Look at Saxonby's mum.'

'Yeah,' Joe sniggered. Sergeant Chris Saxonby at the Savile Row police station had become an instant celebrity in the Met after his mother, seventy-one-year-old Agnes O'Halloran, had crossed over to the pink side, leaving his father – her husband of forty-five years – for a sixty-seven-year-old girlfriend. The shock of his parents new domestic arrangements almost killed poor Saxonby. He went off on sick leave for almost a year, before being granted early retirement on compassionate grounds. Even then, his leaving do had been held in the gayest gay pub in Soho.

'Poor sod,' Carlyle reflected, with feeling.

'Worse things happen at sea,' muttered Joe. 'But, coming back to our Mr Blake, you shouldn't be so binary in your thinking.'

'Why not?' Carlyle asked.

'Because some people will fuck anything,' said Joe philosophically.

'Charming.'

'I know.'

'Still, it's not looking too good for your theory.'

'I don't know,' said Joe, reluctant to give up on his thesis so easily. 'Maybe he was indulging his gay side, his spurmo side then reasserted itself, and there was a falling out. Maybe it was, like the paper says, a sex game that went a bit … wrong.'

'That wouldn't really sit alongside the note, though, would it?'

'No …' Joe pondered that for a second, 'although that could just be something to throw us off the scent. A distraction?'

'It suggests premeditation rather than a crime of passion.'

'Not necessarily. Maybe the killer was a quick thinker.'

'I don't know,' Carlyle was shaking his head. 'It's all guesswork. What else does Facebook tell us?'

'Blake is basically a posh boy who never grew up. He's pushing fifty, but acting like he's twenty-five. He likes skiing, Kate Nash and mojitos …'

'Who's Kate Nash?'

Joe rolled his eyes to the heavens. 'Please try and keep up, old man. She's a singer-songwriter who was flavour of the month – or flavour of the nanosecond – a year or so ago.'

'Never heard of her,' said Carlyle, who couldn't have named any female singer since Kate Bush.

'I just know the name,' said Joe. 'The kids have got one of her CDs, I think, but I've never heard any of her stuff myself. Having said that, she's probably already made more than you or I will earn in our lifetimes ... combined.'

Carlyle grunted. He hated all the irrelevant crap from victims' lives that passed before him in the course of an investigation. The way that people managed to waste time never ceased to amaze him. In the station, they had banned Facebook because too many staff were spending too much time on it, thus sucking up all of the station's bandwidth. On two occasions, the computer network had crashed completely. That was presumably due to the support staff, or at least he hoped so. Wasn't Facebook old-hat now, anyway? Helen, who saw herself as the most socially and technologically literate member of their family, had set up an account but lost interest after about a week. Carlyle was pleased with that, almost as pleased as he was with himself for never having signed up in the first place. He had enough problems with real life, so creating a virtual one would seem madness. The whole thing was bloody dangerous – one of their friends was now getting divorced because her husband had run off with some girl he had met online.

Carlyle stood up, pulled out his wallet and handed over a fiver to Marcello. He waited for the change, and then dropped it in the tips tin. 'OK,' he said, turning back to Joe. 'We're making some progress. Let's get over to Blake's flat.'

'Not possible.' Joe shook his head. 'By the time we got there, we'd have to come straight back again.'

Carlyle made a face. 'Why?'

'For the press conference.'

Carlyle gave him a dirty look. 'What fucking press conference?'

'Oh, yes.' Joe's eyes sparkled as he also got to his feet, and spread his arms wide. 'Why do you think I'm looking so smart today?'

Carlyle looked his colleague up and down for a second time. Belatedly he noticed that Joe's usual outfit – a grubby jeans and T-shirt combo – had been replaced by his basic courtroom attire: a dark-grey Marks & Spencer suit, crumpled white shirt and a maroon tie.

Buttoning up his jacket, Joe made a show of looking his boss up and down, too. 'Not a match on the Paul Smith, of course. That is quality.'

Damn right, Carlyle thought. Glancing at his reflection in the window, he gave a nod of approval. His own suit was a very nice navy, three-button, single-breasted Paul Smith number that he had acquired a few years ago for seventy-five quid from the Oxfam shop just down the road, on Drury Lane. The one item in his wardrobe that he looked after carefully, it was still in reasonable nick. Given the turn of events, he was glad he hadn't gone with his alternative outfit of The Clash T-shirt and jeans. If you looked carefully, you could see that the Paul Smith was a bit worn in places, but it was still several notches above the rest of his wardrobe, fitting in well with the Met Comissioner's new 'anti-scruffy' campaign.

'You should have shaved,' Joe observed.

'You should have shaved better,' Carlyle deadpanned in response.

Joe grinned. 'What about a tie?'

'Don't push your luck,' Carlyle growled. He then closed his eyes. 'Why do we need a press conference?'

'Because Simpson says so.'

SUPERINTENDENT CAROLE SIMPSON was their boss. She was based at Paddington Green Police Station, appearing in Charing Cross when a problem – or an opportunity – presented itself. A woman in a hurry, she was five or six years younger than Carlyle and, unlike him, could still realistically eye another three – or even four – rungs of the career ladder before her time was up.

Carlyle had known Simpson for almost ten years now. Apparently untroubled by any 'history', she had arrived on the scene not long after his own move to Charing Cross. She was, he had to admit, a hell of an operator. Political to her fingertips, she only ever looked upwards, and she had taken to what was essentially a management role like a duck to water. She could be charming too – if you were a man of a certain age (i.e. ten to fifteen years older than her) and she wanted something from you.

But Superintendent Carole Simpson rarely wanted anything from Inspector John Carlyle. In fact, they had an uncomfortable, difficult relationship. She was frustrated by what she saw as his stubborn refusal to play the game, and his inability to hide his feelings towards her. In turn, he hated that sense of being co-opted on to her mission for personal glory.

Simpson, in fact, left Carlyle cold. Somehow, the collective good always seemed to be neatly aligned with the interests of the superintendent. He found her approach to the job completely introverted, indeed almost demented: she was far too busy climbing the greasy pole to worry about anything else. As far as he could see, Simpson combined utter selfishness with the self-awareness of a goldfish. Either way, Carlyle eyed her with a mixture of extreme distrust and antipathy. However, he had to be professional and, with discipline and concentration, he could just about tolerate her so long as their paths did not cross too often. Whenever they did coincide, he always felt as if he was getting too close to speaking his mind in a way that would fatally undermine any hope of maintaining even the most perfunctory of working relationships.

'Why does Simpson want a presser?' Carlyle began massaging his temples firmly, in the hope that maybe the headache that he knew was on the way wouldn't actually arrive.

'Who knows?' Joe raised his hands as if in supplication. 'The media have already got the story, so she probably wants to ride the wave.'

Carlyle looked hard at Joe. 'So, if the press has got everything already, what do we hope to achieve with a bloody press conference?'

Joe shrugged. 'You know what she's like.'

Carlyle nodded. 'Oh, yes.'

'For Carole there is no such thing as bad publicity.'

Carlyle looked at his watch. 'What time is it scheduled for?'

'Three-thirty,' Joe replied. 'They've already been told that you'll be there. I'm just a little bonus.'

Carlyle ground his teeth in frustration. Toying with the media circus would only make their job harder. Press conferences were the first refuge of the brainless and the desperate. As of right now, however, they were a long way from being either. 'What are we meant to be saying?' he asked.

Joe drained the last of his coffee. 'Just the basics. Telling them what they already know. Asking the perpetrator of this horrific crime to give himself up. Calling for witnesses. Yada, yada, yada. Reassuring the public.'

'Do they *need* reassurance?'

'Probably not.'

'No sign yet of mass panic?'

'No.'

'OK, OK.' Carlyle thought about this further. Ten years ago, maybe even five years ago, he would have thought *Fuck it* and bunked off, leaving Simpson to deal with the journalists on her own. But the new, mature Carlyle was more sanguine, or maybe just warier. He knew that there was now a limit to what you could get away with before the myriad of disciplinary processes kicked in and your professional life was strangled before your eyes. Therefore, he would go to the press conference, while vowing to let Simpson do the talking. It was her show, her glory. Let her have it, if that's what she wanted.

'Let's get back to the station,' he said. 'After the presser, we'll head off to Blake's place. I can read all the necessary stuff in the meantime.'

A long evening stretched ahead, therefore sustenance would be required. Carlyle peeked over the counter and smiled. 'Marcello,' he said, 'bag me up that last pastry, please. I'll take it with me.'

Chapter Twelve

THE 'MEDIA CENTRE' at Charing Cross Police Station was a large, windowless basement that no one had ever found another use for. It was always cold and filled with the smell of stale food from the canteen next-door. The harsh strip lighting further helped ensure that no member of the media ever wanted to hang around too long. There were twenty chairs arranged theatre-style, facing a slightly raised platform that could sit up to six people. Behind the stage was displayed a large Met logo, with the legend *Working together for a safer London* spelt out in foot-high letters underneath. At the back of the room, there was space for television cameras, and in one corner a carefully branded mini-studio set where one-on-one interviews could be conducted after the press conference, like those interviews given by a football manager after a game.

Simpson's press conference had drawn a reasonable crowd. They included a crime reporter from the *Evening Standard*, a reporter from one of the local freesheets, a guy from the PA news-wire and a local radio reporter. Television was represented by ITV's London Tonight and BBC London. As usual, they were all willing to hype it up in the hope of breathing some new life into a story that, after fifteen hours, was almost past its sell-by date. At the same time, with what they had so far, none of the journalists was getting over-excited. London might not be the murder capital of the world, but equally it was not the kind of place where a killing, per se, merited too much interest. When it came to getting the journalistic juices flowing, death was necessary but not sufficient. News editors needed a juicy angle involving sex, race, drugs, children or – the mother-lode these days – celebrity, to give the story legs.

Five minutes after the appointed starting time, Simpson, Szyszkowski and Carlyle entered the room by a door behind the platform. They were greeted with indifference by the small gathering in front of them – who continued chatting, talking on their mobiles, filling in their sudoku puzzles or, in one case, actually dozing. Simpson tentatively tapped on the microphone in front of her, but it appeared to be switched off. She raised her voice slightly to compensate. 'Good afternoon, everybody …'

She was interrupted by another door opening at the back of the room. Heads turned, and stayed turned, in recognition of a star suddenly in their midst. In her Chanel suit, BBC reporter Rosanna Snowdon was far too well dressed for her surroundings. Her tan (maybe fake, but not obviously so), hard brown eyes and big blond hair gave her the look of an upmarket 1980s soap star. Carlyle pegged Snowdon at just north of thirty. After a well-publicised skiing accident that had kept her off the air and out of the gym for a month earlier in the year, it looked as if she was now quite a few pounds overweight. But she carried it in a healthy, knowing way that said: *I don't have to be thin to be sexy.* She possessed what he thought of as a 'neutral' face, not friendly, not hostile, always ready to adapt to the situation. Not a chameleon, though, because she was always too focused on the matter in hand – self-promotion – to adapt *too* much to external circumstances. Nothing was for nothing, and everything was calculated.

It took a while for every man in the room to compose himself and return his attention to the matter in hand. Simpson let them settle. 'Good afternoon, Rosanna,' she said with an impressive faux familiarity. 'Very nice to see you here today.'

Snowdon smiled, gave a little nod, and took a seat in the otherwise empty front row.

Simpson paused, quickly introduced her two colleagues, and then launched into the prepared statement. This managed to fill most of the remaining time allotted for the conference, while actually containing no new information whatsoever. The hacks scribbled away and nodded politely, apart from the *Standard* reporter who appeared to be either deaf or suffering from a serious attention-deficit disorder.

Once Simpson finished reading her statement, Snowdon immediately turned to Carlyle. 'Is it true,' she smiled sweetly, 'that you were told about the body in a note, Inspector?'

Carlyle stiffened. 'We are not adding to any detail we have already put out into the public domain,' he heard himself say, robotically.

Snowdon came back at him gently. 'But it has already been reported that there *was* a note ... so any additional colour you can let us have on that would be most appreciated.'

Carlyle forced himself to smile. 'I understand the need for colour in your story, Ms Snowdon,' he replied evenly, 'but I've got my job to do as well. We really have nothing to add at this stage.' He could sense Simpson getting irritated, but felt that he had to stand his ground. This whole event was, nominally at least, supposed to be for the benefit of *his* investigation, after all.

The other journalists sat back, happy to see how far this gentle sparring would continue. Aware that they had ceded her the floor, Snowdon felt it was at least worth giving it one last go. 'I'm sorry to have to repeat the question, Inspector ...'

'But you are going to anyway,' Carlyle shot back.

At this point Simpson intervened, clearly having had enough of Carlyle spoiling her show. 'I think we've already covered that,' she declared, with a rictus grin. 'Are there any more questions?' she asked firmly, scanning the room. After the briefest of pauses, she moved on. 'None? Good. Thank you all for coming. We will, of course, provide you with an update in due course. I will now happily make myself available for any radio and television interviews you might need.' She scanned the audience, willing someone to take her up on her offer. 'Shall we say BBC first?'

With no immediate takers coming forward, the superintendent almost sprinted to the back of the room to get herself in front of the cameras. Even so, the room had almost emptied by the time she got there. People were working on deadline and the ITV crew was busy breaking up its equipment. Their producer had already left, and it was now clear they didn't want a one-on-one with Simpson.

Watching smugly from the platform, Carlyle caught a quizzical glance passing from the BBC cameraman towards Snowdon, asking her *Do we need this?* Snowdon gave him a quick nod and he made a face before resetting the camera for Simpson's close-up. He was used to this: a 'just in case' interview, mainly conducted in order to keep the subject happy.

While the cameraman fussed about, Snowdon and Simpson exchanged business cards and chatted in a rather over-animated fashion. Carlyle wondered what they were talking about, but he knew that it wasn't likely to be the Blake case. Snowdon was not a journalist in the 'hard news' sense. Indeed, she wasn't really a journalist in any sense. In reality, she was just another hustler who saw every news item, every victim, as another step towards realising her destiny as a celebrity presenter on the main national network, with a smug banker husband and regular exposure in *Hello!* magazine. Similarly, Simpson wasn't really a copper – he doubted if she had been out on the streets in the last ten or even twenty years. She was just a politician in uniform.

In short, they were both women in a hurry. Each recognised a kindred spirit in the other. This whole performance was more about networking than it was about the reporting the news or even solving a crime.

Stepping down off the platform, Carlyle moved closer to listen to the interview. For a couple of minutes, Snowdon lobbed a series of easy questions that allowed Simpson to reprise her comments from the press conference.

'That's great,' said Snowdon, after Simpson had delivered the same soundbite for the third time in a row.

The superintendent beamed like a sixteen-year-old who'd just been told that she'd received twelve A grades at GCSE.

'Just one final question.'

Simpson smiled even harder, nodding expectantly.

'Have you spoken to the mayor about this?'

Simpson's smile faded as a look of confusion spread across her face. 'I'm sorry ...' Instinctively, she reached for the microphone, but stopped herself before she pulled it off her lapel.

'That's OK,' said Snowdon, goading gently. 'Let me ask that one again ... The mayor was a close friend of the victim, so how did he take the news?'

Simpson looked blank. 'I'm sorry,' she repeated. 'I don't know anything about that.'

'Fine,' Snowdon glanced at the cameraman. 'We'll leave it there.' She smiled at Simpson. 'Thank you, that was great. Don't worry about that last answer. I'll take one from the top.'

A rather crestfallen Simpson nodded and shuffled off, carefully avoiding eye contact with Carlyle as she headed out of the room.

The Mayor of London, Carlyle thought. *That's the second time he's come up, so far, in this investigation.* That meant he had got to be part of the investigation. *That means, John old son, you are going to have to tread carefully here. Very carefully indeed.*

Chapter Thirteen

Cambridge University, March 1985

ROBERT ASHTON CLOSED his copy of *The Rise of Anglo-German Antagonism, 1860–1914* and stood up from the desk. He felt a fierce thirst, but ignored the tall, narrow glass of water that stood on the corner of the table, next to a pile of textbooks and papers. A dull pain was building slowly behind his eyes. It mingled with the numbness that he still felt after all these months.

A pale shaft of sunlight struggled through the curtains, illuminating a small patch of the worn rug on the floor. Outside was a beautiful spring day: England as it was supposed to be, bright, fresh, almost warm in the sun. Laughter rose from the courtyard outside.

Room 12 was situated on the third floor of Darwin Hall, one of the halls of residence for undergraduate students at Cambridge University. It was basically a large, dark space that Ashton shared with another student, a French waster called Nicolas who had already left for Easter even though there were still ten days until the end of term. That suited Robert just fine, as he liked having the place to himself. Reaching across the table, he picked up the glass of water and stepped cautiously into the middle of the room, careful to avoid stepping on any of the books strewn across the floor. Having picked his spot, he gazed up at the oversized mirror that had been placed above the fireplace. His head cocked to one side, like a concerned fawn, he contemplated a face that he no longer recognised. Then, slowly, deliberately, he threw the glass into his reflection, smashing it to pieces. His heart racing, he stood there for a second, concentrating hard, making sure that the image was gone. After a moment, he realised that his cheek was stinging. Carefully, he extracted a small shard of glass from just below his left eye and dropped it in the fireplace, before wiping away the smallest drop of blood.

From down the hall, he could hear the strains of Mahler's *Symphony No. 2* coming from the room of a seriously disturbed German theology student, who had been playing the same music almost non-stop since September. Turning back to the desk, Ashton extracted three envelopes from under his pile of books and placed them in a row, aligning their edges carefully with those of the table. The brown A4 manila envelope addressed to Professor Box contained his essay on the causes of World War One. It was a day late – the first time he had ever missed a deadline – but, still, he knew it was a good effort, probably deserving of an A, or an A – at the very least. A stickler for deadlines, Box would doubtless even refuse to look at it, but Ashton had finished it, so he might as well send it.

The other two envelopes were smaller, just big enough to contain a couple of the Howard Hodgkin postcards he had bought at the Fitzwilliam Museum a week before. The first envelope, containing an image of Hodgkin's painting entitled *Bleeding*, was addressed to his shrink, a nervous woman who seemed even more disturbed about what had happened to him than he was himself. The envelope containing the second card, *Mourning*, was simply addressed to 'Suzy'. Both cards had been left blank, and both were apologies of a sort. Both, he knew, were pitifully inadequate, not that he cared. They could decipher them or not.

Satisfied that everything was finally in place, Robert Ashton stepped through some curtains and opened the door that led on to the small balcony overlooking the quadrangle. He was wearing just a thin black T-shirt the chill in the air made him shiver. The sun was rapidly sinking in the sky, and already beginning to disappear behind the buildings on the far side of the quadrangle. Squinting, he held up his hand to shield his eyes from the sun's glare. The stone parapet in front of him was about four feet high and maybe ten inches wide. Yawning, he pulled himself up on to it and stood shakily surveying his domain. Forty feet below, people were going about their business, still heading to and from lectures. In the middle of the square was a large oak tree. Near the tree, a fantastically pretty girl was sitting on the grass, lapping up the attention she was getting from two would-be suitors competing for her attention.

For what seemed like an eternity, Ashton waited for the girl to look up and catch his eye. When she finally did so, he pulled back his shoulders and held his arms outstretched. Overwhelmed by a huge sense of relief, he listened to her scream of alarm fade away on the breeze.

Then he stepped off the wall and into space.

Chapter Fourteen

CARLYLE PRIDED HIMSELF on not paying much attention to politicians, but even he knew chapter and verse on Christian Holyrod. Known as 'the Holy Rod', 'the Rod', 'Hot Rod' or 'the hero of Helmand', depending on the mood of the tabloid newspapers on any given day, Holyrod had been enjoying the kind of press that other politicians could only dream of. Two years earlier, he had been Major Holyrod, commander of the 2nd Battalion of the Duke of Wellington's Regiment (motto: *Virtutis Fortuna Comes*, or 'Fortune Favours the Brave'). It was one of the first British battle groups to go into Helmand in south-west Afghanistan, with a mandate to give 'Terry Taliban' hell.

Holyrod's journey from unsung hero to big-time politician began when an American documentary crew arrived to film the story of Operation Clockwork Orange, a mission to capture a terrorist commander inside his mud compound in the middle of nowhere. The mission was a total fiasco, Holyrod's boys were ambushed and a swift retreat followed, but the firefights and general chaos that followed made for great television. Shaky, hand-held pictures of the Major shouting, 'Contact, contact, contact!', while squeezing off rounds from his SA80-A2 assault rifle and trying to drag a wounded squaddie back to his truck, were as gripping as anything that Hollywood could have come up with. They made all the major news bulletins back home in Britain even before the programme was aired in the USA. For almost two days it was the most watched video on YouTube, with more than forty-five million hits around the world. Holyrod became an instant celebrity. He was offered his own radio talk show, signed up to do a newspaper column, acquired an agent and received more than one hundred offers of marriage.

For its part, the Ministry of Defence was, initially, more than happy to let a stream of journalists beat a path to the Major's door, given their desperation for any kind of 'good news' out of a story that had been a complete disaster from day one. Holyrod quite enjoyed the attention, but he was increasingly worried that the MoD had seriously underestimated the task in hand, i.e. fighting the enemy. The tone of his interviews became more and more downbeat as he contemplated 'the big picture'. After telling a very nice girl from the *Sunday Express* that 'the whole thing's gone to rats', he was hauled back to London 'for discussions'. His return to the front line was then cut short after he was caught, on camera, berating the Foreign Secretary, who was in the middle of a four-hour 'tour' of the troops, about Her Majesty's Government's lack of support for 'his boys'.

Of course, the media lapped it all up. So did the public. Opinion polls suggested that Holyrod's approval rating had reached the high eighties. No politician could compete with him. The Major's window of opportunity had arrived, and now he had to decide what to do with it.

It was at this point that Holyrod's political contacts came into play. His brother-in-law was one Edgar Carlton MP, leader of the opposition and, by common consent, prime minister in waiting. After some detailed discussions with his pollsters, Edgar persuaded his old pal to cash in his chips and take the fight to the real enemy – those disgusting, spineless liberals that had taken over Whitehall in recent years.

After a few phone calls, a bit of arm twisting and the promise of a few peerages, Holyrod was installed as Carlton's choice for Mayor of London. After six months of campaigning under the party slogan, *Change That Keeps Changing*, he won a landslide victory over the incumbent, an immensely tired-looking woman with the air of someone who couldn't get out of the job fast enough. The only time Holyrod ever saw her smile was on the night of the election itself, immediately after it was announced that she had lost.

According to received wisdom, the first hundred days are crucial for any newly elected official. That's when the new broom can sweep clean, and you make your mark. After that it's all downhill. For more than three months, Holyrod went in to work each day with a nagging feeling that he should be doing something significant. What, though, he had no real idea. Meanwhile, the less he did, the higher his poll ratings climbed; and the higher his ratings went, the more he was seen as providing the template for Edgar Carlton's first national government, which was just around the corner. As the national election loomed, Holyrod's job was to provide living, breathing proof that the party was fit to govern.

AFTER THE CAMERAMAN had taken the disc out of his camera, and was again breaking up his kit, Carlyle wandered over to join Rosanna Snowdon.

Snowdon watched him approach with a wry smile. 'You don't want us to do you as well, do you, Inspector?'

Carlyle held up his hands. 'No, no,' he said, stepping closer. 'Not my kind of thing.' As discreetly as possible, he breathed in her luxurious perfume. 'I leave that to others.'

'Very wise.'

'I just wondered,' Carlyle probed, as casually as possible, 'about the connection between Mr Blake and the mayor …?'

'It's not a big deal,' Snowdon said, stuffing her notebook into an oversized handbag and pulling out a very bling mobile. 'They know each other from university. Just a minor detail, so not something you guys would necessarily have picked up on at this stage.'

'And how do you yourself know that?'

She shrugged. 'It's just one of those things one knows.'

Carlyle considered asking her about the Mayor's Office using Alethia, Blake's PR firm, but decided to hold back. 'Will that be part of your story?'

'I doubt it. I wondered if it might make a nice angle, but maybe not. It's a bit contrived and I probably won't get anything like enough time to squeeze it in, anyway.' She grabbed the handles of her bag and hoisted it over her shoulder, before holding out a hand. 'Nice to meet you, Inspector,' she said, pulling up a number on her mobile with her free hand, 'but I've got to rush back to the edit suite. I hope that you'll like the piece.'

Before Carlyle had the chance to reply, she was off, already talking into her phone and leaving only a fading whiff of scent in her wake.

Chapter Fifteen

CARLYLE SAT ON a very nice two-seater cream sofa in the living room of Ian Blake's small but perfectly presentable one-bedroom flat in Lennox Gardens in Chelsea. One of the most upmarket neighbourhoods in the city, it was only a mile, give or take, from where Carlyle himself had been born. The flat was smaller than Carlyle's present home, but it was easily worth two or even three times as much. Even with the recent sharp fall in house prices, the place had to be worth around a million quid. Solid, understated, it was the type of property that would never go out of fashion.

The policemen and technicians who had spent the last three hours going over the place had packed up and headed back to the station. They had given no indication of finding anything of note, but they would be doing their job thoroughly and diligently, all the same. In line with the toxicology report on the corpse, they had found a small stash of cannabis which had been inexpertly hidden in a shoebox in the closet. There was nothing to suggest that Mr Blake was anything other than a standard middle-class dabbler.

Last night's exertions were catching up with Carlyle and his attention wandered. He tried to focus on what he might want for dinner since, by the time he got home, Helen and Alice would have eaten and he would be fending for himself. He went through a mental list of what was stored in the fridge, and the likelihood of it still being there when he returned. Nothing grabbed his attention, so it looked like a trip to the supermarket beckoned.

In the corner of the room, a large plasma screen flickered silently, the sound muted while Carlyle waited for the local news to appear. The sofa was very comfortable. Sitting back, he yawned and closed his eyes.

'Wake up! It's on.' Joe grabbed a large remote control from the coffee table and turned up the sound. He flopped down next to Carlyle and dropped the remote in the space between them.

Just over a minute later, it was all over. The highlight was a breathless piece to camera from Rosanna Snowdon, standing outside the Garden Hotel. Carlyle noticed she had undone an extra button on her blouse, providing an enhanced view of her seriously impressive décolletage. So this is why people watch local news, he thought. The piece also included a passport-style photograph of the victim, and a ten-second clip of a suitably dour-looking Simpson describing it as a 'violent and senseless crime'.

'She looks tired,' Carlyle commented.

Joe grunted.

Snowdon signed off with: 'The investigation continues.' Carlyle did not have a speaking role, although he did appear on screen, nodding intently as he listened to Simpson's wise words. Of Sergeant Joseph Szyszkowski, the man in the Marks & Spencer suit, there was neither sight nor sound. Nor was there any mention of the mayor.

Carlyle switched off the television and looked again round the room. 'Like you said ... spurmo.'

'Huh?'

'Not exactly a gay shag pad, is it?' Lost in thought, they both studied the Helmut Newton 'big nude' which dominated the far wall: a black-and-white photo of a naked Amazonian blonde posing beside a motorcycle.

'I wouldn't mind one of those at home,' Joe mused.

'The woman? Or the photo?'

'I'd settle for the photo.'

'I'm sure Mrs Szyszkowski would be delighted to hear you say that.'

Joe shifted in his seat, but made no attempt to stand up. 'A boy can dream. By definition, you don't want your dreams to become reality, otherwise they wouldn't still be dreams.'

'Mmm ... good try, soldier.'

'Anyway, Anita knows that I understand my limitations ... almost as well as she does.'

'Just as well,' Carlyle sniffed. He made a half-hearted attempt to get out of the sofa. 'So where do you think we are now? Have we found anything useful?'

'Not really. Not much of the personal touch here, is there? No photos, address books, stuff like that. His phone was in his hotel room. His BlackBerry is missing.'

'Are we sure that he even had one?'

'Yeah, his office confirmed that. You can't be a proper PR man without one, apparently.'

'So it was taken by the killer?'

'Maybe.'

'Can we track it?' asked Carlyle, operating at the extreme limits of his technological knowledge. 'It's just like a mobile, right?'

'Yeah, but it's switched off. I've checked.'

Carlyle thought about that. 'But if someone took it, presumably they want it for something. So, at some point they might be expected to switch it on?'

'Not necessarily. You can switch it on but keep the wireless turned off. You can then access all the information already on the machine, though you won't be able to send or receive any emails. That way businessmen can play with them on planes without causing a crash.'

'That's good to know,' said Carlyle listlessly. He'd had his own BlackBerry up and running for little more than three weeks now and he hadn't quite managed to work that kind of facility out yet. He wasn't the kind of guy to bother consulting the user manual: a gadget either worked straight away or it went in a drawer. With the BlackBerry, once he had worked out how to use the email and check the latest football news (not necessarily in that order), as far as he was concerned he was away. In his book, whatever else the machine did was over-engineering – the curse of the modern consumer electronics industry.

He stood up and took a step over towards the window. 'This place feels like a hotel suite, or one of those serviced apartments. It doesn't look like we'll get much here. What did the people employed at his company have to say?'

'The usual: shock, horror, surprise.'

'Could it have been a colleague that killed him?'

'Doesn't look like it, but we're still taking statements. Nothing much has jumped out, so far. There are only thirty-five people working there and we haven't heard any suggestion of grudges. The victim was reckoned to be very straightforward: good with clients, good at networking, relatively good with junior staff. Not too pushy. Basically, he seems to have kept his work life and his private life separate. They knew he wasn't married, otherwise he's a bit of a blank sheet of paper.'

'OK, go and have another chat with the Alethia people tomorrow morning and see what you can find out about his clients.'

'No problem.' Joe nodded. 'They don't start early, these folks, so I can take the kids to school for once. Anita will be chuffed.'

'Nice,' Carlyle smiled. 'What about ex-colleagues?'

'Doubtful. The company has only been going a few years, and none of the top people has left yet. Apparently, the way these things work is that you build up the business and then sell it off to someone bigger. You probably get tied in for a while, but then you can bugger off as soon as the cash hits your bank account. They haven't got to that stage yet.'

'What about the more junior staff?'

'Again,' Joe sighed, 'nothing's really come up. It's the kind of place where the secretaries save a bit of money and then go back-packing in Australia. The others are all bright young things, very career-focused.'

Carlyle kept throwing out the questions as they popped into his head. 'What was Blake doing before this job?'

'Dunno. Still checking.'

'Next of kin?'

'Nope. Parents dead. No brothers or sisters.'

'Partner?'

Joe gestured around the sparse room. 'Apparently not.'

'Neighbours?'

'There are six flats in this building. We've managed to speak to someone in three of them so far. Two more are still being chased.'

'And?'

'Nothing.'

'Fucking hell.' Carlyle sighed. 'Give me *something*!'

Joe shrugged. 'They didn't seem that interested, to be honest. Apparently he's been living here for about eight years, but that's about it. Like the people at his work, they found him fairly quiet and polite.'

'Car?'

'Nice motor, an Audi Q7. It's downstairs. There's a garage in the basement.'

'Has it been checked?'

'Yeah. A preliminary search threw up nothing.'

'What about cameras?'

'None. Neither inside nor outside.'

Carlyle raised his eyebrows.

'I know,' said Joe. 'Some of the residents thought it would lower the tone, apparently.'

'Typical.' Carlyle yawned. 'Half a million security cameras all over London, and not one where we actually fucking need it.'

'It's always the way.' Joe struggled out of the sofa. 'We are where we are, then. Let's call it a night.'

'That's a plan,' agreed Carlyle, as he went back to thinking about what he might have for dinner.

THE REMOTE CONTROL missed the screen by about two feet and exploded on impact with the wall behind it, switching the television off as it did so. A few deep breaths saw the frustration subside, but only a little. From the moment she had appeared on the screen,

it was clear that the Snowdon woman was one of those bimbo journalists who shouldn't be let loose on anything more taxing than
a *Hello!* magazine interview. Even then, it was a shocking performance: no background, no insight, no bloody context. No wonder
more and more people were refusing to pay their licence fees.

Breathe!

How difficult could it be for these people to see what was
going on?

Breathe!

On the other hand, these journalists only regurgitated whatever the police told them. If the police themselves were clueless,
why should the journalists be any better?

Breathe!

There was no point in wailing about what had happened. If
people couldn't yet put the pieces together, they could always be
given more help. Next time, it would be spelt out so clearly that
even this bunch of idiots couldn't miss it.

EVA HOLLANDER STOOD in the kitchen with a large glass of Château Puysserguier Saint Chinian in her hand. Dominic Silver
wasn't too keen about his wife drinking before the children had
gone to bed – he didn't want them to see alcohol as something to
be consumed as a matter of routine every evening – but he wasn't
going to make an issue out of it. Their five kids weren't around
to see Mummy's teatime boozing, anyway. They had now fled to
various parts of the house in order to avoid teeth brushing, face
washing, bedtime stories, etc., etc. If he listened carefully, he
could hear the sound of *Modern Warfare 2*, interspersed with bits
of Abba. Everyone was safe and happy under one roof. Domestic
bliss personified, it was the best feeling in the world.

Should he have a bowl of pasta? Or a bowl of cornflakes? Dom was still undecided as Eva tapped him on the shoulder. 'Look,' she was pointing at the small television screen fixed below one of the kitchen cupboards, 'there's John Carlyle.'

She turned up the sound and together they watched the rest of the news report. By the time it had finished, Dom had decided on the pasta.

'He looked very grumpy,' Eva observed, bringing the glass to her lips without taking a sip.

'He always looks grumpy,' said Dom, as he poked around in the fridge for some tortellini.

'It sounds like he's working on a particularly nasty case.'

'That's his job.' Dom finally pulled out a packet of pasta and closed the fridge door. 'He's been doing it for long enough now. It's his choice, and it always has been. It's what he likes doing.'

'I wonder how Helen and Alice are getting on,' Eva mused. 'We haven't seen them for a while.'

Dom carefully opened the packet with a knife and dropped half the contents into a pan. 'Give them a call,' he said, over his shoulder. 'Get them to come over sometime. I'm sure all the kids would love a play date.'

'I THINK THAT was fine ...'

For now, thought Christian Holyrod. He eyed the callow adviser hovering beside him. *Should I have told him about Blake?* There was no use worrying about it now.

'... and the important thing was that your name was kept out of it.'

The boy's fruity aftershave was giving him a headache. 'Give me a minute alone, will you?' he said, and it wasn't a question. 'And close the door on your way out.'

With just the slightest pout, the aide did as he was told. Alone for the first time that day, the mayor turned down the sound on the television and pulled a bottle of Tullibardine 1994 out of a desk drawer, along with a small shot glass, before filling the glass almost to the brim. Sitting back in his chair and lifting his feet up to the desk, he savoured the toffee-apple and sherry smell of the whisky before taking a gentle sip. The bittersweet taste tickled his throat, reminding him of candyfloss. Holyrod took another sip and then drained his glass in one long swallow. Closing his eyes, he contemplated the silence.

Chapter Sixteen

CARLYLE SLURPED AT a cup of lukewarm black coffee, and happily munched on the pastry he'd saved from earlier in the day. The third floor of the police station was deserted apart from a couple of cleaners who were wandering from desk to desk, waving some feather dusters around in a desultory fashion, like a pair of bored performance artists from the piazza nearby. Dropping the remains of his Danish on a napkin, he picked up the pen lying on an A4 notepad next to his keyboard. At the top centre of the page, he wrote IAN BLAKE, drawing a neat box around the name. Below the box he wrote the name of Christian Holyrod.

For several seconds, he studied the yellow paper, searching for inspiration. It was time to start putting the pieces together, and this was the part of the job he liked almost more than any other. After all his time on the Force, he still got a buzz of excitement as he embarked on that voyage of discovery that would inevitably take him to the heart of his case. How he conducted that journey – whether from behind a desk or out on the street – didn't matter just as long as it took place.

'Right ...' He pushed the remainder of the Danish into his mouth, washed it down with the last of his coffee, and started bashing the keyboard. Clicking on to Google, he typed in BLAKE+HOLYROD. The legend 'Results 1–10 of about 12,000 (0.09 seconds)' popped up and Carlyle reflexively hit on the first link, which was a newspaper article entitled *The Merrion Club: Young, rich and drunk*. Carlyle waited for the story to load before scanning it quickly. It informed him that Blake and Holyrod had both been members of an ultra-exclusive Cambridge University fraternity famous in equal measure for its hard drinking and bad behaviour. For reasons that were not explained, the club was named after the Dublin street in which the Duke of Wellington had been born. The story was a trail of booze-fuelled vandalism and famous old boys. Near the bottom of the piece, a quote from a hanger-on caught his eye: 'It wasn't considered a proper night out until a restaurant had been trashed. A night in the cells was par for the course for a Merrion man. So, too, was the debagging of anyone who incurred the irritation of the Club.'

What was a 'debagging'? Carlyle decided he could guess. He now contemplated the accompanying group photograph. Standing on the front steps of some stately pile, all floppy hair, morning suits and sophisticated sneers, they looked like extras from a Spandau Ballet video. In fact, he thought that they looked as though they were boys from a departed era. The picture was taken less than thirty years earlier but it could just as easily have been a hundred and thirty. The caption beneath the image listed the members of the Merrion Club of 1984: George Dellal, Ian Blake, Nicholas Hogarth, Edgar Carlton, Xavier Carlton, Christian Holyrod, Harry Allen, Sebastian Lloyd.

Carlyle read and reread the eight names on the list. 'Well, fuck me sideways!' He continued to stare at the image for a long time.

There was Blake at the back, over to the right. Holyrod, London's current mayor, stood in the middle, waving a cigar. In front of him, the leader of the opposition, Edgar Carlton, was standing next to his brother Xavier, who, if Carlyle remembered correctly, was the shadow foreign secretary. *Fuck knows who the rest of them are,* Carlyle thought. At this rate, he wouldn't have been surprised if the rest of them included the new Pope and some minor European royalty. He understood that the Establishment was tightly knit – after all, that's what made it the Establishment – but this was surely ridiculous.

Quickly scribbling those six new names on his pad, he added little crosses beside the Carltons and Holyrod. Switching his attention back to the keyboard and clicking out of the internet, Carlyle paused to roll up his sleeves. Taking a couple of deep breaths, he prepared to do battle with the Force's internal IT network. The British police were notorious for their terrible computer systems, which were commonly assumed to have let an unknown number of serious criminals slip through the net over the years. A few years earlier, the high-profile failure to vet a school caretaker who subsequently murdered two schoolgirls had encouraged the introduction of a Police National Database linking all forty-three forces in England and Wales. But that was still quite some way off and, knowing that trying to search the whole country was too ambitious, Carlyle decided to stick to London – even if it was hard enough trying to extract information from the different computer systems run by the Metropolitan Police. Many old-school coppers simply could not be bothered trying to access them, but Carlyle realised that, for all their failings, they offered him access to a treasure trove of information of the kind that had helped him solve many cases in the past.

Typing in a second username and password, he accessed a Met database that allowed him to view basic details of all the capital's outstanding homicide cases. Blake he knew about, along with the Carlton brothers and Holyrod, who were all still very much alive. So, one by one, he slowly typed in the other four names: 'Delal, Hogarth, Allen, Lloyd'. Asking for anything showing from the last six months, he waited five, six, seven seconds before NO RESULTS flashed up on the screen.

Carlyle leaned back in his chair. Then he tried again, extending the search parameters, to cover the last two years.

Another short wait.

Again NO RESULTS appeared on the screen.

So much for a quick hit. Carlyle looked at the clock and realised it was way past Alice's bedtime, so it looked as if he wouldn't be seeing her this evening. *Don't rush it,* he told himself. *This could crack the whole thing open.* He remembered the note: 'not the first and not the last'. Someone mentioned in this database had to be connected to Blake. It was worth the effort to try to find them. He pulled his mobile out of his jacket and sent Helen a text saying that he would be working a while longer, before getting up and going for a piss. After fetching another coffee from the machine, he walked twice around the office to stretch his legs and clear his head, before returning to his desk.

Carlyle felt extremely tired but he forced himself to concentrate. 'Third time lucky,' he mumbled to himself, as he looked again at the scrawl on his pad. The handwriting was appalling, almost illegible even to himself. He flipped back to the newspaper story on the internet and ran his finger down the names, double-checking the spellings. With a groan, he realised that he'd missed one *l* out of the name Dellal. Quickly, he punched the correct spelling back into the database, and hit send. He was still cursing his carelessness when it popped up in front of him:

Dellal, George Edward Hazlett
DoB: 16/9/63
Deceased: 12/02/10
COD: multiple stab wounds
Investigating officer: S. Sparrow
Status: OPEN

'Sam fucking Sparrow,' Carlyle smiled, 'come on down ...'

INSPECTOR SAM SPARROW worked out of the Enfield station in north London. He was a straightforward, no-nonsense police-man maybe five or six years younger than Carlyle, with almost as many commendations and considerably better career prospects. The two men had worked together in the late 1990s, when Spar-row had been leading an investigation into Turkish drug dealers in the Wood Green neighbourhood of north London. After the Turks had begun invading rivals' turf to the east, Carlyle, sta-tioned at Bethnal Green at the time, had been drawn into what became a violent and bloody mess, with body parts randomly strewn across both neighbourhoods. Sparrow had proved very easy to work with, and Carlyle had come out of six months' hard slog with both a commendation and a promotion. For a while, he was on a roll. It even looked as if all his 'career issues' might have been sorted out for good. A subsequent run-in with a particularly stupid superintendent quickly put paid to that hope, but it still ranked as Carlyle's most successful period on the force and he remembered it fondly.

He brought up Sparrow's mobile number, and listened to it ringing.

'Yes?' a voice asked sharply.

'Sam?'

'Yes.' There were voices in the background: kids, maybe a television.

'It's John Carlyle. Sorry to bother you at home.'

'No problem. How are you?' Sparrow sounded tired, distracted.

'Fine. And you?'

'All good. What can I do for you?'

Carlyle could sense that it was not a good time, so he got straight to it. 'George Dellal.'

Sparrow waited for more. When it didn't come, he asked: 'What about him?'

'I might have something similar.'

'Oh?' Sparrow gave no indication of being in any way intrigued. 'Yes … this Blake thing?'

'Sorry,' said Sparrow wearily, 'I've been off the last few days. The mother-in-law's been in hospital. Family drama.'

'Sorry to hear that.'

'Don't worry about it,' said Sparrow, with the air of a man who wished he was busy raking through other people's shit rather than dealing with his own. 'These things happen. What's the Blake thing?'

Carlyle wanted to keep it vague, hedging his bets. 'Basically, it's another knife murder. What's the background to Dellal?'

Carlyle listened to Sparrow breathing down the line as he parked his domestic drama for a moment and slowly dredged the basic details of that earlier case out of his memory. 'George Dellal. Found dead in his flat. The neighbours reported the smell. It was very messy.' Sparrow paused as if he'd run out of things to say.

Carlyle prompted him gently. 'I don't remember reading about it in the papers.'

'We kept it low-key. It only made the local paper and a couple of paras in the *Standard*. Since then there's been nothing. Happily, the family didn't want to make a meal of it in the press.'

Again, Sparrow stopped abruptly. Carlyle knew that, if that case was still open, it couldn't be looking too good. He didn't want to rub Sparrow's nose in it – no one wanted to be associated with any of the small minority of murders that didn't get solved – but he wanted to elicit what he could. 'How's it looking now?' he asked, gently.

'No weapon. No leads. We haven't made much progress, so we haven't exactly been shouting about it from the rooftops.'

'No,' said Carlyle. *You're lucky you don't have Simpson hovering at your shoulder,* he thought. Sparrow's boss, Superintendent Jack Izzard, was far less high-maintenance. 'One other thing,' he asked, as casually as possible, 'was there a note?'

Sparrow laughed. 'It definitely wasn't a suicide,' he said, misunderstanding the question. 'No, there wasn't a note.'

'OK.'

'Is there a possible connection with your guy?' Sparrow asked.

The noise in the background increased. Carlyle could clearly hear a child crying and a woman shouting at it to go to bed. 'I dunno,' he said.

'Look, John,' Sparrow said hurriedly, 'I gotta go. I'll be back at work in a couple of days. If you need anything, you know where to find me. And if you find out anything interesting, let me know. Good luck.'

'Thanks.' Carlyle put down the phone and scribbled three points on his pad:

1. *Merrion Club*
2. *6 possibles – Carltonx2, Holyrod, Sebastian Lloyd, Nicholas Hogarth, Harry Allen*
3. *Total shitstorm*

Then he called Joe Szyszkowski.

After five, six, seven rings, Joe answered. 'Hello, boss.'

'Are you sitting down?' Carlyle asked.

'Sure. Why?' Joe sounded relaxed, as if he'd had a glass or two of wine with dinner. Unlike the Sparrow call, there was no background noise. Joe's kids would be in bed by now.

'Things have moved on a bit,' Carlyle said. 'There's good news and bad news.'

'I'll have the good news first, then, please,' said Joe cheerily.

'We know who the next victim will be.'

'Excellent!' said Joe, waiting patiently. He knew that Carlyle would get to the point eventually and, relaxing at home, he didn't feel the need to hurry him along.

'At least,' Carlyle continued, 'I can narrow it down to six people.'

'From seven million to just six, that's not bad,' Joe agreed, suspending his disbelief. 'So what's the bad news?'

'One of them is the mayor.'

'The mayor?' Joe groaned. 'Of London?'

'No, the mayor of fucking Cairo,' Carlyle deadpanned. 'Of course, the Mayor of London!'

'The Mayor of London.'

'That's what I said.'

'Tell me that you're joking,' said Joe, '*please.*'

'Sadly not, and—'

'Jesus,' Joe cut in, 'there's an *and*?'

'Of the six,' Carlyle said slowly, 'one of them is our own dear mayor. Another – according to current opinion polls – is our next prime minister.'

'Are you sure this isn't a wind-up?' Joe asked. 'How do we know all this?'

'Ian Blake went to Cambridge University, right?'

'Right,' Joe agreed. 'He got a 2.1 in PPE, Philosophy, Politics and Economics, the standard-issue degree of our governing classes.'

'Good for him,' said Carlyle. 'Beats my A level in General Studies. Anyway, while he was stuffing his head full of knowledge en route to obtaining that excellent qualification, he was a member of something called the Merrion Club.'

'Never heard of it,' said Joe.

'Me neither until about fifteen minutes ago,' said Carlyle.

'I'm guessing it's not the kind of club we'd get invited to join.'

'No, the Merrion Club was – is, for all I know – a drinking club for rich young wankers.'

'Rules us out, then.'

'Damn right. In this case, rich means *really* rich, as in absolutely fucking loaded.'

'Lovely.'

'The aim was to get blind drunk, have a food fight, smash some furniture and maybe fuck the hired help, if they could still get it up later in the evening. At the end of it all, they'd pay for all the damage with fifty-pound notes.'

'When was this?'

'The early eighties.'

'Blake graduated in 1984?'

'Right. The Merrion class of '84 included Blake and a guy called George Dellal. Plus Holyrod and the Carlton brothers and a few others. Dellal got chopped up in similar fashion to Blake a few months ago.'

'Coincidence?' Joe asked.

'Hardly,' Carlyle replied. 'You've got a 1-in-25,000 chance of being murdered in this city, in any given year. What we have here is two out of this group of eight getting brutally murdered in less than six months.'

'So what have we got?' Joe asked. 'Sounds like *Brideshead Revisited* meets *Friday the 13th*.'

'Something like that.'

'Well, well, well,' Joe chuckled. 'Edgar Carlton and Christian Holyrod? The joint dream ticket of dream tickets.'

'Maybe,' Carlyle snorted, 'if you're a mentally incontinent, *Daily Mail*-reading fascist.'

'Hey,' Joe chided him, 'Anita reads the *Mail*.'

'She should know better,' Carlyle growled.

'What are the odds of those ending up in our investigation?' Joe asked, moving the conversation on.

'About as good as our own chances of getting murdered,' said Carlyle glumly.

'Simpson will most definitely not be happy,' Joe pointed out.

'A silver lining,' Carlyle agreed, 'however faint.'

'So what do we do now?' Joe asked.

'Let's sleep on it,' said Carlyle. 'Keep all this strictly to yourself, for now. We will have to be extremely discreet, especially when it comes to writing things down. No written reports, no emails … at least until we know what the fuck is going on here.'

'Of course.'

'I'll go and see Simpson tomorrow. It's better to do it face to face. Then we'll have to reach out to the gentlemen in question, and see if they can shed any light on why someone might want them dead.'

Chapter Seventeen

HEADING FOR PADDINGTON GREEN police station, Carlyle walked out of Edgware Road tube station. At the station entrance, he paused to let his eyes adjust to the gloom. There was no need to hurry, as Simpson regularly stayed holed up in her office to late into the night. She was not the best when it came to handling bad news, and therefore Carlyle was in no rush to give it to her.

As he approached the station, he was struck by its shameless ugliness. Paddington Green police station was a brutalist cube from the 1960s that almost made its Charing Cross counterpart seem elegantly designed. Straight out of the couldn't-give-a-flying-fuck school of architecture fashionable at the time, it eroded his spirit still further. Five minutes later, waiting in the anteroom outside her office, he picked up a magazine that had been discarded on the seat next to him. Flipping the pages, he realised it was the same magazine he'd been reading in the clinic on Harley Street while waiting for Ferruccio Pozzo to come round from his operation. Finding the correct page, he picked up the article about *The Golden Twins*, Edgar and Xavier

Carlton, where he'd left off before arresting the now-deceased
Mafioso.

Both brothers have worked hard to cultivate their voter-
friendly image. Each is physically imposing (Edgar is 6'1"
and Xavier 6'2"), with the looks of a pair of matinee idols.
Both have the regulation exotic political wife (Russian for
Edgar, while Xavier's is Italian) and an impressive number
of suitably cute and precocious children (four and three
respectively).

The third leg of this proto-political dynasty is provided
by half-sister Sophia, who is married to close political ally
Christian Holyrod, the former soldier whose election as
Mayor of London last year was very much seen as a fore-
runner of Edgar's assault on No 10. Sophia has her hands
full with the five children she has popped out for Holyrod in the course of their eight-year marriage, but she is
still seen as a powerful behind-the-scenes influencer. Last
year's Christmas card, a group shot of the three families
at a polo match under the legend *Wishing You a Carlton
Christmas*, was, in effect, the party's manifesto encapsu-
lated in full.

The door to Simpson's office opened, and a young woman stepped
out. She didn't introduce herself, but Carlyle assumed she must be
his superior's assistant.

'Sorry for keeping you waiting.'

'That's fine,' Carlyle smiled. He had already resigned himself
to a long wait, so it was relatively easy to be gracious. The PA was
a chunky girl, in her twenties, with mischievous grey eyes and

an arresting lime-green bra clearly visible under her transparent white blouse.

She let him gawp at it for a few seconds. 'Can I get you anything?'

'No, I'm fine.'

'If you *do* need anything, just let me know.' She smiled before disappearing back into the office.

Carlyle filed the bra in his bank of happy thoughts, and returned to reading his article.

The brothers are poster boys for 'the new posh', the fashionable, knowing, *ironic* elite who can beat the liberals at their own game. So, by and large, they keep their fancy cars in the garage (Edgar has a Porsche Cayenne 4×4 and Xavier not one but two Maseratis), but they make sure that they are only ever photographed driving their matching, environmentally friendly Prius hybrids.

Xavier has also embraced a bicycle, some say at his brother's behest, regularly cycling to work at the Commons. 'It takes me back to my days at Eton,' Xavier said recently, 'the happiest days of my life, obviously. And, at the end of the day, when you look at the big picture, you can see how it's also about freedom of the individual and taking one's own action over an overbearing nanny state which wants to kill our spirit and rob us all blind.'

Camping (it's not like the boy scouts; instead think drinking Chablis in a £5,000 yurt while barking down your iPhone at your PA and complaining about your WiFi), music festivals and British seaside holidays have all got the Carlton thumbs-up. Times may be tough, but they are laughing in the face of recession. It's all therefore about the quality of life. Is it all bogus, though? Of course it is. But if everything is bogus, then nothing is. What is a dream if it's not reality?

The door opened again. This time, Simpson herself dashed out, bouncing along the corridor without even acknowledging him. Less than a minute later, she bounced back.

'Sorry to keep you waiting, John. I won't be long.'

She didn't wait for his reply. He didn't utter one, being too busy worrying because she had used his first name.

Such is this picture of domestic and political perfection that even 'the race issue', the one thing that some of the more antediluvian political commentators speculated could halt their blitzkrieg through the establishment, has been completely neutralised. In a recent pressyour button.co.uk poll for *Political Stud* magazine, 42 per cent of respondents didn't even realise that they were black. As Edgar himself put it recently: 'I'm not black, I'm *privileged.*'

Carlyle felt a familiar vibrating feeling against his chest, and pulled out his phone. Seeing that it was Joe, he hit the receive button.

'How's it going?'

'There's not a lot to report, boss,' Joe replied. From the sounds in the background, he had either gone home already or he was watching the Cartoon Channel in the office. 'Did you speak to Simpson?'

'Still waiting. Anything new in the media?'

'No, it's all gone quiet.'

'Good. I'll give you a call right after the meeting.'

'OK.'

'Give my best to Anita and the kids.' Carlyle ended the call and put the phone back in his pocket. *Lucky sod*, he thought. *I wish I was at home, too.*

Of course, neither brother has ever worked in the real world, moving seamlessly from Cambridge to safe seats, one in London, one in the country, after a few years spent travelling and setting up their respective families. At that time, Edgar spent a year at the Society for Freedom, Progress and Innovation, currently the party's favourite policy think-tank. Colleagues at the time have suggested that he was a stranger to the concept of a five-day working week, but he still managed to be credited as the co-author of a pamphlet called '*Heading South: The case for internal migration in the UK*', which argued that northern cities like Liverpool and Newcastle have 'lost much of their raison d'être', their private sector economy and their ability to generate wealth. It argued that the citizens in such godforsaken places should head south to places like Oxford and Cambridge, offering better job prospects. Needless to say, this paper caused a storm of protest. The idea has now been disowned and it is not expected to appear in the party's election manifesto.

His phone went again. This time it was a text from Helen: *We've eaten, so you're on your own for tea. x*

Carlyle ignored his rumbling stomach and focused on finishing off the article.

With the election looming, it seems that nothing can stop Edgar and Xavier Carlton from realising their political ambitions. According to a former colleague: 'There was never any doubt that they were ultimately going to run the country.' A bold statement, but an accurate one. If there ever was any doubt before, there isn't now.

He closed the magazine and let his gaze lose focus. Nothing he had read made him feel any happier. What the hell was he going to do with these people? The Carltons wouldn't want to be seen anywhere near his case, even if it turned out that they were right in the middle of it. People like that didn't get to where they were by worrying about little things like a murder enquiry. At best, they would ignore him. At worst ...? Well, who knew?

It was the ultimate no-win situation.

HAVING BEEN MADE to wait for more than an hour, it was almost 7.45 p.m. when he was finally invited to enter Simpson's office. The assistant had put her coat on and was ready to leave. This time round, she did not grace him with a smile, merely pointing in the general direction of her boss, while grabbing her bag and heading in the opposite direction.

As he walked through the door, he realised that he had never been inside this particular office before. However, if he had been looking for clues as to the content of her character, he would have been sorely disappointed. Aside from the furniture, it was spectacularly bare save for a photograph of a middle-aged man who Carlyle assumed was her husband. Sitting at her desk, scribbling some notes on a pad, she gestured him to sit with a curt wave of the hand, without even looking up. Prim, proper and poised,

Carlyle thought she had the air of someone who had already done a full day's work, thank you very much, and now had a top-notch dinner party to go to, offering the chance to mingle with people far more interesting than himself.

Five minutes later, once he had explained the situation, the same dinner party was off. As expected, Simpson did not take the news well. Listening to him in silence, she clasped her hands together as if in prayer, while gnawing on her lower lip. In fact, she seemed to have aged ten years during the short time that he had been speaking.

Carlyle thought she might burst into tears at any moment. All in all, that made him feel a lot better.

After taking a moment to compose herself, Simpson spoke. 'John, you know how careful we must be here?'

'Yes.'

'You realise just how … sensitive this is?'

No fucking shit, thought Carlyle. 'Absolutely.'

'Who else knows about this?'

'My sergeant,' Carlyle replied. 'No one else.'

'Good. It goes no further than that,' Simpson said quietly, a steely determination colouring the words. 'If the press get hold of this, I will have your balls … and Szyszkowski's.'

Spare me the macho bullshit, thought Carlyle. 'Understood,' he replied, in his most clipped, no-nonsense manner.

She looked him up and down. 'Do you have any idea who is doing this? Or why?'

It was a tricky question that called for a straight answer. 'No.'

Simpson gave no indication of being surprised. 'Well, maybe I should see what I can do to help you move this along, Inspector.'

'That would be very kind. I would be most grateful for any assistance.'

'Let my office reach out to the remaining Merrion Club members, appraise them of the situation, and then we can take it from there.'

My office? She even talks like a politician, Carlyle thought, *not a policeman.* He nodded and said nothing as he watched the light bulb coming on above Simpson's head. It was clearly beginning to dawn on her that this case might not prove a total pile of shit after all. It could offer her the chance to do some favours for some of the most important men in the capital, and therefore in the country. And, if everything turned out well, another promotion beckoned.

'Once I have made the initial contact,' Simpson continued, 'it will become easier for you to speak to them.'

Carlyle kept his expression neutral. 'Thank you.'

'These are very important men, so we have to approach them correctly.'

'Of course.'

Simpson looked him up and down, searching for evidence of sarcasm or unreliability in one of her least favourite officers. Carlyle gave her none. Having laid down the rules of engagement, she switched tack. 'On the plus side, at least the mayor and the prime minister and his brother will have their own security already.'

'He's not the prime minister,' Carlyle pointed out evenly.

'Yes,' said Simpson, clearly put out at being pulled up. 'A Freudian slip.'

'Easy to make,' Carlyle smiled.

'Yes, indeed. He will be prime minister, of course. And sooner rather than later. Do you look at the polls?'

Carlyle made a non-committal gesture.

'He's got the biggest lead since polling began.' She seemed quite excited.

'I thought his lead was slipping,' Carlyle said mischievously, vaguely remembering reading something about it in *The Times* that morning.

'You always get the odd rogue poll,' she replied. 'It doesn't matter. He's a certainty.'

Carlyle looked at Simpson carefully: 'That doesn't make any difference, though, does it?'

'To what?'

'To the way we handle the case.'

'Of course not,' she said stiffly. 'What it means is that the killer, if he is after these remaining gentlemen, is very unlikely to be able to get close to at least three of them. Out on the stump, in the public eye and surrounded by security, they're pretty safe.'

'Unless our guy changes his MO,' Carlyle mused.

'The thing to do,' said Simpson, ignoring this thought, 'will be to concentrate on the others … once I have spoken to them.'

'Understood,' he repeated.

'Remember,' Simpson said with some feeling, 'there absolutely must be a media blackout on this. It cannot be allowed to … pollute the election. You know how the Met would get the blame. The mess would cover us all. Maybe we should get a DA-Notice out tonight?'

'Good idea,' said Carlyle, injecting a little false enthusiasm into his voice, trying to sound supportive. 'But maybe that would be a bit over the top.' DA-Notices were issued by The Defence, Press and Broadcasting Advisory Committee, requesting that editors not publish or broadcast items on specified subjects for reasons of 'national security'. This present case might be a serious matter, but describing it as a national-security issue would be rather stretching it a bit. 'A Defence Advisory Notice is probably inappropriate here, and this is not really a matter for the Press Complaints Commission,' he continued, 'but we could go through the Society of Editors. That's what the Palace did a while back, when one of the young princes went to Iraq.'

'Very brave of him,' Simpson mused.

'Far better for him than rolling around in the gutter outside some nightclub,' Carlyle muttered, recalling one of the same young royal's other hobbies.

'What?'

'Nothing.'

'Now is not the time for any lack of focus, Inspector,' Simpson said with smooth menace.

Carlyle ignored her tone and ploughed on. 'Editors might accept a purely voluntary "understanding", in return for special access later on.'

Simpson thought about it for a minute. 'I would need to agree that with their people.' *Their people* meaning the Carltons' entourage.

This game is getting very complicated, Carlyle thought.

'In the meantime,' Simpson continued, 'let's avoid any leaks. And, of course, the quicker we can get this solved, the fewer problems there will be. Let me have a full verbal report every twenty-fours hours. Whatever you need to get the job done, take it.'

'Thank you,' he said, forcing himself to maintain eye contact.

'John,' Simpson smiled one of the fakest smiles he had ever seen in his life, 'I am always here if you need me. You know that, don't you?'

'That is a great help,' Carlyle lied.

'Good. I'm glad,' Simpson lied back. Picking up one of the papers on her desk, she began reading it.

This was his cue to leave, and he took it.

FEELING MUCH HAPPIER than when he had arrived, Carlyle quickly left the station and sauntered down the Edgware Road. Heading south, in the direction of Marble Arch, he realised that he was in London's North African neighbourhood and therefore spoilt for choice in terms of coffee and cake. He passed a succession of cafés with men in shalwar kameez smoking oversized hookah pipes at pavement tables. Taking a right turn, he passed the north end of Connaught Square, glancing up at the inevitable pair of heavily armed policemen guarding the fantastically expensive town house of a previous prime minister. It had been bought a couple of years just before he left office and as the lucrative lecture and non-executive director circuit hove into view. With his current successor struggling so badly, it looked as if Edgar Carlton would soon be the third PM in short order. All political careers end in failure, some more quickly than others, Carlyle reflected. He knew that, within twelve months of getting the job he so shamelessly coveted, Carlton's ratings would be lower than a snake's belly in a storm drain. People might want the old guy back, even though they had hated him when he was in the job. What a shit job: it was even worse than being a policeman.

Fifty yards down the road, Carlyle took a seat outside the Café du Liban and ordered some of their thick, strong, black coffee sprinkled with cardamom seeds, along with a heavy, sticky pastry. At this time of the evening, the place was basically empty, since he had been lucky enough to hit the gap between office workers leaving for home and the locals arriving for a post-dinner coffee and gossip. Enjoying the peace, Carlyle settled down to turn things over in his head and map out what to do next. However, with his mind flitting from one thing to another, he found it impossible to focus on the case.

Letting his gaze roam over the middle distance, he was distracted by the sight of a dwarf chatting with a *Big Issue* seller on a street corner across the road. The dwarf was waving his arms about, and the magazine vendor was scratching at his beard and nodding vigorously. *I'm in one of the crazier David Lynch movies*, Carlyle thought unhappily, rummaging in his pockets for his BlackBerry and his different mobiles. If he couldn't process information in his head, he could at least do it on his various machines.

As it turned out, the only thing of note on any of them was a voicemail from Rosanna Snowdon on his 'work' mobile (as opposed to his 'private', untraceable, pay-as-you go phone). Snowdon hinted at some new development in 'the story' and asked him to call her. He wondered how she had got his number. The message was timed at 4.20 p.m., so he assumed that he'd missed her deadline for today. He would give her a call tomorrow, even if only to discover what she knew. Carlyle saw journalists primarily as people to get information from, rather than the other way round. On that basis, he liked them well enough. He understood the rules of the game, and so did Rosanna. When the time came, both of them would be happy enough to share.

Carlyle was about to switch off his phone and return it to his pocket when it started vibrating again. A text told him he had another message. Irritated, he pulled up the number for his answerphone and hit the call button.

'This is a message for Inspector John Carlyle. My name is Harry Allen. I was looking to speak to you about Ian Blake …'

'Fuck!' Carlyle punched the recall button.

'I'm sorry,' said a prim electronic voice, 'but the number you are calling is not available. We are unable to connect you ...'

'Fuck, fuck,' he looked at the handset with a mixture of resignation, disbelief and genuine hatred. Punching another button, he waited for the message to return.

'This is a message for Inspector John Carlyle. My name is Harry Allen. I was looking to speak to you about Ian Blake. I am out of the country at the moment, but I should be back in London next week. I will give you another call when I return.'

'When you return?' Carlyle hissed at the phone. 'When you fucking return? This is a murder investigation, for God's sake! What is wrong with you people?' Flicking through his missed-call list, he also had a 'no number' from three minutes ago. How could I miss that? he thought. The bloody thing just didn't ring. Resisting a strong urge to throw the handset under a passing taxi, he wondered if there was some way he could trace that call. At the very least, he could get Joe to track down Allen's number, and they should be able to get hold of him eventually. The good news was that at least someone was offering to talk.

His coffee arrived along with a generous slice of baklava. His attention now focusing on the humble delights in front of him, Carlyle finally dropped the mobile into his pocket and began to let the vexations of the day slip from his mind.

Chapter Eighteen

As instructed, the Range Rover Vogue SE pulled into parking space U3A28 Horseferry Road car park in Westminster, just a few blocks north of the Palace of Westminster. Killing the engine, Nicholas Hogarth switched off the Coldplay CD that had been burbling along in the background during his journey into town. The drive from Heathrow airport was easier than expected, and he was actually fifteen minutes early. He undid his seat belt and sat in silence, listening to his heartbeat ticking over in syncopation with the cooling engine.

After yet another sixteen-hour day, he felt exhausted but elated. The four espressos on the plane (and another in the airport) were doing their job. It was a relief that he was finally back in London, for advising on the restructuring of Moscow's Dzhugashvili Bank had been hard going. Russia was still very much the Wild West of global capitalism, which was saying something these days, and everything there was chaotic. With the financial markets in freefall, floating the bank on three different stock markets simultaneously – a tricky manoeuvre at the best of times – was taking much longer than it was supposed to. This latest trip had been scheduled to last three days, but, eventually, he had been stuck out there for almost two weeks. His Russian clients were driving him mad, too, but at least he had been paid this time, which was another reason to party.

Nicholas liked to party. His wife wasn't expecting him home for another twelve hours and, for the first time in a long time, he could enjoy a little freedom.

Outside the car, the top floor of the garage was silent, bathed in an industrial yellow glow from the sporadic strip lighting dotted about the concrete ceiling. Most of the parking spaces were empty, and he had seen no other people since he arrived. Gripping the steering wheel, he rocked slowly backwards and forwards in his seat, feeling a huge surge of adrenaline as he thought about what was coming next.

Within half an hour, he would get to fuck a total stranger with abandon. This was always the best part of these sessions: the anticipation of imminent, guaranteed, greedy sex. Exotic sex. Strange sex. Degrading sex. Expensive sex. Sex that was all about *him*.

That was what Serenissima was all about.

Serenissima was a Swiss-based agency that he had been introduced to by a business contact in Zurich, three years ago. It was a 'complete-experience agency', and he used them every couple of months. Usually at the end of a tough business trip like this one, or when his regular life just became too boring for words.

The agency was invisible. It billed one of his trading partners in Liechtenstein, so that the cost was lost amongst the thousands of transactions that went through the books at his financial services boutique in St James's every year.

He paid Serenissima to take control, and its slogan was *No limits, no boundaries, no preconceptions.* He set the time; they set the where and the how. And the who.

It could be anyone, male or female, aged eighteen to seventy. That was part of the delicious pleasure of the game: the freedom from choice. When you met your host, you could say 'No, thank you', of course. But if you ended it then and there, it was your loss ... and your cost. He always accepted what he had paid for, and had found that there was an important lesson there, too – don't prejudge things. The regulation-pretty girls were fine, but they were the least eager to please, the least imaginative and the least welcoming. On the other hand, the best session he'd ever had was with a sixteen-stone, sixty-two-year-old black lady who had jumped straight on to his dick and fucked him raw for three hours straight. He could barely walk for days afterwards. Thinking about it later, he'd decided that it was probably the best sex of his life, even better than the Peruvian triplets he'd enjoyed in Chiclayo one time. He'd tried to re-book her, but that was not allowed. Serenissima's strict rule was that everything was a one-time-only arrangement.

Another agency rule was no artificial time limits – once you come, they go. He therefore knew all about the dangers of getting too excited too quickly. The one encounter where he had felt short-changed had lasted barely five minutes, from start to finish. The boy had deliberately brought him to a frenzy in record time. The little whore had then spat out his juices, got dressed and was out the door almost before Hogarth realised what had happened. It was, he thought ruefully afterwards, probably one of the most expensive blowjobs in history.

From then on he had always made sure that he got value for money. As part of his pre-Serenissima ritual, he now reached into the glove compartment and pulled out a packet of tissues. From a bag on the back seat, he fished out an Armenian porn mag that he had acquired on his trip, and propped it up against the dashboard. With a contented sigh, he unzipped his fly and got to work.

After a couple of minutes' uncomplicated pleasure, he had completed the job. Dropping the used tissues out of the window, he felt sated, and wondered if he might not just go home. But, before he could reach a conclusion, there was a click, the passenger door opened, and a modest frame slid into the seat next to him. There was a glimpse of flesh and the sound of leather against leather.

'I see you've started without me,' said an amused voice.

'Well …' Hogarth gasped as a cold hand gently grasped his still exposed member.

'Leave the talking to me. Just sit back, eyes front.'

He did as he was told, bringing his breathing under control as the hand was replaced by something else. Hogarth let his mind wander, relaxing completely as he was gently brought back to life.

Several minutes later, the oral ministrations came to an abrupt end. He opened his eyes, but found it hard to focus.

'Get out of the car.'

Slowly he did as he was told.

'Face the windscreen. Hands on the bonnet. Spread your legs.'

Hogarth moved around the front of the car, watching his reflection in the cool Galway Green paintwork. From behind, he felt a pair of hands roughly undo his belt buckle and push his trousers to the floor. His underpants quickly followed. A hand came up between his legs, caressing his balls. Something cool tickled his anus. He was completely hard again now, and poised to explode. *Don't rush it*, he thought. *Slow down.*

When the explosion came, however, it was at the base of his neck, rather than in his groin. He tried to push himself up off the car, but instead found his head being smashed back on to the bonnet. His nose exploded, and blood mixed with the tears welling in his eyes. Dazed, he felt his legs buckle. His vision blurred and then there was darkness.

'Wakey, wakey!'

Hogarth regained consciousness as a bottle of water was poured over his head. Confused, with a throbbing ache behind his eyes, he took a moment to remember what had happened. Slowly, the world stopped spinning around him. He was lying face down, on the car bonnet, with his arms raised as if in surrender. The bonnet still felt warm, suggesting he hadn't been unconscious for long, and there was a sickly smell in his nostrils. Grunting, he tried to push himself up, but to no avail.

He was stuck.

Literally.

'Don't struggle, or you'll do yourself some serious damage.'

As his eyes regained focus, he saw the knife resting on the windshield. Next to it was a small photograph. Unable to move his head, it was hard to make it out clearly – but he could guess. A hand snatched up the blade and Hogarth clenched his whole body, in anticipation of the imminent blow.

'Help me,' he whispered, but only so that he could hear the sound of his own voice one last time. 'Please, help me.'

Hopping from foot to foot to try to stay awake, Carlyle stood as far away from the body as he reasonably could without looking too much like a wimp. He fiddled with his BlackBerry and looked over at Joe Szyszkowski, who was talking to one of the other policemen attending the scene. Even at this distance, the smell was appalling. He could feel the bile rising in his throat and he was only glad that his stomach was empty.

It was ten to five in the morning and he felt like shit. Those bastard students who rented the flat below him in Winter Garden House had woken him up at two a.m. with their bloody computer war games. It was the third or fourth time this had happened in recent weeks. They would stay up all night playing *Mercenaries: World in Flames* or *Call of Duty: World at War*. The first time it had happened, Carlyle literally thought that a bomb had gone off inside the building. It wasn't much better once he realised that it was only a game. There would be stretches of silence and then a monumental explosion. It was like World War III was taking place right under his fucking bed. Every time Carlyle went to complain, they would sheepishly apologise and call it a night. Then a few days later they'd start again. The fact that he was a policeman didn't seem to concern them in the slightest. He started giving serious consideration to having the little fuckers arrested for something. Better still, he would ask Dominic Silver to send someone round to trash their games consoles and break their fingers.

Carlyle really needed his sleep: anything less than seven hours and he was in bad shape for the next day. In the event, he had managed to grab less than an hour because, what had seemed like only two minutes after his eyes had finally closed, he had received the call about the body. Joe had picked him up just after four, and they reached the scene in less than ten minutes.

The body had been identified from a marketing brochure found inside the Range Rover. There was the by now familiar knife sticking out of his arse, and a pool of congealed blood extended several feet away from the body. Nearby, an extremely impressive stream of vomit had run almost the whole length of the vehicle.

Joe wandered over.

'Why is he still here?' Carlyle asked.

'They superglued him to the car,' Joe explained, trying to stifle a giggle. 'The paintwork is going to be ruined.'

'What?'

'He is stuck to the bonnet. They found a jumbo bottle of Lockdown "brush on" superglue.' He gestured to a small group of officers gathered by the car, lowering his voice a little.

'Lovely.' Carlyle already knew that superglue was a more common problem for the police than most people would imagine. Once, in East London, he had been called to a flat where a man in a wheelchair had starved to death after his upper and lower jaws were glued together. The coroner recorded an open verdict, but for a long time afterwards Carlyle wondered what had happened. Was it an accident? Or suicide? They were real teeth, so how could you glue them together by accident? If the guy had done it deliberately, then what a truly terrible way to kill yourself. Or maybe someone else had done it to him? Carlyle had lain awake at night trying to work it through, but a plausible explanation would always elude him. Another time he had to deal with a man suspected of breaking his bail curfew, who had glued himself to his girlfriend in an attempt to avoid being arrested. Carlyle packed both of them off to the station and had her charged with obstruction, before making himself scarce so that he didn't have to hang around for the business of separating them.

'Why do you think they did that?' he asked Joe, gesturing towards the corpse.

'Presumably to hold him in position,' Joe replied, 'so that we would find him exactly like this, with the knife sticking out of his arse.'

'Just like Ian Blake. And similar to George Dellal.'

'Yes, it's the same MO – different type of knife, but clearly the same MO.'

Carlyle thought about it for a minute. 'How are they going to get him off?'

'They're discussing that with the pathologist and a forensics guy right now. It's going to be tricky. They've already tried soap and water with no joy. Someone suggested nail-polish remover, but they don't have any handy. Now they're thinking of calling the Fire Brigade.'

'That will go down well,' said Carlyle wryly. 'Let's make sure we're gone before those guys turn up.'

Carlyle felt his phone start buzzing in his jacket. He fished it out and glanced at the screen. There was no name or number; it just read 'call'. Thinking that it was probably Simpson, he left it buzzing and dropped it back in his breast pocket. 'How exactly did they manage to do it?' he asked casually, nodding in the direction of the crime scene.

'They smeared glue on his palms, then pressed them down on the bonnet,' said Joe, who did not share Carlyle's squeamishness. 'And also on one side of his face.'

'OK.'

'And they glued his knob, too,' gasped Joe, his shoulders bobbing as he finally lost the fight against mirth.

Despite the early hour, the smell, and everything else, Carlyle couldn't help but smile too. 'Seriously? His knob.'

'Apparently,' Joe coughed, wiping away a tear, 'it's stuck to the badge on the grille.' He somehow managed to grin and grimace at the same time. 'I didn't look that closely myself, but I have it on good authority from those that have.'

Carlyle allowed himself another peek from a distance. It did indeed look like the guy was trying to fuck his Range Rover. What a shocking way to treat a seventy-grand motor.

One of the men in the group discussing the glue problem peeled away and came over.

'Joe ...?'

'How's it going, Matt?' Joe replied. 'This is my boss, Inspector John Carlyle. Boss, this is Sergeant Matt Parkin.'

'Inspector.' Parkin extended a hand.

'Good to meet you,' said Carlyle, 'despite the circumstances.'

'It is a bit of a mess,' Parkin agreed.

'Yes, Joe was telling me. What have you got?'

'The body was found about two this morning,' said Parkin. 'The sick belongs to the woman who found him. She must have puked half her body weight.'

'Nice,' said Joe.

'We've identified the man as Nicholas Hogarth, from some documents found in his car,' Parkin continued. 'He was on a flight from Moscow last night. Picked up his car from Heathrow and drove straight here.'

'Do we actually know that he came straight here?'

'Yeah,' Parkin nodded, 'we've got the timings down precisely. According to the Congestion Charge people, he entered central London just before midnight. According to the garage staff, he arrived here just after midnight.'

'Where does the Hogarth family live?' Carlyle asked.

'Highgate.'

'So this wasn't exactly on his way home?'

'No, clearly it looks like there was a bit of extracurricular going on. We found some tissues that suggest Mr Hogarth at least managed to get his rocks off before he expired.'

'Good for him.' Carlyle had seen enough. 'Any sign of any drugs?'

'Haven't found anything yet.'

'Apart from the woman who discovered him, did anyone else see anything?'

'No witnesses, as far as we know. This place is pretty dead at that time of night.'

'CCTV cameras?'

'There are twelve on each level and also one in each of the three lifts. Three of them cover the spot where the Range Rover was parked, but the lenses on those three, plus in one of the lifts, were smeared with Vaseline. This was very carefully planned. We are checking all the other cameras, plus those in nearby streets, but it will take time.'

'OK. It would be great if you could keep us posted.'

'Of course,' Parkin nodded. 'The other thing we've got at the moment is this.' He handed Carlyle a small, see-through plastic, Ziploc bag. Inside was a photograph, about the size of a playing card, with a white border. Slightly over exposed, it showed a smiling young man in a T-shirt and jeans, taken on a summer day somewhere in the countryside. 'We found this under one of the windscreen wipers of the Range Rover.'

Carlyle looked it over and then handed it to Joe. He turned back to Parkin. 'We'll need some copies.'

'No problem,' Parkin replied.

'I'll give you a call this afternoon,' Joe added.

Carlyle looked over at the body one last time. 'Thanks for your help,' he said. 'Now, tell me, where can we get a decent cup of coffee round here, at this time of the morning?'

Chapter Nineteen

Southwark, London, November 1985

HALFWAY BETWEEN THE Elephant and Castle and London Bridge, PC John Carlyle sat by the window in an all-night greasy spoon café, staring into space. The place was run by a Lebanese family who had escaped the civil war in Beirut five years earlier. After months patrolling the local streets of Southwark, the young constable wasn't sure that they'd made the right choice.

Sitting on the opposite side of the table, his partner of the last three weeks, Constable Kevin Slater, an amiable idiot from Manchester, shoved a bacon roll into his mouth and began chewing noisily. Staring into his empty coffee cup, Carlyle tried to ignore the brown sauce that was trickling down Slater's chin and dripping on to his uniform. The pair of them were six hours into a ten-hour shift. Once it was over, Carlyle would have three days off. Not just any three days, because a crucial weekend loomed. Carlyle was in love.

Crash, bang, fucking wallop. He was in *luurve*. Thinking back to how it happened made him smile. On a day off, a week or so earlier, he had been mooching around the West End with no money in his pockets, and no plan of action. He was standing in Leicester Square looking at a movie poster for *Rocky IV*, which was due to come to the Empire in January, when the heavens had opened. Running down St Martins Street in search of shelter, he ducked into Westminster Reference Library. Behind a pile of books at a desk near the door sat the prettiest girl he had ever seen in his life. She looked up as he walked in. Carlyle caught her eye, and for a moment he couldn't move. It was as if he had stepped into a different universe. Trying to recover the power of motion, he almost immediately tripped over a waste basket. While the girl tried to stifle laughter, he stumbled over to a chair some way off and spent the next hour staring at her over the top of a three-month-old copy of *Farmer's Weekly*. Finally, as she was getting ready to leave, he stood up and introduced himself.

As a result, he got a date. She was due to meet him outside Leicester Square tube station in about seventeen hours' time. London was their oyster. Now he had to come up with something, something damn good. He could not, under any circumstances, fuck this up. If he did, he was convinced that Helen Kennedy would never give him a second chance.

A monster burp from his partner tore Carlyle away from his thoughts. Having finished his roll, Slater went off in search of another. 'Sure you don't want one?' he asked, waving an empty plate in Carlyle's direction. 'They really are excellent.'

'Nah.' Shaking his head, Carlyle turned away from his partner and stared out of the window in search of romantic inspiration. But in the middle of the night, on Trinity Street in SE sodding 1, there was none to be found. The rundown street was a mix of small shops and workshops, all of them closed at this time of night. The place was deserted. Not a single car was parked at the roadside, and no one had driven past for over ten minutes.

These were hard, unforgiving streets, streets with a history of violence and no future to speak of. More than eighty years earlier, during the General Strike, the police had fought pitched battles with the workers only a stone's throw from where he was sitting. Barely two months ago, just down the road in Brixton, prison riots had left one person dead and fifty injured; more than two hundred were arrested. The trouble there had been sparked by the accidental police shooting of a Jamaican mother of six, who was left paralysed below the waist. North of the river, the Broadwater Farm housing estate in Tottenham was still under martial law after riots there resulted in the murder of a police constable, a forty-year-old father of three. Another policeman had been shot. Meanwhile, a local politician had crowed that the police had received 'a bloody good hiding'. The shit never fucking stopped.

Carlyle had turned all this over in his head, time and again, as he walked his beat. It had been almost nine months since he had visited Dominic Silver. He hadn't taken up the offer of a job, of course, but he couldn't help remembering Dom's words: 'There will always be an "enemy within" ... You'll be doing someone else's dirty work forever.' Carlyle had to admit, if only to himself, that it was looking as if like Dominic bloody Silver was right.

Slater returned with his second bacon roll and a mug of tea, just as two white youths came into view, walking at a steady pace towards the café. They were big blokes, easily six foot plus, broad as well as tall. Stopping in front of the window, they stared at the two policemen inside. It was only then that Carlyle realised that one of them had a brick in his hand. A second later, the window exploded and he was covered in glass. Without letting go of his roll, Slater toppled backwards in his chair. Leaving him on the floor, and abandoning his helmet and radio on the table, Carlyle rushed out of the café door and gave chase.

He shouted for the youths to stop. Unsurprisingly, they ignored him. Trying to run in his standard police-issue boots was agony. Almost immediately, his chest felt tight and he was struggling for breath. *You need to start exercising some more*, Carlyle told himself. Breathing through his mouth, he kicked on, pushing himself harder. He wasn't gaining on the two men, but they weren't losing him either. Fifty yards down the road, he saw them duck into an alley to his right. Looking over his shoulder, he could not see Slater anywhere. He felt a surge of annoyance, but there was nothing he could do about that now. Head down, he took the corner at speed and tripped straight over an outstretched foot, crashing headlong into a pile of rubbish bags that had been stacked against the alley wall. Carlyle flipped himself on to his back and just lay there, catching his breath. *In the gutter,* he thought, *looking up at the stars. Or where the stars should be.* Aware of the shadows moving just beyond the edge of his vision.

Someone took a step closer. There was the dull clink of metal on brick. 'Get up!'

Slowly, Carlyle worked himself into a sitting position. One of the bags had burst and some spoiled fruit had spilled out. He plucked a rotten banana skin from his tunic and, as casually as he could manage, tossed it in the direction of the voice. Pushing himself out of the garbage, he stood up, looking at a third man now in front of him, with the two he had been chasing leaning against the wall further back.

'Hello, Trevor.'

Trevor Miller tapped the length of lead pipe against the leg of his jeans. In the semi-darkness, he looked bigger and uglier than Carlyle remembered. 'I warned you, Carlyle. Why did you go and talk to that tart's lawyer? Why did you put me in the frame?'

Carlyle could feel his heart going like the clappers under his uniform. 'Why didn't you leave her alone?'

Without replying, Miller stepped forward and chopped the pipe into Carlyle's ribs. A searing pain shot through his torso and he went down again. 'My career could have been fucked because of you.'

'You're a big boy, Trevor,' Carlyle said, struggling to his feet and glancing back down the alley. 'You have to take responsibility for your own actions. Anyway, I don't think you were ever going to make Commissioner.'

Trevor had caught his glance, and also looked back towards the street. 'No one's going to come and help you,' he spat, waving the pipe in front of his face. 'Everyone knows you're a complete cunt. When I fuck you up, loads of people will be cheering. You have to take it.'

Carlyle decided that his only chance was to run for it. There was only Miller between him and the entrance to the alley. The other two were maybe ten yards further back, each enjoying a cigarette, neither paying a great deal of attention. *If I could sell Trevor a dummy,* Carlyle thought, *I might get a couple of yards start. Who knows?* That dickhead Slater might even put in an appearance. At the very least, he could have called for assistance.

Carlyle knew that he might not be able to outrun all three of them, but worrying about that wouldn't help. He sprang forward, feinting to Miller's right, before pushing off with his left foot and sprinting, head down, arms pumping, to his left. Miller, momentarily wrong-footed, screamed in fury. Carlyle felt the pipe whistle past his head before clattering to the ground. Reflexively he ducked but didn't stop running. *Bloody hell*, he thought as he reached the mouth of the alley, *I'm going to make it!* Then his right foot went down and gave way beneath him as he slipped on the same discarded banana skin. Careering into a wall, Carlyle fell in a heap by the side of the road.

The footsteps behind him stopped and were replaced by mocking laughter. Someone kicked him in the back, and then he took a boot between the legs that, literally, made him see stars. Dazed, he was dragged by his legs back into the darkness of the alley. This time, all he could do was curl up as tightly as possible and wait for his beating. The next blow hit him behind the left ear. His last thought before blacking out was that he still had no idea where he should take Helen on their first date.

Chapter Twenty

'WHO IS IN charge of the police investigation?'

'Err …' William Murray glanced at his boss, who nodded his approval, before leaning forward and speaking slowly into the star-shaped conference phone in the centre of the table. 'He's called …' he checked his notes, 'Inspector Carlyle. He works out of the Charing Cross station.'

'But it was a woman at the press conference.' This time it was Xavier's voice that crackled down the line, fighting to be heard above the background traffic noise.

The Merrion Club was back in session – sort of. This morning, however, expensive booze and obnoxious behaviour were off the menu. The club's surviving members had dialled in to a conference call to discuss the unfortunate situation that they now found themselves in. While Edgar and his aide sat in a private room in Pakenham's Gentlemen's Club in central London, Xavier was busy campaigning somewhere in Surrey. Christian Holyrod was also out on the election campaign, while the other two – Sebastian Lloyd and Harry Allen – were both abroad.

'The woman who conducted the press conference yesterday,' Murray replied, looking down at his papers again, 'is a Superintendent Carole Simpson. She is the inspector's boss.'

'Simpson will doubtless be very helpful in all this,' Holyrod remarked. 'Her husband is Joshua Hunt, who runs McGowan Capital.'

Murray waited for some sign of recognition on Edgar's face. When none was forthcoming, he whispered, 'He's a member of the Pack.'

'Don't use that expression,' Edgar snapped, quickly hitting the mute button on the phone. The so-called 'Wolf Pack' was a group of City investors who had each given the party a donation of at least a million pounds at the beginning of the year, in anticipation of the upcoming campaign. The details of who had donated what had been duly disclosed, as part of Edgar's much-hyped commitment to financial transparency. Sadly, the fact that a couple of Pack members had made more than three hundred million each by unpatriotically shorting sterling during the recent financial crisis had not gone down so well in the press. The row was still bubbling along. Edgar, who could be thin skinned on certain matters, needed the money, but hated the hassle. He now eyed Murray like he was a naughty schoolboy in line for a caning. 'Even in private,' he hissed, 'we never call them that.'

'Yes,' said Murray quietly, looking down at his hands.

Edgar felt his anger fade. 'Loose lips sink ships, and all that,' he grinned.

'Yes,' said Murray again, wondering what the hell his boss was talking about.

Edgar sighed and tried again. 'Don't start using the language of the media, because that will only help them destroy us.'

'Anyway,' said Murray, trying to find his way back to the matter in hand, 'it has to be convenient for us to have a connection with Superintendent Simpson through Mr Hunt. Although, I suppose that to her it might appear a potential conflict of interest.'

'A mere coincidence,' Carlton sniffed. 'Anyway, it's not like it's actually her case, is it?'

'No,' Murray stood corrected. 'It seems this guy Carlyle is in charge of the investigation.'

'But she was the one made the running with the press?'

'Yes,' Murray nodded, 'as far as we can tell.'

'Edgar? Are you still there?' It was Sebastian Lloyd, speaking from halfway up a mountain in Chile or Peru, or somewhere. Wherever it was, he was safe enough. 'I've got to go in a minute.'

Edgar unmuted the phone. 'Yes, sorry. Let's wrap it up, then. Rest assured that we will deal with this problem at our end, and we will also make sure it's dealt with as quickly and efficiently as possible.'

There was silence for a few seconds, and then Harry Allen spoke: 'That's fine, Edgar, but just remember that we're all in this together and there is more to worry about here than just your bloody career.'

'It's being dealt with,' intervened Xavier huffily.

For the first time, it crossed Edgar's mind that some of his so-called chums might not even care to vote for him. He shook his head impatiently and leant over the phone. 'Xavier is right. It is being dealt with. And you are absolutely right, we *are* all in this together. So we must deal with this quickly, efficiently and in the best interests of the Club and its members. Good to speak to you all this morning, gentlemen. If we need to arrange another of these calls, William Murray will let you know. But, meanwhile, don't worry. You can consider the matter resolved.' Without waiting for any comeback, he ended the call with a quick stab of his finger. Closing his eyes, he slumped back into his seat.

'That was fine,' Murray ventured.

'Yes,' Carlton yawned, 'but the last thing I – we – need right now is this kind of problem. I must get back on the campaign trail. I need to be out on the road, like Xavier and Christian.'

'Yes,' Murray nodded.

'And we need to draw the public's attention away from the polls.'

'Yes.'

'Better still, we need some new bloody polls.'

'Yes.'

'Ones that show us what we damn well want to see.'

'Yes.'

Three days of narrowing polls meant that Edgar Carlton's lead was slipping towards single digits, just as the election itself headed towards its penultimate week. Unbelievably, given their appalling track record, the other side was regaining some momentum. That had to be stopped – and fast. The last thing he could afford now that he was fighting for his political life, was to be dragged into a multiple murder case.

'I wish we could have more confidence in the way the investigation is currently being handled,' Edgar mused. Why the police needed to crank up media interest by holding a damn press conference was beyond him. Indeed it was galling beyond belief that these people were so *unbelievably* incompetent when it came to handling the media. But it was a fait accompli. 'This Simpson woman, does she know about the … context of the case?'

Murray sucked in his cheeks, then exhaled. 'No, I don't think so. The police don't seem to have put the pieces together yet. But, of course, we have to assume that they will get there in the end.'

'What about this Carlyle chap?' Edgar asked breezily. 'Should we just get rid of him? See that it's handed to someone else?'

'I think that would be premature,' Murray replied. 'There's no obvious need at this stage. If it becomes necessary, Simpson can easily take care of Carlyle.'

'So, what about the good inspector? What do we know about him?'

The aide took another peek at his notes. 'Well … he seems a bit of a strange one.' He shuffled some papers. 'He's a Londoner, joined the police in 1979, has done various jobs at various stations, received several citations. But there's nothing that impressive in his file, and his career seems to have flat-lined in recent years. You get the impression that he's never been able to fit in that well. Wherever he goes, he seems to do OK for a while, but then every couple of years the wheels come off. After the latest such incident, it was made clear to him that he really should be thinking about retirement.'

This sounds good, thought Carlton. 'What happened?'

'For some reason, a few years back, he was put on Royal Protection Duty—'

'Seems a strange decision. Do we know why?'

'Probably just some administrative error. Anyway, on one particular occasion he was responsible for looking after a couple of the young royals while they were conducting their civic duties at Pomegranate.'

'I know it well,' Edgar nodded. 'At least, I've been there a few times.' Personally, he felt that the Chelsea nightclub in question was like a school disco with silly prices, but he had been there quite regularly since royal patronage had made it ultra-fashionable among his own set. After all, it was good to show that you could still get down with the kids. Getting his picture in the newspapers along with 'the boys' – the two young princes who alternated between playing at being soldiers and playing at being playboys – didn't hurt either. And the fact that his wife Anastasia wouldn't go near the place was another big plus.

'It gets to three a.m.,' Murray continued, 'and Carlyle's charges fall out of the club, blind drunk as usual.'

'Well,' Carlton said airily, 'everyone's entitled to some fun.'

'Of course,' Murray nodded. 'But then one of the young chaps got into an altercation with a press photographer.'

Carlton yawned. 'So far, so unremarkable.'

'Yes, but the suggestion was that Carlyle was rather slow to step in and sort things out. It was even suggested that he let the snapper – a big chap who had been in both the South African army and the French Foreign Legion – give HRH a few hard slaps, before he dragged the boy away, covered in his own blood and vomit.'

'Mmm.' Carlton scoured the farthest regions of his memory. 'I think I remember the pictures. It looked to me fairly much like a normal night out for His Highness.'

'There was an investigation but nothing could be proved. The young royal in question wanted Carlyle kicked off the Force, but it was considered that might cause too much of a scene, particularly if the Police Federation got involved.'

'Ah, yes,' Carlton nodded, 'the most obnoxious trade union in the world.' He would make very sure that his own government did nothing to annoy them. Best to let sleeping police dogs lie, and all that.

'In the end, Carlyle was simply yanked off royal duties and put back on the taxi rank, to wait for whatever else came along.'

'So, he's a bit of a republican?' Carlton shook his head in disbelief. 'How can a man like that become a policeman in the first place?'

'It's not entirely clear,' said Murray. 'Generally, he's thought to be a bit too liberal for the police, or maybe just a bit too ... cerebral.'

'So you mean he thinks too much,' Carlton frowned. 'Great, that's all we need. How in the name of sweet Jesus did we end up getting someone like him?'

Murray shrugged. 'You're always going to get one or two like that in an organisation as big as the police.'

Pouting unhappily, Edgar checked his watch. It really was time he should be getting along to the House of Commons. 'Anything else we know about this Inspector Carlyle, other than the fact that he is completely unreliable? What's his family situation?' He gave Murray a stern look. 'You're probably now going to tell me he lives in a hippie commune with a gay lover called Gerald, who runs a basket-weaving collective.'

Murray made a face. 'No, he has a wife and daughter.'

'First marriage?'

'Yes. The wife works for a liberal charity called Avalon. It sends doctors to the Third World, begs for money, moans about "imperialism", that kind of thing.'

'And the kid?'

'She goes to City School for Girls in the Barbican.'

'Good school,' said Carlton, impressed. He himself had four children, two boys and two girls, and all were attending top-notch London schools. Public schools like City. 'Public' as in 'private'. It seemed a very English way of using the language, hiding the reality behind the words.

'Expensive,' Murray commented.

'I'm sure,' Carlton shivered. The fees for his brood had been killing him even before the damn credit crunch had started kicking in. God knows what Mr Plod made of it, despite having only the one kid to worry about. 'We thought about sending our girls to City a few years ago,' he mused, 'and the cost was pretty impressive even then. Presumably she is on a scholarship?'

Murray shook his head. 'No, they're paying full whack, for the moment at least. Apparently that school doesn't hand out any scholarships before the age of eleven. I'm sure they'll be trying to get one when the child is older, but they'll have to cough up for a while yet.'

'That must eat into the family budget, so it explains why he is not too interested in retirement. A police pension is not going to be anywhere near enough for our inspector, not if young ...'

'Alice.'

'Not if young Alice doesn't then deliver on the scholarship front. Imagine having to take her out of City School for Girls and drop her back into some local state school. What a nightmare! I'm sure Mrs Carlyle would never forgive him.' He paused, reflecting, not for the first time, on the reality that domestic hegemony was far harder to achieve than high political office. 'But good for them, anyway, for not taking the easy option. For being ambitious for their daughter. For being fans of private education. Maybe we can count on their votes, after all.'

Chapter Twenty-one

CLEMENT HAWLEY MIGHT be considered a Renaissance man for the early twenty-first century. He was a trader in the highly pressurised world of the London money markets, as well as running a lucrative sideline in recreational pharmaceuticals. This allowed him to deploy his considerable social and marketing skills while exploiting the synergies that existed between those two jobs. The boys in the City want to make money and do drugs, often in large quantities and at the same time, while Clement was at hand to help facilitate either, or both, of those ambitions.

Young master Hawley had stumbled out of the Sir John Lydon Imperial Grammar School for Boys in Canterbury more than fifteen years earlier, wandering the beaches of Thailand and Goa for a while before strolling into London's booming financial services industry. There, in the bright, gleaming, non-judgemental, ultra-short-term, fuck-everything-and-then-fuck-it-again world of high finance, he found his metier through dealing in foreign exchange. He established a niche in obscure currencies like the Turkish lira, Lebanese pound and Israeli shekel. These had a tendency to gyrate wildly against the major currencies – namely the dollar, sterling and the Euro – with every car bomb and airstrike occurring in the Middle East, of which, of course, there were plenty. It didn't matter what was going up or down because, as long as things were moving, you could trade. If you could trade, you could make a profit, which was good for your end-of-year bonus, or a loss involving someone else's money.

Trading forex was a nice little earner, but it was nowhere near as profitable as the drugs Hawley sold on the side. His was an uncomplicated business, essentially providing grass, ecstasy and cocaine to between sixty and a hundred recreational users within his extended social set. Clement observed certain standards: he didn't sell crack, the drug of choice for the truly degenerate, and he didn't sell anything to those that he didn't know, or to anyone who didn't arrive at his table with a personal recommendation from an existing customer. Even without chasing every last pound, it was a very lucrative set-up, and Clement was comfortably clearing three hundred thousand pounds a year. Added to the money from his trading job, this sideline pushed his overall income towards half a million.

There were scores of dealers like Clement throughout London. For the police, most were a useful source of market intelligence, people to trade information with rather than to close down. Arresting them was pointless, since there was always someone else to fill the void. Better to make use of them out on the street.

Clement had been arrested just twice, once for being drunk and disorderly, the second time for possession. The first time, three years ago, he was taken to Charing Cross, where Carlyle, after a short but frank discussion regarding the six grand's worth of ecstasy in his pockets, had him released without charge (but minus the drugs). The second time he was arrested, eight months later in Camden Town, Hawley declined his right to a phone call and asked for Inspector Carlyle, straight off the bat. All in all, Carlyle felt that he had built up a lot of credit at the Bank of Hawley, and now it was time to make a small withdrawal.

Hawley's normal stomping ground was Brick Lane, in the heart of a run-down East London neighbourhood just east of Spitalfields Market, and less than five minutes' walk from the Liverpool Street offices of the Australian bank where he worked. One of the poorest districts in the whole country, it was historically famous for housing successive waves of immigrants: the Huguenots, the Irish and the Jews. It gained a small but important mention in twentieth-century British history with the Battle of Cable Street in 1936, when anti-Nazis fought the British Blackshirts. More recently, it had become a centre of the Bangladeshi community and was now famous for its curry houses. It was not an area that Carlyle knew well but, constantly changing and full of hustle, bustle and hardship, it lay at the heart of what made London the heaving, restless metropolis that it was. As a Londoner, therefore, he felt that he could relate to it well enough.

Brick Lane had once been home to more than twenty pubs. With names like the Duke's Motto, the Jolly Butchers, the Seven Stars and the Monkey's Tackle, they had eagerly competed for the pound in the working man's pocket. Now, with a decent round of drinks easily costing well north of thirty quid, just one of them, the Frying Pan, remained. The others had been turned into more profitable businesses: Indian and Chinese restaurants, cafés, a hairdresser's shop, clothes shops, fast-food outlets, a canoe centre (who went canoeing in E1?), a money-transfer kiosk and a church for some religion that Carlyle had never heard of. There was also a travel shop offering Jack the Ripper tours – the Ripper being the leading local celebrity.

Landlords in the 'wet trade' had taken a right kicking in recent years, victims of falling custom, the smoking ban, higher taxes and ridiculously cheap supermarket beer. By the more nostalgically inclined, pub closures were seen as a symbol of the death of London's community spirit. Carlyle, who was most certainly not nostalgically inclined, personally considered this a load of old bollocks. For the fastidious inspector, the demise of these hovels, offering crap service and plenty of second-hand smoke, had to be considered a good thing. As far as he was concerned, that fake East End bonhomie, mixed with an undercurrent of prejudice and menace, would never be missed. More than a hundred London pubs might have closed during every year for the last decade, but he still didn't notice any great shortage. That meant that there were still plenty of options for the likes of Clement Hawley to go about their business.

Carlyle tried to think of the last time he'd been inside a pub, other than for the purposes of work. He reckoned it had to be at least three years. Probably so he could watch Fulham lose to some fellow no-hopers on one of the various subscription-TV services that he couldn't afford at home.

Now, he deliberately chose a corner table far from the door, after eyeing the half-dozen or so other patrons scattered about the place, who were drinking pints of lager and studiously ignoring each other. There, Carlyle sat down and waited, nursing a glass of Jameson whiskey, straight with no ice.

CLEMENT HAWLEY WAS fresh faced and energetic. He was also completely predictable. As soon as he walked in to the Frying Pan, he started scanning the interior for his regular clients. He clocked Carlyle immediately and did a sharp U-turn. Why he was trying to escape was anyone's guess. They knew where he worked and they had already checked that he had turned up there today. And he would have to get back to his desk sooner rather than later, in order to close himself out of the trading positions he had taken that morning. It was far better for Clement that Carlyle spoke to him here in the pub, rather than back at the bank.

So why did he try to run? Perhaps it was the stash in his pockets. Perhaps it was his criminal DNA. Perhaps it was just sheer fucking stupidity. Whatever, he didn't get very far. As Clement approached the door, Joe walked in off the street, flipped him round again, and gave him a gentle push in the direction of his boss. Carlyle smiled to himself. It was nice when these things went according to plan.

With a shrug, Hawley allowed himself to be ushered towards Carlyle's table. He was probably pushing thirty-five but had retained his boyish good looks, and his own personal drug use was keeping the extra pounds at bay. From a few feet away, he could have almost passed for a new graduate starting out on his career in his first work suit. All in all, it was a good effort for a bloke who managed to hold down not one but two stressful jobs.

'Inspector.' Clement gave a meek wave.

'Clement.' Carlyle looked past his guest, and eyed the two City boys who had just appeared at the far end of the bar. They had finished buying their pints and were now giving Clement the once-over, trying to read the situation. Was he open for business or not?

Turning back to Hawley, Carlyle nodded towards the stool next to him. Clement knew what had caught Carlyle's eye, but he fought the urge to sneak a glance at the punters. He ignored the stool. 'I'm, um, a bit pushed for time.'

Carlyle let his hand tighten around his whiskey glass. 'Sit!' he growled.

Clement sat down and Joe took a seat next to him.

'Looks like you've just lost some customers,' Carlyle said, watching the duo drain their pints in double-quick time and head for the door. Maybe they could manage to get through the afternoon under their own steam, after all.

'Yes, well,' Clement smiled, 'you know the score.'

'I know the score,' Carlyle nodded, 'but do you?'

"Course I do, Inspector,' the trader smiled. 'I'm all yours. How can I be of assistance?'

'First, empty your pockets and give the stuff to Joe. Then we need to have a quick chat.'

'Inspector!' Clement protested, his face scrunched up in pain, like an eight year old just reminded for the final time that it was bedtime. Nevertheless, he did as he was told. Joe shoved the stuff into his jacket pocket, without looking at it.

'There's no chance of a receipt, I suppose?' When neither Carlyle nor Joe bothered to answer his question, Clement took a deep breath and rubbed the back of his neck for a few seconds. This type of police harassment was frustrating but, at the same time, it was factored into his overall business plan as part of the cost of doing business. When he turned back to Carlyle, the scowl had been replaced by philosophical calm.

Carlyle decided that they'd had enough preamble. 'How's your brother?'

'Paul? He's fine.' Clement looked surprised, then worried. 'Unless you tell me anything different.'

'No, no,' said Carlyle hastily. 'It's nothing like that.'

'Good,' said Clement, relaxing slightly.

'Is he still at Cambridge?' Joe asked.

'Yeah,' Clement smiled, 'he finally got a job. The shock almost killed him. Assistant lecturer or something.'

Paul Hawley was eight or nine years older than Clement. He had gone up to university in the 1980s and never left. Clement was proud of his brother in the way that everyone likes having an academic in the family. To people who didn't know any better, it suggested intelligent genes.

'Did he ever finish his PhD?' Carlyle asked.

'It only took him seventeen bloody years!' Clement made a face. '*Drinking cultures in the early and middle Middle Ages*. Published too – you can find it on Amazon, but I haven't seen it in the bestseller lists yet.'

'Maybe you shouldn't have been bankrolling him for quite so long,' Carlyle smiled. Clement had once revealed that he had been covering his brother's costs to the tune of two thousand pounds a month.

'Hah!' Clement laughed. 'That's not going to change. He might have a job, but he's still not making any money. Can you guess how much he's earning?'

Carlyle shrugged. 'No idea.'

'Sixteen thousand a year!'

'Bloody hell!' said Joe.

Clement threw up his hands in despair. 'Can you believe it? Sixteen grand. A fucking year! That's not even the average wage, nowhere close. Why would you bother?'

Carlyle shook his head in genuine disbelief. Even he earned more than that, in fact a multiple of that. He tried to work the precise number out in his head, in terms of monthly income, but it was taking him too long, so he moved on. 'I'm trying to find out about something called the Merrion Club. It's a drinking society for well-heeled Cambridge students. I don't suppose Paul was ever a member?'

Realising that they were not interested in him personally this time, Clement relaxed. 'I've heard of the Merrion,' he said, eager now to please. 'It's not like it's a secret society, or anything, but Paul would never get invited to join something like that. It's not something you just sign up for at fresher's week. "Well-heeled" doesn't quite do it justice, because it's the crème de la crème de la crème. Paul's not in that league. In fact, almost no one is.'

'But he would probably have come across them?' Carlyle persisted. 'Might he know anyone who was a member?'

'He might.' Clement shrugged non-committally. 'Cambridge is a small place. A very small place compared to London. Anyway, what do you want to know about?'

'Never you mind,' said Joe firmly. 'We just want to go up there and talk to Paul. Nothing heavy, just to pick his brains. Can you tell him to be there to meet us?'

'Sure,' Clement shrugged. 'Term finished last week, but he's still there. He's marrying one of his students, so they're doing up their house.'

'Isn't that illegal?' Joe asked. 'Knocking off your students, I mean – not doing up your house. Isn't it a violation of teacher-student ethics, or whatever?'

'You would have thought so. But she's switched her course from Medieval English to Media Studies, so it looks like he's got away with it. She's Serbian, twenty years younger than him, with a hell of a body. He's a lucky sod.'

'Rather him than me,' said Joe.

Amen to that, thought Carlyle. *Nice body or not.*

'You've got to be careful with East Europeans, though,' Joe continued, graciously prepared to share the wisdom of a second-generation Pole who was married to an Indian. 'The girls are fantastic, some of the best-looking babes in the world, but they don't age well. They go from thirty to sixty in about three years. By the time she's thirty-five, she'll look even older than him.'

'I'm not sure he'll care by then,' said Clement wistfully.

'Give us Paul's mobile number and we'll give him a call to let him know when we know when we'll be coming,' interrupted Carlyle, boring of the chat. 'And remember to tell him it's not a big deal, just a few general inquiries. It will be nothing taxing. Not like an academic test.'

AFTER CLEMENT HAD gone back to the bank to churn a few billion of this and that, just in order to help keep the world's currency markets in business, Carlyle sat in the corner of the Frying Pan pub, pondering what to do with the rest of his afternoon. Joe had returned to the station to book in Clement's stash (every little helps for the year-end performance tables!) and prepare for making a court appearance in the morning. This had already been cancelled three times, but one never knew. Carlyle thought about heading for home, or maybe going to the gym. Realising he still had most of the whiskey in front of him, he lifted the glass to his lips and drained it in one go. He thought about another but decided against it, heading for the door via a quick trip to the gents.

Stepping out into the street, he was assaulted by a grubby, muggy afternoon. He could already feel beads of sweat forming on his forehead. A couple of streets away, someone was digging up the road, and the drilling just upped Carlyle's discomfort level a notch further. Still trying to formulate a plan, Carlyle pulled out his 'private' mobile and switched it on. The Nokia 2630 was one of the cheapest, most ubiquitous pay-as-you-go models currently on the market. Carlyle had bought it for cash, and would top it up for cash at random newsagents well away from his usual haunts. He didn't flash it around, and gave out the number to very few people. Even then, he changed both the handset and the SIM card every three or four months. This didn't guarantee complete secrecy, but it meant that no one was routinely checking his calls. It allowed him some privacy, and for that the additional hassle and cost was worth it.

Crossing the road, he stood at the corner of Brick Lane and Chicksand Street, and scrolled down the list of names. He stopped at 'DS' and hit the call button.

The response was immediate. 'Yes?'

'Dominic? It's me.' No one else called him Dominic.

'What can I do for you?' The tone was neutral, not exactly guarded but not welcoming either.

'I'd like to have a chat.'

'About what?'

'I'm just after some background information. Business-related, obviously, but nothing in any way related to you.'

'Why not speak to your little pal Clement?'

Jesus, how could he know? Was he fucking psychic? 'I already have. I'm just moving on up the food chain.'

There was a sigh at the other end, some muffled noises in the background. 'OK, meet me at the usual place in an hour.'

THEY MET SIMPSON in a discreet room on the fourth floor of Port-cullis House, the £235-million office block for MPs, located across the road from the House of Commons, facing the north side of Westminster Bridge. This close to the election, the place was completely deserted. Gratifyingly, the superintendent seemed suitably desperate to do whatever they wanted from her. Straight off the bat, she had promised a media blackout 'better than the prime minister's when—'

Edgar stopped her with a gentle wave of the hand. 'Everyone knew about that anyway,' he sniffed,

'Maybe in Westminster,' she replied politely, 'but it didn't make the papers.'

Xavier snorted: 'Who cares about it not being in the media, when all your peers know anyway?'

'Yes,' said Simpson, nervously standing her ground, 'but the situation here is rather different.'

'Yes, it is.' Edgar smiled graciously.

Xavier watched his brother moving into campaign mode. He had seen it so many times before when they needed to build the 'hired help' up, not knock them down. It was now time to throw a bone to one of the little people.

'You are absolutely right.' Edgar's smile grew wider still.

'Indeed,' Xavier nodded.

'It is,' Edgar continued, 'in the absolute best interests of all concerned – especially the victims and their families – that this most unfortunate and difficult situation is dealt with quickly. A total information blackout, while the matter is resolved, would therefore be a good thing.'

'Yes,' Simpson agreed.

'That should help your people catch this lunatic soon.'

'I have already explained that to my people,' Simpson concurred.

'I am sure,' Edgar said gently, 'that our people will be able to help you, too.'

Our people?

Simpson made no comment at all when she was informed, in so many words, that William Murray would be dispatched to mark Carlyle's card and report back to Edgar Carlton himself.

'Your Inspector Carlyle,' Edgar said casually, as they were finishing up the conversation, 'he seems quite ... unusual.'

Simpson finally lifted her head and tried her best to smile. It merely made her look constipated. 'He has had some issues over the years, yes. To be frank, there are some who consider the inspector an inverted snob with a chip on his shoulder. He is not well liked and amongst ourselves ...' She paused, glancing at the two politicians, wanting to believe in their discretion.

'Of course,' Edgar said gently, 'nothing that is said here today goes beyond the three of us.'

I've heard that, too, thought Xavier, smirking.

'Well,' Simpson continued, 'I think it is reasonable to assume that he is now in the slow lane to retirement. As I am sure you know, he has had more than a few problems with authority down the years.'

'That's not really what we need here, is it?' Xavier piped up.

'No,' Simpson agreed gently, addressing Edgar rather than his brother, which pissed Xavier off considerably. 'But it would be more trouble than it's worth to take him off the investigation at this stage. It might lead people to ask awkward questions.'

'My thoughts entirely,' said Edgar, shooting his brother a sharp look.

'Anyway,' said Simpson, 'Carlyle has a reasonable track record when it comes to actually closing cases. There's a chance that he will be able to wrap this business up quickly. If not, and if he takes a few wrong turns, it will be easier to have him replaced later.'

'That all makes great sense,' said Edgar Carlton sweetly. 'Thank you for giving us such reassurance. We'll leave it in your capable hands.'

Chapter Twenty-two

Brixton, London, June 1987

YAWNING WIDELY, LARRY GUTHRIE strolled down Mostyn Road on his way to the New World café round the corner. It was a beautiful day, temperature in the mid-twenties, with a slight breeze and the occasional cloud skipping across a sharp blue sky. It was the kind of day that should make you happy to be alive, but the weather currently didn't interest Larry very much. It had been a late night and the seventeen year old could have done with more than a couple of extra hours in bed. Sleep, however, would have to wait. Right now, Larry was hungry. And he was also on a schedule. There was more work to be done this afternoon too, and his was not the kind of job that allowed you to throw a sickie and hide under the duvet. People needed their gear for Saturday night and therefore business would be brisk. Anyway, some pancakes and coffee would keep his tiredness at bay. Tomorrow, he promised himself, he wouldn't get out of bed at all.

Looking up from his plodding feet, he glanced at two young boys playing on the swings in Mostyn Gardens. Only a few years ago and that had been him. In a few years' time, if not sooner, this life of his would be theirs. Sticking his hands deeper into the pockets of his hooded sweatshirt, Larry returned his gaze to the pavement and increased his pace. Eyes down, he didn't see the man with the lengthening stride walking towards him. Nor did he see the man pull out a gun and aim it at Larry's stomach.

When the gun went off, the noise was so shocking that Larry didn't even realise he'd been hit. His hands went to his ears, rather than his guts. Then, once he went down, everything went silent. He could hear nothing but his beating heart and the blood pulsing in his temples. He blinked repeatedly, trying to focus on the gun that was now hovering barely six inches from his face. He wondered if he would be able to see the bullet approach. In the event, as the muzzle twitched again, there was only darkness.

FEELING LIKE A spare prick at a whore's wedding, Constable John Carlyle watched the forensics team going about their business and wondered what exactly he himself should be doing. For a while, he just stood there looking at the blood-splattered trainers of Larry Guthrie sticking out from under the dark green sheet that had been casually dropped over the boy's body. Carlyle recognised the Nike high-top Dunks from a recent spread in *The Face* magazine, and he felt a stab of envy: the sneakers were way out of his price range. The favoured footwear of various local gangs, such as Young Thugs, the Cartel Boys, the Alligator Crew and the Superstar Gang, they weren't even on sale in the UK yet, but had to be brought over from the United States at a cost of several hundred dollars a time. Carlyle looked on as a technician removed the trainers from Guthrie's sockless feet and placed each one in its own evidence bag. At least he died with his boots on, he reflected, smiling grimly to himself.

One of the detectives standing over the body finally took offence at his idleness. 'Don't just stand there gawping, sunshine,' he shouted. 'Get across the street and start knocking on some bloody doors.' Reluctantly, Carlyle trooped off to report for duty with the sergeant who was out organising the canvassing of potential witnesses.

Ten minutes later, some old codger was bending his ear: 'The area has become really terrible,' the man complained. 'It's a war zone. Every night you can hear shouting and bawling. Gunfire, too, sometimes. Gangs of kids shouting in street slang. No one feels safe here. You're constantly looking over your shoulder when you're out and about. It's the folk with young families that I feel sorry for.' He pointed in the direction of the body. 'How do you explain that to a six year old? It's a disgrace and you people should do something about it.'

Carlyle stood there, nodding absentmindedly.

You people? Thanks.

He glanced up at a VOTE LABOUR poster in one of the neighbouring windows. He'd have thought that the residents inside would have taken that down by now. It was more than thirty-six hours since Margaret Thatcher had recorded her third crushing election victory on the bounce. According to the media, they were all now officially 'Thatcher's Children'. If it was difficult to remember what life had been like before she arrived, it was becoming increasingly impossible to imagine what life might be like after she departed – that was if she *ever* departed.

Several hours and dozens of interviews later, Carlyle felt hot, hungry and hacked off. Lots of people had heard the screaming, lots of people had heard the police sirens, lots of people had an opinion on how the neighbourhood was going downhill, and everyone had an opinion on the unbelievably piss-poor job that the police were doing. No one, however, had seen anything or had any useful information to share. He was delighted when the end of his shift finally approached, having turned down flat the sergeant's offer of overtime. Carlyle needed a shower and something to eat. He was taking Helen to see *Angel Heart* at the Ritzy, and was looking forward to an enjoyable Saturday night. The job could fuck right off.

Carlyle was now four months into a stint working out of the station on Brixton Road. If anything, it was a rougher beat than his previous postings at Shepherds Bush and Southwark, but he was enjoying it immensely. In the locker room, someone had scrawled the legend 'Twinned with Fort Apache, the Bronx'. A not unreasonable comparison considering this was the kind of place where everyone took pretty much in their stride the shooting of a local gang member in broad daylight in a residential street.

Even here in battle-hardened Brixton, the news that the gun that killed Larry Guthrie was a Browning BDA sent a frisson of nervous excitement through the ranks. The BDA was a modern, Belgian-made, 9 mm semi-automatic pistol, therefore a very fancy piece of kit indeed for a bunch of local hooligans to be using. Even more surprising was the fact that it been deliberately tossed away at the scene. Local criminals getting hold of guns was one thing; being well connected and well resourced enough to casually discard them once they'd been fired was another. At the station, the gossip was that this Guthrie killing threatened the start of a new round of drug-related violence that would have a posse of local and national politicians down on their backs in their usual search for easy answers and quick results.

At least it's not my problem, thought Carlyle, as he stepped out of the station. It was just after six in the evening and he was looking good in his best grey and red Fred Perry polo shirt, a pair of black Levi 501s and a new pair of Doc Martens. With plenty of time to spare, he wandered slowly along Brixton Road, before turning into Coldharbour Lane in search of some food. He was standing by a set of traffic lights, waiting to cross the road, when he heard a nearby driver blast on his horn.

'John!'

He looked up to see Dominic Silver leaning out of the driver's window of a rather knackered-looking, copper-coloured Ford Capri. 'Get in,' Dom shouted, popping his head back inside and pushing open the passenger door. The lights changed back to green and the drivers behind Silver began noisily expressing their impatience. 'Hurry up!'

Carlyle jogged over and jumped into the car. He pulled on his safety belt as Dom accelerated away from the crossing, while sticking one arm out the window to flip a finger at the drivers behind.

'Good to see you, man!' Dom said with a grin, returning both hands to the steering wheel. 'Long time no see.'

'You, too,' said Carlyle, staring into the traffic ahead. He wondered what Dom wanted. More to the point, why had he himself been so quick to jump into his bloody car? They hadn't seen each other for more than a year and this part of south London wasn't anywhere close to Dom's turf. With a sinking heart, Carlyle knew that this wasn't likely to be merely a social call.

'You OK for time?' Dom asked, picking out a sign for Black-heath and heading east.

Carlyle made a show of looking for his watch. He had agreed to meet Helen back at Brixton tube station in just under two hours, as the film started half an hour later. 'I've got about an hour,' he said cautiously.

'Perfect,' Dom grinned. 'Let's go and have a little drink.'

The traffic was light for a Saturday evening. Less than twenty minutes later, they were sitting in the beer garden of the Railway Arms in Blackheath Village. Carlyle wasn't much of a drinker but, at the end of a hard day, the cold lager tasted good. A couple of pretty girls in short skirts and skimpy T-shirts were talking ani-matedly at a table nearby, and he casually gave them the once-over. Nothing special, but worth a look. Feeling the alcohol kicking in, he began to relax and waited for Dom to talk.

After a few minutes, Dom put down his glass. 'Do you know what the "Great Stink" was?'

Carlyle thought about it for a second. 'No.'

'I forgot,' Dom grinned, 'you didn't pay much attention at school, did you?'

Carlyle made a face and took another swig of beer.

'The Great Stink,' Dom continued, 'was in 1858. Back then, the smell of sewage in the Thames was so bad that it, quite liter-ally, got up the noses of the politicians in the House of Commons. They eventually demanded action, and the great Joseph Bazalgette came to their – and our – rescue.'

'Who?'

'The chief engineer of the Metropolitan Board of Works. He spent seven years building a 1300-mile system of sewers and pumping stations.'

'I'll remember that the next time I take a dump.' Carlyle wondered what the hell Dom was on about.

'It was a truly fantastic achievement.'

'The history of shit.' Carlyle took another sip of his lager. 'How interesting. I don't remember them teaching us about that at school, at all.'

'I know,' said Dom, shaking his head. 'It's criminal really. Joseph Bazalgette was a truly great Londoner. He got a knighthood in 1875 and there's a small monument to him on the Victoria Embankment. Altogether, it's a very, very small recognition of his genius. Any idiot can get a knighthood. Did you know that all civil-service permanent secretaries get them as a matter of course? What do *they* ever do?'

Carlyle shrugged. He forgotten how Dom could go off on one, once he'd picked a subject on which to pontificate.

'The same goes for senior judges,' Dom continued, warming to his theme, 'and generals and ambassadors. At the very least, Joseph Bazalgette – the man who sorted out our shit – deserved a statue in Parliament Square. Or they could have named a bridge named after him, or ... something.'

'And the relevance of all this is?' Carlyle smiled, demonstrating his willingness to indulge his 'mate'.

'The relevance of all this, Constable,' said Dom, not missing a beat, 'is that one of Bazalgette's finest monuments is the Abbey Wood sewage works, which is not all that far from here.'

'And?'

'And ... that's where you'll find the body.'

Carlyle glanced round. The plain girls had gone. Checking that no one else was within earshot, he looked at Dom. 'What fucking body?' he hissed.

'The body of the muppet that shot Larry Guthrie this morning. It's in one of the settlement tanks. There are a few … I'm sorry I can't be more specific.'

'Guthrie?' Carlyle struggled to get his brain into gear. 'That was only eight hours ago.'

Dom shrugged modestly. 'We … they moved quickly. No one wants this thing to get out of hand. Both sides have lost a soldier. Additional compensation will be paid. It is time to call it quits and move on. All this cowboy bollocks is bad for business.'

'So it was a drugs-related killing?'

Dom raised his eyes to the heavens and said nothing.

'What's the name of this "muppet"?' Carlyle asked, gulping down another mouthful of lager.

Dom finished his pint. 'Does it matter?'

'Did this guy really do it?'

'Absolutely.'

Carlyle frowned. 'Evidence?'

'Guthrie's blood is on his clothes. Along with his own now, of course.'

Carlyle put his glass carefully on the table and looked Dom in the eye. 'You didn't …?'

'Don't be fucking stupid!'

'So why are you telling me this?'

'It needed sorting. You don't need … you don't want to know the details. This way, everybody wins: You look good, while keeping my name out of things, and I get kudos on my side for putting this business to bed, police investigation included. The message gets out that this thing is over, a score draw, and the streets are that little bit safer again for the Great British public.' He waved his empty glass at Carlyle. 'One for the road?'

Carlyle shook his head. 'And just how am I supposed to have come across this info?'

Dom grinned. 'Sources, old boy. Informants. Just make sure you don't have to go in there yourself. I'm told that the stink really is something terrible.'

'Thanks for the tip.'

'My pleasure.' Dom got up and gestured in the direction of the bar. 'Sure you don't want another one?'

Carlyle shook his head. While the shit expert went inside, he sat biting his lip, trying to keep in check his annoyance at being patronised. This was all bollocks. No way was he going to end up with any glory. He was a police constable, for fuck's sake. Dom was really dropping him in it, and treating him like an idiot to boot. There was no chance he could get away with closing a murder case in just a matter of hours and not find himself questioned very closely about it. If he didn't come up with a decent explanation, he would be under investigation himself. He couldn't even think what a decent explanation might be.

After a little while, Carlyle decided that there was only one thing for it. He stood up and walked round the side of the pub to an old-fashioned red phone box that he'd noticed on the way in. Stepping inside, he dialled 999. Putting on a hopeless Irish accent (that being the only one he felt he could do), he relayed the details to a bored-sounding girl, mentioning the Browning BDA in the hope that would help convince her that this was more than just another nutter calling in with a useless tip. That was as much as he could do. Ultimately, they could check it out, or not; he couldn't really give a fuck.

Finishing the call, he walked back to the table, while Dom was steadily draining his second pint.

Carlyle didn't sit down. 'I think we better get going now.'

'No problem. I'll drive you back.' Dom emptied his glass and stood up.

'Thanks.' Carlyle took a final mouthful of his own beer, which has lost its cold edge and now felt warm and flat. 'Let me just take a leak first.'

Chapter Twenty-three

THEIR USUAL MEETING place was one of a string of properties Dominic Silver now owned in central London. Over the last couple of decades, he had steadily built up a London portfolio that was worth easily north of £20 million, even after the recent market crash. This one was a small Georgian house on Meard Street, a short pedestrianised alley between Dean Street and Wardour Street, in the heart of Soho. It was set back from the pavement, behind a wrought-iron gate, with a small plaque on the door that said NO PROSTITUTES HERE. Carlyle pressed the buzzer and the door clicked open. A voice on the intercom said, 'Come right to the top.'

The house was home to Gideon Spanner, a former paratrooper who was currently Silver's number one bodyguard, debt collector and personal trainer. Carlyle found both men in a large room that covered almost the whole third floor. It was empty apart from a sofa and two armchairs, which were positioned facing a fifty-inch Panasonic plasma TV screen. Carlyle stood in the doorway, eyeing the two men watching a boxing match. The fighters were really going for it and the commentary was reaching fever pitch.

There was a station logo in the corner of the screen, but he didn't recognise it, probably another one of those premium sports channels he didn't subscribe to. Carlyle knew next to nothing about boxing, but this bout clearly wasn't live. It looked like a tape of an old fight from the 1970s or the 1980s.

'Drink?' Dom looked up from the screen long enough to wave his glass in Carlyle's direction.

'What is it?'

'Guavas, mangoes and goji berries. Not bad.'

'Sounds good.'

'In the kitchen, downstairs. Help yourself.'

'It doesn't matter.'

'No, go on.' Dom nodded at the screen. 'This is nearly finished.'

It took Carlyle five minutes to find the kitchen and pour himself some juice. When he came back, he plonked himself in the free armchair, and they all watched the boxing in silence. After a couple more rounds, one of the fighters called it a day.

Dom muted the TV and turned to Carlyle. 'Leonard-Duran Two, generally considered one of the greatest fights in history.'

Carlyle made a non-committal kind of noise in response.

Dom looked at it him. 'You know what I'm talking about?'

'Not really,' Carlyle admitted.

'Sugar Ray Leonard and Roberto Duran – the artist and the street fighter. Both of them were great, great fighters. They had three famous contests, back when we were kids. This was the second and the most famous one.'

'The *No Más* fight,' said Gideon, who may not even have been born when the fight actually took place.

'*No Más* meaning "No more". That's what Duran was supposed to have said when he quit in the eighth round.' Dom gestured at the screen with his chin. 'Duran denies saying it, but it's such a good story. *No Más* – what a great ending. No one was going to let the truth get in the way of a story like that.'

'Interesting,' was all Carlyle could think of to say. Other people's passions invariably left him bemused.

'Anyway,' said Dom, 'it's nice to see you, John. You're looking well.'

'Thank you,' Carlyle replied, bowing his head slightly. 'You too.' And it was true. Dom was one of those annoying guys who looked better in his late forties than he did in his early twenties: richer, healthier, more relaxed. Carlyle wished that he could say the same about himself. Dom's cheeky-chappy demeanour had been long since jettisoned, replaced by a professional/academic look that was underpinned by a degree in Business and Management from Queen Mary College on the Mile End Road. Dressed in Comme des Garçons, with rimless spectacles, greying, shoulder-length hair, and some flattering lines around his eyes, he was currently on top of his game.

Finally finishing his trip down boxing's memory lane, he gave Carlyle his full attention. 'What can we do for you?'

'That remains to be seen,' said Carlyle, smiling.

'As always.' Dom turned to Gideon. 'The inspector and I go back a long way.'

Gideon kept his eyes on the silent screen. 'Uh-uh.'

'Yes,' Dom smiled, 'John is one of my earliest comrades. We've worked together a lot over the years.'

Carlyle said nothing. Dom was right, up to a point. They had known each other for a long time and the relationship was both stable and cordial. It wasn't complicated but it wasn't clear either. Neither of them would necessarily have wanted to create it from scratch if it didn't already exist, but they could both see its advantages ... as well as its disadvantages.

Dominic Silver had left his old picket-line mates like Carlyle a long way behind. He had built up his business slowly, one step at a time, wherever possible avoiding conflicts and solving problems without needlessly resorting to violence. As the years turned into decades, his reputation grew. In a business where to survive two years was rare, to have survived two decades was a miracle. He had never been arrested, never mind convicted of any offence. In the last few years, he had reached his peak, settling comfortably in the third or fourth tier of the capital's drug-related entrepreneurs. Near the top but not aiming for the top. This was not a bad place to be, reasonably comfortable and avoiding the problems facing those above him and those below him. His operation was turning over maybe low millions each year, with clients including a swathe of minor celebrities and some of the newer entries in *Who's Who*. Before the recession took hold, he even had a couple of corporate clients, major City financial institutions who bought on account.

Business school had shown Dom how to build up a portfolio of assets and diversify risk. With all of his property and other investments, drugs probably now accounted for less than a third of Dom's income. However, it wasn't the kind of business you could easily retire from. Similarly, despite the risks, Carlyle could not easily walk away from their relationship which, after all this time, was almost as much personal as professional. Dom, like Carlyle, was a family man. He'd had the same girlfriend for more than twenty years and, as far as Carlyle knew, they enjoyed a happy, monogamous relationship, one which had been blessed with five kids. The families knew each other well, and Alice had played with the Silver kids plenty of times over the years.

Carlyle drained his glass of guava, mango and goji. Dom was right; it was good. 'I'm in the market for some information.'

'Obviously.' Dom sat further forward on the sofa and eyed Carlyle intently. 'What kind of information?'

'I'm interested in five men specifically. Their names are George Dellal, Ian Blake, Nicholas Hogarth, Harry Allen and Sebastian Lloyd.' He wasn't yet ready to mention Holyrod and the Carltons.

Dom made a show of thinking about that for a few seconds. 'This is the thing you were on the TV for last week?' he asked.

'Yes.'

'Not making much progress, then?' He grinned. 'So what do you want to know?'

'The usual. At least some of them use drugs, cocaine mainly and a bit of ecstasy. Where do they get them from? Who do they like to indulge with? What else do they get up to? Any interesting peccadilloes?'

'Interesting peccadilloes?' Dom laughed. 'We all have some of those.'

'You get the picture.'

'Sure. Give Gideon the list and we'll see what we can find out.'

'I appreciate it.' Rummaging through his pocket, Carlyle found a piece of paper, a receipt for a sandwich he'd bought the day before. While he scribbled down the five names, he thought about whether there was anything else he could get from his host. Things needed to be pushed along a bit, so he showed a little more of his hand. 'Do you ever supply the concierge at the Garden Hotel?' he asked, without looking up.

Dom glanced at Spanner and turned back to Carlyle. 'Alex Miles? Yeah, now and again. Only the odd bit of business, though, nothing major. He likes to use different people. He wouldn't make "my top hundred clients" list.'

'Blake was the stiff found in his hotel last week.'

Dom made a face to signify: *OK ... and?*

Gideon Spanner meanwhile kept staring blankly into space.

'Blake was a fairly high-end drug user,' Carlyle continued, 'the type of guy who might buy from the likes of you through someone like Miles.'

'There's lots of those,' Dom smiled. 'Just leave it with us. We'll doubtless dig up something. We usually do.'

'I know.'

'I'll walk you down the stairs.'

At the front door, Dom followed Carlyle out into the street. 'How's the family?'

'Fine,' Carlyle said. 'You?'

'Good. The eldest two are at secondary school already.' He grimaced. 'The fees? Bloody hell!'

'Tell me about it. Alice is at City in the Barbican now.'

'That's an excellent school.'

'Yes, it is. We're very pleased.'

'How can you afford that?'

'Good question.'

'If you ever—'

'No, no,' Carlyle interrupted quickly. He wasn't going down that road again. 'We're fine. She'll get a scholarship soon ... I hope.'

'Good luck.'

'Thanks.'

Would Carlyle ever take Dominic's cash? It didn't get any less tempting as the years went by. He'd discussed it with Helen a few times, in a *What if?* kind of a way. But it was never a serious possibility. They knew that if he ever crossed that line, he could never go back. The bottom line was that it wasn't worth it, since it would be incredibly stupid to risk everything just for money. Never say never, of course, but things would have to become truly desperate.

Dom moved the conversation quickly on to less choppy waters. 'We should get the kids together over the summer hols.'

'Helen would like that. She's always worried about Alice not having enough company, being an only child.'

'Excellent.'

Dom wasn't always this chatty, so Carlyle thought he might as well do a bit more fishing. 'How's business? Getting squeezed by the recession?'

'Nah ... well, maybe. Like you, I'll never be out of work. It might be tough for a while, though, as I'm a discretionary spend.'

'Sometimes.'

'Yeah, sometimes,' Dom laughed. 'But, I'll tell you this, we've just turned off easy street and on to shit street. The good old days are over. The easy money has run for the hills and the dirty money is getting dirtier. Things could get quite nasty for your average punter.'

'Sure.' *A sociology lesson from a drug dealer*, Carlyle thought. *That's just what I need.*

'You think about it, no more buying a house in London, watching the price going up, and then thinking you're Warren Buffett. We're off on a bumpy ride: industrial unrest, unemployment, stagflation – back to the bad old days of the seventies and eighties. You remember them?'

Yes, Carlyle thought, *I do indeed.*

Dom was off again on one of those monologues he's perfected over the years: 'Back to the days of power cuts, the rise of the

National Front – or, rather, the bloody BNP,' Dom continued. 'Back to the days of mortgage rationing, holidays in Southend rather than Jamaica.'

Carlyle, who hadn't been on holiday anywhere more exotic than Brighton since before Alice was born, said nothing. Dom probably spent more on his holidays than an inspector's annual salary afforded.

'We're running out of power, too,' Dom continued, really on a roll now. 'Our ageing power stations are closing and we haven't bothered to build new ones. Power cuts, shutting down the tube service, reducing hospital services, three-day working weeks, Alice doing her homework by candlelight … it's all on the cards.'

'Maybe.'

'No maybes about it, mate. Civilisation requires electricity. Without it, it's chaos and anarchy, here we damn well come. I wouldn't want to be stuck at the top of your block of flats when the power fails.'

'Thank you for that happy thought.'

'Have you got a gun?'

'Are you kidding?'

'I wouldn't rule it out,' Dom smiled. 'We are in serious, serious shit here. History is repeating itself in ever shorter cycles. Scumbag capitalism has been running out of control. The Russians are invading other countries again. They've even remade *Brideshead Revisited*. Even worse, that bunch of idiot public schoolboys will be running the country soon, or trying to.'

'Helen wants me to take her to some film about the Baader-Meinhof,' said Carlyle glumly. He couldn't understand why his wife would want to spend two hours watching a film about German terrorists. Maybe it offered a gossamer thread to her lefty past.

'Great date movie,' Dominic sniggered. He flashed one of his trademark, old-style smiles. They were rarer these days, and usually of the sixty-watt rather than the hundred-watt variety, but this one was a decent approximation of the days gone by. 'At least all this shit makes it interesting, eh? Just as long as they don't bring back Spandau fucking Ballet.'

ON HER KNEES in a bathroom at Party HQ, Yulexis Monagas slipped Xavier Carlton's penis out of her mouth and began gently flicking its tip with her thumbnail.

Xavier grunted with a mixture of surprise and pleasure. His member twitched on the brink of orgasm.

Yulexis released her grip and carefully moved her face out of the line of fire. She looked up at her boss. 'Xavier?' she said quietly.

'Yes?' he gasped.

'Xavier … I'm pregnant.'

His eyes widened in surprise but he was incapable of speech as a stream of ejaculate flew past her left ear.

Yulexis quickly moved backwards and handed him a small towel. 'I'm pregnant.'

He frowned, not wanting to believe it.

'Almost twenty weeks,' she added.

'Twenty weeks?' Xavier sniffed. That sounded quite a lot. He looked her up and down and felt himself begin to harden again. Shouldn't he be able to notice that sort of thing? She didn't look any different. Giving himself a quick wipe, he resisted the urge for seconds and zipped up his trousers. 'Are you sure it's mine?'

Buttoning up her blouse, she fought back a sob. 'Of course it's yours. Who else's could it be?'

'Don't worry,' he said airily, 'we can get it sorted. I know a good man in Harley Street.'

'What do you mean?' Yulexis asked, taking a step backwards.

Xavier frowned. He was beginning to think this girl was a bit dumb. 'Well, you can't keep it, obviously.'

'Xavier! It's too late for an abortion! Anyway, I want to keep it.'

The look that passed across his face made her shiver. But then he managed a smile. Not much of a smile, but a smile nonetheless. Taking hold of her shoulders, he reached over and kissed her on the top of the head.

'Don't worry,' he said. 'I'll get an appointment arranged.'

Chapter Twenty-four

HARRY ALLEN STEPPED through the non-existent Customs check and into the arrivals hall, scanning the assorted taxi boards until he found the one with his name on it. Nodding curtly to the driver, he handed over his bag and followed him out to the waiting car. Settling in the back seat, he reached into his pocket, and instantly realised that he'd left his mobile in the bag which was now secured in the boot. Cursing gently to himself, he thought about getting back out to retrieve it, but he couldn't summon up the energy. Half a bottle of wine on the plane had made him sleepy, besides he'd be home in an hour. There was nothing so important that it couldn't wait until then.

Allen opened the car window an inch, as they pulled away from the kerb and into the slowly moving traffic. For once the weather was fine, but that only served to make him more depressed to be back. London was a place designed for poor weather: whenever the sun came out, you should be somewhere else. Closing his eyes, he tried to tune out the traffic noise and began planning his next trip.

THE NEXT THING he realised was that they had come to a stop. Slowly, he opened his eyes, yawned and stretched. His body felt stiff after his nap, his legs ached and his mouth was dry. The atmosphere inside the car was stuffy and he felt dizzy. Fumbling with the handle, he tried to open the door. It was locked.

'Hello?' he said in a feeble voice that could barely be heard even inside the car.

Where was the driver?

More to the point, where was Allen?

Shielding his eyes against the glare, he looked around. The car was parked by the side of a single-lane road in the middle of a patch of wasteland that stretched for as far as he could see. In the distance rose some electricity pylons. To his right, a goods train slowly made its way across the horizon. A jet screamed low overhead as it approached the airport.

Fully awake now, he could feel his heart racing. He tried the door again, to no effect, and began banging his palm on the window.

'Hello? HELLO?'

The sudden beep made him flinch. For a second, after the door popped open, he didn't move. Then, pushing himself up, he stumbled out of the car. Standing with his hands on his hips, he took a moment to clear his head. Feeling a little better, he started walking. Knowing that he had no idea of where he was, he struck out in the direction of the train tracks, walking away from the road. He kept up a steady pace without ever quite breaking into a run.

Minutes later, the sound of the car engine starting up again made the hairs on the back of his neck stand on end. Beginning to jog, he immediately felt his chest tighten and cursed the fact that he hadn't done enough exercise for years. Behind him, the car gently bounced towards him over the uneven ground. Ignoring the pain, Allen started to run. But the vehicle was on him in seconds. When he sensed it right behind him, he finally turned to look – just in time to glance off the left-side wing and cartwheel into the air, before landing in the dust in a broken heap.

Spitting blood from his mouth, he gasped in agony. Rolling on to his back, he tried to sit up but fell back into the dirt. Through the tears in his eyes, he squinted up at the sky. The excruciating pain in his left leg told him that it was broken even before he saw bone protruding through the skin. But that was a mere distraction from the footsteps now steadily heading towards him. Allen turned his head to see a pair of dirty trainers stop just inches away from his face. Looking directly into the sun, he could only make out the silhouette of a man. There was something glinting in one of his hands.

'Who are you?' Allen croaked through teeth gritted against the pain.

'Don't worry about me.' The shadow leaned forward to show him the knife. 'You just worry about this.'

Allen felt the toe of a trainer in his back as he was flipped on to his stomach. A mixture of soil and gravel shot into his mouth and up his nose. He was crying like a baby now, as he realised that he would be found like this.

Humiliated.

Destroyed.

Violated.

'Don't hurt me,' he whimpered, 'please.'

'You people are all the same,' the silouette grunted. 'Stop whining. I haven't got much time to waste. This won't last long.'

Chapter Twenty-five

WITH THREE DAYS left until the election, Carlyle had read in the paper that Edgar Carlton would be holding a press conference to discuss his party's social policies. Despite the narrowing opinion polls, victory still seemed the most likely outcome for the golden twins. The conference was scheduled to start at 10 a.m. at the Royal Academy of Engineering building, close to St James's Park. Joe Szyszkowski had left for Cambridge, to visit Clement Hawley's brother, so Carlyle decided to decamp to the park with a coffee and a copy of *The Times* while he waited for the presser to start.

It was a beautiful morning, with a clear blue sky. The temperature had not yet climbed above fifteen or sixteen degrees, so there was a pleasant nip in the air. He sat on a bench, with Buckingham Palace way off to his left, Downing Street on his right, and watched other people going about their business while he himself took a short time out. If he wasn't exactly feeling blissed out, there was still a distinctly positive vibe flowing through the Carlyle veins. Things were moving now. Harry Allen's death had been a new blow to the investigation, though not as big a blow as it had been to Allen himself. *The silly sod should have spoken to me sooner*, Carlyle thought. But at least his death showed that it was still game on. While that was the case, he remained confident that they would get their man.

Thinking of Allen, he pulled out his phone and deleted the dead man's voicemail. No sense in leaving that hanging around in case there were any accusations of slackness further down the line. With hindsight, Carlyle knew that he should have tracked Allen down while he was abroad, rather than waiting for him to come back to London. He didn't need Simpson or anyone else using that mistake as a stick to beat him with later.

Closer inspection of the phone indicated that he had missed another three calls. When did that happen? How come he had never heard the bloody thing ring? There was one voicemail as well, but he wasn't going to check it just yet. It would doubtless be Simpson, and he didn't want to speak to Simpson until after he'd seen Carlton. At the earliest. Instead, he called home and gave Helen an update on the situation.

'Looks like you're still quite a bit behind the game,' she said, gently pulling his leg.

'I know,' said Carlyle, laughing, 'but at least now I can start to shake things up a bit.'

'You could be in for a busy few days?'

'We'll see,' he said, watching a duck waddle towards him. It stopped about two feet away and looked at him expectantly. When he didn't come up with some bread, it turned around and crapped on the path, before heading back the way it had come.

'Be careful,' she added.

'Of course.'

'I'm serious, John,' she said reproachfully, 'these are not normal people you're dealing with here.'

'They never are.'

'I know,' she said, 'but this is the other end of the spectrum. Normally you're wading through the bottom end of the gene pool. This is different.'

'You mean I'm playing out of my league?'

'Yes.'

'Thanks a lot,' he said, with mock indignation.

'Don't be silly. It's not about you. With people like that, it never is. It's all about them. Don't get in their faces.'

'Me? Never!'

Helen sighed loudly. 'You never learn, do you? Just be careful. And good luck. I've got to get Alice to school now. Let's talk later.'

'Give her a kiss from me. Tell her I'll try and take her sometime soon.'

After hanging up on his wife, Carlyle scoured the back pages of the newspaper for any decent football news. Finding nothing of interest, he folded the paper and tossed it on to the bench beside him, before checking his emails. There was nothing of interest on his BlackBerry either, so he moved on to his private mobile. There were yet more unanswered calls and another message, timed at 8.30 the previous evening. This time he checked his voicemail.

Dominic Silver's message was short and to the point: 'Why didn't you tell me about the Merrion Club? Call me back.'

'Why do you think?' Carlyle said to himself. He switched the phone off and stuck it back into an inside pocket of his jacket. That was another conversation to be delayed until later in the day. Yawning, he got up from the bench and stretched. It was almost twenty past eight now and the rush hour was in full swing. The park was getting busier, with a steady stream of people using it as a pleasant short cut on their way to work. Carlyle picked up his newspaper and dropped it in a nearby bin.

Then he headed off to see Mr Carlton.

EVERYONE LIKES A winner, and the Royal Academy of Engineering was full to bursting. Simpson would kill for a crowd like this, Carlyle thought. More than a hundred journalists and a dozen camera crews had turned up to listen as Edgar Carlton, flanked by two severe but eager-looking women, whom Carlyle didn't recognise, revealed the secret of how precisely he was going to fix Britain's 'broken society'.

Waiting for it to finish, Carlyle quietly sat at the back, playing the BrickBreaker game on his BlackBerry. After about twenty minutes, they went to Q&A. After another ten, a PR flunky called a halt to the proceedings. Immediately, the journalists and cameramen swarmed to the front of the room to grab the man of the moment and ask him the same questions all over again.

Carlyle moved in the direction of the crowd. He was happily hovering behind a rather foxy-looking German reporter when he felt a hand on his shoulder.

'Good morning, Inspector,' said Rosanna Snowdon, 'how nice to see you again.'

'Er ... yes. You too.'

'You didn't return my call,' Rosanna said sweetly.

He casually feigned ignorance. 'Sorry?'

'I left three or four messages on your mobile.'

Three or four? He vaguely remembered one.

She gave him just the slightest pout. 'You never called me back.'

Had that been deliberate or not? He couldn't remember. 'Sorry.'

'Never mind,' she said, in a cheerily forgiving manner. 'I can't even remember what my message was about.'

He assumed that was a lie. Rosanna Snowdon didn't strike him as the kind of woman who forgot anything. 'Ian Blake, perhaps?'

'Who?'

Don't over-egg it, he thought. 'The guy who was killed at the Garden Hotel,' Carlyle reminded her. 'You came to our press conference.' He gestured at the continuing throng. 'Not quite as big a deal as this.'

'Ah, yes,' Snowdon nodded, 'Carole Simpson. The superintendent is a very impressive woman. It must be great for you to be working with her.'

Carlyle said nothing.

'Anyway,' said Snowdon, moving on, 'what brings you here?'

Carlyle realised that there was no point in trying to bullshit his way out of it. 'I'm looking for a quick word with Mr Carlton.'

She smiled at him, in a very disconcerting way. 'Ah, yes, that would be in relation to the Merrion Club, I suppose.'

Seeing the discomfited look on Carlyle's face, she reined in the smile and returned her beautifully manicured hand to his shoulder to give him a reassuring pat. 'Don't worry, Inspector. Who am I going to tell? Your superintendent has everyone in line on this one. And if the papers don't run it, the BBC isn't going to touch it with a bargepole. We would never have the stomach for a legal dispute like that. Anyway, it is not the kind of publicity that Edgar needs right now. So, tell me, how is your investigation going?'

'It's going,' Carlyle replied tersely, unable to manage a smile of his own. He glanced quickly around the room. The scrum of journalists was slowly thinning out, so Carlton himself would be off soon. Carlyle would have to try to grab his chance while he could.

'I'm surprised you haven't managed a chat with Edgar before now,' she prodded.

Carlyle said nothing.

'Come on,' she said, taking his arm, 'I'll introduce you.'

In front of them, the PR flunky was trying to close it all down. 'That's it for this morning. Thank you all for coming. If you have any further questions, please call our press office.' The remaining journalists ignored him and kept on hurling questions at his boss.

Rosanna pushed her way through a couple of cameramen until she was almost facing Carlton. 'Edgar!' she cried, stepping deftly in front of the German reporter and planting a kiss firmly on Carlton's cheek.

'Rosanna! How nice to see you,' Edgar replied warmly, before kissing her on both cheeks. Carlyle was amused to see him firmly squeeze her backside at the same time.

'You were on good form this morning,' she remarked.

'Thank you.' Edgar glanced at Carlyle, who was hovering at Snowdon's shoulder like a lost schoolboy, and casually removed his hand from her left buttock. 'Do you need an interview?'

'No,' Rosanna replied, 'I think we'll take a clip of the bit where you talked about your "iron will to repair the shattered hopes and dreams of a generation".'

'Very good.'

Grabbing Carlyle by the arm, she dragged him forward. 'I wanted to introduce you to a friend of mine.' She took a half-step to one side. 'Edgar, meet Inspector John Carlyle.'

The German reporter didn't notice the cloud pass over Carlton's face as he turned towards the policeman. It passed in the brief moment that it took Edgar Carlton to set his jaw, but Carlyle caught it. Nice to be welcome, he thought, resisting the urge to get out his badge and start flashing it about.

'The inspector is investigating the death of Ian Blake,' Rosanna continued.

'A terrible business.' Carlton bowed his head slightly.

'I was wondering if I could have a couple of minutes of your time,' Carlyle said, smiling.

'Absolutely,' said Carlton, smiling back.

'I just wanted to ask—'

Carlton held up his hand. 'We will have to do this later, because I'm afraid now is just impossible. I'm already behind schedule and, as you can, imagine, we've got a lot to get through today.'

'Just a few minutes would be much appreciated,' insisted Carlyle gently.

Carlton gestured to his flunky, who had by now ushered all the journalists out of the room. 'Speak to Mr Murray here, and we will get something in the diary. Today is a desperately busy day, but I'm sure that William can arrange to get you a slot sometime this week.'

'Well …' Carlyle started to protest, but Carlton had broken eye contact and was already moving off. Clearly, as far as he was concerned, the policeman no longer existed.

'Come on, Rosanna,' Carlton said, taking her arm, 'you can escort me to my next appointment.'

'See you later, Inspector,' she said, looking over her shoulder.

Once they were gone, Carlyle stood facing the flunky. He looked about twelve years old and wore an expression that suggested Carlyle was about as welcome as a piece of shit on his well-polished shoe.

'William Murray.' He held out a limp hand. 'I'm one of Mr Carlton's special advisers.'

'And what does that mean?' Carlyle asked.

'I'm sorry?' Murray looked confused.

'What do you do?'

'I advise,' the boy said, as if it were the most obvious thing in the world.

'Advise on what?'

'On whatever comes up.'

Carlyle gritted his teeth, realising that he had to get out of there before he tried to strangle this little tosser. *Focus on the matter in hand,* he told himself. *Keep breathing. Stay neutral. Don't let this little shit wind you up.*

'So when can I have ten minutes with Mr Carlton?' he asked.

'I don't know,' Murray sniffed.

'But he said ...'

'I will need to consult with the PA in charge of Edgar's diary and then I'll get back to you.'

Carlyle handed Murray a card. 'My boss told me that I would receive Mr Carlton's full co-operation.'

Murray briefly turned the card over in his hand, before dropping it into his pocket. 'You can be assured of our full co-operation. We are the police's biggest supporters.'

Glad we cleared that up, thought Carlyle. 'Let me know a time as soon as possible.'

'Of course. But, remember, there is an election going on.'

He had expected a card from Murray in return, but none was forthcoming. 'This is just a matter of routine,' Carlyle said, 'but it is nevertheless important. People have died, and this is a murder investigation. I have a job to do, just the same as you do. Just the same as Mr Carlton does. If you delay my enquiries any further, I will start making a considerable fuss.'

'A considerable fuss?' Murray smirked. 'We wouldn't want that, Inspector. Not at all.'

'Good,' was all Carlyle could think of saying.

'Don't worry,' Murray said, 'we will be in touch.' With that he skipped away, leaving Carlyle to find his own way out.

Chapter Twenty-six

WHILE CARLYLE WAS getting the brush-off in London, Joe Szysz-kowski was sitting down to a cup of tea with Paul Hawley, assistant lecturer in Medieval History at the University of Cambridge. They were sitting in Starbucks on Vimeiro Road, in the centre of the city. The place was fairly empty and they had managed to find a pair of very comfortable armchairs by the window. Across the road stood the imposing front gates of Wellesley College. They were closed for the summer holidays and as a result the place appeared devoid of life.

Paul Hawley looked like a slightly more careworn but friendlier version of his forex-trading, drug-dealing brother Clement. His hair showed streaks of grey, with just the first signs of a receding hairline at the temples. He had a couple of days' worth of stubble on his chin and looked as if he had not enjoyed any sleep for a month. *Maybe it's all the DIY*, thought Joe. *Or maybe it's that Serbian girlfriend?*

Paul took a sip of his Chai tea. 'So, Sergeant, how do you come to know Clement?'

'We deal with him professionally,' said Joe, 'from time to time.'

'Oh?'

'Don't worry, this is not about him.' Joe sniffed at his own Zen tea – 'an enlightening blend of the finest green teas infused with mint and lemongrass, to calm the mind' – and wondered whether a mocha might not have hit the spot better. Along with a cinnamon swirl for that perfect caffeine-sugar rush.

'That's a relief.'

'He seems fine,' Joe added, 'but ultimately it's a very tough business that he's involved in, and there's a lot to be said for getting out while you're ahead.'

'That's a fair point,' Hawley said evenly. 'I'll mention it to him. He's coming up here this weekend.'

'That sounds good.'

'So,' said Hawley, relaxing now that the preliminaries were over, and he felt reassured that his role in the policeman's current investigation was just, well, academic, 'how can I help you?'

Joe leant forward. 'We want to know about the Merrion Club.'

'What's to know? It's just a bunch of rich kids who don't have any brains or any manners – like clones of Lord Snooty who keep turning up year after year.' Hawley sighed theatrically. It was the sound of a man who had spent the best part of two decades writing a thesis on medieval drinking habits. 'It was ever thus.'

'Do you actually know any of them?'

'Well, technically, there isn't any Merrion Club at the moment. The current crop of über-alpha males have all left to join the army or make their squillions in the City. Those few that are left will take over when they come back from their summer in the Hamptons, or wherever, and they will then oversee a new intake.'

'Have you ever taught any of them?'

'As a research student, I ran a couple of introductory under-graduate courses for several years. There have been a few attending my classes, but only one or two. Medieval history isn't the type of subject these boys generally go for.' He thought about that for a second, then let out a harsh little laugh. 'In fact, there isn't any type of subject boys like that really go for.'

Joe made a sympathetic face, but it was himself he was now feeling sorry for. He wondered if Paul Hawley could ever manage to just stick to the point. This man's lectures must be a real draw.

'The number of graduates that we, as a country, churn out every year has doubled over the last decade, but it's amazing how academia still very much remains the preserve of thick rich people.' Hawley was working himself up into a state of indignant anger. 'People like me are just an irritation while we pass through the system.'

Joe pointed out through the window at the college standing across the road. 'Are they always based over there?'

'Yes, the club is always housed in Wellesley. That way it is the most elitist club in the most elitist college. The senior members always come from there. They occasionally co-opt outsiders, but that's quite rare, I think.'

Joe wasn't getting much yet for his thirty-five-pound train fare, but he ploughed on. 'What kind of scandals has the club been involved in?'

'They don't really do scandal, Sergeant.' Hawley shook his head. 'That is the whole point. What you or I or Mr and Mrs Smith from Acacia Avenue might consider "scandalous" is considered de rigueur for these people. That's what the club is basically for. It is a way of showing us that they don't have to play by the rules. Meaning the rules that the rest of us have to obey.

If you can't sufficiently annoy the little people, you're not fit to become a member.'

'Where would I be able to find out more information about the club down through the years?'

'How far back do you want to go?'

'I'm not sure,' said Joe warily, not wanting to give too much away. Even Mr Medieval Boozing must be aware of the current crop of ex-Merrion celebrities. If he started gossiping around town, the investigation could still find its way into the press. 'Maybe thirty years or so.'

'There's a student newspaper called *Grantebrycge*.'

'What?'

'Gran-te-bry-cge … it's what Cambridge was called, back in the Middle Ages.' Hawley spelt it out, letter by letter, so that Joe could scribble it into his notebook. 'The paper has been going since just after the First World War. It comes out every two weeks during term time. How specific is the information you're looking for?'

'I don't really know.'

'A fishing exercise?' Hawley smiled. 'Well, you might get lucky. Some American internet company started digitising the magazine archive as a PR stunt last year. Some of it might be online, but I don't know how far they've got.' He pointed along the street. 'Their offices are just down the road. God knows if there's anyone around at the moment, though.'

'I'll check it out, thanks.' Joe took one last look at his Zen tea and decided to leave it. 'Let me know if anything else comes to mind.'

THE OFFICES OF *Grantebrycge* were housed in what looked like a small shop on a side street running towards the station. In the window was a copy of what Joe presumed was the front page of the latest edition, which was by now more than a month old. There was a website address above a cover feature about undergraduate hookers, headlined 'Students for Sale'. More than half the page was given over to an image of a statuesque blond, wearing little more than her underwear, climbing out of a Porsche. Both her face and the car's number plate had been pixelated out. In the top left-hand corner of the illustration it said: 'As posed by a model.' Joe scribbled down the email address and made a mental note to check out the 'special investigation' that was promised on pages four and five, once he next got online. Standing with this nose up against the window, he peered further inside. The place looked empty. He tried the door, which was locked.

Hovering outside the newspaper office, Joe watched a pretty blond girl walking up the road in his direction. From a distance, she looked similar to the model in the picture. However, there was no sign of any Porsche-driving punter on the mean streets of Cambridge that afternoon.

For want of anything better to do, he called Carlyle, but the inspector's mobile was going straight to voicemail. Joe didn't want to leave a message admitting that he'd found out next to nothing. Hoping that Carlyle was having a better day than himself, he wondered how long he would have to wait for a train back to London.

The blonde, meanwhile, had reached the *Grantebrycge* office. To Joe's surprise, she stopped and smiled at him. In his experience that was not what pretty girls normally did.

'Can I help you?' she asked.

Unconsciously, Joe pulled in his gut and pushed back his shoulders. He gestured at the front page displayed in the window.

'I was hoping to speak to someone at the magazine about back issues.'

'You can find those online,' the girl replied.

'I need to go back a long way, maybe twenty-five or thirty years.'

A look of understanding breezed across the girl's face. 'Ah, yes, back when you were a student?'

'Jesus,' said Joe, 'do I really look that old?'

'Sorry,' said the girl. 'We get a lot of people wandering through here trying to dig up old stories to prove that the good old days actually happened.'

'I didn't go to university,' said Joe, a tad defensively.

'OK.'

'But, if I had, it wouldn't have been much more than a decade ago.'

'Sure,' the girl said doubtfully.

'Anyway ...' Joe then belatedly managed to explain who he was and, in broad terms, what he needed.

'Well, you're in luck,' said the girl, after she'd taken a careful look at his warrant card. 'I was just popping into the office now. This is probably the only time for the next two months that you'll be able to get in.'

After unlocking the door and inviting him inside, she turned and said: 'I'm Sally McGurk, by the way. I'm a research student in Accounting and Finance, and also the deputy editor of *Grantebrycge*.'

'An accountant *and* a journalist.' Joe grinned. 'How schizophrenic.'

'No prizes for guessing which career path my parents are keener on me pursuing,' Sally laughed.

'No,' Joe smiled. 'I'd be delighted if my two kids became bean counters.'

'And if they turn out to be journalists, instead?'

'I might have to drown them in the Thames.'

She pulled a memory stick out of her pocket and waved it at him. 'Right now, I'm two weeks late with my MPhil dissertation.'

'Is that a big deal?'

'It sure is,' she grimaced. 'It's thirty thousand words and it represents a third of my final mark. I need to get three copies on my professor's desk by ten o'clock tomorrow morning, before he heads off to Umbria for the summer, or else I fail.'

'Bummer.'

'It's no biggie. I need an hour or two on the computer here, and then I'll be able to print them out in about ten minutes flat.'

'Why not just go to the library?'

'Too many distractions. Always someone wanting you to go for a coffee with them or chat about what a shit their latest boyfriend is.'

'Ah.' Joe tried his best to look knowing.

'Here I get guaranteed peace and quiet.' She tossed him another dazzling smile. 'At least I did until you came along.'

'Sorry,' said Joe.

'Don't worry about it.' She pointed towards a computer at the back of the room. 'Park yourself over there and get it switched on. Then I'll come and see if I can help you in the right direction. What years are you looking for?'

'1981 to 1985,' Joe replied. The Carlton brothers had been at Cambridge until 1984, but he thought he should allow himself a little extra room at the back end, in case they'd hung around after graduating.

By now, Sally was already bashing away at the keyboard of another machine by the door. She paused to explain, 'I don't know if we've got that stuff on the system yet. Last I'd heard, they'd got as far back as 1988, but that was a few months ago, so you never know.'

After a bit of random groping around, Joe located the on-switch for his machine. 'I could always look at the hard copies, I suppose?'

'You could,' she called over, while scanning the words on her own screen, 'but they're not kept here. Some are in the library, but most are stored in a warehouse out of town somewhere. That could take a while.'

IN THE END, accessing old copies of the newspaper proved much easier than he could have hoped. Not only had all the editions of *Grantebrycge* back to 1977 been put online, but an excellent search facility allowed him to compile lists of stories referencing both the Carltons and the Merrion Club. However, after more than an hour of scanning articles about binge drinking, trashing of restaurants, urinating in the street and other by now familiar types of student naughtiness, Joe was feeling quite fatigued, and fearful that he wasn't really any further forward.

'How's it going?' Sally asked. 'I'm almost finished here.'

'OK,' said Joe, rubbing his eyes as he scanned a story from April 1985 headlined 'Merrion legends a tough act to follow.' He noted down the names of Edgar and Xavier's successors without any great enthusiasm.

'Got something?'

'Not really. Joe pushed back his chair, rolled his shoulders and stretched. 'I think I'm just about ready to wrap it up.' He was hungry. Maybe he should offer Sally a bite to eat. 'Fancy a drink?'

Switching off her computer, Sally eyed him carefully. 'Maybe a coffee.'

'Great.' Pulling his chair back towards the desk, he reached for the mouse and moved to hit the close button. Then he noticed the story next to the one that he had been reading.

'Ready?'

'One minute.'

He rubbed his jaw and stared at the photograph appearing at the top of the piece. Then he scratched his head and stared at it some more. 'Well, fuck me.'

'What?' said Sally McGurk, startled.

Chapter Twenty-seven

THE GENERAL BUZZ of activity was punctuated by the regular clink of metal on metal and the occasional grunt of effort throughout the gym in Jubilee Hall, an old warehouse on the south side of Covent Garden's piazza. The atmosphere was thick, steadily heading towards fetid. Though all the windows were open, the heat of the day was slow to dissipate, and it was still easily above eighty degrees inside. The heat, however, was not going to put Carlyle off. The double espresso he'd downed ten minutes earlier was kicking in, as planned, and he was good to go. His T-shirt stuck to his chest and he felt a bead of sweat descend the length of his spine. He mounted a Life Fitness cross trainer standing in the middle of a row of eight identical machines, and fiddled around with his iPod shuffle. A Christmas present from his wife, it made his exercising easier and had belatedly dragged him into the world of digital music, allowing him to return to some of the music of his youth as well as try out the odd new tune. It didn't really matter what the music was, as long as it got him going. He skipped through six or seven tracks until he found something from Stiff

Little Fingers that was guaranteed to get his blood pumping and his legs moving. He turned the volume up close to maximum, cutting out as much of the background noise as possible. 'Nobody's Hero' began blasting into his brain. Gritting his teeth, he stomped down on the machine and sought out a rhythm. It was time to leave all the stresses of the Blake case behind, if only for a short while. With as much violence as he could muster, he chased that endorphin rush that would surely clear his head and reinvigorate his mind.

Being given the brush-off by Edgar Carlton irritated him hugely. Worse, Carlton's special adviser, William Murray, had still not come back to him with a time for their promised meeting. As Carlyle saw it, they were clearly playing for time. After the election was over, and they had their hands on all the levers of power, they could easily have the whole case buried.

'Bastards!' Carlyle grunted as he upped the pace on the cross trainer. 'Fucking bastards!' He hated being messed about by people who thought that they were somehow above the law. And, even more, he hated not being able to do anything about it.

SHOWERED AND RELAXED, Carlyle strolled out of the changing rooms, to find Joe Szyszkowski nursing a coffee in the gym's café.

'Helen told me you were here,' explained Joe, by way of introduction. 'I tried to ring your mobile earlier, but it went straight to voicemail.'

'Do you want another drink?' Carlyle asked, dropping his Adidas holdall on the floor next to a display for sports nutrition supplements with names such as Hurricane and Scorpion Extreme.

'No, I'm good, thanks.'

Pulling out a chair, Carlyle glanced up at a list of the day's 'specials' chalked on a blackboard above the counter. He didn't really need to look: they may still have been 'special' but he couldn't remember the last time they had varied. Ordering an orange juice and a hummus wrap, he sat down at Joe's table. The post-work rush hour was over by now, and the place was emptying quite quickly. Looking across the gym, Carlyle clocked a well-known actor hanging out by the free weights. He had appeared in a movie that Helen had brought home a few weeks ago, the details of which Carlyle had already forgotten before the final credits had finished running. The man was wearing a hooded top, baseball cap and sunglasses, which Carlyle thought was a bit over the top. Though he was not actually doing any lifting, he was making very sure that everyone noticed he was there.

'Good session?' Joe asked.

'Not bad,' Carlyle mumbled, in a way that he hoped said *Food first, talk later'*.

Plastered on the wall beside them were flyers announcing all different kinds of classes, from Kendo to Russian Military Fitness (*Train the Red Army way, with genuine Spetsnaz instructors!*) to Hot Bikram Yoga. There were also adverts for a number of one-on-one personal training services. One ad fascinated and appalled him in equal measure. 'You're never too old for a six-pack', it proclaimed, over a stunning black-and-white picture of a smiling guy in his sixties with a set of abs of such perfect definition that they defied belief. Not for the first time, he felt awestruck and oppressed at the same time.

Tired, wired and not particularly impressed with his boss's apparent lack of interest in communicating, Joe tried to rouse Carlyle from his thoughts. 'Did you get to speak to Carlton?'

'Yeah,' said Carlyle, feeling the post-exercise hunger kick in now, and hoping that his food would hurry up. 'For about ten seconds. The Rt Hon Edgar Carlton MP, Leader of the Opposition, told me he would deign to see me later.'

'When?' Joe asked.

Carlyle adopted what he hoped was his most philosophical demeanour. 'I have absolutely no idea.'

Joe frowned. 'Does he actually realise just how serious this is?'

'Does he care, more to the point?' Carlyle asked. 'These people all see this as our problem, not theirs. They have other priorities, and they're certainly not working to our timetable.'

Joe lowered his voice slightly. 'But we are talking about multiple murders here.'

Carlyle glanced around. The actor was still gossiping away with one of the weightlifters. 'I don't notice that the world has stopped turning.'

'Have you spoken to Simpson about it?'

'I've left her a message, but what's she going to do?' Carlyle shrugged. 'Probably, the way she sees it is that she works for them, we work for her. Who's the dog here and who's the tail? This is one of those situations where we're just supposed to sit tight and do what we're bloody told.' The endorphins were fast wearing off and he felt a whole new type of fatigue. A good *I've-got-off-my-arse-and-done-something* type of fatigue, but a fatigue nevertheless. 'Anyway, how was Cambridge?'

Finally receiving his cue, Joe took up two pieces of paper that had been resting on his lap and handed them over. One of them was a copy of the photo they had seen so early in the morning at Horseferry Road car park. Carlyle, in fact, had another copy of the same picture in his pocket, which had been emailed over by

Matt Parkin, the sergeant handling the Nicholas Hogarth crime scene, just before Carlyle had left the station. The other item was a short newspaper article, consisting of a single column underneath a photograph. It was no more than maybe a hundred and fifty or two hundred words. Carlyle scanned it, glanced at Joe, and perused it again, more slowly.

By the time Carlyle had finished reading it the second time, his order had arrived. Thanking the waitress, he drained half of the orange juice and took a bite from the hummus wrap.

'It's the same guy,' said Joe.

Carlyle chewed carefully and swallowed. 'Certainly looks like it.'

'Could even be a cropped version of the same photo?'

Carlyle looked again. 'Yes, it could,' he agreed. The photo featured in the newspaper was a head-and-shoulders shot with a clear sky in the background. It wasn't great quality, but it looked very much as if it had been copied from the same photo left behind the windscreen wiper of Nicholas Hogarth's Range Rover.

'The article comes from the Cambridge University newspaper,' said Joe. 'It was published in April 1985, almost a year after our friends sat their finals.'

In order to appear suitably impressed, Carlyle read the story a third time:

Student Suicide Tragedy

Family and friends of Robert Ashton are struggling to come to terms with the popular third-year Law student's tragic death. Ashton, 21, jumped from the balcony of his room on the top floor of Darwin Hall on 3 March. According to media reports, a suicide note was subsequently found. The police have said that they are not looking for anyone else in connection with the incident.

University friends were shocked by the terrible news. Some have reportedly claimed that Ashton was behaving strangely in recent months, but he had a one hundred per cent class-attendance record and tutors described his work as 'outstanding'. His parents have issued a short statement celebrating 'a wonderful loving son with his whole life ahead of him' and thanking people for their support at this difficult time.

There will be a memorial service for Robert Ashton at St Mungo's Church on Boot Street on 2 May at 4.30 p.m. The family has asked for no flowers, and anyone wishing to make a charitable donation is requested to support the NSPCC.

Carlyle took another bite of his wrap, saw that there was not much of it left, so stuck it all in his mouth.

'Not going to win a Pulitzer Prize, this piece, is it?'

Joe ignored his boss's sarcasm. 'The police investigation was literally open and shut. The coroner's verdict was "killed himself whilst the balance of the mind was disturbed".'

'That's the standard verdict,' Carlyle remarked. 'What's his connection to the Merrion Club?'

'We don't know,' Joe replied. 'He doesn't seem to have been a member, but Paul Hawley said that that they sometimes co-opted lesser mortals.'

'What was he like?'

'Hawley, you mean? He wasn't much use really: a bit of a moaner always straying off the point. He did put me on to the university newspaper, though.'

Carlyle thought about it all a bit more. 'A suicidal would-be lawyer doesn't seem much like proper Merrion material.'

'No, not really,' Joe agreed, 'Of course, the whole thing could be a false trail.'

'False or not, it's the only one we've got. Is there anything else of interest about this guy Ashton that might be relevant?'

Joe shook his head. 'There was nothing else I could find out today.'

'Do we know if he had any previous problems?'

'I don't think so. He'd had no run-ins with the local police, at least.'

'What about his academic record?'

'Haven't been able to check that out yet,' said Joe. 'But, if that article is anything to go by, it should have been fine.'

Carlyle finished his orange juice, and took the empty glass and plate back to the counter. He was still hungry, so he ordered a double espresso and a slice of fruit cake, before heading back to their table.

'He was an only child,' Joe continued. 'Seems that his parents never got over it.'

'Well, you wouldn't, would you?'

'The mother had a stroke a year later and the father spent years fighting colon cancer. He died in 1997.'

'The poor bastard,' said Carlyle, as he eyed a very attractive redhead, cheeks flushed from her workout, sauntering towards the exit. 'The poor fucking bastard.'

'Which one?'

'The father.' Carlyle paused to acknowledge the arrival of his coffee and cake. He took a mouthful of the latter, and continued: 'Imagine losing your kid and your wife like that, so close together, and then getting fucking cancer.'

'Maybe the stress brought it on.'

'Quite possibly,' Carlyle mused. He nibbled at the cake approvingly. It was dark, moist and heavy, just the way it should be. He dropped the rest of it back on the plate, just to stop himself scoffing the lot in one go. 'What else did you find out in Cambridge?'

'That's about it.' Watching Carlyle stuff his face was making Joe hungry, too. His wife had sent him a text earlier to say that she had made them a curry. He hoped that the kids had left him some, and wanted to get home to find out. 'Everyone's buggered off for the summer holidays. The "Come back in two months" signs are out.'

'Well, hopefully, we've got what we need from up there already,' said Carlyle, draining his coffee. 'Well done, Joe. Not a bad day's work.' He stood up and reached into the inside pocket of his jacket, searching for his wallet. 'Now we think we know *who* this is about, maybe tomorrow we'll find out *why*.'

'Maybe the killer will send us a note explaining it all,' Joe smiled.

'His continued help would be very nice,' Carlyle agreed. 'After all, it's just about the only way we've been able to make any progress in this fucking case, so far.'

CARLYLE WAS BRUSHING his teeth when he heard an electronic yelp from the bedroom. Still brushing, he wandered out of the bathroom and picked up the mobile from the small table on his side of the bed. Without checking who it was, he hit the receive button.

'Yes?'

'John? It's Carole Simpson. Apologies for not returning your call earlier. I was caught up in a budget meeting that went on for more than six hours.'

'No problem,' said Carlyle, as he headed back into the bathroom and dropped the toothbrush in the handbasin.

'So where are we now on the investigation?' Simpson asked.

Carlyle spent the next couple of minutes filling her in on recent developments.

After he was done, she said: 'Progress at last. Well done. It sounds like Joe Szyszkowski has done a good job here.'

Szyszkowski? Carlyle thought. *That pseudo-Polish bastard? What about me?* But he restricted himself to a clipped, 'Thank you.'

'And where do we go from here?'

Carlyle perched himself on the side of the bath. 'As you can imagine, I really need to speak to the two Carltons and Christian Holyrod, now more than ever. I saw Edgar Carlton very briefly yesterday, but I still haven't had a time arranged for a proper meeting. One of his advisers, a guy called Murray, is supposed to be getting back to me.'

'I know William Murray,' Simpson said, 'or, rather, I've met him a couple of times. My husband says he's one to watch – a potential rising star.'

'Someone ready to cover up his boss's dirty work?' Carlyle suggested.

'Someone who is very bright and has worked incredibly hard to get to the position where he is now,' Simpson replied sharply. 'Apparently he went to school at some troubled inner London comprehensive, but still got a first in Political History from Cambridge. He's seen as a poster boy for the non-privileged wing of the party.'

'Good for him,' Carlyle sneered.

'I will speak to Murray or someone in Edgar's office, and get this moving,' she said firmly, choosing to ignore the inspector's petulance. 'This has taken too long. I want to get it resolved as quickly as possible.'

'Thanks.' Carlyle was surprised by the note of determination in her voice. Maybe she was feeling some pressure as well.

'In the meantime,' she added, 'we have to keep an open mind. The Merrion Club may end up having nothing at all to do with this case. Once you've spoken to them, let me know how it went.'

'Of course.'

Carlyle ended the call and went back to brushing his teeth. He had barely finished that when his mobile went again.

'Inspector Carlyle?'

'Yes.'

'This is William Murray.'

Jesus, that was quick, Carlyle thought. He assumed his most official tone. 'Yes, Mr Murray, what can I do for you?'

'Would eleven a.m. be possible for your meeting with Edgar Carlton?'

'Eleven tomorrow, you mean?'

'Yes.'

'That would be fine.' *Only two days before the election,* Carlyle reflected. *That is a turn-up.*

'Good,' Murray purred. 'The meeting will take place at the offices of Badajoz Consulting, 132 Half Moon Street, just off Piccadilly.'

'Who are Badajoz Consulting?'

'They are ... advisers to the Carltons.'

Carlyle snorted. 'I thought that was *your* job.'

There was a pause, then, 'Inspector, if you are preparing to run the country, you really do need the broadest range of top advisers.'

'I'm sure you do,' Carlyle agreed.

'132 Half Moon Street.'

'Hold on a second.' Carlyle went back into the bedroom, found a pen in his jacket pocket. 'Half ...'

'... Moon Street.'

'Got it.' He jotted the address down above a half-finished Sudoku puzzle that Helen had left beside the bed. 'I'll see you there.'

'It will be our pleasure, Inspector.'

Sitting up in bed, a little later, Carlyle told his wife about his upcoming meeting with Edgar Carlton.

'It will be interesting to see what you make of him,' Helen said, peering over her glasses at the newspaper, seemingly more interested in her puzzle than in his work.

'I think we know that already.'

'I know,' she said, jotting down some numbers before immediately scrubbing them out. 'But how often do you get to see people like that close up in the flesh? Maybe you'll see him in a different light, afterwards.'

'I doubt it.'

'Aren't you supposed to keep an open mind?' she sniffed, not lifting her eyes from the page in front of her. 'Isn't it your job not to prejudge things?'

'We'll see,' he said, non-committally.

'Oh, by the way ...' Helen finally gave up on the Sudoku, letting the newspaper drop to the duvet and removing her spectacles. '... I forgot to mention it earlier but I spoke to Eva yesterday.'

Eva as in Eva Hollander, otherwise Mrs Dominic Silver.

'Yes?'

'She suggested that we get our kids together during the school holidays. I think Alice will love it.'

'I agree,' said Carlyle. He knew how much Helen worried about her daughter having playmates during the holidays, being an only child.

'Eva said that you'd already spoken to Dom about it,' Helen added.

'Not really,' said Carlyle, rather defensively. 'I saw him in Soho for a quick chat the other day ... mainly about business.'

'What would *he* know about Carlton?' Helen asked.

'It's what he can find out that I'm more interested in.'

'Well, maybe he has found something out.' Helen reached over to switch off her bedside lamp. 'Eva says he's been trying to get hold of you. You need to give him a call.'

'I will.'

She quickly dived under the duvet.

Switching off his own light, Carlyle sat for a while in the darkness, reflecting.

Chapter Twenty-eight

BADAJOZ CONSULTING IDENTIFIED itself by a shiny brass name-plate alongside the nondescript door of 132 Half Moon Street, a thoroughfare which was home to a mix of offices housing companies that you had never heard of and stores housing luxury goods brands that you had. Offering 'bespoke management solutions', the firm occupied the upper three floors. On the very top floor, Edgar and Xavier Carlton and Christian Holyrod had been closeted in the company's boardroom for over an hour. They eventually talked themselves to a standstill. Strewn across the Italian-designed, dark-oak boardroom table were used coffee cups, glasses and half-empty bottles of carbonated and still Highland Spring water. The shades had been partially drawn, while the air-conditioning kept the temperature at a steady sixty-five degrees.

The trio had been reviewing the 'overall situation', and the mood was now tetchy. With just two days to go, the election campaign had still failed to catch fire, and the polls were continuing to narrow. As far as anyone could tell, the voters were not particularly minded to support anyone. For the first time, one or two newspaper articles had begun speculating that the Carltons could actually snatch defeat from the jaws of victory. Meanwhile, the ongoing police investigation showed no signs of reaching a conclusion. The possibility loomed large of the whole thing exploding in their faces just before polling day.

At one end of the room, Christian Holyrod paced about in front of a monster, sixty-inch television screen, set up for video conferencing but currently blank. Feeling pale and bloated after a couple of years out of the army, the mayor was uncomfortable in his £3,000 suit and £750 Italian loafers. He was also distinctly uncomfortable at being here in the Badajoz boardroom. Above all, he was annoyed at himself for getting dragged into this sorry mess. As far as he could see, the whole thing was nothing to do with him. It wasn't his problem and he wasn't going to take any flak for Edgar's wretched brother.

As far as Christian was concerned, Xavier had meant trouble ever since he'd known him. If he were to finally get his comeuppance, that would be no bad thing. Christian smiled to himself. He was a politician now. A *professional* politician, just as he had been a professional soldier, someone who could see the big picture. Holyrod was well aware that this situation could work out very nicely for him in the longer term. For anything that damaged Xavier could see Holyrod emerge as Edgar's natural successor. Potentially, in less than a decade, he could be the country's first soldier turned prime minister since Churchill. Winston bloody Churchill! There was a thought to put fire in the belly and stir the blood!

Christian glanced around at his brothers in arms. 'Let's get on with it, then,' he said, gesturing towards the door. 'We can't leave them out there forever.'

'Yes,' Xavier agreed, 'let's do it. I have a lunch appointment in an hour' – he rolled his eyes to the ceiling – 'with the bloody Women's Institute!'

'Fine.' Edgar gestured to William Murray, hovering nervously in the shadows. 'Bring them in.' As the special assistant headed out of the room, Edgar turned to the other two. 'Leave this to me. I'll do all the talking.'

Two minutes later, Carlyle and Joe Szyszkowski were ushered into the room and offered the chairs closest to the door. Immediately to their left, Edgar took his seat at the head of the table. Murray slipped round to sit on Edgar's right, pen and paper in front of him, ready to take notes. Xavier and Holyrod sat down a couple of places down, directly facing the two policemen.

'Our apologies for keeping you waiting, Inspector,' said Edgar as he poured himself a fresh glass of sparkling water. 'I think that you will know everyone round the table, by reputation at least.'

Carlyle nodded.

'Good,' Edgar smiled. 'I also thought it would be useful to have our head of security present, too.' He nodded at Murray, who again skipped out of the room, returning almost immediately with another man.

Entering the room from directly behind Carlyle, the new arrival offered nothing by word of greeting, merely moved around the table and dropped heavily into the seat next to Edgar Carlton, depriving Miller of his place. For several seconds, time stood still. The new arrival eyed the two policemen, silently, only the slightest of smiles playing across his lips. It took Carlyle a moment to accept the reality of the situation. He hadn't seen the man facing him for more than twenty-five years – and he wished he was not looking at him now.

Carlyle bit down firmly on the inside of his cheek and took a deep breath.

'Hello, Trevor.'

Time had not been kind to his old adversary. His face looked worn, greyer; the hair was largely gone and he had gained a lot of weight. He could easily pass for a man ten or even fifteen years older. But, beneath the additional layers of fat, Carlyle could still make out the same petulant child. More than anything, it was the eyes. They were the same: dead, and sullen and dangerous.

Looking uncomfortable in his suit and tie, Trevor Miller glanced at his boss and grunted.

'Of course,' Edgar smiled warmly, 'you two already know each other.'

'We go back a long way,' Carlyle replied evenly.

'That's good,' Edgar said cheerily. 'Anyway, Inspector, you now have our full attention.' He glanced at his watch. 'We only have a little time, so how can we be of help to you?'

Carlyle looked him straight in the eye. 'What can you tell me about Robert Ashton?'

Edgar took another sip of water and prepared himself. 'What happened to Robert was tragic, truly tragic. He always did appear to have a self-destructive streak, but no one thought that he would go that far. I will remember his suicide as long as I live.'

It was a well-rehearsed opening. *Bloody Simpson*, Carlyle thought, *she's marked their card. This meeting is going to be a complete charade.*

'I attended the funeral,' Edgar continued. 'So did Christian here.'

'It's not something you are ever going to forget,' added Holyrod.

'What was his connection with the Merrion Club?' Carlyle asked.

Edgar looked slowly around the table before his gaze settled back on Carlyle. 'We knew him ... he was an acquaintance.' He paused. 'No, he was more than that; he was a friend. But he was not a member of the club.'

'So why are former members of the Merrion Club being killed off now, after all this time?' Joe asked. 'And what has it got to do with Robert Ashton?'

Carlyle looked at Miller, but the man's eyes were focused on some imaginary spot in the middle distance and he refused to make eye contact.

Edgar's smile grew even wider. 'That is what we are hoping the inspector here is going to tell us.'

Carlyle slowly gazed around the room.

Holyrod stared at a space above Carlyle's head.

Xavier fought to hide a smirk.

Head down, Murray scribbled notes on his pad.

'Tell us, Inspector,' Edgar purred, 'how is your investigation going?'

'We are making progress,' Carlyle replied evenly, 'but what I need to know from you is whether someone out there could somehow hold your club responsible for Ashton's death?'

Edgar spread his hands out in front of him. 'I don't see how.' He looked for confirmation to the others, who shook their heads on cue. 'Robert committed suicide,' he repeated. 'That *was* the official verdict, wasn't it?'

Carlyle nodded.

'We had all already left Cambridge by then,' Edgar continued, 'but, of course, it was no less shocking for that.'

'Yet something happened there that is coming back to haunt you almost thirty years later,' Carlyle said, almost casually. 'Why don't you tell me what it was?'

'We are simply not aware that suggestion is correct,' replied Edgar stiffly.

Xavier lowered his gaze to the table.

'What else can you tell me about Robert Ashton?' Carlyle asked gently. 'Was he ever ... injured in some way by members of the Merrion Club.'

'No.' Edgar expressed no hesitation. 'Never.'

'I'm not sure that you are being totally open with me,' said Carlyle, again without any edge to his tone.

Miller, no longer distracted by something on the ceiling, eyed Carlyle angrily, but still said nothing. Edgar leant forward slightly across the desk, the slightest hint of irritation creasing his brow. 'I'm sorry to hear you say that, Inspector.' He spoke carefully and slowly. 'I can assure you that we have offered you, and we will continue to offer you, any and every assistance possible. The very fact that we are here now confirms that.'

The others nodded.

It illustrates that you're shitting yourselves, Carlyle thought. 'That is indeed reassuring,' he said, 'but it appears that there is still a serious threat to each of you. My job is to try to ensure your safety.'

'We have plenty of security of our own, thank you, Inspector,' said Xavier. 'Mr Miller here is very thorough.'

'That is good to know,' Carlyle replied, now looking directly at Xavier, 'but it doesn't change the nature of the job that Sergeant Szyszkowski and I are tasked with.' He turned back to face Edgar. 'We must always keep an open mind about the possibilities, but it seems that Robert Ashton is the key to all of this. There must be some connection here, and it is very difficult for me to believe that you gentlemen are not aware of what it is or, at least, what it might be.'

Edgar thought for a minute. 'We are straightforward men, Inspector. What are you suggesting here?' Frowning, he forced himself to take a deep breath. 'Do you think there's been some kind of … conspiracy of silence?'

'I don't usually believe in conspiracies,' Carlyle replied evenly, 'but cock-ups, yes. You see them all the time. And cover-ups, too. Accidents happen. Things go wrong. People make bad choices.' Carlyle paused for effect. 'I know how extremely sensitive an issue this is, and how poor the timing. Therefore we are making strenuous efforts to avoid this business becoming public, as you know. No one wants a media circus.'

'For which we are very grateful,' Holyrod said.

'But' – Carlyle looked at each of them in turn – 'I wouldn't want to see anyone making any more bad choices here, not after all this time.'

'Is that a threat?' Xavier bridled.

'No,' replied Carlyle calmly, 'absolutely not. I am simply doing my job. Unfortunately, I have seen a lot of difficult situations made worse by poor decision-making.'

'Our decision making is excellent,' Xavier snapped. Edgar gave him a dirty look, but he ignored it. 'We don't need any lessons on exercising our judgement from you.'

'I'm sure you don't,' said Carlyle, letting the reproach slide off him. He was trying to sound as humble as possible while resisting the urge to reach across the table, grab that little wanker Xavier Carlton by the throat and squeeze the truth out of him.

'Do you have an actual theory about what's going on here, Inspector?' Trevor Miller lent back in his chair. 'Or, indeed, any proof?'

Carlyle ignored the question and the questioner. He had rattled their cages enough for now, and decided to back off. He would play the dumb copper looking for leads. Turning back to Edgar, he asked, 'Could this be about something else entirely?' He waved his hands in the air in a vague fashion, ignoring Joe's quizzical glance. 'Those club members that have died, was there any other connection between them that we may be missing still?'

'It's possible.' Edgar made a face. 'We will meanwhile put our heads together and see if we can come up with anything.' He stood up, which was a signal that the meeting was over. 'In the meantime, thank you for coming to see us. If you need anything else, you can contact us through William' – he nodded in the direction of Murray, sitting in the corner – 'or Trevor, of course.'

Before Carlyle could respond, Murray had jumped up and rushed to open the door. Within seconds, they were out of the boardroom and back in the lift heading towards the ground floor. Glancing at his watch, Carlyle saw that their whole session had lasted barely eight minutes.

Back on the street, an extremely well-dressed but heartbreakingly ugly woman walked by, with a massive shopping bag in each hand. Shutting his eyes, Carlyle wondered if that meeting had taken place at all, or if he'd simply dreamt it.

'What do you think?' Joe asked.

Hands on hips, Carlyle looked up and down the street. He hadn't been expecting a blast from the past like Trevor Miller to drop into the middle of an already troublesome investigation, and therefore felt distracted and agitated. *Calm down*, he told himself, *then you can think straight.*

He turned to Joe and smiled: 'I think it's time for an early lunch.'

HAVING WANDERED BACK towards Piccadilly, Carlyle steered them into the excellent but normally largely empty News Café in the basement of the massive Seringapatam & Mysore bookstore on Lower Regent Street. Few of the people browsing the bookshelves upstairs even realised that the café existed. The food was a bit expensive, but you could borrow a magazine from the nearby racks for a free read while you ate. Carlyle particularly liked it because you could usually guarantee getting a table to yourself. He didn't like being squeezed in between strangers while he was eating.

A copy of *France Football* caught his eye. It promised an in-depth interview with the French national coach, who apparently used astrology and tarot to help him pick his team. It was a bizarre thought, but no one would have batted an eyelid if their results hadn't been so crap. Given that the magazine was in French, Carlyle wouldn't be able to read it properly, but he would still be able to get the gist and look at the pictures. Perfect.

Magazine in hand, he was weighing up the relative merits of a Summer Bean & Herb Soup or a Chicken Avocado Salad, when his phone went. With a sigh, Carlyle pulled the handset from the breast pocket of his jacket and peered at the screen. It took him a second to realise that it was blank. It was Joe's phone that had gone off, rather than his.

The sergeant was no happier at being interrupted than his boss was, and he pondered for a couple of seconds before deciding to answer it.

'Hello? ... Yes ... Hold on a second.' He tapped Carlyle on the shoulder and held out the phone. 'It's for you.'

Still pondering whether to go for the soup or the salad, Carlyle felt reluctant to take the call. 'Who is it?'

'I don't know,' Joe shrugged. 'They didn't say.'

Carlyle sighed. Sometimes his sergeant's lack of curiosity seemed quite baffling. He took the mobile and stepped away from the chilled cabinet. 'Hello?'

'Why don't you ever answer your damn phone? Do you want me to solve this bloody case for you, or not?'

Carlyle stepped further away from Joe. 'I'm sorry, Dominic. We've been busy.'

'Have you sorted this thing out yet?' Dom asked, well aware what the answer would be.

'No.' Carlyle then remembered the message Dom had left on his voicemail. 'How did you find out about the Merrion Club?'

'Have you ever heard of something called Google?' Dom grunted. 'It's really quite handy. I typed in the names you gave me, and it took me to the heart of this particular matter in about zero-point-zero bloody zero of a second.'

'I see,' said Carlyle, embarrassed.

'You could have just laid it out for me and saved us a bit of time.'

'About zero-point-zero bloody zero of a second,' he couldn't help echoing.

'Don't be a smart-arse,' Dom snapped. 'I can't be expected to help you if you go all Inspector fucking Clouseau on me.'

'Sorry.'

'It's not like I'm going to blow your cover.'

'No.' Carlyle wasn't in the mood for this conversation. He was hungry, and he didn't want an argument.

'Who am I going to tell?' Dom continued. 'I see even the papers are keeping a lid on this one.'

'Thank God!' Carlyle sighed. 'So far, so good.' He knew that the media blackout could only last for so long.

'I couldn't sell the story even if I wanted to,' Dominic teased.

'OK, you're right. I'm sorry. I could have been more forthcoming. I should have mentioned it at the time.'

'Apology accepted.'

'So … what have you got?' Carlyle asked.

'Where are you now?' Silver asked.

Carlyle explained his location.

'Meet me in St James's Square in twenty minutes. You can bring us some lunch.'

'It will be my pleasure.'

'Yes, it will,' Dom said cheerily. 'I'll have a tuna sandwich and a pomegranate juice. Maybe a banana, as well.'

Chapter Twenty-nine

Trafalgar Square, London, March 1990

THE WOMAN WAS clearly in shock. She stood less than ten feet away, staring at him or, rather, through him, oblivious to the background roar of the crowd. Still gripping her *Socialist Worker* 'Break the Tory Poll Tax' placard, she was caught in a small sliver of no-man's land between her fellow protesters and a group of police in riot gear, who were holding small, round shields in one hand and batons in the other. Blood dribbled out of the corner of her mouth, dripped off her chin and splashed on to the road. This being a very English type of riot, both sides politely ignored her. Feeling like a voyeur, Sergeant John Carlyle looked away.

He was on duty, but out of uniform. Over a Combat Rock sweatshirt, he wore a red body-warmer which had PRESS spelt out on the back in black marker pen. An expensive Nikon SLR camera hanging from his neck added to the effect. Working out of Paddington Green police station, Carlyle had been assigned to Counter Terrorism duties for two years now. He had turned up today at the anti-Poll Tax rally in Trafalgar Square to see if some of his charges – a ragbag collection of domestic terrorists, otherwise scumbags who had hitched their wagon to the Animal Liberation movement and the Class War anarchist group – had decided to join in the fun.

Looking out for thirty or so 'names' in the midst of this crowd, perhaps as much as one hundred thousand strong, wasn't the most sophisticated form of surveillance ever undertaken by the Metropolitan Police. But, despite the likelihood that it was wild-goose chase, Carlyle had been curious to see how the day would develop. Everyone knew that not enough overtime had been put on the table to cope with this one, and with too few police available to be deployed, serious trouble was always on the cards.

And so it proved. By the time he had arrived, just before 6 p.m., the rally was well on the way to becoming one of the worst riots seen in the city for a century. Cars had been overturned and set alight; local shops and restaurants had their windows smashed and were forced to close; nearby tube stations were shut; and many streets had been cordoned off. People were milling around with nowhere to go and, since many had been drinking all day, violence was inevitable. The atmosphere was tense.

Standing on a traffic island in the middle of Duncannon Street, Carlyle watched a half-brick come flying through the evening sky, catching one unfortunate constable on the back of the head. *Been there, son*, thought Carlyle, *done that*. He watched the dazed officer being helped into the back of the ambulance by his clearly agitated colleagues, already knowing what would come next. Once the ambulance was on its way, the sergeant in charge gave the nod, and police on either side of him waded into the motley collection of demonstrators, with batons flying.

Carlyle saw men, women and even a couple of children go down under a hail of kicks and blows. Some were so close he could almost reach out and touch them as they fell. For maybe five minutes he just stood there watching, feeling a strange sense of detachment. He was finally woken from his daydream by seeing the woman with the smashed face. Picking his way through the mêlée, he headed away from the trouble, walking north towards Charing Cross Road.

From outside the National Portrait Gallery, he then watched a group of mounted riot police try to clear the corner of Trafalgar Square immediately in front of the South African High Commission. A group of about thirty youths was trying to fight back with wooden sticks pulled from placards, or metal poles extracted from nearby scaffolding. Further down the road, a building was now on fire. Having seen enough, Carlyle turned to leave, just as he felt a hand on his shoulder.

'Having fun?' Grinning from ear to ear, Dominic Silver seemed rather overdressed for the occasion. In a crisp white shirt, open at the neck, and an expensive-looking jacket, he appeared as though he was on his way to an important dinner party. In fact, he probably was.

Silver took Carlyle by the arm and began walking him briskly in the direction of William IV Street and Covent Garden. 'It's quite a show,' he said, excitement evident in his tone. 'I hear they're trashing Stringfellow's.'

'So I guess we're not going to take in a lap dance, then,' Carlyle deadpanned, allowing himself to fall in step with his mate. 'What are you doing here anyway?'

'I just need a quick favour.'

Two minutes later, they were standing in Chandos Place, at the back of Charing Cross Police Station. The entire street had been cordoned off. Behind the tape, ten or twelve police vans were parked haphazardly, occupied by a mixture of bored-looking policemen and policewomen, annoyed at missing out on the real action, and some arrested-looking demonstrators whose disappointment looked even greater. Standing on the corner of Bedfordbury, along with a few gawkers and people searching for their friends, Dominic outlined the situation. 'Two of my guys are inside there,' he said, pointing to a van parked twenty feet away.

Carlyle sighed. He knew where this was going.

'They're holding,' Dom continued. 'Quite a lot, as it happens.'

'That was clever,' Carlyle scowled. 'What the hell am I supposed to do about it?'

Dom put on a pained expression. 'C'mon, John, they haven't been processed yet. It'll last forever to deal with this lot, so it'll take nothing for you to sort this out for me.'

'Easy for you to say,' Carlyle huffed.

'Surely you can have a quiet word with one of your colleagues, and then the problem is solved?' He gestured at the scene in front of them. 'It won't make any difference to all this. Your arrest figures today are going to be extremely good, regardless.'

'For fuck's sake,' Carlyle glared at him, struggling to keep his voice down. 'Do you only hire these types if they are terminally stupid? What the fuck were they doing here, anyway?'

Dom spread his arms wide and laughed nervously. '*Mea culpa*, mate, *mea culpa*. I know it's a big ask. A very big ask. I'll owe you big time.'

'Fucking hell, Dominic.'

'I'll get you anything you want,' he said, hopping from foot to foot. 'Anything.'

Carlyle gritted his teeth. 'Don't start that again. How many times …? I don't fucking want anything. If I take stuff from you, that's only going to get me into more trouble.'

'I understand, of course, I do.' Dominic stepped closer. 'Anyway, it doesn't have to be like that,' he said, with a slight desperation in his voice that Carlyle had never heard before. 'You know how it works. I've helped you before. I have contacts. I can get information. I can help you again.'

Carlyle started pawing the ground with his right boot. He knew that the smart thing here to do would be to just walk away.

'C'mon,' Dom pleaded, 'this will be a great investment in your future career.'

Carlyle rubbed his neck, not even wanting to think about it. He looked at Dom. 'What are their names?'

'Pearson and Manners. Nice middle-class boys, both.' He gestured at the chaos around them. 'Fit right in with this mob.'

'Fucking idiots.' Pushing his hand into the back pocket of his jeans, he pulled out his Police ID and ducked under the tape. 'Wait here.'

Chapter Thirty

FIFTEEN MINUTES AFTER speaking to Dominic Silver on the phone, Carlyle headed into St James's Square carrying a small see-through plastic bag containing lunch for them both. Before entering the garden in the middle, he stopped by the simple memorial erected to Yvonne Fletcher to pay his respects. A round plaque told him what he already knew: twenty-five-year-old WPC Fletcher had been shot in the Square on 17 April 1984. She had been on crowd control, looking after a small demonstration outside the Libyan People's Bureau. Twenty-five years later, her killer had yet to be brought to justice. Carlyle hadn't worked with her personally, but he knew that she had been well respected as a decent, friendly copper, and also a good colleague.

Carlyle stood there for a minute as the cars rushed past and people went about their business. His thoughts were the same as always. How unlucky was it to have died on what should have been a routine shift in the heart of London? A year after the shooting, Carlyle had stood to attention in the same square while Prime Minister Thatcher had unveiled Fletcher's memorial. In her speech, Thatcher had signed off with a quote from Abraham Lincoln: 'Let us have faith that right makes might; and in that faith let us, to the end, dare to do our duty as we understand it.' *We'll dare to do our duty*, Carlyle often told himself in the years afterwards, *if only we're allowed to by the politicians.*

By the time he entered the garden, Dominic Silver was waiting for him on a bench under a tree. The day was warm, but there was a pleasant breeze, and Dom had managed to commandeer the best of the available shade. The park was quite busy, with office workers spread out on the grass to enjoy the sun. Without introduction, Carlyle handed over the plastic bag. Dom rooted about in it for a few seconds, taking what he wanted before handing it back. Together, they sat eating in happy silence for ten minutes or so. When they'd finished, Carlyle gathered up all the rubbish and dropped it in a nearby bin.

'Thank you for lunch,' said Dom, as Carlyle returned to the bench.

'No problem.'

'It's a great day to be sitting here in the square,' Dom said, wiping some crumbs off his Neil Young 'Like a Hurricane' T-shirt.

'Sure,' said Carlyle, letting the food settle in his stomach.

'The world's most expensive house used to be over there.' Dom, the property guru, pointed a finger over his left shoulder. 'Number eight went for more than a hundred million, once upon a time. The Russians have pissed on that amount many times over in the last few years, of course.'

'You wanted to talk about the Russians?' Carlyle was bemused.

'No,' Dom smiled, 'I wanted to talk about Susy Ahl.'

Carlyle made a face that said *Be my guest.* A pigeon was trying to stick its head into a discarded crisp packet on the grass. It wasn't having much success and he knew how it felt. By now he was getting used to everyone else being at least one step ahead of him on this case. 'And who, pray tell, is Susy Ahl?'

'Susy Ahl,' said Dom casually, '*was* Robert Ashton's girlfriend, back in the day. She is the woman you need to speak to about the Merrion killings.'

Carlyle turned to look at him, interest finally overriding his irritation at being shown up. 'And how do you know this?'

Dom waved a hand airily above his head. 'I know lots of things.'

'Come on,' said Carlyle, getting a bit exasperated now, 'this isn't about *lots* of things.'

Now he'd had some gentle fun, Dom's expression became more serious. 'Did you know that Eva went to Cambridge?'

'No.' Carlyle knew next to nothing about Eva Hollander, other than that she was Dom's common-law wife.

'Eva's a very smart girl, got herself a first in History. Thought about doing a PhD, her subject being the cultural legacy of the Weimar Republic.'

'But she hooked up with you instead,' Carlyle quipped.

'I didn't meet her until later,' Dom corrected him. 'Instead of doing research, she got married. Her scumbag husband was actually a client of mine in the early nineties ...' He let those reminiscences trail off.

With his famed empathy, Carlyle kept on digging. 'Let me guess,' he said. 'You lost some money, but won the girl.'

'Don't be flippant, John.' Dominic sat up and stared him straight in the eye. 'I wouldn't take the piss out of your family, would I?'

'No, sorry.' Carlyle tried to get the conversation back on track. 'So Eva knows this woman?' he asked.

'She knows her sister. They shared a house together in Cambridge, for a year.'

'Small world.'

'It sure is. Six degrees of separation, and all that.'

'How did you make the connection?'

'It was Eva,' said Dom, grinding the toes of his black Converse All Stars into the dirt. 'I got Gideon to do some basic research, since he's quite good on the old Google and the various other databases we use to keep an eye on our clients ...'

Other databases? But Carlyle didn't enquire further.

'... and when we pieced together what you were *actually* interested in,' Dom shot Carlyle an amused look, 'I spoke to Eva about it. I knew that she'd been there around the same time, and she remembers the Ashton kid topping himself. You know what teenagers are like, melodrama-wise. It was a big deal back then.'

Carlyle sat back, prepared to be impressed. 'So how did Eva connect Robert Ashton to the Merrion Club?'

'The housemate's sister.'

'This ...?'

'Susy Ahl. A-H-L.'

'Ahl. OK, got it.'

'She was Ashton's girlfriend.'

'OK,' said Carlyle, genuinely interested now.

'After the kid killed himself, Susy Ahl went off on one big time, apparently ...'

'As you would.'

'As you would indeed. But she blamed the Carltons and the rest of their crew for driving him to it.'

'Why?'

'That,' Dom said, 'I don't know. According to Eva, Ahl kicked up quite a fuss. But no one took her seriously, and she disappeared fairly soon afterwards. Eva graduated that summer, 1985, then she went travelling for a bit. After she got back, she married the moron-stroke-junkie tosspot who made her life hell for the best part of ten years. She was too busy trying to get the shithead clean to bother keeping in contact with all her old pals, so she lost touch with the housemate, too.'

Carlyle idly wondered what role Dom had played in trying to get the 'shithead' off drugs, himself being a drug dealer and all. Again, he kept his mouth shut.

'Then I came along, and we had the kids, and things just moved on. It's been a busy couple of decades. Now, hey presto, it's twenty-five years later and now we're caught up in our own little episode of *A Week in Westminster* meets *Crimewatch*.'

'Where do I find the sister, Eva's old flat mate?' Carlyle asked eagerly.

'She's in Canada.'

'Fuck, you're kidding?'

'No, I'm not.' Dom watched a look of exasperation cloud Carlyle's face, and he smiled. He then dug into the back pocket of his Levis, pulled out a scrap of paper and handed it over. 'Sarah, the sister, is living somewhere west of Calgary. She married a cowboy or something. They have even more kids than Eva and me, apparently.'

'That's good to know,' Carlyle said gloomily.

'Susy Ahl, on the other hand,' Dom grinned, 'is right here in London.'

Carlyle stared at the address on the piece of paper and smiled. 'Are you sure?'

'Unless she's done a runner in the last fourteen or fifteen hours. Eva tracked down Sarah through her mum. Happily for you, the dear old mum has been living in the same house in Winchester for the past forty years.'

'Nice.'

'Yeah.' Dom stood up and gave his legs a stretch. 'Thanks again for lunch.'

'My pleasure,' Carlyle smiled. 'You're a cheap date.'

'Yes, I am.' Dom scratched at Neil Young's head, around the spot where his own left nipple should be. 'By the way, one other bit of background info for you ...'

'Yes?'

'... my man Gideon served under Christian Holyrod in Afghanistan, three years ago.'

'What did he think of him?'

'Gideon doesn't talk that much, about anything. I think he probably has some kind of post-traumatic stress disorder. That or he's just bored shitless at being home. Either way, I think he felt that Holyrod was basically fine.'

'Insightful.'

'It tells you something,' Dom shrugged. 'Guys like Gideon, they're in it for the buzz, essentially. It's like extreme sports with automatic weapons, and you can actually kill people. Can you imagine the rush that must provide?'

'No.' Carlyle had never even held a gun in his life, for which he was very grateful. He didn't want to think about what it might feel like.

'Well, you always did lack a certain imagination.' Dom smiled. 'Anyway, as regards your average squaddie, as long as the public-schoolboy officer class don't spoil their fun too much, they put up with them. Holyrod was well enough liked, I think. Gideon could equally take him or leave him.'

'Not exactly a ringing endorsement,' Carlyle said.

Dom fixed him with a firm stare. 'At least he didn't take out his Browning Hi-Power and put a 9 mm slug in Holyrod's back halfway up some mountain somewhere.'

'So?'

'So ... Holyrod was a proper soldier, John. He's not really a politician – not deep down in his DNA. He's had experience of doing a *proper* job.'

'So?'

'So, he's probably someone you can do business with.' He paused. 'Or, at least, he's more likely to be someone you can do business with than the rest of them are.'

'I'll bear it in mind,' Carlyle said, and sat for a minute in silent contemplation. The pigeon made one last foray towards the crisp packet before giving up and wandering off in search of a handout from some tourist. For a second, he even felt a bit sorry for the bird, before quickly returning to his own problems. 'What do you think this is all about, Dom?'

'I don't know, mate,' Dom sniffed, 'and really I don't care. That's your job.'

'Apparently.'

Dom eyed at him carefully. 'I know that *you* must understand just what a tricky situation you currently find yourself in.'

'Yes.'

'So it doesn't need me to tell you how careful you need to be in dealing with people like this.'

'Why not?' said Carlyle, smiling. 'Everyone else has.'

'That's good,' Dom grinned. 'It means people are looking out for you. Be grateful, you dumb fucking plod, and accept their advice.'

'I will.'

'I'll look out for your case on the news. Let me know how it goes.' The mobile in the back pocket of Dom's jeans started ringing, but he ignored it. 'And remember ...'

'Yes?'

Dom cranked up his air guitar. 'Keep on rockin' in the free world, baby!'

NEIL YOUNG STARTED playing inside Carlyle's head as he watched Dom saunter out of the garden, and back into the hustle and flow of the city. What should he do next? He had started making a list in his head, when his own phone went.

'Inspector?'

'Rosanna, how are you?' He was happy enough to get the call, since it delayed the need for him to do anything else.

'You recognised my voice!' she chirruped happily.

Carlyle stretched out on the bench and stifled a post-prandial yawn. For most people, lunch hour was now over and the garden had largely emptied. Carlyle had the place pretty much to himself, aside from a bag lady asleep on a nearby bench and a couple of tourists who stood consulting a guidebook. 'I don't have that many celebrity contacts,' he replied.

'So that's what I am?'

'To me, everybody is another contact.'

She laughed. 'Then I guess that's something we have in common. How did your meeting with Edgar go?'

Christ Almighty, Carlyle thought. Did everyone know *all* of his business? In real time? He proceeded with caution. 'It was fine. I saw him earlier today. He was very helpful.'

'That's good.'

'Yes. Thank you for introducing me the other day. It was very kind of you.'

'My pleasure.'

Meaning: *What are you going to do for me in return?*

Carlyle ploughed on. 'One thing I was wondering ...'

'Yes?'

'How do you know him?'

'Edgar?' She seemed surprised by the question.

No, the bloody Queen of Sheba, he thought. 'Yes.'

'We go back a long way ...' He listened patiently to a pause, while she wondered whether what she said now might be significant. 'I went to school with his wife Anastasia and his sister Sophia who is now Mrs Christian Holyrod.'

'I see,' said Carlyle. 'Isn't that all a bit, well, incestuous?'

'Do you think?' she asked. 'It's a very close social set, but that's fairly common, I think.'

Carlyle tried a bit more fishing. 'Mr Carlton is really quite impressive,' he lied.

'Oh, yes,' she gushed. 'I've known Edgar since I was eight or nine, and he really is a lovely man. Very charming and thoughtful.'

'And Xavier?' Carlyle asked.

'Less of a charmer,' she mused.

'More impetuous?'

'He's more the kind of man to dominate you by force of will and the power of his emotions,' she said, with a strange kind of relish. 'He sweeps you off your feet.'

'Is that a good thing?'

'There's a time and a place for both. Edgar's the boss, of course, but I think they complement each other quite well.'

'I can see what you mean.'

'So how's your investigation going?'

'Nothing to report at the moment,' replied Carlyle stiffly. 'We are making progress.'

'That's a very straight bat you're playing, Inspector.'

'You wouldn't really expect me to say anything different, though, would you?'

'No,' she laughed, 'I wouldn't. But you know that I want the exclusive when something big happens.'

'Even if it's a story that your friend Edgar wouldn't like?' Carlyle asked.

'What?' Her voice changed as the tone of the conversation went up a couple of gears. 'Is Edgar a suspect?'

'No, no,' Carlyle said, hastily trying to backtrack. 'But, inevitably, this case may throw up things that are embarrassing.'

'Like what?'

'Who knows?' said Carlyle, trying to sound as casual as possible. 'The investigation still has to run its course.'

'Well, when it does, I definitely want a heads-up, whatever the outcome.'

'I understand.'

'You have to remember two things,' she said primly. 'A story is a story, so it will get out somehow, and, just as important, I am a journalist first and foremost. I don't burn my contacts. Rule number one from journalism school is that you always protect your sources.'

It sounded a well-rehearsed spiel. 'You went to journalism school?' he asked.

There was a pause. 'No … but I respect the rules of the game. Therefore I respect you.' She sounded quite annoyed at having to spell it out for him.

'I'll bear all this in mind,' said Carlyle, happy to get off the subject.

'Jolly good,' she said, recovering her brighter tone. 'You've got my mobile number. Give me a ring. It's always switched on.'

'I bet it is,' Carlyle said with a smile.

WITH NO OTHER distractions, he finally had to get on with things. First, he called Joe Szyszkowski and told him to find out whatever he could about Susy Ahl. Then, in a newly found spirit of openness and co-operation, he called Superintendent Simpson to let her know what the day had so far revealed. For once, Simpson was not ensconced in a meeting.

His update to her, while leaving out any reference to Dominic Silver, was comprehensive. 'This woman Ahl,' he concluded, 'appears to be the link between Ashton *then* and the Merrion people *now*.'

'Do you think she can explain it?' Simpson asked.

'You would have to hope so. She – or somebody else – has been carefully leading us down this path of inquiry. There has to be an explanation.'

'Is she a suspect, then?'

'Maybe,' Carlyle said evasively. The reality was that he had no clue. 'We have no physical evidence. I want to see what she has to say first, and then we'll take a view.'

'All the same, let's keep an open mind.'

'Always,' said Carlyle. 'Are you intending to speak to Carlton about this?'

There was a pause. 'I promised that I'd keep him informed.'

'It would be a help if I could speak to the Ahl woman first.'

'I understand.'

Was that a yes? Carlyle wondered. Promising, as always, to keep Simpson updated, he ended the call. His thoughts turned next to paying Ms Ahl a visit. He looked again at Dom's piece of paper. In addition to a home address, it had a landline number and a mobile number. He tried them both. Each time he got voice-mail. He didn't leave a message on either. Presumably the woman had a job, so he decided to wait until the evening before paying her a visit at home. Reluctant to go back to the station, he called Helen and scored a few brownie points by promising her that he would head over to the Barbican and pick Alice up from school.

Chapter Thirty-one

FULHAM PALACE GARDENS, the grounds of the former official residence of the Bishop of London, lay just north of Putney Bridge in west London. It was barely a ten-minute walk from where Carlyle had grown up, on Peterborough Road. Even after becoming a policeman, he had lived at home for almost three years. His parents still lived there, in the same modest council flat in a small block called Sullivan Court. Tonight, however, he wouldn't be paying them a visit.

Enjoying the last warmth of the summer evening, he watched the planes as they made their final descent into Heathrow, further to the west. Every two minutes without fail, another one appeared overhead, following the one in front, leading the one behind. Back when he was a kid, in the 1960s and 1970s, he couldn't remember much about watching any planes, although there certainly must have been some.

Heading further away from the river, he slipped into Stevenage Road, passing Craven Cottage football ground on his left. Details of Fulham Football Club's first pre-season game of the summer were posted on a wall by the Putney End turnstiles. It was less than two weeks since the last season had ended, but the euphoria of the team's last-gasp escape from relegation was long since dissipated. Carlyle had yet to renew his season ticket for the Riverside Stand, and he wondered if this time he would actually get round to it. He had been going to watch Fulham ever since he had been eight years old, but every year it seemed harder to justify the cost. If he put his mind to it, he could doubtless think of a dozen other things to do with the six hundred pounds, while Helen could probably think of a few dozen more.

Walking fifty yards on past the football ground, he turned right into Harboro Street. It was the same as dozens of other roads in the area, and hundreds of residential streets in the surrounding inner suburbs. There was a long row of two-storey terraced houses on either side, with a cross-section of cars, from tiny Fiats to huge Porsche 4×4s – parked tightly together against the pavement.

Crossing the road, he walked about halfway down before he found number 99. This was the address that Dominic Silver had given him.

The house was set back no more than twelve feet from the street, behind a small paved front garden. It appeared clean and in good repair, with a newish-looking coat of white paint on the brickwork and a flower box on the ledge of the ground-floor bay window. Three bedrooms, Carlyle guessed, and probably worth about half a million, if not more. Not for the first time, he felt a deep pang of regret that his parents had shown no interest in getting on to the London property ladder forty-odd years ago.

The front gate stood ajar, so he stepped quickly up to the front door and rang the bell. When there was no reply, he stepped forward to give it another ring, then noticed that the door was slightly open. Gingerly he gave it a push and stood peering along the hallway.

'Hello?'

There was no reply.

Carlyle stepped inside the narrow hall. In front of him rose the stairs: to his right was what must be the living room. The hall continued alongside the stairs towards presumably a kitchen located at the rear.

As he took another step forward, he could hear voices coming from the back of the house.

'Hello?' he called again, louder.

Still no answer. Hearing some movement in the living room, he moved a couple of paces further along the hall and stuck his head round the door. An immaculate-looking Labrador immediately jumped off the sofa and padded over to give him a friendly sniff. Carlyle indulged it with a quick tickle behind the ears and moved back into the hallway. He moved slowly towards the voices, with his new friend now in tow.

'HELLO!' he shouted. 'This is the police!'

The voices instantly stopped, and a woman stepped out of the kitchen. There was a large cook's knife in her hand.

Instinctively, he took a small step backwards. 'I'm Inspector Carlyle of the Metropolitan Police.'

'Yes, you are,' she said, letting the knife drop to her side.

'I tried calling from the door, but got no reply,' he explained, still keeping his distance.

She smiled. 'Apologies, Inspector, I didn't hear you back there. I was listening to the radio: an interesting report on the current conflict in northern Uganda.'

'Uh-uh,' said Carlyle, who was blissfully unaware of that particular war.

With her free hand, she reached into the pocket of her shirt and tossed the dog a biscuit. 'I see you've met Arthur.'

'Yes.'

A thought suddenly struck her. 'How did you get in, by the way?'

He gestured back down the hall. 'The front door was open.'

'God, I'm always forgetting to close it properly. I've got to stop doing that, haven't I, Arthur?' The dog wagged his tail happily, perhaps anticipating another biscuit. 'Maybe I'm losing my marbles.' She looked past Carlyle, down the hall. 'I didn't also leave the keys in the lock, did I?'

'No.'

'Thank goodness for small mercies.'

She was a striking woman, in good shape with an athletic build and easily a couple of inches taller than Carlyle, even in her bare feet. Well preserved, she looked around his age, or maybe a few years younger. He noticed how her striking green eyes shone with what looked like the effects of no little alcohol.

A few minutes later, he was sitting on the sofa recently vacated by Arthur, nursing a small cup of black coffee. Susy Ahl sat in an armchair opposite him, with a large glass of Château Miraval Rosé. The three-quarters-empty bottle stood on the wooden floor by the foot of her chair.

'Were you expecting me?' Carlyle asked, once they were both sitting comfortably. 'You seemed to know who I was.'

'I saw you on the television,' she said matter-of-factly, though not making eye contact. 'I assumed that you'd want to speak to me sooner or later.'

He didn't see a television in the room, but that didn't mean anything. Maybe she had one in the kitchen or up in her bedroom. Anyway, there were plenty of other ways she could have seen Superintendent Simpson's press conference.

'That was a few days ago,' he said.

She smiled weakly. 'Was it?'

'Yes.'

'Time flies.'

'You didn't think of coming to see me?' he asked gently.

'I've been busy. Out of the country.'

'On business?'

'Yes.' Gingerly she stood up and lifted a business card from the mantelpiece above the empty fireplace, in which stood some kind of potted plant. Handing the card over to Carlyle, she continued. 'My firm has a number of clients in the Middle East, so I've been shuttling between here and Dubai every couple of weeks for the last nine months.'

She sat back down, as he studied the card. In navy script, it said: *Susy Ahl, Partner, Escudo & Caspian LLP.*

'What's LLP?' he asked.

'Limited Liability Partnership. Escudo & Caspian is a law firm.'

'What kind of law?' he asked, tensing slightly.

'Property. We mainly help investors buying and selling commercial property in London.'

How boring, thought Carlyle, suppressing a smile. 'Isn't that quite tough at the moment?' he asked.

'It's not as easy as it was, but at least my clients still have some cash. Thank God for dumb Arab money.'

'Dumb?'

'That's the stereotype, that they always get suckered into paying tourist prices. In reality, they're very smart; very smart indeed. They tend not to overpay and they now own large chunks of London lock, stock and barrel.'

Carlyle could not care less about that, one way or another. What he needed now was to get this conversation back on track. 'I'll need the precise dates of your business trips.'

'Of course. Call me at my office in the morning and I can give you a full list.'

'I'll do that.' Carlyle slipped the card into his jacket pocket. *Enough of the preliminaries*, he thought. 'Tell me about Robert Ashton.'

This time she kept her eyes directly on him, as she took a large mouthful of wine. 'What exactly do you want to know?'

'Just let me hear your version of it.'

'Well,' she put her glass down on the floor, 'I assume you know that Robert was my boyfriend at Cambridge.'

Carlyle said nothing.

'We had been going out for a couple of years before he killed himself.' She said it quietly but calmly, without any emotion in her voice.

Very controlled, thought Carlyle, *but, then again, it's been a long while.*

'We were going to get married.' She snatched up the glass and took another slug of wine.

Fuck! Carlyle thought. *It's soap-opera time.*

'I was pregnant.'

Fuck! Fuck! He quickly scanned the room. There were no photographs. No sign of any children. No sign of any family at all.

'It was not a good time.'

'I can imagine,' said Carlyle gently. The reality was that he couldn't begin to imagine, but what else could he say? He watched her drain her glass and fill it up immediately with the remainder of the bottle. *Keep on drinking*, he thought, *the more the better*. He waited to let her take another sip.

'Why did he kill himself?'

A look of genuine surprise crossed her face. 'Don't you know by now?' She put her glass back on the floor, next to the now-empty bottle. 'I thought that's why you were here.'

Me? I don't have a clue, he thought. 'I want to hear it in your own words.'

'They killed him.'

'Who?'

'The Merrion Club.'

Here we go, thought Carlyle. He placed his coffee cup carefully on the arm of the sofa, trying not to look too keen to hear her story. 'How?'

Suddenly, Susy Ahl looked quite pale, as if she was going to be violently sick. 'Excuse me a minute,' she said, standing up. 'I just need to use the bathroom.'

As his hostess went up the stairs, Carlyle counted to five and quickly slipped into the kitchen. A quick look around showed it to be cramped and unremarkable, not much bigger than his own kitchen in Winter Garden House. The knife that Ahl had been brandishing when he arrived was now slotted in a glass and metal knife block, alongside four others. The brand on the blade read '*evolution*', which was different from the ones that they had found at the murder scenes. A quick look through various drawers didn't offer up anything else of interest. *Face it*, he thought, *if she's smart enough to get this far, she's not going to make it that easy for me*. He stepped in front of half a dozen photographs stuck to the fridge door. Curiously, only one of them included Susy Ahl herself – Ahl from maybe ten or so years ago, posing in front of a pyramid alongside a young boy. Was that her son? Maybe, but it was impossible to tell.

The toilet flushed upstairs. Carlyle quickly retreated to the sofa. Less than a minute later, Susy Ahl was back in the armchair in front of him, looking more composed now. 'So ...where were we?'

'You were explaining Robert Ashton's involvement with the Merrion Club.'

'Ah, yes,' she said, trying to inject a little levity into her tone. 'Robert, he was a brilliant student. A lovely, gentle boy but a little shy.'

Carlyle said nothing. He looked her directly in the eye, but didn't move a muscle. It was now or never.

She picked up her wine glass, but didn't drink from it. 'We took a first-year philosophy class together. I had to almost force him out on our first date. If I'd waited for him to make the first move, it never would have happened.'

For a nanosecond, he felt acutely jealous of Robert Ashton. No girl had ever forced Carlyle out on a date. He'd literally had to beg Helen to go to the cinema with him.

'He lacked self-confidence,' Ahl continued, 'which at Cambridge was a very bad thing. I suppose it still is. You don't get very far unless you think you're God's gift to the entire universe, and are not afraid to let everyone know it.' She finally took another sip. 'But they took him under their wing.' A bigger sip this time. 'I don't know how it started, but he managed to become friends with a couple of them, Xavier Carlton in particular. He wasn't a member of their club, but they kind of adopted him.' This time she drained the last of the wine in one gulp. 'For a while that seemed like a good thing. It boosted his confidence. He became less shy, but without becoming the kind of stereotypically smug little git which Cambridge is far too full of.' She lifted the glass to her lips again, not seeming to realise that it was empty. 'Then they destroyed him.'

'What do you mean?'

'It was the end of the academic year in which Xavier and the others were graduating. They were going out in style with the party to end all parties, a monster binge lasting days. At the end of it, they were all off their heads on all kinds of drink and drugs ... and they raped him.'

Looking at her sitting there with eyes now blazing, Carlyle tried to process what she had just told him and quickly put the pieces together. She was fast losing her composure, so he knew that he would only get away with a few more questions. There was a clock on the mantelpiece, and he watched the second hand count off a minute before he spoke again. 'Who raped him? Xavier?'

'All of them. They held him down and took turns. It was brutal. Xavier Carlton was the most vicious, apparently. He did the most damage. Robert was half-dead when I found him.'

'Why did they do that to him?'

'I don't know. Because they could, I suppose. For fun, even? I spent a lot of time afterwards wondering whether it was already planned or just a spur-of-the-moment thing.'

'Does that matter,' asked Carlyle, 'as far as you're concerned?'

'No,' she said firmly.

'Did you go to the police?'

'When we got to the hospital, one of the nurses called the police. Robert was in such a terrible state, one of the doctors insisted that they got involved. After an hour or so, a couple of young constables arrived. They were even younger than us, and they treated it just like it was a joke. One of them whispered something about unsafe sex, then the other one got the giggles so badly he had to leave the room.'

Sounds about par for the course, thought Carlyle.

'Not that Robert would have made a complaint anyway. Under the circumstances, who would?'

'No.'

'I can understand his reasoning,' she said. 'You're not going to go up against guys like those. You're not going to hold up your hand and admit to anyone that it happened. Everyone would assume – like those policemen at the hospital did – that you let it happen, even if you couldn't have fought them off. They were leaving Cambridge, anyway, but *he* had to go back. And he did go back. I was very proud of him for that.'

'Yes.'

'I was proud of us for sticking together.'

'I can understand.'

She looked as if she was desperate for another drink, but she kept going. 'We had a quiet summer and put it behind us – or so I thought. When we returned in September, Robert had gone back into his shell, somewhat. He was a bit more clingy, but it wasn't all that different to how he'd been before hooking up with those guys in the first place.'

Carlyle nodded to signal that he was keeping up.

'I felt that he must be getting over it. He was attending all his classes, enjoying his studies. And we started having sex again.'

Carlyle blushed slightly. 'Yes?'

'Yes,' she said, almost defiantly. 'It wasn't the full-on, greedy, needy fucking of the early days, but that goes anyway, doesn't it?'

'Er ...' Carlyle's brain had temporarily stopped sending signals to his mouth, which remained stuck, immobile, in a slightly open position.

'I always had to take the lead, and it took us about four or five months, but he was able to perform again. At least he made the effort, and we were getting back to something like you might call a normal relationship. Or so I thought. And then I found out that I was pregnant, during the January ...'

She suddenly stopped.

Carlyle managed to re-establish lines of communications between his brain and his vocal cords, but he still couldn't bring himself to ask about the kid.

'So ... when Robert dies ...?'

She slowly met his gaze. 'So, when he threw himself off that balcony, it was a hell of a shock, yes.' She put her empty wine glass back on the floor and stood up.

'Did you make another complaint after his death?' Carlyle asked, trying to move the narrative along.

'I made as much fuss as I could, but I was in a bit of a state.'

'Not surprising.'

'And then I thought to hell with it. One morning, I just got up, packed my bag and left Cambridge. It took me a while to get my act together, but the baby helped. After our son was born, I was able to move forward. Eventually, I went back to university.'

'To Cambridge?'

'No, I couldn't face going back there, so I ended up studying Law at UCL. Being in London was a lot easier, and I was able to get on with my life.'

'And now?'

'And now,' she smiled, 'I have a very boring life.'

'And your son?' Carlyle asked casually.

'Travelling.' She eyed him carefully.

'Where?'

She smiled. 'Right this moment, I'm not exactly sure. Somewhere in Thailand, I expect.'

Another Trustafarian waster, no doubt, Carlyle thought. He changed tack. 'Do you have any photos of Robert?'

'Just the one. I keep it upstairs in my bedroom.'

'Can I see it?'

'Of course.'

What she handed him a couple of minutes later was a slightly faded photograph in a simple oak frame. It showed a younger, slimmer Susy Ahl sitting outside a café with Robert Ashton, his pretty-boy good looks preserved there for all time. She had one arm round his shoulders and they were laughing in a way that didn't look at all posed for the camera. It was clearly not the same photograph that had been left beside Nicholas Hogarth's corpse.

'That was the Easter before it all happened,' she explained, as Carlyle handed the picture back to her. 'We took a holiday in France, near Lake Annecy. It was incredibly beautiful and serene – the Venice of the Alps and all that. We had the most perfect time.' She gave him a fleeting, fragile smile. 'It was probably the happiest moment of my life, but I suppose you don't realise things like that 'til much later, do you?'

'No.' Carlyle left her reflection on the transient nature of happiness hanging in the air for a few seconds. Now it was time for the sharp end of the conversation. 'And, with what happened afterwards, the past is the past?'

'The past is the past,' she agreed.

'And your son?'

Her eyes narrowed. 'What about him?'

'Does he know about what happened to his father?'

Susy Ahl blanched, but quickly composed herself. 'He knows about Robert's suicide, yes.'

'And the rest?'

'No,' she said sharply, 'absolutely not. What would be the point of that?'

'I understand,' Carlyle nodded.

'That is the one thing I ask of you, Inspector,' she said slowly. 'He is a sensitive boy, like his father in many respects. I do not want him to have to face all that being dug up after all this time.'

'I understand,' Carlyle repeated. *Good luck*, he thought. 'So what about the Merrion Club now?' he asked, edging the conversation forward.

'What about them?'

'It's the General Election tomorrow,' Carlyle mused.

'So?'

'It must be galling to see Robert's attackers having such power, sitting smugly there at the top of the tree.'

She grimaced. 'Let them do what they like. The past always catches up with people, don't you think?'

'Do you want them dead?' he asked quietly.

She stared at him quizzically. 'Do you expect me to answer that?'

'Yes,' he said firmly, 'I do.'

'Am I a suspect?'

'I should say so,' Carlyle said gently. 'You are connected to all the people involved, and you have a motive. A very good motive, if I may say so.'

'I do?' she said, almost coyly.

'If revenge is a dish best served cold,' said Carlyle, 'it might appear that you are taking your meal out of the freezer.'

'What a tortuous metaphor, Inspector.'

It struck Carlyle how people always addressed him as 'Inspector' when they were patronising him. He took a deep breath and vowed to rise above any slight. 'Let me ask it another way,' he continued. 'Do you care that some of them are dead?'

'No.' She did not flinch from the question. 'It really doesn't make any difference to me.'

'And if the others were to be killed?'

'The same. *Inshallah*, as my Arab clients might say. It is the will of God.'

'That is not an answer that encourages me to look elsewhere for suspects,' he reproached her, as sternly as he could manage.

'I guess you have to use your professional judgement,' she sighed.

'Yes, yes, I do.'

She looked at him carefully. 'But maybe they deserve to die.'

A lot of people deserve to die, Carlyle thought. 'Maybe,' he replied, 'I wouldn't know.'

'Someone has to judge them.'

'No, they don't.' He strove to sound reasonable. 'They haven't yet been arrested or charged with any crime.'

'That means nothing,' she pouted.

'Life is not about right and wrong,' he shrugged. 'It's about who gets to choose. You don't get to choose ... neither do I, for that matter.'

'You have to set your sights higher than that, Inspector. Remember Jeremy Bentham: "Publicity is the very soul of justice. It is the keenest spur to exertion, and the surest of all guards against improbity. It keeps the judge himself, while trying, under trial.'"

Carlyle was lost. 'Who?'

'Jeremy Bentham. He was a philosopher and jurist who lived two hundred years ago.'

'Ah.' Carlyle didn't have a clue who she was talking about. Philosopher and jurist? The only Jeremys he could think of were a couple of TV presenters.

'At UCL they still have his skeleton on display,' she grinned, 'dressed in his own clothes, and with a wax head on top.'

'Lovely.'

'It's what he said he wanted.'

'Maybe I'll go for something similar myself,' Carlyle joked, 'but in the foyer at New Scotland Yard.'

All trace of her smile vanished as the lawyer inside took over. 'I can see I'm wasting my time here,' she said sharply, 'so let's cut to the chase. What evidence do you actually have?'

I wish people would stop asking me that, thought Carlyle. 'The investigation is proceeding in a fairly normal manner,' he replied lamely.

'So how can I actually help you?' she asked neutrally.

'Are you assuring me that you had absolutely nothing to do with the deaths of Hogarth, Blake and the others?'

She stared at him blankly. 'I'm telling you that those types of questions will require the presence of my lawyer.' She took a second business card from the mantelpiece and handed it to Carlyle.

He looked at the name on it. 'Different firm?'

'Yes,' she said. 'At our place, we don't have anyone who special-ises in ... this type of thing. And, anyway, it is not something that you really want to discuss with your colleagues.'

'No.'

Arthur the Labrador reappeared, looking for another biscuit. Susy Ahl gave the dog a big smile and idly patted his back. 'Are you arresting me?'

'No.'

'Not yet?'

'Not yet.'

The smile grew bigger. 'No evidence?'

Carlyle said nothing.

She headed towards the door. 'I need another drink. Can I get you anything?'

'No,' said Carlyle, 'I'll be going now. Just one final question: are you planning on leaving the country on any more business trips?'

Under the effects of the wine, she took a few moments to mentally flip through her diary. 'I am due back in Dubai in something like ten days' time. Let me know soonest if that's not allowed.'

'I will. We may also ask for your passport. And, we might need to take your fingerprints and a DNA sample.'

'Don't worry, Inspector,' she said, waving an ever so slightly inebriated hand in his direction, 'I know that you have a job to do, and I will not impede you in any way.'

'Thank you.'

Her eyes suddenly focused on him sharply. 'But I won't do your job for you, either.'

She then showed him to the front door. Standing there on the doorstep, she turned to him and said: 'What's the worst thing that's ever happened to you, Inspector?'

Exhaling deeply, Carlyle thought about it. 'I don't know,' he said eventually. 'Nothing really springs to mind. I suppose I've been quite lucky.'

'You can't really judge me, then, can you?'

'No, that's true. It's not my job to judge, though, is it?'

'Maybe, maybe not.'

'It's not,' he said firmly. 'All I would say is that, even when terrible things happen, the world doesn't stop turning. That may sound callous, but it's the truth. If you've still got a life, get on with it. Don't crucify yourself. Don't become a victim. No one else really gives a toss.'

'Good night, Inspector,' was the only reply he got.

He heard the front door click as, this time, she closed it properly.

As he walked back down Stevenage Road, the procession of planes above his head continued unabated. Lost in thought, Carlyle paid them no heed.

Chapter Thirty-two

The restaurant Kami no Shizuku, translated 'Drops of God', aimed to provide diners with a thoughtful, almost spiritual environment that would ensure the emotional calm required to spend thousands of pounds on a single meal. The celebrated Italian designer Simone Mestaguerra had chosen the finest natural materials to provide the place with a sophisticated image of timeless luxury that kept just on the right side of decadence. Drawing on the aura of a medieval monastery, the main dining area was a serene space detached from the wearisome realities of the everyday world. Exactly the right marble, the perfect limestone, the best hardwoods, they had all been sourced from around the globe to create a template for perfection.

Owner Kanzaki Carew thought about Mestaguerra's €250,000 consultancy fee and uttered a silent prayer for his salvation. This evening, however, the timeless luxury didn't make the place look any less empty. Business was slow, whereas this time last year it could have easily taken diners up to four months to secure a table. Back then the joke had been that reservations were so sought after that they were traded on the futures market. Well, no one was joking now: this market, like so many others, had collapsed.

Like everyone else, Kanzaki had become a victim of the recession. The private dining-room bookings from American finance houses had completely dried up over the last few months. The lunchtime trade – made up largely of City wives, media creatives, spin doctors and entrepreneurs – had similarly evaporated. And the days when bankers would spend tens of thousands on wine during a meal – a common enough occurrence for Kanzaki to have then instituted a house rule that the food was always free when the wine bill climbed beyond twenty thousand pounds – were a very distant memory indeed.

With a nervous sadness, he glanced at a framed bill displayed behind the cash register and vowed to take it down. It was undoubtedly bad karma. The highest bill ever charged in Kami no Shizuku's history now mocked the penury of the present. It had been run up by a dozen bankers at the height of the boom, celebrating the closing of a monster deal by indulging in a nine-hour beano. The bill had once excited him and he could still recite it from memory, like his very own Lord's Prayer:

> *Four bottles of 1995 Dom Pérignon at £6,750 each;*
> *A magnum of Mouton Rothschild 1945 at £20,000;*
> *Three bottles of 1982 Montrachet at £2,400 each;*
> *A 1945 Pétrus at £15,600, a 1946 Pétrus at £11,400;*
> *A 1947 Pétrus at £13,300; and*
> *A 1900 Château d'Yquem at £10,700.*

The tip alone had come to thirteen thousand pounds – half of which had gone straight into Kanzaki's own pocket. The bankers had all been regular customers, but six of them had since been sacked. Of those still in a job, two were now working in Hong Kong and another two in Dubai, while another was trying his luck in Mumbai. Only one of them was still managing to keep his head above water in the bombed-out London market, and he, Kanzaki reflected bitterly, hadn't been seen in the restaurant for more than three months.

Kanzaki knew that this record bill would never now be beaten. Indeed, no one would get anywhere close. Tonight, for example, none of his diners would end up spending much more than three thousand, tops. That kind of return was just not enough to keep the place going, and he now bitterly regretted splashing out more than three hundred thousand pounds on refurbishing his kitchen earlier in the year. At the top of the market, he had employed forty cooks; now they were down to less than half that number and he had plans to let another five go. Two of his three sommeliers had also departed, along with half a dozen other front-of-house staff. It distressed him to let his people go – they were a great team, professional, knowledgeable and charming – but he had no choice. The carefully stocked wine cellar would soon be quietly shipped out to Switzerland and sold. Plans to roll out Kami no Shizuku as a global brand, backed by a Chinese or Indian investor, were now totally dead in the water. With every quiet night that passed, Kanzaki was increasingly resigned to closing the place. There was no point in hanging on. Another two months like this and the costs would start seriously eating into whatever money he'd made for himself in the better years.

Sitting in the restaurant's VIP section, Joshua Hunt watched Kanzaki Carew pacing the floor, and felt a stab of sympathy for his restaurateur friend. Joshua looked at the empty tables all around them and did some quick calculations in his head. The place had to be losing at least fifty grand a week, so it couldn't be long before it closed. Joshua gave it two months, tops. He didn't like to see Kanzaki suffering but, of course, life went on. Ultimately, it wasn't Joshua's problem. There would still be plenty of other places to choose from.

He felt a stab of pride that he himself could make money regardless of the economic situation. Whether the market was going up or down made no difference to Joshua and his computer programmes. His company, McGowan Capital, had run three of the best-performing investment funds in London for each of the last four years. This year, thanks to a timely move out of equities, property and oil and into gold, government bonds and, above all, cash, there was a good chance that they would win the top three places by some considerable margin.

Glancing at his Omega Seamaster, Joshua failed to stifle a yawn. The dinner seemed to have gone on for hours, so it was a relief when his two guests had finally called it a night. Now that he had been liberated from the client and his wife, he was in no hurry to leave. The abalone with goose web had been a delight that he wanted to spend some time ruminating on.

He never came to Kami no Shizuku simply for work alone, but for the whole experience. Tonight, having dealt with business, the exquisite meal demanded an extended period of reflection. Even more importantly, his two-grand bottle of 1982 Château Lafite-Rothschild still had some wine left in, it and he certainly wasn't going to waste it. He stared into his glass and smiled, before raising a gentle toast to his wife. 'Thanks for putting up with that.'

'What?' Carole Simpson had already forgotten about the couple they had spent the last two and a half hours dining with.

Rather, she was wondering about the wisdom of having chosen the sticky toffee pudding for dessert. It had been delightful, as always, but she shouldn't have let Kanzaki talk her into it. Once consumed, it became just a pile of additional calories that she didn't need. Despite her surroundings, she still saw herself very much as a regular police officer, and was therefore embarrassed by the amount of time she spent sitting on her backside behind a desk. Her attempts to keep in shape were tortuous enough.

'Thanks for coming tonight,' he said, pouring the last of the wine into his glass.

'My pleasure,' said Simpson. 'Well, not really, but you know what I mean.'

'Yes, I do,' her husband agreed.

'Remind me. Who were they?'

'Shane is a mid-level backer,' said her husband casually. Mid-level meant someone who had put between fifty and a hundred million pounds into one of McGowan Capital's funds. 'He's not nervous about the funds, which is just as well, considering he is locked in until next March, but he happened to be in town with his wife, and ...'

Carole smiled. 'And some reassurance and a free meal never do any harm when the stock market is in freefall.'

'Exactly,' Joshua agreed, suppressing a slight feeling of annoyance. He had explained all this to his wife at least three times in the preceding days, but by now he was used to her not paying much attention to his work. She seemed merely amused that he made so much money by pushing numbers across a computer screen. To a police officer it just didn't seem real.

Her casual attitude didn't really bother him, however, since he didn't have much interest in her job either. They were more than secure financially, so there was no actual need for her to work. The way Joshua saw it, the police thing was less of a job now and more like a hobby. But neither of them had ever given thought to the idea that she might quit. The Job was a core part of her being, always had been, and he knew that she would never give it up voluntarily.

For a few minutes they sat in comfortable silence, while, not for the first time, Simpson eyed her husband with a mixture of bemusement and deep affection. How he had transformed himself from the rather unworldly Imperial College computer scientist that she had married into a razor-sharp financial investor, in ten short years, amazed her. She was just glad that the five-bedroom house in Highgate, the expensive restaurants, the needy clients and the political networking had not turned Joshua into a completely different person, robbing her of what she had seen in him in the first place. And it amused her that they could now mix in circles that were way beyond her previous expectations. Many of her social experiences were consequently way beyond the aspirations of even her most senior bosses in the Metropolitan Police. It was fun but it wasn't what she had signed up for, and, if it all disappeared tomorrow, Simpson knew that she could happily go back to the way things had been before.

The meal had been pleasant enough, but now she felt deeply tired. Tomorrow would mean another extremely early start and, as always, the new day would bring more committee meetings and less policing. Responsibility without power was wearisome. The backlog of cases that she was ultimately in charge of was getting far too long for comfort. She wondered if John Carlyle had tracked down the Ahl woman yet. He should have given her an update this evening, but she knew how he hoarded his information carefully. All in all, he made her extremely nervous, and she even hated him for that. Why couldn't the little rat-faced cynic just do what he was bloody well told, she wondered, not for the first time.

The problem with Mr John Carlyle, she had concluded long ago, was that he possessed too much of a sense of his own importance. Sudden heartburn sent a spasm of discomfort through her chest. She should have insisted that he bring the Ahl woman straight in to Charing Cross for questioning. Things would be far more straightforward once they had made an arrest. It was still Carlyle's investigation, but Simpson knew that she had the bigger picture to consider. Maybe it was time for her to give him a sharp nudge. Getting this case off her desk would represent a big step forward.

Joshua was thinking about a cigar, but saw how tired his wife looked and decided against it. Instead, he caught Kanzaki's eye and gestured for the bill. Turning back to his wife, he said: 'The gossip is that the mayor is finally ready to take out the commissioner. After the election is out of the way, and Holyrod's chums are settled in Downing Street, your man Osgood is a goner.'

Carole Simpson smiled. Like everyone else on the Force, she knew that the rumours had been gathering pace for some time. The present commissioner, Luke Osgood, had nailed his colours too closely to the mast of the old regime. Christian Holyrod, as trailblazer for the incoming Carlton regime, was busy flexing his muscles ahead of a change of government in Westminster. Changing Britain's top cop was a good way of showing everyone just who was in charge now.

'Luke was always his own worst enemy,' she remarked airily.

'Past tense?' her husband asked.

'Past tense,' she agreed. 'When he goes, no one will be surprised. He's always been seen as too close to the current government. With them on the way out, he's been a dead man walking for a while now.'

'How loyal,' he teased.

'I am loyal,' she smiled. 'To his memory.'

'Very funny.' He gave one of those fake for-the-client laughs that she hated so much.

'Seriously,' she pouted, 'in many ways, Luke was a great policeman. London is now a very safe city, and he should get some of the credit for that. But you know what they say …'

He played along. 'What do they say?'

She grinned. 'They say that all political careers end in failure.'

Joshua sipped his wine. 'When he goes … it will shake things up?'

'Absolutely.'

'That's got to be good for you?'

'You'd hope so, but we'll have to wait and see.' She didn't want to get carried away, but Simpson knew that she was still on the way up and the possibilities were exciting. And it would be a lie to suggest that she hadn't given the matter some considerable thought over recent months. At the very least, she should be able to skip chief superintendent and go straight to commander. From there, an assault on assistant or even deputy commissioner beckoned. She could see it all falling into place, especially if they sorted out this other business quickly and discreetly.

'By the way, how is the Carlton thing going?' It was as if he was reading her mind.

Simpson took a dainty sip of her peppermint tea and replaced the cup carefully on the saucer. 'It looks like we are finally making progress. My inspector has tracked down a woman called Susy Ahl, who is the nearest thing we've got to a suspect.'

'Interesting.'

Kanzaki silently appeared at his shoulder and placed the bill on the table. Joshua Hunt gave it a cursory glance and fished out his American Express Centurion Black card.

'Apparently, Ahl was the girlfriend of a boy called Robert Ashton. Ashton killed himself at Cambridge in 1985,' Simpson said quietly, once Kanzaki had retreated a respectful distance. 'It was Ashton's photo that was left at the Hogarth crime scene.'

'So it's a revenge thing? You think she did it?' her husband asked, as the restaurant owner returned with the hand-held card reader.

Simpson waited while her husband typed in his PIN and collected the receipt. When they were alone again, she replied. 'She's the only lead that Carlyle seems to have at the moment.'

'If it really was her,' Joshua asked, 'why would she leave such an obvious clue?'

'Who knows?' Simpson sighed. 'People like that are, by definition, not very good at thinking straight.'

'Or maybe she wants the publicity,' Joshua mused.

'Perhaps,' Simpson agreed. That was what really worried her. 'A killer who wants to get caught ...'

Simpson shot her husband a look that said: *Don't make me join the dots for you ...*

'Shouldn't you arrest her?' Joshua asked.

'That's a very good question, but for the moment it's Carlyle's decision. He wants to size her up first. As he sees it, she's not an immediate threat. There's no chance she can get anywhere near the remaining members of the Merrion Club.'

'Isn't that taking a bit of a chance?'

'It's Carlyle's call.'

'I see.' Joshua Hunt slowly swallowed the final drip of wine. It tasted truly wonderful, but the knowledge that he himself could still drop two grand on a bottle of plonk in times like these tasted even better. After a while, he said: 'You know that I'm seeing Edgar tomorrow morning.'

Simpson sipped more tea. She had completely forgotten about her husband's big breakfast meeting. Another ten thousand pounds for providing a cup of terrible coffee and a muffin, she supposed. She didn't understand why her husband was so keen to cozy up to Edgar Carlton, but it was Joshua's money and therefore that was his prerogative. On top of the million-pound cheque he had written at the beginning of the year, he had signed up to something called 'The Leaders' Group', which gave the party fundraisers carte blanche to bleed him dry at every opportunity. Simpson herself merely saw it as an expensive hobby, but it still puzzled her. It wasn't as if Joshua needed these people to help McGowan Capital make money. Maybe he had dreams of becoming an MP? Or maybe it was just something in his home-counties DNA. Whatever, if that was as far as his mid-life crisis went, she knew that she should be grateful.

'It's an Election Day working breakfast,' Joshua smiled, 'for myself and a couple of dozen other top donors. But I'm sure that I'll get the chance to speak to him.'

'Won't he be too busy tomorrow?'

'No, they're very relaxed. Despite the polls, they know it's in the bag. Edgar is spending the whole day in London, as he doesn't want to be seen to be rushing around like an idiot, chasing every last vote.'

The whole business filled her with a sense of endless boredom: a bunch of boys rushing around drunk on self-importance. 'Isn't that what politicians are supposed to do?' she asked sweetly.

'That's the whole point,' he said huffily. 'This lot are breaking the mould. Anyway, if I don't get to speak to Edgar, Xavier is seated on my table. I will definitely get to talk to him, at the very least. Shall I mention the woman?'

You just want to demonstrate to them that you're in the know, Simpson thought. *Show off a bit.* But she indulged him. 'All right, if the opportunity arises, mention her to them, but please remember to be discreet. This is an ongoing investigation, and one that I am ultimately responsible for.'

'I know.'

Simpson's heart sank. She always knew when her husband wasn't listening. 'For goodness sake,' she repeated, 'be discreet. Be extremely discreet.'

'Of course.' Her husband flashed her the kind of smile that he usually reserved for his largest clients. 'I always am.'

Chapter Thirty-three

IF THE GERMANS had won the Second World War, the world would be a very different place. Nelson's Column, for instance, would have been dismantled and moved to Berlin. Christian Holyrod was reminded of this fairly pointless factoid as he stood one hundred and eight feet below the great admiral and tried to avoid any shit from such pigeons as had managed to survive the cull organised by one of his predecessors. He was increasingly of the view that being mayor was not a job for a grown-up. Not for the first time, he thought about all he had given up when he had left the army. As a man used to being in control of his environment and the people around him, he was still coming to terms with how little actual control of his day-to-day life he now enjoyed.

Holyrod wiped the sweat from his brow. He was not a great one for what-ifs, but he couldn't help thinking that if Vice-Admiral Horatio Nelson, first Viscount Nelson, first Duke of Bronté had, in fact, made that 600-mile journey east into the heart of the thousand-year Reich, then at least Holyrod himself could have been somewhere else today. But here he now was, feeling very warm and more than a little sheepish. Whichever adviser had put him here, in Trafalgar Square, on Election Day, the hottest day of the year to boot, to promote cycling in London, should be shot. *Just one more photocall*, he told himself, *and then it's all over.*

Surrounded by a posse of Lycra-clad lovelies, he took a deep breath as the clicking of camera shutters reached a crescendo.

'Over here!'

'Mr May-yor!

'Christian!'

'Look this way!'

He smiled with as much conviction as he could muster for the benefit of the collection of snappers and camera crews ranged in front of them. After a minute or so, a nubile television presenter – the token media 'celebrity' attending the event – jumped on a bike and started on a wobbly lap around the fountains, chased by a couple of the more energetic cameramen. Taking that as his own cue to leave, Holyrod slipped on a pair of Ray-Ban 3025 Aviators and started walking towards the north-east corner of the square.

Holyrod had already dismissed out of hand a suggestion that he cycle to his next engagement. However, not wanting to set the wrong tone at his departure, he had agreed to meet his driver at a more than discreet distance away, out of sight of any camera lens. His Jaguar was parked on Bedfordbury behind the London Coliseum, home of the English National Opera on St Martin's Lane. At most, it was a three-minute walk.

Keeping his head down, he set off at a brisk pace in the hope of deterring well-wishers or any persistent hacks. It took him less than a minute to cross Trafalgar Square and reach the National Gallery on its north side. As he did so, a man fell in step beside him.

'Mayor Holyrod?'

Expecting an autograph hunter, Holyrod slowed his pace slightly and turned towards the voice. He was surprised to recognise the plebeian policeman beside him.

'Inspector.' The mayor quickly resumed his previous energetic pace.

'Mr Holyrod,' Carlyle upped his own pace, 'I would like a word, sir.'

'Not a good time,' said Holyrod stiffly, upping his pace some more, 'I have an appointment.'

Already feeling hot and uncomfortable, Carlyle was not going to start jogging. Putting a firm hand on Holyrod's arm, he ignored the surprised look on the mayor's face, and stepped closer.

'I have been very polite, so far ...'

'And we have appreciated it,' said Holyrod, looking down at his unwanted companion in a way that made his exasperation clear.

The former soldier was a good three or four inches taller, but Carlyle was not prepared to be intimidated. 'However,' he continued, ignoring Holyrod's sharp tone, 'if you don't stop fucking me about right now,' he snarled, 'I will arrest you. On the fucking spot.'

Holyrod snorted in astonishment.

'And,' Carlyle gestured back in the direction of the Square, 'I will take you down there in front of the camera crews, in handcuffs, while we wait for a car. That should take about twenty minutes, I expect, and might prove a slightly bigger story than your bike thing. Wouldn't that be a bit of a bugger on Election Day?'

Holyrod sighed. 'Miller told us you were a complete arsehole.'

Carlyle smiled. 'That's Trevor for you. He always was an excellent judge of character.'

A bodyguard, who had been hovering in the background, stepped forward, but Holyrod waved him away. He looked back towards Nelson's Column, down at the ground and then over Carlyle's shoulder.

'Let's go over there,' he said, quickly heading in the direction of the church of St Martin-in-the-Fields, on the opposite side of the road.

Pleased that his bluff had not been called, Carlyle followed as Holyrod slalomed through the stationary traffic and bounded up the steps, before disappearing through the open doors of the church. He knew that if the mayor had decided to simply walk away, arresting him would have been out of the question. Apart from anything else, Carlyle had left his handcuffs behind at the station.

CARLYLE TOOK HIS time in getting to the church entrance, giving the mayor a couple of minutes to ponder what might be coming next. As he approached, he watched a steady trickle of tourists wander up the steps and stick their heads through the door, before retreating back towards the dissolute chaos outside.

Inside St Martin's, the air was musty but the mood was calm. Light flooded in from the windows on the east wall of the building, bouncing back off the white ceiling. A notice board by the door informed Carlyle that there would be a lunchtime prayer session at 1.15 p.m. He checked his watch: happily there was no chance of getting caught up in that. Another poster announced a performance of the Bach Cantata series. However, the thing that caught his attention was a poster for the church's Thought For The Week. It proclaimed: 'The truth will set you free.' *Amen to that*, Carlyle smiled. If only more people could appreciate that counsel, his life would be a lot easier.

Holyrod was sitting waiting for him in the front pew on the right, out of the direct sunlight. 'This must be your local church, Inspector,' he said, as Carlyle sat down beside him.

'I suppose so,' said Carlyle vaguely, the truth being that he had never set foot inside St Martin's before.

'You should get to know your neighbourhood,' Holyrod chided him. 'This is one of London's finest baroque churches. During the First World War, it was a refuge for soldiers on their way to France. More than 6,000 homeless people still take refuge here every year.' The mayor paused, pleased that he had remembered so much from his recent meeting with the vicar of St Martin's, who, for a man of the cloth, had made a surprisingly slick pitch for city funding.

'That's very interesting,' said Carlyle, 'but it wasn't really a history lesson I was after.'

'So, what exactly did you come for?' Holyrod asked, barely trying to conceal his obvious contempt.

'The truth.'

'Ah.' Holyrod raised his eyes to the heavens. 'That's tricky.'

Carlyle waited for a stray tourist to wander off out of earshot. 'Why didn't you tell me about Susy Ahl?'

An expression blending confusion and resignation crossed Holyrod's face.

'We're in church now.' Carlyle was a devout atheist, but Holyrod might have a different take on the meaning of life, so an appeal to a higher authority was always worth a try. He nodded back towards the entrance. 'The current thought for the week is "The truth will set you free." I'm not taking any notes now. This conversation is just between us.'

Holyrod gave no indication of being spiritually inclined, however. 'I don't recognise the name.'

'She was Robert Ashton's girlfriend.'

'Ah, yes.' Holyrod nodded. He raised his hands in a gesture maybe supposed to signify sincerity. 'I'm with you now. I am aware of the person you are referring to. Her name never registered because I don't know that I ever actually met her.'

'I suppose that's progress,' said Carlyle.

'Why do you ask, anyway?' A sly smile crossed the mayor's face. 'Is she a suspect? Have you arrested her?'

'The investigation is proceeding.'

'I'll take that as a no, then. If she's your woman, I would suggest that you just get on with it, Inspector.' Holyrod finally stopped staring at nothing in particular and turned to face Carlyle. 'That is your job, after all.'

'Is what she claims happened to Robert Ashton true?'

'What did she say?'

'That he was brutally raped, and driven to suicide.'

'Do you really believe that?'

Carlyle shrugged. 'It's not my job to believe anything.'

Holyrod dropped his pseudo-patrician demeanour and showed the hard-faced soldier that still lived underneath. 'Either way, it's not much of a defence for committing multiple murder, is it?' He affected a shrill, girlish voice: 'My boyfriend was on the wrong end of some rough sex.'

Carlyle looked at him, nonplussed.

'What happened to Ashton wasn't exactly unique,' Holyrod resumed his normal tone, 'even if it did drive him to kill himself. Which, of course, is a matter of complete conjecture and speculation on your part. It might get your woman some extra counselling, while she spends the rest of her life in jail, but that's about it.'

My woman? thought Carlyle. 'That's an interesting perspective on things,' he persisted. 'It's not quite how Ms Ahl explains it.'

'I'm sure it isn't.' Holyrod now threw his hands open wide. 'Come on, Inspector. When you get to our age, it doesn't count for much, one way or another. What about all the shitty things you got up to at university, yourself? The things that still make you embarrassed today?'

'I didn't go to university.'

Holyrod started to reply, but thought better of it, making do with a look that said: *I'm finished wasting my time here.* He stood up. Carlyle did the same. This time, the Mayor put his hand on the policeman's shoulder and gripped it firmly. 'What you've got to remember is that she wasn't there.'

'No, but—'

'Neither were you.'

'No—'

'And neither was I.' Holyrod let go of Carlyle's shoulder, which began throbbing slightly. 'Not for the meat of the matter, anyway.' He smiled. 'Whatever happened, I was not a party to it. Neither, for that matter, was Edgar Carlton.' He paused. 'You know how important our reputations are to us.'

'Yes,' Carlyle nodded. 'Particularly for the next twenty-four hours.'

Holyrod made a face that was part saint, part executioner. 'For the next twenty-four hours, for the next twenty-four years – and longer even than that. We are men of honour, do you understand?'

How can people believe this kind of bullshit? Carlyle wondered. But, for once, he bit his tongue and nodded. 'I do.'

'I wonder.' Holyrod looked him up and down. 'This has been handled pretty well, so far. Now it needs to be finished. Do your job, Inspector, no more, no less.'

Without waiting for a reply, Holyrod turned on his heel and headed for the exit. Carlyle listened to footsteps echoing on the stone floor as Holyrod marched out of the church. After the mayor had gone, he quietly said to himself: 'Well done, John, that worked perfectly. Exactly as planned. Another triumph beckons.'

TREVOR MILLER GENTLY returned the phone to its cradle and looked up. 'OK,' he said quietly, 'we've found her.'

'You know what you've got to do?' Edgar Carlton inquired dreamily.

'Yes.'

'Good. That's very good.'

PASSING THE GARDEN Hotel, Carlyle glanced inside and caught sight of the concierge, Alex Miles, making a fuss of some newly arrived guest. It was little more than a fortnight since Ian Blake's body had been found in a hotel room upstairs. Carlyle tried to recall the details. What was the number of the room? How many people had slept in there since? He also wondered if they had installed a new bed; they would have had to replace the mattress at the very least.

He tried to remember what it had been like on walking through that door to see the blood, the empty eyes, to smell the stench of death. None of it came back to him. Nothing had lingered in his memory any longer than last night's television. Already, Ian Blake had become a dim and distant memory, a minor footnote in his own murder investigation. After only a couple of weeks, did anyone miss him? Did anyone even remember that he had ever existed? The inspector felt a sense of melancholy descend on him that he knew would be hard to shake. *Don't be a victim*, he thought to himself as he hurried on. *Don't ever be a victim.*

AVOIDING A RETURN to the Station, he went home, had a shower and then a cheese sandwich. When Helen got home from work, they took Alice to the polling station at Dragon Hall, just off Macklin Street. It was something of a family tradition that they all went voting together: Alice would hand over the polling cards and collect the voting papers, then she would take each of her parents in turn into the booth and put a cross beside their chosen candidate. Then she would fold the papers and put them in the ballot box. The place was quite empty when they arrived, so they were in and out of there in minutes. Carlyle had very mixed feelings about the whole thing: he knew that his vote counted for nothing; on the other hand, he didn't want his daughter to grow up as cynical as himself.

He left them at the door to Winter Garden House, with a hug and a kiss.

'When will you be home?' Helen asked.

'I don't know,' Carlyle shrugged. 'Late … maybe very late.'

'OK,' she sighed. 'Do what you have to do, but be careful.'

'I will,' he said, shuffling off round the corner, into Drury Lane.

Chapter Thirty-four

IT WAS WELL after six o'clock when he got back to Charing Cross Police Station. Joe Szyszkowski had not yet reappeared, so Carlyle sat at his desk and watched the BBC's rolling news on a monitor suspended from the ceiling. The sound was off, but subtitles scrolled across the bottom of the screen, allowing him to follow what was being said. The stock market wasn't waiting for the result of the election, before it collapsed. Some know-nothing news pixie was explaining how share prices were plunging, the capitalist system was doomed, and everyone would be living in caves by Christmas.

'You don't want to listen to that rubbish,' said Joe, wandering across his line of vision. 'It'll only make you depressed.'

'There's never been a better time to be poor,' Carlyle said mirthlessly, grabbing a remote from the desk behind his own and turning the news pixie to black, with a flourish.

'That's handy,' Joe grinned.

Carlyle tossed the remote back on his desk just as he felt his mobile start vibrating in his pocket. For once he had managed to pick up a call! Recognising Ahl's mobile number on the screen, he hurriedly pushed the receive button.

'Hello?'

The line immediately went dead.

He rang back but got a 'network busy' signal.

Bastards!

He tried again, but got the same thing.

Bastards! Fucking shit technology!

He somehow resisted the temptation to throw the handset at the wall. At the third attempt, he got through, but it went straight to voicemail. Once again, he didn't leave a message. Why was she ringing him? Maybe she had come to terms with the fact that the game was up.

In anticipation of their evening's work, Joe had booked a Mitsubishi Shogun from the station garage. The previous user had still to bring it back in, however, and the car pool was empty apart from a couple of Smart electric cars that were currently being trialled by the Met. No self-respecting copper, including Carlyle and Joe, would be seen dead in one. Carlyle thought about catching the tube, but he couldn't be arsed to slog his way through the rush hour. Anyway, they still needed a car to bring Ahl back to the station. It was time to wait.

Waiting had always been a key part of the job, and by now Carlyle was quite good at it. For the next hour and a half, he and Joe kicked the case around, looking at what they had, what they lacked and what they had missed. In the end, they called a halt, finding themselves back where they had started. As far as anyone could tell, Susy Ahl had killed three members of the Merrion Club in revenge for what they had done to Robert Ashton all those years ago.

Was the woman crazy? That was for a doctor to decide. It was not for Carlyle himself to judge. Crazy or not, he had to admit that taking down four members of the Merrion Club was a hell of a result, far better than a lone, middle-aged, female lawyer could have hoped for at the outset of her killing spree. The icing on the cake would be to destroy the political careers of the Carltons and also Holyrod. To do that, she needed to be caught. She wanted her fifteen minutes of fame.

And who, Carlyle thought, *are we to deny her that?*

THE JOURNEY ACROSS London had taken the best part of an hour, so it was after 8 p.m. when they parked on Atlanta Street, at the south end of Fulham Cemetery. With the end now in sight, Carlyle felt shattered. He got out of the car and stamped the ground, trying to rid his body of the lethargy. The street was quiet and the air was still. The edge had come off the mugginess and the sky was getting darker by the minute. That meant it was going to rain very soon. Unprepared, as usual, he knew that a soaking beckoned.

Atlanta Street was just across the Fulham Palace Road from Susy Ahl's house on Harboro Street. Access to Harboro Street itself was blocked by roadworks. A twenty-yard stretch of it was littered with the usual items of machinery scattered around a trench about a foot wide and three feet deep, which had been cut into the tarmac along the middle of the road. It was all cordoned off behind temporary metal fencing on which hung a notice informing them that the thoroughfare would remain closed until late July. Pedestrians could still squeeze past by using a three-foot gap left open on the pavement to his right.

Carlyle heard a growl of thunder. It was quickly followed by a large raindrop landing on his head. Cursing, he tried to shrink

inside his jacket, while lengthening his stride. Almost immediately, the rain came spearing down, bouncing off the road and
drenching him. He had planned on making his dramatic entrance
rather differently, but nothing could be done about that now.
Trusting that Joe was keeping pace behind him, he began jogging
towards the house.

Only when he was about fifty yards away from his destina-
tion did he look up. The rain had driven everyone from the street
except for a couple of kids and an old bloke sheltering under a
tree with its roots in the pavement. One of the kids was using his
mobile phone to record video of an ambulance as it slowly pulled
up at the kerb, the siren off but its blue lights illuminating the
gloom. Switching the lightbar off, the paramedics pulled on their
anoraks. They showed no desire to get out of the cab in a hurry,
which told Carlyle that they were not here to deal with a living
patient. Eventually, they stepped down into the street and jogged
back to the vehicle's rear. Opening the doors with a flourish, they
pulled out a trolley and carried it past the thoroughly pissed-off-
looking constable still standing at the front gate.

Feeling a bit like a man who had just turned up late for his own
funeral, Carlyle headed across to the opposite side of the street,
with Joe following immediately behind. He was no longer worried
about the rain, focusing rather on the sinking feeling in his stomach. It was clear that he had overplayed his hand, and now wasn't
the time to go rushing inside.

After a couple of minutes, the ambulance crew reappeared.
They stowed the draped body in the back of the ambulance and
slammed the doors shut, before climbing aboard and moving off.
Ten yards down the road, the driver realised that his exit was

blocked by the roadworks ahead. He performed a tortuous three-point turn and headed back the way he had come.

The gawkers took this as their cue to leave. Watching them depart, Carlyle tried to snap himself out of his funk. Then, just as he was about to step across the road, Trevor Miller emerged from the house. He stood on the pavement for a second, pulling up the collar of his raincoat. Looking up, he caught Carlyle's eye. Acknowledging him with the slightest of nods, Miller stuck his hands into his pockets and hurried off in the direction of the river.

The rain began easing as Carlyle showed his ID to the copper posted on the gate. He was just sticking it back in his pocket when Simpson herself walked out of the front door, carrying an umbrella.

'Ah, there you are, Inspector.' She stopped to put up the umbrella before stepping towards him. Nodding a greeting to Joe, who was hovering a yard away, she placed a gentle hand on Carlyle's elbow and guided him a few yards back along the street, to where a driver was waiting for her in a BMW. She stopped by the passenger door and looked Carlyle up and down.

'Why are you looking so glum, John?'

Partly sheltered under the umbrella, he was even more conscious of the rain slipping under his collar and trickling down his spine. 'What happened?'

Simpson pursed her lips, ignoring the question. 'You've got a result ... one way or another. It's job done, and case closed.'

'What are you doing here?' Carlyle asked, struggling to keep any trace of emotion from his voice. The sick feeling in his stomach had dissipated. It was now being replaced by the kind of gentle numbness that came at times when things were going spectacularly tits-up.

A small, brittle smile appeared on Simpson's lips. 'Mr Miller called me personally, after he found the body. Apparently, Ms Ahl had called up Edgar Carlton to demand a meeting.'

'What kind of meeting?'

Simpson shrugged. 'It looks like we shall never know that. Carlton decided to send Miller. He arrived here about 6.30 and found the door was open.'

'Miller? Carlton's head of security? On Election Day?'

Simpson paused there, eyes shining, saying nothing further. The rain had now stopped and the air suddenly felt fresher than it had for weeks.

'Was there anything suspicious about the death?' Carlyle asked, trying and failing to keep a hint of desperation from his voice.

Simpson executed a small hop on the spot, like a small child desperate to go to the toilet. 'Not as far as I could see.' She lowered the umbrella, giving it vigorous shake before closing it. 'When Miller went in, he found her hanging from the banister, so he rang 999, and then he rang me.'

'Suicide?'

She let her gaze fall to the pavement. 'Yes, I'd say so.'

Carlyle clamped his jaw tight and fixed his gaze on a point in the middle distance, before nodding at her carefully rehearsed answer.

'Why wasn't I called?'

'I tried your mobile,' Simpson said gently, 'but I couldn't get through. The network was busy. I rang the station, and they said you were on your way.'

He tried to work it through in his head, to see if that timing made sense. It was difficult to say.

Simpson radiated calm. She glanced towards Joe, still standing on the pavement outside Susy Ahl's house. 'You must pass on my congratulations to your sergeant, as well, John. It's excellent work that we've managed to clear this thing up without too much ... fuss. Good for our performance stats as well. You know that it all comes under SCD in the end, but I will make sure that you both get the proper recognition you deserve.'

Carlyle shivered. As far as he was concerned, the Specialist Crime Directorate could take whatever credit they wanted. He sneezed.

'Bless you,' said Simpson, reaching down to open the car door. 'I know that you'll have some more questions, but don't hang around here any longer than is necessary. The officer in charge of the scene is a Sergeant Longmead, and she seems very efficient.' Simpson gestured towards the house. 'She's inside right now. Go and speak to her, and let me have your final report first thing in the morning.'

'Final' meaning final. Meaning: *Kindly fuck off back to the day job, the muggers and the drunks, and try to stay off my radar for a while. A long while.*

'Any loose ends?' he asked, giving it one last push, more in hope than expectation.

'Not really.' Simpson had already lowered herself into the car and seemed keen to close the door. 'Not really. There was an empty vodka bottle on the floor. The provisional time of death is around five p.m.'

Carlyle thought about his missed call. His brain was now slowly getting into gear. 'What about a suicide note?'

'No note,' said Simpson, with just the slightest hint of levity in her tone, as if she might have just taken a stiff drink herself. 'But that's not unusual. After all, she knew that we were closing in.'

'I should have arrested her yesterday.' He said it to himself more than to Simpson, but he saw the first sign of irritation flash across her face.

She looked up at him sharply. 'People hang themselves in jail, too, as you well know. Who's to say that she wouldn't have done exactly the same thing inside? Look at it this way, you've saved the taxpayer the cost of a trial. That could mean hundreds of thousands, if not millions, of pounds. Not to mention the thirty thousand or more a year necessary to keep Ms Ahl in prison for the rest of her life.' Simpson did the mental arithmetic in her head. 'Let's say a couple of million pounds – one and a half minimum. That more than pays your way.' She grabbed the inside door handle firmly. 'Not a bad night's work, I'd say. Once again, well done. I'll call you once I've read your report.' With that, she finally pulled the door shut and allowed herself to be driven off into the night.

CARLYLE DIDN'T BOTHER talking to Longmead or even taking a final look round Ahl's house. Instead, he led Joe to the Eight Bells pub round the corner, on Woodlawn Road. As befitted his designated driver status, Joe was carefully sipping a half pint of London Pride bitter. Damp and dismayed, Carlyle had ordered a double measure of Jameson whiskey. After knocking that back in one, he was now nursing a second.

Did I get that woman killed? he wondered grimly. *Is this one on me?*

'What do you think?' asked Joe, trying to break his boss free of his dark mood.

Carlyle sneezed again. 'I think I'm going down with the flu.'

Joe was not in the mood for handing out any faux sympathy. 'You know what I mean.'

'It doesn't matter what I think,' Carlyle said gloomily. 'Not in the slightest.'

'So what do we do now?'

'What do you think?' He sucked down the remaining whiskey. 'You drive me back, and then I write my report.'

'OK.'

Carlyle looked down at his glass. 'Tell you what, I've got a better idea. *You* go and write the report, and I'll sign it in the morning. I feel like one for the road.'

Joe shrugged, not caring one way or the other. It was the hanging around picking over the bones of failure that he hated. Now, it was time to move on, find some other bastards to get worked up about. 'Sure.' He pulled the car keys from his pocket and weighed them in his hand. 'See you in the morning, boss.'

'Thanks, Joe.'

Carlyle ordered another double at the bar and took it back to his seat. For the next few minutes he wanted nothing more than to enjoy his drink, stare vacantly into space, and hope that all the frustrations of recent weeks would fade as he began to get increasingly pissed.

Behind the bar was a television with the sound turned right down. Carlyle looked up to see Edgar Carlton, on the steps of party HQ, making an 'impromptu' speech to his cheering campaign workers. Edgar was surrounded by faces that had become all too familiar in recent days, all of them busy nodding and clapping as if their very lives depended on it, waiting for the polls to close so that the celebrations could begin in earnest.

'Almost there now, aren't you, you tossers,' Carlyle slurred to himself. 'Got what you wanted, your bloody birthright.'

He took another mouthful of whiskey and decided that tonight would be an excellent night to get totally shitfaced.

'Tossers!'

The barman stopped pouring a pint and gave him a dirty look.

'But they are,' Carlyle grumbled under his breath.

Maybe he should just go to bed.

On the screen, the picture zoomed in on one bright, shining face hovering behind Edgar's left shoulder. With the shot glass poised at his lips, Carlyle froze.

'Holy fucking shit!'

This time, the barman looked ready to come over and sort him out.

Ignoring him, Carlyle jumped to his feet and bolted for the door.

Chapter Thirty-five

'COME ON, COME ON!'

Hopping from foot to foot, Xavier Carlton sipped his beer nervously and glanced at the second hand skipping round the face of his TAG Heuer Carrera. It was 9.59 plus ten ... eleven ... twelve seconds.

His heart was beating so fast, Xavier thought it might burst out of his chest at any moment. This waiting was killing him. The final hour before the polls closed had dragged interminably, going on for what seemed like days. But now, finally, in less than a minute, they would know the outcome of the election.

... twenty-three ... twenty-four ... twenty-five ...

The excited hubbub died down as everyone gathered round the television monitors placed all around the room, waiting for the news. The final opinion polls still had them in front, if only by five per cent or so. That should still be enough to give them a small but workable majority in the House of Commons, assuming that the polls were right.

... forty-eight ... forty-nine ... fifty ...

Letting his eyes slip away from the massive cinema screen at the far end of the hotel ballroom, Xavier glanced at his brother. With his head bowed, Edgar looked gaunt and exhausted. They'd had it in the bag for so long now, all they really wanted was the relief of knowing it was all over.

In the distance, Xavier thought he could just make out the faint chimes of Big Ben, half a mile down the road, as it struck ten o'clock. For a second, all of the screens within the room went blank.

Heart pounding, Xavier held his breath.

Suddenly, finally, Egar's face appeared on the screen.

There was a split second's delay, then a massive cheer went up. All around, people were shouting and screaming, hugging each other and punching the air in celebration. One of the girls close by burst into tears.

Xavier stepped over and hugged his brother.

'Thank God!' Edgar closed his eyes and gave silent thanks.

'Amen,' said Xavier, feeling his knees buckle slightly. Regaining his composure, he grabbed Edgar by the arm and quickly led him past a couple of Trevor Miller's security guys and down a hallway leading away from the noise. Round a corner, he swiped a key card that gave them access to the sanctuary of their own private hotel suite. Strict instructions had been given that absolutely no one, other than a handful of their closest circle, was to be allowed access. Even friends and family had been parked in rooms on the floor below, the brothers having insisted on a space which was for them alone. Those years of having, literally, their every move watched, exposed, dissected, debated and criticised were over. The campaign to claw back some of their privacy started here.

Grabbing a fresh beer, Xavier dropped on to the sofa in the middle of the large sitting room. On a TV mounted on the wall the presenter proclaimed: 'The polls have now closed in today's General Election. And tonight it looks as though Britain has a new government. We are predicting that Edgar Carlton will become the next prime minister, with a majority of twenty seats in the House of Commons.'

In the ballroom outside, the music started up as the victory party proper finally got under way. Xavier felt his brother's hand rest on his shoulder as he gulped down his beer. Neither man said anything, their elation drowned in sheer relief.

They were still lost in their thoughts when the door swung open and William Murray fell into the room, eyes gleaming.

'Congratulations!' shouted the special adviser. 'You've done it!' In each hand, Murray held up a magnum of chilled Krug 1995, beads of condensation quickly forming on the dark green glass. An unlit Romeo y Julieta Short Churchill was wedged between his lips. Standing unsteadily on one leg, he kicked the door shut behind him with the other.

The little sod's drunk, thought Xavier. *But why not? I will be, too, soon enough.* Everyone should get blasted on a night like this. The night of a lifetime.

'Thank you, William.' Edgar stepped forward, smiling broadly. The emotion of the moment had subsided, and he was regaining his composure. 'And thank you for all your work on our behalf over the last few years.'

Tears in his eyes, the young man bowed his head. 'It has been an honour ...'

'You have been a vital member of the team,' Edgar burbled, 'and, as I have always said, this is simply the beginning of our adventure.' He gestured towards the door. 'Please let everyone know that Xavier and I will be coming out right away. Let's get the party started. Tonight we want everyone here to have a great time. Goodness knows, they deserve it. Can you tell them that we'll be with them in a few minutes.'

Murray stared at him blankly. 'No, I really don't think so.' Tossing one of the bottles on to the sofa, he skipped straight towards Edgar. Grabbing it by the neck with both hands, he lifted the remaining bottle high above his head. The two politicians appeared mesmerised. For a millisecond, as he struggled to keep his balance, it looked as if Murray might tip over backwards. Then, grunting with the effort, he brought the Krug bottle smashing down right on to Edgar's head with a dull clunk.

'What the ...?' Xavier watched in disbelief as his brother crumpled under the heavy blow. He tried to stand up, but Murray was upon him before he could force himself out of his seat. The first blow glanced off his arms, raised in defence, but the second caught him full in the face, sending him spiralling into darkness.

XAVIER REGISTERED THE smell of burning flesh before he heard the scream.

'No-ooo!'

Reluctantly opening his eyes, it took Xavier another second or two to realise that he was lying face-down on the carpet, his hands tied behind his back and his feet taped together. Worse still, he was totally naked. The worst headache he had ever known was scouring at the inside of his skull, and he badly wanted to puke. Slowly, he turned his head in the direction of Edgar's cries.

Lying about six feet away, his brother was also bound hand and foot, naked from the waist down. Edgar's right buttock sported a nasty red burn about the size of a fifty-pence piece, clearly the result of William Murray's casual deployment of the now lit cigar.

'Help! Help! HELP!' Edgar's face turned crimson as he screamed with all his might. However, against the sound of Kylie Minogue thudding through the intervening wall from the party outside, it amounted to barely a squeak in his brother's ears.

Xavier struggled to lift his head far enough from the floor to see Murray's face. When his gaze reached the jagged neck of the bottle still clutched in Murray's right hand, he felt his bladder spasm and a fearful warmth spread through the carpet beneath his groin. Scanning the boy's face, he tried to make meaningful eye contact, while praying that someone else would finally wonder where they were and come to their aid.

'What do you want?' he gasped.

Murray stood between the two brothers, flushed, exultant, not flinching from Xavier's gaze, but saying nothing. For a moment, the two men eyeballed each other, both ignoring the steady, heaving sobs of the soon-to-be prime minister of the United Kingdom of Great Britain and Northern Ireland. Xavier realised that he had never really looked Murray up and down before. Now, on closer inspection, he realised that there really was nothing to the boy at all. Although he had been one of their inner circle, and a senior trusty, he was but one of dozens, if not hundreds, of similar helpers. If he were to leave tomorrow – and now, after this comical breakdown, he *would* be leaving tomorrow, if not sooner – there were plenty of others queuing up to take his place. All of them were young, bright, fiercely ambitious, and utterly disposable.

Utterly disposable.

Like a cheap razor. Or a tampon.

Xavier started laughing.

Maybe Murray had flipped simply because he was worried that he had already passed his sell-by date.

Maybe he'd just started partying too hard, too quickly. Maybe he had taken too much ecstasy and had suffered a brain meltdown. If that was the case, he certainly wouldn't have been the first.

Maybe ...

'Oh my God!' Looking deep into the boy's eyes, Xavier suddenly realised what was going on. Struggling to breathe, his eyes misted up as he was transported back half a lifetime – to the true night of a lifetime.

Murray gave him a crooked smile.

'Oh my God!' Xavier repeated.

Murray took a contented puff on his cigar.

'You!' Xavier pulled ineffectually against his restraints. 'It was you all along.'

Murray nodded.

Xavier let his forehead sink back to the floor: 'Icarus, the boy who flew too close to the sun ...'

'Not a very original choice of name.' Murray spoke quietly, flicking some ash on to the carpet, his words almost getting lost against the music. 'Not *his* name, of course.'

'Of course,' Xavier nodded subconsciously.

Murray flicked some cigar ash towards Edgar, who had fallen silent. The shock had finally kicked in, and it looked as if he had passed out. Probably just as well, Xavier thought. Where the fuck was that useless fat bastard Trevor Miller? Probably out in the ballroom getting drunk and trying to grope one of the secretaries.

'His name was Robert.'

'Yes.'

'The name of the man you killed was Robert Ashton.'

'But—'

'He was my father.'

Murray dropped to his knees and pulled Xavier's head up by his hair, bringing the broken bottle neck close to his neck. For a few moments, the noise outside died down as Kylie's singing gave way to another thumping dance track.

Out of nowhere, Xavier summoned some new reserves of spirit. 'You'll never get away with it!' he hissed.

'I don't want to get away with it,' Murray snarled. 'I want everyone to know what you people did.'

'It wasn't me. I wasn't even there,' a voice snivelled. Edgar had obviously reawakened.

'Yes, you were!' Xavier retorted angrily. He wasn't going to let this lunatic have the pleasure of watching either of the brothers grovel.

'Only at the end,' Edgar protested. 'I didn't—'

'You didn't fuck him,' Xavier hissed. 'Big deal, so what? You still got your rocks off. We all did.' Craning his neck, he turned back to face Murray who had dropped the neck of the broken bottle on to the carpet and was now fumbling with a mobile phone.

Edgar grew even more agitated as Murray started filming the grotesque scene that he had staged.

Laughing, Murray gave him a sharp kick. 'Keep it up,' he jeered. 'This will make for better viewing. You'll be an internet sensation.'

Screaming like a stuck pig, Edgar obliged the crazed auteur. It struck Xavier that his brother looked like the victim in a splatter movie, which, in a sense, he was.

'You don't like it so much when the tables are turned, do you?' Murray grinned, dancing about in front of them, as if he was in a trance.

To hell with it, Xavier thought. *If I ever live through this, a bloody video will be the least of my worries.* Waiting until the camera was focused straight on him, he let rip. 'You murdering bastard, I'm not ashamed of having buggered your old man.' With a monumental effort, he adopted a leering grin. 'We both enjoyed it at the time. And I have to say, William, your dad was a rather good shag.'

'You total fucking bastards!' Murray screamed, hurling the phone at Xavier's head, but missing wildly. Tears poured down his face as he fumbled about on the carpet for the broken bottle. Grabbing it by the remaining neck, he rose slowly to his feet.

'Now it's your turn to die ...'

The rest of his words were drowned out by a tidal wave of noise filling the room. To the soundtrack of The Prodigy's 'Omen', the party's election theme tune, Xavier watched open-mouthed as Trevor Miller slammed the door and launched himself through the air, taking Murray out with a tackle aimed at neck height. His head smashing against the wall, Murray collapsed to the floor, narrowly avoiding impaling himself on the jagged glass of the bottle still gripped in his hand.

Miller jumped up, kicking Murray's weapon out of his grasp. He then crossed the room and locked the door. Taking a Swiss Army knife from his pocket, he hacked at the tape binding Xavier's hands until he could pull them free. Leaving him to untie his own feet, he then moved on to Edgar.

Xavier winced as he pulled the tape from around his ankles, tugging away several follicles of hair in the process. Jumping up, he found his trousers and quickly pulled them on. Then he turned to watch Edgar, slowly struggling into his underwear with a glazed expression on his face.

'Let's get this sorted out,' Xavier declared grimly.

Edgar did not respond.

Pulling on his shirt, Xavier shifted his gaze to Miller, who was now standing over the prostrate body of Murray. 'Is he dead?'

Miller gave the body a firm kick, which managed to elicit a groan. 'Sadly not.'

'What shall we do with him?' Xavier asked.

Miller shrugged. 'Your call.'

Buttoning up his shirt, Xaxier stared Miller in the eye. 'He cannot leave this room alive.'

After a moment's reflection, Miller pulled aside the curtains covering most of the wall opposite the door. Behind them was a pair of sliding doors that gave access to a small balcony. Opening the doors, Miller stepped out on to the balcony itself, put his hands on the guard rail and peered over the edge. After checking that Murray was still immobile, Xavier headed over to do the same.

They were currently on the top floor, and the balcony overlooked a large atrium rising through the centre of the hotel. They were more than a hundred feet up, and only twenty feet below the atrium's glass roof. This level of the hotel was deserted – all the neighbouring suites having been kept empty on security grounds.

After a few moments of silent contemplation, Miller turned to Xavier and grinned. 'That'll do nicely.'

CARLYLE FOUND HIS access to the Carlton brothers' suite barred by Miller's security men, who showed no interest in either his warrant card or any demands for them to step aside. With his adrenaline pumping, and in no mood for further argument or delay, he headed over to a nearby fire alarm and smashed the glass, setting off a hellish cacophony of alarms and bells.

'What the fuck are you doing?' One of the guards reached out to grab Carlyle by the throat.

Joe Szyszkowski rabbit-punched him on the back of his neck, then gave him a kick to the back of his left knee. 'Consider yourself arrested, my friend.' As the man sank to the carpet, Joe slapped on a pair of cuffs, and then gave him another kick for good measure.

'Thank you,' Carlyle smiled.

'My pleasure,' Joe replied cheerily.

As the bells continued to ring, people began leaving the ballroom, heading for the stairs as they evacuated the building.

The second guard looked from Joe to Carlyle, as if eyeing up which one of them to smack first.

Taking a step backwards, Joe pointed at a sign reading *Exit*. 'It's time for you to go.'

'If you're still here when I get back,' Carlyle shouted over the noise, 'you'll be arrested for assault as well.'

Disgusted but impotent, the man shook his head and started for the stairs.

Carlyle jogged round a corner of the corridor just in time to see the door to the suite open and Edgar Carlton pop his head out. He looked very confused and didn't seem to recognise the inspector. 'What's going on?' he wailed, sounding as if he was about to burst into tears.

Lengthening his stride, Carlyle pushed his way through the door and on past the befuddled politician. 'Just a false alarm,' he smiled cheerily. 'Nothing to worry about.'

PERSPIRATION BEADING ON his brow, a grim smile spread across Trevor Miller's face as his eyes flicked between Carlyle and the sergeant. 'Oh, look,' he snarled, 'it's the fucking cavalry!'

The first thing Carlyle noticed in the room was the smell: a strange mixture of cigar smoke, piss and burning flesh. 'Fuck me,' he quipped, 'this place smells worse than a kebab shop on Tottenham Court Road!'

Not for the first time in his life, he saw a joke fall flat. Carlyle didn't even have time to laugh at his own gag before being rendered speechless by the scene in front of him.

'Fuck me!' Joe echoed from the doorway.

Miller stood on a balcony, holding a bruised and bloodied William Murray in a headlock. Up against the bulk of the ex-policeman, Murray seemed almost like a child. His eyes were glazed and he barely seemed conscious. Unable to put up any resistance, his face was turning red as the air was choked out of him.

'What are you doing, Trevor?'

Miller automatically took a step backwards, thus propping Murray up against the balcony rail. 'Just fuck off out of it, *Inspector*,' he snarled.

Signalling for Joe to stay back, Carlyle took a careful step forward, then another. His mouth was dry and his heart was pounding. For the briefest moment, it was just like the old days, when he was speeding his tits off on the picket line. He felt giddy, almost euphoric.

'What happened here?' he asked gently. 'What did he do, Trevor?'

'He's our man.' As Miller eased his grip slightly, Murray started twitching.

'I know,' said Carlyle, edging towards the balcony. 'That's why we're here.' The pair of them were only ten or eleven feet away from him now, but Carlyle realised that he had no room for manoeuvre. 'That's why you have to hand him over to me.'

'You haven't learned very much over the years, have you?' Miller looked past Carlyle, in the direction of the Carltons, who were both hovering in a corner.

'What do you mean?'

'What I mean is …' Miller was in mid-sentence as Murray's eyes opened wide and he started struggling. 'Fuck!' Miller started punching the aide in the face with his spare fist, eventually smashing his nose and showering them both with blood.

Jumping forward, Carlyle made a grab for Murray, but a brutal smack across the face from Miller stopped him in his tracks. As he staggered backwards, it felt as if he had been hit by a frying pan, and Carlyle was sure that the ringing in his head wasn't just the fire alarm.

'Boss?' Joe asked, moving to Carlyle's shoulder. In the distance, they could make out sirens. The police and the fire brigade would be here within minutes at most.

'It's OK.' Carlyle straightened himself up, anger mixing with the agony. 'I'm OK.' Waiting for his head to clear, he eyed Miller and smiled. 'That's it, Trevor. Time to hand him over.'

A strangulated squeak emerged from Murray.

'I don't think so,' Miller hissed, tightening his grip.

'Trevor …'

'Fuck off, Carlyle.' Pulling Murray upwards and backwards, Miller flipped both of them over the guard rail.

For a split second, Carlyle stood there staring at the vacant space where the two men had been.

'Shit!' Rushing over to the rail, he peered down in time to see the two bodies hit the surface of what looked like a small swimming pool below. From the balcony, the splash sounded like a gentle ripple of applause.

Joe appeared at Carlyle's side and looked down. 'Ouch!' he grinned. 'That's got to hurt.'

Carlyle turned quickly away and scanned the room. Both politicians had disappeared. On the carpet, amidst the broken glass, was a smouldering cigar. Stepping in from the balcony, he stamped it out with the toe of his shoe. As he did so, he caught sight of a light flashing under the sofa. Dropping to his knees, he pulled out an expensive-looking mobile phone, quickly dropping it in the pocket of his jacket before he stood up.

Joe was still peering over the rail. 'Looks like there's some kind of movement down there.'

'Come on,' Carlyle groaned, 'let's see if the fuckers can swim.'

FIGHTING THEIR WAY past the stragglers on the stairs, it took the two policemen the best part of ten minutes to make it down to the basement. At least the alarms had stopped by the time that they reached the swimming pool. Finding the entrance locked, Carlyle pressed his ear to the door and listened. Other than the hum of the air-conditioning, there was nothing. Once, twice, three times he tried and failed to kick the door in. For a moment, he stood there catching his breath, trying to ignore the pain in his right foot and glaring at Joe, who was struggling to stifle a laugh. 'You try it then, you fat bastard,' Carlyle snapped, stepping away from the door.

'OK.' Joe, whose experience of kicking doors in was much more current, jogged ten feet back along the corridor, then turned round at a crouch. 'One, two, three ...' Springing forward, he charged the door head-down, looking like an enthusiastic baby rhino. Carlyle grimaced in expectation of the imminent crunch of bone against wood. But, with Joe just inches from his target, the door suddenly flew open.

Carlyle watched open mouthed as his sergeant steamed through the doorway, tripped over a small flight of steps and belly-flopped into the pool beyond, splashing alongside the face-down floater that the inspector instinctively knew had to be William Murray. A moment later, Trevor Miller stepped out from behind the door. Although soaked from head to foot, he showed no sign of being injured by his fall.

Bloody typical, Carlyle thought, Miller lying face down in the pool would have been a decent result.

The security chief had a large white towel draped round his neck while vigorously drying what remained of his hair with another. 'Well done, Carlyle,' he grunted from somewhere behind the fabric. 'Another crime scene compromised.'

'Fuck you, Trevor,' Carlyle snarled, 'you're under arrest.'

'Am I indeed?' Miller tossed the used towel on the floor and picked up a fresh one from a pile stacked on a white plastic chair nearby. 'For what?'

Carlyle said nothing. What had he just seen? Murder? He was sure of it. He was equally sure that he couldn't prove it – even before one considered the queue of people who would be ready to cover it up.

'You really haven't learnt anything, have you?' Miller sneered. 'Even after all this time, you stupid, stupid little shit.' Towelling himself down as best he could, he stepped towards the door, tossing the wet towel at Carlyle. 'Come anywhere near any of our people and we'll fucking crucify you. It's case closed. This has finally been dealt with, no thanks to you.' He jabbed a meaty finger towards Carlyle's face. 'Ironically, you might even get a bit of glory if you play your cards right. I'll at least let you have that.'

'I don't think so,' Carlyle snarled, but he was struggling to put on a brave face. Already, he could see how it would all play out.

The meaty finger retreated into a clenched fist. 'Don't fuck it up again,' Miller smiled. 'Remember which side you're on.' Then, pushing Carlyle out of the way, he squelched out through the door and disappeared along the corridor.

'Give me a hand, boss!' Joe called as he struggled to get himself out of the pool.

Ignoring him, Carlyle turned and left.

Chapter Thirty-six

EDGAR CARLTON THREW a large glass of Rémy Martin XO down his throat, followed quickly by another. Feeling suitably relaxed, he plastered what he hoped was a confident smile on his face and stepped out of No 10 Downing Street to address the world. Gripping the lectern that had been placed out in the street, he acknowledged the assembled journalists corralled behind barriers on the pavement, and waited for the flash photography and the whirr of camera motors to die down. Clearing his throat, he fixed his gaze on a point just above the tallest head in the throng, and launched into his statement:

'Her Majesty the Queen has asked me to form a new government, and I have accepted. I came into politics because I believe deeply in public service. I love this great country of ours and I think that its best days still lie ahead. I want us all to work together to help to build a society with stronger families and stronger communities. We should remember the words of St Francis of Assisi when he said: "Where there is discord, may we bring harmony. Where there is error, may we bring truth. Where there is doubt, may we bring faith. And where there is despair, may we bring hope." I believe that together we can provide that strong and stable government that our country needs based on those values – rebuilding family, rebuilding community and, above all, rebuilding responsibility in this country. These are the things I care about. These are the things that I will now start work on delivering. Thank you very much.'

Before he had even finished, the hacks began hurling an avalanche of questions at him. Turning quickly away, Edgar fled back inside.

CARLYLE SAT IN a small office, looking out over the empty newsroom: an open-plan arrangement of desks and monitors, with a small studio set in the far corner. On maybe twenty separate screens, he could see images of Edgar Carlton proclaiming his victory on the steps of Downing Street.

'How did you make the connection?'

'Huh?' Carlyle returned his gaze to Rosanna Snowdon. On the desk in front of her lay William Murray's mobile phone, recovered from the Carlton brothers' hotel suite. She eyed it nervously, as if it was radioactive.

'Between father and son? What made you realise that William Murray was Robert Ashton's kid?'

'It just came to me,' Carlyle shrugged. 'I was sitting in a pub as the polls were closing. Edgar appeared on the TV screen, and William Murray was at his shoulder. Then it hit me ...'

'And his mother was covering up for him?'

'Yes. We don't know the precise balance of power in that relationship, but they were in it together.'

'Madness.'

'Was it?' Carlyle exhaled. 'If someone did that to my family, well ...'

Rosanna drummed a perfectly manicured fingernail on her desk. 'Are you actually condoning murder, Inspector?'

'No,' he said stiffly, quickly descending into a bit of jargon in order to mask his opinions. 'But at least you can put together the pieces and, at the very least, begin understanding the motivation of the perpetrators. That is not the same as condoning it.'

'It's an amazing story ...'

'It certainly is,' Carlyle agreed.

'... but I can't use it.'

She looked up at Carlyle, with a pained expression. 'Why have you brought me this?'

'I thought you wanted an exclusive,' he said evenly.

She gestured at the mobile. 'Not this kind of exclusive.'

Carlyle shifted in his chair. Maybe coming here wouldn't be the brightest decision he had ever made – even in the course of this current investigation, which would certainly be saying something. 'What kind is that then?'

'The kind that will never see the light of day,' she replied.

He waited for her to explain.

She screwed up her face. 'How can I use this? It's not a story.'

'It seems like a story to me,' Carlyle said, not convinced himself now. He felt a creeping embarrassment at his stupidity. Why was he even here? What was he thinking? Edgar Carlton was in his first week as prime minister. William Murray and Susy Ahl were both dead. No one cared about their deaths. Robert Ashton may or may not have been successfully avenged.

Who had chosen Carlyle as the one man to shine a light on this dark little corner of the past? He wasn't even doing his self-appointed task very well. There wasn't going to be any 'closure'. All he was doing was digging himself into another hole.

She sat back and gave him a rather pitying smile. 'That's why you're the policeman and I'm the journalist. A story is only a story if I can report it. No one can use this. The lawyers wouldn't let us go anywhere near it.'

Feeling like a complete idiot, Carlyle sat in silence.

'You think this security guy ...?'

'Miller.'

'Yes, Miller. You think he murdered the aide and also his mother?'

Carlyle nodded.

'And maybe that other guy ... the one killed out near the airport.'

'Allen?' Carlyle shrugged. 'Maybe. I don't know, but it's possible.'

'Why would he have done that?'

'Well, unlike the rest of them, I think Allen was ready to talk. Talk properly that is. He had agreed to speak to me once he returned to the country. If he had spilled the beans, then that would have been a problem for all of them.'

'But you can't prove any of this, otherwise you'd nick Miller.' The word 'nick' was delivered with a childlike relish.

'That is correct,' Carlyle admitted.

'So you dangle it in front of me,' she smiled broadly, 'hoping that I can stir up some trouble.'

'But publicity is the very soul of justice,' he said primly.

'How profound,' she said sarcastically. 'Where did you pick that up from?'

It took Carlyle a second to dredge the name from his memory. 'Jeremy Bentham – he was a philosopher.'

'I know who he was,' Rosanna laughed, 'but he never worked for the bloody BBC. And, anyway, I don't think he meant that journalists should allow themselves to be used as a tool of revenge by frustrated coppers.'

Carlyle could only smile. She had him sussed out.

After a few seconds, she added, 'And you could never arrest them, could you?'

Them being the Carltons.

'No,' he conceded. 'Never in a million years.'

Her face lit up at the thought of it. 'Although that would certainly be a story and a half. Nicked during your first week as prime minister! Who'd have thought old Edgar Carlton might be so interesting?'

Carlyle sighed. 'No one will ever face any charges in relation to any of this. Ashton was too long ago, and the Murray problem has been solved to the satisfaction of everyone ... except me.'

'Exactly!' She folded her arms in triumph. 'See? I can't run this story even if I wanted to.'

'Can't ... or won't?' he asked petulantly.

She leaned forward in her chair. 'Inspector, if I could stand this up, get interviews on camera, put it all together *and* get it past the lawyers, it would be a bloody miracle.'

'But if you were a miracle worker?'

'If I was a miracle worker, and I could get all the pieces to fall into place, sure I'd run it.' She gave him another one of her coy smiles. 'A grizzled old detective like you might think that I'm a bit of an airhead ...'

Grizzled? He frowned. She was teasing him now, and he quite liked it.

'... not that I would care, but I *am* a journalist. I'm a friend of Edgar Carlton sure, but my professional reputation is worth much more than any friendship. A story is a story and I will be a journalist for a lot longer than he is prime minister. I'm not in the business of burying things.'

'I understand,' he nodded, poised to spring out of his chair, suddenly keen now to be on his way.

'But I'm not in the business of flogging a dead horse, either.'

Carlyle looked out at the monitors in the newsroom. Edgar had disappeared back inside his new home, and the screens were now showing some cartoon.

'Like I said,' Snowdon continued, 'it's got no legs. Even if I could run a piece, which I can't, who's going to follow it up? At best, I might get a mention in a couple of newspapers that hate the Carltons anyway. Who cares? Their powerful allies in the media will simply rubbish such "smears". So the boys may have got up to a bit of high jinks at university. So what? Isn't that what boys are supposed to do?'

They were distracted by a tired-looking man tapping on the window, signalling that he needed Snowdon. She nodded at him and held up her right index finger to signify that she would be only another minute.

'I need to go and record a trailer,' she explained, standing up.

'Of course,' Carlyle finally got out of his chair. 'Thank you for your time.'

'No problem. However, I think you're being a bit naive, Inspector, and frankly that's a bit of a surprise.'

Was that a compliment? Or an insult?

'Still,' Snowdon continued, 'I'm going to do you a favour, a big favour.' Tentatively, she lifted Murray's mobile phone from the desk and began pressing some buttons. Then she looked up at him like a schoolteacher who was about to tell a none-too-bright pupil how best to avoid flunking his exam. 'This case is closed, right?'

'Yes.'

She waved the phone at him. 'This evidence is not part of any official report?'

'No.'

'You haven't copied this? Or sent it to anyone?'

'No.' It was easy to slip in the lie among a collection of truths. Casually patting his jacket pocket, he reassured himself that his pay-as-you-go mobile was still there. The one to which he'd already sent a copy of William Murray's video nasty.

'Or posted it on YouTube?'

Carlyle shrugged. 'I wouldn't know how.'

'OK, good.' Snowdon picked up the handset from her desk and pulled up Murray's video. For a second, Carlyle caught a glimpse of Xavier Carlton's contorted face. Then Snowdon hit the delete button, and the screen immediately went blank. Standing up, she tossed him the phone. 'That's sorted, then. Take my advice, Inspector, and just forget that you ever saw it.' Stepping from behind the desk, she took him by the arm and ushered him out of her office and through the newsroom, heading for reception. Catching the eye of her producer, who was hovering nervously, she shouted, 'Just coming!'

At the door, she turned to Carlyle and pulled an imaginary piece of lint from the lapel of his jacket. 'Don't get me wrong, Inspector. I really appreciate you thinking of me.'

'My pleasure,' he mumbled.

She grinned. 'In the meantime, that's another favour ... another two favours ... you owe me.'

'Favours?'

She counted them off on her fingers. 'One for providing the initial introduction to Edgar, one for deleting that stuff on the phone, and one for not telling our prime minister that you wanted me to run the story and thus destroy his honeymoon period with the voters.'

An uncomfortable look crossed Carlyle's face.

'Don't worry.' She took him by the arm. 'Remember, I need stories … exclusives, particularly crime stories. Crime reporting has not been one of our strengths in recent years. It's an opportunity for me to make a splash, and you can help me with that. You can also help me broaden my range of contacts within the police.'

'I understand,' he said rather wearily.

'Good.' She was pleased to discover that this rather slow pupil was finally beginning to show some promise. 'I think we're going to have a beautiful relationship.'

I'm fucked, he thought.

'YES! COME ON!'

Xavier Carlton felt as if he was finally getting his mojo back. A couple of good nights' sleep, and the prospect of no more electioneering for the next five bloody years, had done wonders for his spirit, not to mention his libido. Later in the day, he would be off on his first official trip as foreign secretary. First, however, he had to finish servicing young Camilla or Cressida, or whatever the hell her name was. He grimaced at the sight of the young party worker bent over the desk, with her Boden crinkle cotton skirt bunched up around her waist and her knickers discarded on the floor, while thrusting as hard as he could.

'Yes!' She mimicked him, without much enthusiasm.

Xavier tugged on the girl's hair, forcing her to turn and face him, so that he could enjoy the mixture of confusion and boredom in her eyes. *You'll never have much of a career in porno movies*, he thought, slapping her hard on the buttocks.

'Faster!'

'Yes! Yes!' She thrust backwards with such vigour that it almost knocked him off his feet.

'For God's sake!' Slipping out, Xavier closed his eyes and inhaled deeply the smell of shit. Smearing the girl's bodily waste along the length of his shaft, he started stroking himself vigorously. After a few moments, he brought up an image of Yulexis, on her knees, tickling his balls while she sucked him off like an angel on crack. Almost immediately, he felt himself quiver uncontrollably. Pushing himself back inside the girl, he lent forward and started pawing at her chest.

'Oh, sweet Jesus!'

'WAS THAT GOOD, Xavier? Better than me?'

He opened his eyes. The real Yulexis was standing before them, a very nasty-looking kitchen knife in her hand and hatred blazing in her eyes. As she raised the weapon, Xavier thought that he could finally make out the increased curve of her stomach. Had she refused to go to Harley Street? Or had he simply forgotten to make that appointment for her abortion?

As he struggled to recall, Yulexis hammered the blade into his chest. There was a sickening crack as she forced the steel through his breastbone. With the knife stuck firmly in his chest, Xavier collapsed, a confused expression on his face, blood rapidly staining his shirt. *But I was thinking of you*, screamed a voice in his head. *I was thinking of you!*

THE GIRL LOOKED pained rather than scared. Standing up, she pulled down her dress and involuntarily passed wind. Yulexis wrinkled her nose at the stench of excrement, but said nothing. Blushing, the girl looked at Xavier's crumpled body lying on the floor.

'Is he dead?' she asked.

'I truly hope so,' said Yulexis, carefully feeling her bump. 'It's the very least that the sick bastard deserves.'

AFTER ESCAPING FROM Snowdon, Carlyle wandered aimlessly up Marylebone High Street. Stopping at a café, he ordered a take-away latte. From a radio behind the counter came a round-up of the day's news. After the soap opera of the election, it was back to business as usual. The world was not going to dramatically change.

The presenter rushed through the stories, as if not wishing to delay the adverts.

'The aide to Prime Minister Edgar Carlton, who accidentally drowned in an election night tragedy, has finally been officially identified.'

But William Murray did not even merit a name check.

'And Spandau Ballet are to regroup for a series of concerts in the autumn.'

Spandau fucking Ballet, Carlyle, thought. *Jesus! What is the world coming to?* He thanked the girl who handed him his coffee, took a careful sip and smiled. For once it was extremely hot, just how he liked it.

Out on the street again, his phone rang. Seeing Joe's number on the screen, he punched the receive button. 'Hi.'

'You're not going to believe this,' was Joe's opening gambit.

'I'll believe anything.' Carlyle laughed.

'I've just had a call from Commissario Edmondo Valcareggi ...'

Carlyle took a mouthful of coffee and felt it scald the back of his throat. 'Oh yeah?' he coughed.

'Apparently Ferruccio Pozzo wasn't Ferruccio Pozzo.'

'The liposuction guy?'

'Yeah, the one who was killed in prison.'

'But Valcareggi said he had DNA ...'

'The lab messed up, apparently. Either that or someone fiddled with the test results.'

'So,' Carlyle sighed, 'the guy we nicked – who was he, then?'

'No idea,' Joe said cheerfully. 'But Valcareggi reckons that the real Pozzo is going to be in London next week. He wants us to help him arrest him.'

Carlyle gave this some thought as he watched a very pretty girl in a very flimsy T-shirt and no bra stroll slowly past him, walking a very small dog on a very long lead. Only by gritting his teeth and summoning up the willpower of ten men did he resist the temptation to turn round and gawp at her backside as well.

'What do you think?' asked Joe.

Carlyle unclenched his jaw. 'Tell him to fuck off.'

Ending the call, he turned round. The girl was already gone. Smiling to himself, he walked into Paddington Street Gardens and squeezed into the small space that was free on a bench in the shade of a tree. Slowly drinking his coffee, he thought about the phone in his pocket with a copy of William Murray's video nasty on it. Would he ever do anything with it? He had no idea. Would it make any difference to anything, even if he did share it with the world?

His mind went completely blank.

Finishing his coffee, he tossed the empty cup into a nearby waste bin. A car pulled up at a nearby red light, The Clash's

'London Calling' blasting from its stereo. Singing along under his breath, Carlyle watched a young boy happily chasing a pair of pigeons across the grass, oblivious to the couple snogging enthusiastically right in front of him. Behind their heads, a poster stuck to the outside of a phone box proclaimed 'Capitalism Isn't Working'. Inside the booth, the selection of cards offering a wide range of services from 'Japanese schoolgirls', 'Indian models' and pre-op transsexuals suggested otherwise.

After a short while spent contemplating all of the city's bounty, Carlyle left the shade of the tree, heading for home. Feeling the sun on his back and the stone beneath his feet, he smiled.

About the Author

JAMES CRAIG has worked in London as a journalist and consultant for almost thirty years. He lives in Covent Garden with his family.

www.james-craig.co.uk

Visit www.AuthorTracker.com for exclusive information on your favorite HarperCollins authors.